Quantum Spark

Quantum Spark

V. C. Lawrence

ISBN 979-8-223-49902-2

Table of Contents

John...1
Kunuk...3
The Ship..9
The Phenomenon...16
Puerto Deseado..39
Angel...61
Tzabar..79
Denudasdi...85
Anguta..109
Winterfell...114
Vitrified..131
The Cracked Pan..140
Surprises...148
A fantastic night to die...164
The Wall..187
Dark Fog...192
The Sphere..209
Aklujji Matu..236
Conflict...250
Revelation...261
Brothers..288
Chang..302
The Quantum Spark..308
Abulkur...325

John

My body lies sprawled on the rough asphalt, surrounded by a chaotic blur of images that worsen my pounding headache. The acrid smell of burning rubber fills the air, mingling with thick smoke that invades my lungs.

Flames dance over the wreckage of crashed cars, casting an eerie glow on the debris scattered across the road.

Pain crashes through my body in waves, and it's a struggle just to sit up. I wipe the back of my hand across my lips and find it coated in half-dried blood and dirt.

Through the haze of confusion, my mind flashes to a strange scene - a beautiful woman and a young child, traveling together at night, their laughter and song filling the air.

"Dad, look at me! I solved the puzzle!" the kid says, beaming, skillfully balancing four interlocking metal pieces in his hands.

"Very well, Sebastian! We'll show it to your uncle Angel and surprise him with how you solved the riddle before him." I can't help grinning. "Only 5 kilometers left. We'll be there in 15…"

Before I finish, a scream pierces the air, jolting me back to the present. "Watch out!"

Instinctively, I turn the wheel to the left, barely seeing a figure frantically waving on my right. The blinding glare of headlights consumes my vision before everything goes silent and dark.

As consciousness slowly returns, I feel an agonizing pain in my chest, as if knives are being dragged across my throat.

Struggling to move, I muster all my strength to pull myself toward the wreckage. The sight is all too familiar - the car partially engulfed in flames and suffocating smoke. Nearby, lying motionless among the scattered debris, is a woman.

Despite the pain, hope flickers. I crawl toward her, fighting through the few feet that separate us. With trembling hands, I brush aside the long hair that conceals her face, and something in me goes very still.

Agony rips through me, and I collapse back to the ground.

Melissa's lifeless body lies on the road, and though my eyes see it, my mind refuses to believe it. A vision of my son's face cuts through the despair - a flicker of hope, crushed at once as I find him slumped in the seat, his head covered in blood.

Everything fades again into darkness, silence, emptiness. Then a familiar voice cuts through the void. "John! John, wake up. John!".

Kunuk

An icy symphony envelops the Arctic wasteland's endless expanse as the relentless wind howls in ghastly harmony with barking dogs. Two men, bundled in heavy fur coats, struggle against the raging storm, seeking refuge from its wrath.

"Suluk! Come on, son. I'll finish up here with the sleds, and then we can head back to the tent," a man calls out over the howling wind, his words almost swallowed by the gusts.

"Yes, Dad! I'm just about done feeding the dogs!" Suluk hollers back, braving the onslaught of snowflakes assaulting his face.

"Kunuk, Suluk!" another voice calls out from a nearby tent, barely audible amidst the howling gales.

"What is it?" Kunuk strains to discern the origin of the call, squinting against the blinding snow.

"Olev needs to speak with everyone. Please, come inside." The man in the thick, fur-trimmed leather coat struggles to make his words heard amidst the relentless wind.

"Alright, Lev. We'll be there in a few minutes!" Kunuk responds, motioning for Suluk to hasten. "I could use a warm drink before we join them," he shouts, making his way toward the tent.

"Okay, Dad. I'll join you shortly," Suluk replies, still catching his breath as he battles to regain warmth in his numbing limbs.

As Kunuk steps into the tent, he sheds his coat and gloves, shaking off the clinging snow. He places a kettle of ice on the stove and relishes the radiating heat as it seeps into his frigid hands.

"It's bitterly cold out there today," Suluk states, entering the tent with snow-laden gusts, his breath visible in the chilled air.

Kunuk pours steaming hot drinks for both of them before settling down with his own mug. Suluk takes a moment to catch his breath, the chill refusing to release its grip on him.

"I don't know how you endure this bone-chilling weather," he says, affection plain on his face as he gazes at his father.

"I am a true Inuit, hardened by the ice and wind," Kunuk chuckles.

"Why do you complain so much, son? Look at you, a young Inuit, taller and stronger than anyone I know."

"Come on, Dad, do you think I'm a weak Inuit?"

"What? No! Son, I was just teasing you. I'm proud of you."

Suluk puts an arm around his dad's shoulders, playfully causing him to sway. "Hey, old man, where's that Inuit vigor I've heard so much about?" he teases, pretending to hold his father up.

"I'll show you my vigor with this spear if you don't apologize." Kunuk grabs a spear leaning against the tent and throws it playfully at his son.

"Calm down, old man." Suluk laughs, raising his arm to protect himself. "Don't get too excited. Your heart might not be able to handle it."

Kunuk drops the spear and embraces his son tightly.

"How are you feeling about finally returning home?" asks Suluk, getting up and putting on his coat.

"It's been too long since we've seen our village, and they made us endure more than we agreed upon," Kunuk grumbles.

"At least we're being paid by the day," Suluk smirks. "But I think you're annoyed because we're getting closer to Anguta Matu. I've noticed you looking worried every time we head further north."

"You're right," Kunuk says with annoyance. "We shouldn't be so close to that mountain."

"I know you believe in all these legends," Suluk says, skeptical. "Anguta Matu, the forbidden entrance to Abulkur, the underworld of the gods. But come on; it's just a mountain with rocks and ice." Suluk strides out of the tent, pulling his coat tightly around him to shield himself against the biting wind. "I respect our people's stories and beliefs, but I think they're just myths," he continues, unaware of the hurt look on his father's face.

"These stories, which you mock, have been passed down from generation to generation, from the earliest days of our ancestors," Kunuk says, looking saddened.

"They were learned from the first men, the gentle giants, and those who came after them. They taught us to respect these stories because they contain the secrets that have protected us since the beginning. That's why we preserve them and pass them on to our children.

It saddens me that you don't respect our customs and traditions. That disappoints me."

Kunuk's shoulders sagged as he pulled up his hood and trudged towards the tent where the Russians awaited them. Suluk trailed behind, sensing his father's unhappiness and choosing not to provoke him further. This conversation would only deepen the rift between them.

As Kunuk walked, a distant memory resurfaced, harking back to the time when he had defied the rules of his tribe. He had been younger than Suluk, driven by a fiery determination to embark on a solo expedition to Anguta Matu. Braving the relentless blizzards, he had ventured alone through the unforgiving white desert, enduring harrowing moments of panic under the night sky. Demons and disturbing visions had plagued his sleep, yet he had pushed forward and reached the mountain.

Regrettably, Kunuk had no recollection of his time on Anguta Matu. All that remained were fragmented memories of the steep price he had paid upon returning to his village, where the entire community had awaited him. It had been a week of enduring a cleansing ritual that hadn't been performed in generations.

The images from that time were seared into his mind, the pain and psychological trauma etched deeply into his soul. The ritual had seemingly succeeded, for he had never again defied the rules of his people. Yet, what troubled him the most was the haziness surrounding his adventure on the sacred mountain. Whenever he attempted to recall it, only fleeting, cold flashes of disjointed images came to him.

Approaching the tent, the comforting glow of warm light and the harmonious chatter of men engaged in conversation and laughter fostered a warm, easy camaraderie.

Suluk pulled back the tarp to enter, and Kunuk took a steadying breath before following his son inside.

"Good afternoon, gentlemen," Suluk greeted as they entered, finding three men seated around a kettle and five metal cups. "Apologies for the delay."

"Thank you for coming. Would you like a hot drink?" asks Olev, a formidable figure standing 1.9 meters tall with a sturdy build, gesturing towards the large kettle by the fire. His gray beard was the only indication of his age, well into his fifties, and the leather jacket and cap hinted at his former role as a commander in the Russian Navy.

Seated beside him were two more men - Ivan Pavel, a Civil Geologist in his forties, and Lev Anthony, a Russian navy geographer also in his forties.

"Are the dogs alright? Are they protected from the storm?" Olev asks.

"Fed and safe. Don't worry, the dogs are fine," Kunuk reassured as he settled down with the group. "The weather is improving as well. The winds will die down tonight. We can expect a calm day tomorrow."

"Excellent," Olev exclaimed with enthusiasm. "Before we go into details about the plan for the next few days, I would like to express my gratitude to the best Inuit guides in the northern hemisphere: Kunuk and Suluk," he says, rising to his feet and addressing them directly.

"Thanks to you, we were able to map the coastline all the way to Seal Bay, surpassing our original plans. To Kunuk and Suluk!" He lifted his mug in a toast, and the other men followed suit, raising their metal cups in salute to the blushing Inuit guides.

"Our expedition has been a resounding success. Tomorrow, we will return home with hearts filled with pride for what we have accomplished despite the challenging weather conditions. Let's raise a toast to everyone," Olev continued, reaching into his bag and triumphantly producing an unopened bottle of vodka.

"Look, look! The commander had been hiding this bottle of vodka from us all this time," Ivan Pavel crows, joining in the laughter that filled the tent.

"To all of us and a special cheers to the commander!" Lev shouted, standing up and directing his mug towards Olev.

Kunuk and Suluk remained seated, taken aback by the unexpected exuberance in the air.

"Gentlemen, we don't drink alone here!" Olev booms, turning his attention to the two Inuit guides. "Get up and grab your mugs! Let no one have an empty cup while there's still something left in the bottle."

Reluctantly, the two Inuit rose to their feet, gradually immersing themselves in the festive atmosphere, fueled by Olev's vodka. More toasts were made, and jokes were exchanged, as the spirits soared.

As the night progressed, the atmosphere mellowed slightly, with contentment etched on their faces as they reminisced about their adventures over the past few days.

"I propose that we prepare and pack our equipment before retiring for the night, ensuring everything is in order for an early departure in the morning," Olev says.

"Let's hope the weather remains favorable, and our journey goes smoother this time. I've had my fill of wind and snow," Lev commented as he began wrapping and packing the instruments.

"Ivan, here's your magic camera."

"Wait, don't touch anything," Ivan exclaims, startled. "I'll take care of it." He reached out, retrieved the wooden box from Lev, and carefully placed it on the floor, ensuring its safety.

With anticipation, Ivan delicately opens the box, revealing a rectangular black object adorned with a glass lens. As he presses a hidden mechanism, a triangular skin beneath expands, exposing a lens at the top.

"Did you capture the images you were hoping for?" Lev asks.

"I certainly hope so. However, I need to process the film plates first," Ivan replies, his eyes fixed on his prized invention.

"This is the first time I've put it to the test in these unique light and humidity conditions. I'm eager to see the outcome of the images," he adds, pride unmistakable in his voice.

Lev teases him playfully, "I'm also looking forward to the results. You claim these plates register and fix the images onto paper, but I still find it hard to grasp the concept."

"I believe these photographs will serve as a visual documentation of our expedition, showcasing what we've witnessed and the efforts we've put in," Ivan explains confidently, relishing the thought of the amazement his images will evoke.

Kunuk rises from his seat, followed by Suluk, and bids the group goodnight, "Gentlemen, we shall retire to our tent and prepare for tomorrow. We'll double-check the dogs and sleds. Sleep well."

"Goodnight, everyone. Until tomorrow," Olev responds, taking one final gulp of vodka before parting ways for the night.

The Ship

The tempestuous fury from the ocean finds its mirror in the disarray within the dilapidated cafeteria. The atmosphere hangs heavy with the acrid scent of fuel, while whiskey bottles, upturned chairs, and shattered glass fragments create a scene of chaotic aftermath strewn across the floor. A solitary mug sways in tandem with the rhythmic cadence of the waves, producing an incessant, haunting clinking sound.

Through the rusty circular windows, a blanket of gray clouds covers the horizon. The crashing waves relentlessly assault the ship's hull.

A man is lying on a table, his head resting on his arms. In his forties, with tanned skin, he wears a worn brown leather jacket. A crimson streak cuts through his long, unkempt black hair. His face is marked by scars and stubble, with dried blood and saliva trailing from his lips.

A hand gently shakes his shoulder, accompanied by a pleading voice, "John! John. Wake up. John!"

Startled from his slumber, John stirs, grumbles, and slowly raises his head to survey his surroundings, his voice hoarse and gruff, "What is it? Rachel is that you?! What do you want?"

"The captain is looking for you, John," Rachel replies.

He attempts to sit up, rubbing his weary eyes, running his fingers through his scruffy beard, and wiping away the dried blood. He gazes at the woman in her mid-thirties, clad in a winter jacket with a fur-lined hood. She meets his gaze with a blend of pity and irritation.

"Damn, what did we eat yesterday? There's this awful fishy taste in my mouth," John remarks, licking his lips.

"Where is everyone? This place was packed just a while ago..."

He scans the surroundings, attempting to clear his foggy thoughts. "What does the captain want now? What time is it?" He cradles his head in his hands, bowing down. His stomach churns, and the pounding in his head gets worse.

"You caused quite a scene last night, as usual." She doesn't bother hiding her exasperation. "But the crew managed to handle you this time.

Make your way to the captain now. We're almost reaching the harbor. Finally," she says, breathing out at last. "Once you're done speaking with the captain, it would be great if you could help us with the equipment."

Without waiting for a response, she swiftly turns and heads toward the exit. John rises from his seat, leaning on the table, and drops his head into his hands, shaking it in frustration.

"Damn it, I fuck it up again," he mutters under his breath, pushing the bottle aside, causing it to topple over and spill its remaining contents onto the table. He gathers himself, placing the chair back on the table and running his hand through his hair to ease the tension in his body.

Approaching the bar, he picks up a mug containing some cold coffee and takes a sip, grimacing as he spits out the coffee grounds that caught his tongue. He gently touches the wound on his head, which is marked with dried blood. After placing the mug on the counter, he leaves the cafeteria.

Outside, the aging and rusted freighter is buffeted by the relentless waves, creating an unsettling sway. The dim morning light casts a gray hue on the horizon, while a few icicles dangle from the ship's railings and cables.

John struggles up a ladder, his dizziness exacerbated by the rolling of the waves. Before entering the bridge, he peeks through the grimy glass door, observing two men inside. One, younger and clad in a yellow waterproof jacket with a thick sweater underneath, stares intently at the horizon as he steers the rudder. Beside him stands an older, sturdy man wearing a worn nautical jacket and a crumpled, dirty hat, scanning the horizon with his binoculars.

Taking a deep breath, John opens the door, welcoming the sound of crashing waves and the chilling, salty breeze into the bridge. He addresses the captain, "Good morning, Captain Holmes. Rachel informed me that you wished to see me," closing the door behind him and grasping the nearest support to steady himself against the persistent waves and the nausea they induce.

The captain remains focused on the binoculars, issuing instructions to the pilot without acknowledging John's presence. Finally, he turns his gaze toward John.

"And ensure that everything is ready for Dr. John Saladi and his crew upon our arrival at the dock. We must avoid drawing excessive attention while unloading their equipment," he adds, casting an ironic smile while assessing John from head to toe.

"Good morning. You look terrible. Ensure that you're ready to disembark within 45 minutes to prevent any complications. I want all of you off my ship as soon as possible."

"Thank you for the information, Captain. Rest assured, we will be prepared on time, and we won't cause any further trouble," John replies, feeling a bit uneasy as he extends his hand to the captain.

"You're welcome. I hope you encounter no issues at the port. Although we arrived early, I advise you to exercise discretion," the captain says, shaking John's hand and attempting to offer a smile.

John turns away from the captain, closes the door, and descends the metal stairs to the ship's hold. There, he finds a group of three people working diligently, despite the cold, dark, and cramped surroundings.

He observes them silently for a moment, attempting to compose himself. He adjusts his hair and slaps his face lightly to awaken his senses before approaching them.

The group engages in cheerful conversation, relieved to conclude their arduous journey while organizing and arranging various boxes and equipment within two sturdy nets on the floor.

John approaches and slows down, forcing a smile on his lips.

On top of a wooden box, Rachel is standing coordinating the team's activities.

"Good morning, everyone," John greets, receiving only brief and tense responses in return.

"Rachel, how are things going here? Is everything prepared?" he asks, attempting to overlook the cool reception from his teammates. "The captain informed me that we would be arriving in less than an hour.

We must have everything in order before we disembark," he says, taking a seat on one of the boxes.

Rachel's expression shifts as she glances at him.

"It's good to see you awake and coherent... well, I hope so. We have everything organized and nearly ready. Steve needs help with your special boxes," she indicates a cluster of long, heavy boxes bearing labels that read 'Danger. Do Not Open.'

"Ensure the weight distribution in the net is balanced when you group them," she adds.

"Yes, ma'am! At your command." John throws in a mock salute and heads over to Steve. "Hey, Steve. How can I help?"

"It appears you've had another one of your nights. You look dreadful, man," Steve says, eyeing him with open disdain. "It would be great if you could lend me a hand with these boxes. They're too heavy for me."

"Fine. Let's get it done." John doesn't look up. "I'll grab my things afterward."

As he bends down to pick up a box, a sudden wave of nausea overwhelms him. In an instant, a forceful bout of vomit sprays onto the floor and the box in front of him, prompting everyone to recoil in disgust.

"Damn it, John! That's repulsive!" Rachel exclaims, covering her face with her hand. "Please go sit in the corner and keep quiet."

John obediently finds a spot away from the group, raising his hand apologetically. As the nausea subsides and the unpleasant taste fades, he rests his head between his knees, taking deep breaths.

"I don't know how we're going to accomplish our mission with all this happening," Marta grumbles.

Rachel looks at John and lowers her head in despair. Steve sits in the opposite corner, his gaze fixed on the ground, filled with disappointment.

"Does anyone have any water? Could someone pass me some water, please?" John requests, raising his head and attempting to stand, relying on a stack of nearby boxes for support as his legs feel weak.

"Here you go," Rachel offers, handing him a bottle.

He rinses his mouth and spits onto the floor, remaining silent as he watches the water slowly seep through the floorboards.

"John, this journey has already strained the group's morale. Your behavior the last few nights only exacerbated the situation. You need to restore the team's spirit, or this expedition will crumble before it even begins," she implores, trying to reason with him.

"Alright, Rachel. You're right, and I apologize," John says, struggling to convey sincerity. "I know I haven't been at my best. But don't worry; things will change once we reach land. We just need to get off this damn ship."

Despite his words, the team does not seem convinced, returning quietly to their respective tasks.

"Let's pick up the pace." John pushes himself up gingerly, leaning on the nearby crates for support. "We must disembark swiftly and without drawing excessive attention. We need to evade inspection at the port."

"Well, let's stop talking and get this over with. I can't fathom how the university got involved in this," Marta retorts, her gaze fixed sternly on John.

"I'm confident that the university is well aware of both the risks and opportunities associated with this expedition. As you were selected because you were the best in your fields, they did not choose me for my pretty face to lead the expedition. You should focus on your responsibilities and let me worry about the rest." John's jaw tightens.

"My dear John, my concerns specifically revolve around your ability to handle anything. In addition to your penchant for drinking yourself out of your grip on reality and always ending up in a physical confrontation, like the spectacle you put on last night and the nights before. At least, this last time, you didn't intimidate the sailors. I'm relieved they settled the scores from previous nights." Marta doesn't soften. "Take a good look at yourself. I still can't comprehend how you became the leader of this expedition. You lack any sense of responsibility or leadership skills."

Marta turns her back on John, returning to her previous task and refusing to engage in further discussion. John's eyes narrow with anger, but Rachel's gaze helps him maintain his composure.

Suddenly, the captain's voice reverberates from the top of the stairs, jolting them all. "We'll be docking in less than 30 minutes. Prepare to unload your equipment," he bellows, sparing John from addressing Marta's comment directly.

"We'll be ready in 15 minutes, captain. Don't worry, we have everything under control," Rachel shouts back, even though the captain has already moved away from the stairs.

The team exchanges anxious glances, waiting for someone to take charge.

"Come on, what are you all waiting for? Expecting the captain to help us unload?" Steve jokes, breaking the tension with a hint of sarcasm.

The morning unfolds peacefully, with scattered clouds adorning the sky.

On the bridge, the captain observes as his crew prepares to secure the ship. A sailor approaches him and hands over a piece of paper. "Just received this, captain."

"Damn it," the captain mutters under his breath after reading the message.

"Get Dr. John on the line immediately!" the captain shouts through the bridge door, pulling out his cell phone and stepping away from the doorway.

The Phenomenon

Inside their tent, Kunuk and Suluk are preparing for bed when Kunuk notices Suluk's edginess.

"Suluk, what's wrong? You seem tense," Kunuk observes.

"I don't know, Dad. It's the dogs," Suluk responds, getting up to check on them outside. "They've been acting strangely for a while now."

While Suluk stares outside the tent, a clear, starry night does not reveal any sign of the dogs' restlessness. Some are cowering in the sleds, whimpering in distress, while others growl restlessly, their ears perked up and their gazes darting toward the sky.

Inside their tent, Olev and his companions continue packing their belongings, unaware of the animals' unease.

Suddenly, the dogs stop howling and remain silent, in an alert position, with their gaze fixed on the sky. Tensions rise as they begin to grow agitated; some express their unease through low growls, while others opt to retreat with quiet whimpering.

A heavy silence descends upon the scene. Out of nowhere, a persistent, piercing screech cuts through the night, growing louder with each passing moment.

Conversations within the tents come to an abrupt halt as everyone falls silent, their ears attuned to the sound. The dogs bark ferociously. Just as suddenly as it had begun, the noise abruptly falls silent, shrouding the night in a heavy cloak of anticipation. However, the breathless suspense proves short-lived. A mere few seconds later, a deafening, thunderous blast erupts, its sheer force rattling everything and everyone to their very core, leaving them utterly stunned.

"What the hell was that?" Ivan reacts first, leaping to his feet and gazing at his companions in confusion.

"Did you hear that?" Suluk bursts into the tent, followed by Kunuk, both looking frightened and bewildered.

The dogs outside bark frantically.

"Did you see anything strange out there?" Olev asks, his gaze focused on each of them intently.

"We didn't see anything. We have no idea what just happened," Suluk replies, his voice unsteady.

Olev moves towards the tent's exit, followed closely by Lev and Ivan.

"It looks like something fell and exploded," Lev comments, scanning the night sky.

"It must have been a meteorite or something. There's nothing else around here. We're in the middle of nowhere. It had to be a meteorite," Ivan suggests, searching for a plausible explanation. Meanwhile, Kunuk and Suluk try to calm the agitated dogs.

"Look! Look at that mountain over there!" Lev exclaims with excitement, startling everyone. He gestures toward a distant, enigmatic mountain on the horizon, veiled in an unusual mist, bathed in the brilliance of a radiant light that casts mesmerizing hues of both yellow and blue.

Suluk joins the others, captivated by the glow surrounding the mountain, unaware of his father's growing unease.

"Why haven't we seen that mountain before? It's not on our maps," Ivan remarks, his intrigue piqued.

"It could be because of the bad weather. Since we arrived, visibility has been poor, and the mountain might have been concealed," Lev speculates, unable to tear his gaze away from the mesmerizing display.

The mountain's ethereal play of light and shadow lends it an otherworldly, supernatural aura. A moment of silence envelops the group as they become entranced by the phenomenon.

"This is a sign, a terrible sign. Suluk, we need to leave this place," Kunuk murmurs, distress thick in his voice. He approaches his son, desperately pulling on his arm.

"Father, please calm down," Suluk pleads, torn between fear and curiosity. It is difficult for him to divert his attention from the mountain that holds him in its grip. "We have to go and see what happened."

Kunuk is desperate, his grip on Suluk's arm tightening. He understands that he won't be able to dissuade his son from going, but he cannot let him venture alone either.

"We must investigate what happened there and take this opportunity to explore the mountain," Olev asserts, furrowing his brow at Kunuk and Suluk. "You should have informed us about it, even if it deviated slightly from our planned route."

"Please, don't blame my father. I will explain," Suluk says. "That mountain is called Anguta Matu. It is a forbidden place for our people, and it holds the sacred breath of the gods. The perpetual mist that shrouds it protects it from the curiosity of men."

Olev and his companions fall silent, looking at Suluk in disbelief.

"Gentlemen, change of plans!" Olev announces, newly energized and quickly recovering from the initial shock. "Let's gather our belongings. Kunuk and Suluk, please prepare the sleds. We have a new mission."

Kunuk watches in horror as the group's mood drastically shifts. Fear is replaced by excitement, and everyone moves frantically, eager to uncover the reason behind tonight's phenomenon.

Suluk is torn between his people's rule forbidding them from approaching the mountain and the magnetic fascination it holds for him. He looks at his father, who appears disturbed and grumbling, unlike the rest of the group.

"Is everyone ready? Can we depart?" Olev asks in a commanding voice.

"I'm ready," they all respond simultaneously. Olev looks at each man with a youthful smile and shouts, "Okay! Let's go!"

A sharp crack of the whip triggers the dogs' enthusiastic barking. The sleds glide swiftly towards the enigmatic mountain, taking advantage of the clear night and perfect visibility. The wind has almost completely subsided.

As they draw closer, the peculiar rock formation ahead reveals its intricate details through the intense glow of the flames. The rocks are strangely devoid of any trace of snow or ice.

Dark spiers project more than a thousand meters in an ominous column from the massive black boulders piled at the base. Its smooth and precisely carved walls exude an air of foreboding.

The sleds come to a halt a few hundred meters from the mountain's base. While the rock formation captivates their attention, the radiant light from the flames reflected in the mist limits their visibility.

Its progression falters as the dogs begin to get nervous. Their pace slows down and they refuse to move forward.

Olev instructs everyone to stop and abandon the sleds. They grab their backpacks, lamps, and weapons, preparing to continue on foot.

"I will stay here with the dogs," Kunuk says with a compromised voice, staring at Olev with dismay.

"Good. I was about to ask you to do that. Thank you," Olev responds, understanding Kunuk's discomfort with the taboo surrounding the mountain.

Before Suluk joins the group ready to leave, Kunuk pulls his son aside and speaks to him in a hushed voice, his gaze fixed on him. "Son, be careful. Please, do not step into the black fog."

"Okay, Dad. Wait. What do you mean? What fog?" he asks, intrigued and surprised by his father's words.

"It doesn't matter now. There isn't enough time. Just remember what I've told you," Kunuk replies, turning his attention to the dogs and avoiding Suluk's curious gaze.

"Suluk, let's go!" Olev calls out, interrupting Suluk's thoughts and prompting him to join the group.

"Okay, I'm coming," Suluk shouts back, turning to his companions and casting a suspicious glance at his father, wondering what he meant by the black fog.

With cautious steps and weapons at the ready, they circle the base of the mountain, fear in every step. Their gaze remains fixed on the increasingly intense glow emanating from behind the cliffs in front of them.

After passing a large rock, they witness something enormous burning brightly in the ice, merely a hundred meters from them.

They approach, trying to shield themselves from the intense heat and acrid smell. Even from a distance, they can feel the hellish heat of the fiercely burning blue flames.

"Something massive crashed here, and it doesn't appear to be a meteorite," comments Lev.

Fifty meters to their right, a deep and wide groove in the ice leads towards the flames.

"Can anyone make out what's burning?" Ivan asks as his eyes adjust to the firelight, and the shape of the burning object becomes more discernible.

"It looks like a large metal machine," Lev says, squinting his eyes in an attempt to discern any patterns within the burning structure.

As they get closer to the wreckage, wonder and fear war within them.

The twisted metal structure is unlike anything they've ever seen, and they can't help but wonder where it came from and how it ended up here in the snowy desert.

"I would say it resembles a massive warship, although it's unlike anything I've ever known or seen. It can't be one of those new flying machines people are talking about. This is too big, and I don't see any wings," says Olev, his gaze fixed on the burning structure.

"It's undoubtedly a machine, but I have no idea what kind it is," Lev says, his eyes drifting to the starry sky above. "There's no way something of this magnitude could fly."

As Ivan sets up his tripod to capture images of the strange structure, Olev suggests splitting up to explore the area. He proposes that he and Suluk go to the right while Ivan and Lev explore to the left. They agree to be cautious and call out if they encounter anything unusual.

As they search the surroundings, taking advantage of the light provided by the bright flames, Ivan notices a group of metal plates stuck in the ice a few meters away, devoid of any fire. The plates bear unfamiliar inscriptions and symbols. He calls the others' attention to them.

Lev examines the inscriptions closely, trying to make sense of the characters and symbols. "I can't recognize any of these. They're completely unfamiliar," he mutters, perplexed.

"Have you felt the texture of this metal?" Ivan runs his hand over the smooth surface of the plate, marveling at its velvety feel. He takes out his camera once again to document the discovery. Both men are captivated by the enigmatic materials and collect some smaller objects, stowing them in their bags.

On the other side of the wreckage, Olev and Suluk stumble upon a peculiar green glass shape concealed behind a metal block. They are drawn to a glass dome lying on the ground, mesmerized by its flawless condition.

Suddenly, Suluk notices something on the floor behind it.

Approaching cautiously, Suluk realizes a person is lying on the ground. He grips his spear tightly, curious despite himself, unease coiling in his stomach. "There's someone here," he murmurs nervously to Olev.

Olev joins him and exclaims, "You're right. And look at the size of him. He's nearly three meters tall!" Wonder lights his face, a sharp contrast to Suluk's growing apprehension.

The stranger is clad in a tight, one-piece suit that seems entirely unsuitable for the frigid climate.

On his head rests a helmet made of the same material as the green glass dome that caught their attention.

Suluk curiously asks, "Is he dead?"

Olev examines the motionless figure and responds, "I don't think so. I don't see any visible wounds, but I also don't see any signs of breathing."

Their attention is abruptly diverted when Suluk notices another figure nearby. This one is not lying unconscious but is instead crouched and actively searching for something. Despite being hunched over, they can discern that this individual is also unusually tall and slender.

"Shouldn't we call the others?" Suluk whispers.

"Not yet, let's wait," Olev replies, pulling back his hood to expose his head. With his shotgun pointed towards the ground, he calls out to the stranger, "Hello. Do you need help?"

The stranger jumps in surprise, turning towards them. Their view of his face is obstructed by the opaque helmet, but it's clear that he's trying to communicate something. Suddenly, another stranger appears next to him, eyeing them nervously.

Olev grips his shotgun tightly, but he keeps it pointed down, showing no hostile intent. "Can we assist you? Your companion seems to be in need of help," Olev offers, gesturing toward the injured stranger.

The tall strangers continue to gesture anxiously, seemingly engaged in a heated argument. Olev and Suluk exchange puzzled glances, unable to hear their words. The situation starts to make them uneasy, their apprehension deepening.

Without warning, a blinding flash illuminates the surroundings, followed by a muffled explosion that reverberates through the air. Everyone is thrown to the ground, dazed and disoriented. The impact leaves them temporarily deafened and momentarily blinded by the intense glare. Olev manages to lift his head and sees Suluk lying motionless nearby. A sharp pain throbs in his head, and he too succumbs to unconsciousness.

Meanwhile, Kunuk, who stands with the dogs, shares in the surprise brought on by the unexpected flash and deafening blast. While the physical impact is absent, panic and unease grip him just the same, his thoughts consumed by worry for Suluk. Strangely, the dogs appear unperturbed, their senses seemingly untouched by the event, adding to Kunuk's bewilderment.

With a heavy heart with worry, his gaze remains fixed on the smoldering wreckage, the place where his son and his companions should be.

From this distance, the true magnitude of the chaos remains shrouded in uncertainty, leaving him in agonizing suspense.

"Suluk," he mutters, his face etched with anguish, wrestling with the fear of the looming mountain and the torment of uncertainty about his son's fate. After a brief internal struggle, he resolves to suppress his fear and search for Suluk. He wrestles with the restless dogs, attempting to urge them forward, but their resistance anchors him to the spot.

Summoning all his determination, Kunuk manages to overpower the dogs' stubbornness and finally guides the sleds toward the location where he hopes to find his son.

Lev and Ivan lie on the ground, still reeling from the explosion. Ivan's camera rests on the floor beside him, still attached to the tripod.

"Ivan, what just happened? Are you alright?" Lev asks, sitting up and surveying his motionless companion. "Ivan, can you hear me?" he calls out again, growing increasingly worried by the lack of response from his friend. The weight of silence bears down on him as he attempts to rise to his feet.

"Lev, what in the world happened? Are you okay?" Ivan asks, still feeling a bit dizzy as he raises his body, searching for his companion.

"Thank goodness," Lev sighs in relief. "I think I'm alright. How about you?"

"I don't feel anything seriously wrong, just a bit dizzy. What the hell was that? Did you see what happened?" Ivan asks, trying to regain his composure.

"I have no idea. It felt like an explosion or something. But I don't see any smoke or any other signs that could explain what happened," Lev says, struggling to get back on his feet.

"We need to check on the others," Ivan says, scanning their surroundings. "Yes, you're right. Let's find them. I hope they're alright."

He dismounts the tripod and slings the camera over his shoulder. Acting cautiously, they call out to their companions, hope and anxiety coloring their voices. They search the area carefully and on alert, anticipating any potential future surprises.

Continuing along the path their companions took, they come across the lifeless bodies of two tall, slender strangers lying amidst a pile of metal plates embedded in the icy ground. A few meters away, Olev and Suluk, along with another stranger, lie unconscious.

"Who on earth are these guys? Look at their size. Is that a helmet on their heads?" Lev asks, slowing his pace as they approach the strangers.

"Do you think they're dead? But what the hell clothes do they wear? They must be frozen."

"I have no idea. Let's first check on Olev and Suluk, and then we can try to make sense of these individuals," Ivan suggests.

He kneels beside their companions. "They both appear unconscious. I don't see any visible injuries," he says, relieved.

"Ivan, Lev, are you alright?" a familiar voice startles them, causing them to spin around.

"What's happened to Suluk and Olev? Is my son hurt?" Concern sharpens Kunuk's voice.

"Kunuk, it's good to see you. I'm so relieved you're here," Lev says.

"They don't seem to be injured. Where are the sleds?" Ivan asks.

"I left them at a safe distance and came on foot," Kunuk explains, kneeling beside Suluk with a nervous expression. "What's wrong with Suluk? Is he hurt?"

"No, I don't think so. I can't see any wounds on them," Ivan replies, trying to calm the anxious Inuit.

"I hope they regain consciousness soon. I don't feel safe here. We don't know what happened or what could still happen. We should find a more secure area," Ivan says, uneasy.

"Kunuk, bring the sleds. We'll take them back behind those boulders where we stopped earlier," Lev adds.

Kunuk stands up and nods. Before heading toward the sleds, he points at the fallen strangers ahead, alarm spreading across his face.

"Are the Sdax dead? Did you take them down?" Kunuk's words catch Ivan and Lev off guard.

"What? Who are the Sdax?" Ivan asks, confused.

"I don't know. They appear unconscious. But why would we have taken them down?" Lev is startled by Kunuk's question.

"Why did you call them Sdax? Do you know them?" Ivan asks, his curiosity piqued.

"No, not at all. I'll go get the sleds," Kunuk evades the questions, visibly uncomfortable. Keeping his eyes on the strangers, he turns and heads toward the sleds.

"What the hell? Does Kunuk know something about these strangers?" Ivan wonders aloud.

"I was thinking the same thing. Did you notice how he didn't even react to their unusual appearance? It was as if he'd seen them before. And his avoidance when you asked about the name 'Sdax.' Something's off, and I don't like it," Lev expresses his concerns.

"Well, our priority now is to get our comrades to safety and help them recover," Lev says, glancing at Olev and Suluk lying on the ground.

"Okay. Give me a moment. I want to take some pictures of the strangers while we wait for Kunuk. We will need proof or no one will believe us." Ivan opens his camera, approaches the strangers, and captures photos of each of them.

Soon after, Kunuk returns. They carefully load Olev and Suluk onto the sleds. However, Kunuk remains fixated on the strangers. "Did you see how they arrived? Were they alone?" he asks, unable to hide his unease.

Ivan and Lev exchange surprised glances, taken aback by Kunuk's questions and his noticeable nervousness, constantly scanning their surroundings, especially the sky.

"We don't know. They were already here when we arrived, just like Olev and Suluk," Ivan responds.

"But why are you asking these strange questions? Who did you expect them to be with?" Lev confronts Kunuk, making him visibly embarrassed and unable to provide an answer.

"Let's go now. Our priority is our companions. We'll figure out what to do with the strangers later," Ivan says, realizing Kunuk's discomfort and his unwillingness to discuss the matter further.

Kunuk stands up, nodding in agreement. Before turning towards the sleds, he looks again at the fallen strangers.

#

Suluk is the first to regain consciousness, attempting to move his body.

"Son, how are you feeling?" Kunuk asks, supporting Suluk's head and providing him with something comfortable to rest on. Olev stirs and groans, his face contorted in pain.

"Olev, my friend, how do you feel?" Ivan calls out to his partner, mimicking Kunuk's actions.

Suluk looks at his father, attempting to sit up. "Dad, what's happening? Where are we?"

"You're safe now. Don't worry. You were unconscious, but everything is fine. Drink some water. Your lips are dry," Kunuk reassures, adjusting Suluk's position and offering him a sip from the canteen.

"What the hell happened? Where are we?" Olev asks, struggling to sit up and casting an unsteady gaze at his companions.

"Welcome back, comrades. We were concerned about both of you," Lev says, letting out a sigh of relief and placing his arm around Olev's shoulders.

"There was some kind of explosion, or at least that's what it seemed like. All of us were knocked out," Ivan explains, relieved to see his teammates recovering. "Lev and I regained consciousness after a while, but it took longer for you two. Luckily, Kunuk arrived with the sleds and helped us bring you to this safer location. As far as we can tell, nobody is injured. Do you guys remember anything?"

"No, nothing. I don't know... Wait," Suluk tries to recall, but Olev cuts in, excitement rising in his voice. "The tall strangers! Yes, now I remember," he says, gripping Lev's shoulder.

"Some incredibly tall strangers wearing strange clothing and a green glass helmet. Do you remember, Suluk? Did you see them too?" Olev eagerly looks to Suluk for confirmation.

"Yes, it's true. I remember now. There were three of them, right?" Suluk replies, his excitement growing as he locks eyes with each of his companions.

"Yes, you're both correct," Ivan acknowledges, trying to temper their enthusiasm.

"Lev, Kunuk, and I also saw them. When we found you, they were unconscious, one next to you, and the other two about 10 meters away. They might still be there. We should check on them. How are you feeling now?" Ivan asks, eager to capture images of the mysterious strangers.

"NO!" Kunuk shouts, startling everyone with his sudden outburst. "I disagree! We should return to camp. All of this is a bad omen. We shouldn't remain here," he frantically looks around, attempting to persuade them to leave.

"Kunuk, what's happening? What are you afraid of?" Olev asks, feeling unsettled by Kunuk's behavior.

"We should check on the three strangers and find out who they are. They might need our help. Aren't you curious about them?" Lev questions, surprised by Kunuk's agitated state.

"Suluk, it's time to go." Kunuk firmly holds onto Suluk's arm, disregarding Lev's words. "This is enough. We shouldn't even be here."

"We should return to camp and then head home. Let them stay if they wish. We've already completed our task. That's enough, son. Let's go," he passionately argues with his son in their native language, making Olev and the others uncomfortable as they are unable to understand.

"I'm sorry, Dad. I understand your fear of being here. But I also need to understand what's happening and who these strangers are. There are too many intriguing things unfolding for me to walk away," Suluk says, maintaining eye contact with his father and gently releasing his arm.

"Suluk, Kunuk, what's going on? We don't understand anything you're saying. Please explain to us," Olev expresses his frustration.

"Dad, you can go back to camp if you want," Suluk now switches to Russian. "I'm sure no one will stop you. But I'm going with them."

He turns towards one of the sleds, checking the dogs' harnesses and avoiding eye contact with his father or the others. Suluk feels guilty for defying his father in this way, a knot forming in his stomach. Even if he wasn't so curious about the strangers, he knows he would still go with the group. Something inside him has awakened, and he feels the need to assert himself before his father for the first time.

An awkward silence descends upon the group as Kunuk sits on his sled, stunned by his son's attitude.

He smiles as he gazes at his son, realizing that his cub has grown into a capable man who can make decisions and stand by them. If he doesn't take care of him, who will? Kunuk knows he will never forgive himself for leaving his son alone on this adventure.

Despite his fears and the taboos that once held him back, Kunuk couldn't bear to miss the opportunity to embark on this daring adventure alongside his son. The uncertainty of the future weighed heavily on him, making him realize that there might not be many more chances like this to create lasting memories together.

He stands up and prepares his sled, determination in his eyes. Suluk approaches him, sadness shadowing his face. "Dad, I'm sorry for my words. I hope you understand. I don't want to disappoint or anger you."

"Don't worry about your stubborn old father. I'm not angry with you. I'm very proud. But you won't get rid of me so easily," Kunuk says, climbing onto the sled and calling for the dogs. "Let's go then. Let's see if the strangers are still there," he says, bringing a smile of relief to everyone's faces.

"Welcome, Kunuk. It wouldn't be the same without you," Olev says with a wink.

With a shout to the dogs and a crack of the whip, they set off toward the smoldering wreckage. The flames from the main wreckage still burn, casting intense light and aiding their search. They leave the sleds near a cluster of non-burning metal plates and walk the final few meters until they reach the green dome. The three strangers remain motionless on the ground, just as they left them.

Approaching cautiously, they keep a lookout as Kunuk stays by the sleds, sitting near the dogs and soothing them with his touch.

Ivan grabs his camera, eyes lit with excitement as he prepares to capture the scene, carefully selecting the best angles. He envisions his pictures being praised and showcased at the Academy, with leading newspapers in the country vying to publish his images. Who knows, perhaps even worldwide recognition.

Olev moves towards the first stranger and kneels beside the body. Ivan holds the camera in his trembling hands as his companions stay a few steps behind him, their weapons firmly gripped.

"From what I can see, the body structure appears human," Olev remarks, avoiding direct contact with the stranger and maintaining a composed posture as he describes his observations.

"But the body is much more elongated and slender than that of a human. They must be about two and a half meters tall.

The clothing they're wearing is delicate and lacks any fur covering, which is highly unusual and unsuitable for these temperatures," he adds, glancing at the other two bodies lying on the ground from a distance.

The three strangers wore what appeared to be sleek, thin boots, or perhaps their shoes were integrated with the suits they wore. The helmets that covered their heads were made of green glass, seamlessly connected to the rest of the suits. Olev had never seen anything like it before.

Lev approached, leaning over one of the strangers to get a closer look.

Suluk, wary and fearful as he'd always been taught to be, held back from joining the others in their curiosity. Throughout his life, he had learned to fear and respect his people's values and beliefs, especially anything associated with Anguta.

"Can you see their features?" Lev gestured toward the stranger.

"No, I can't see anything through the helmet. It's completely opaque," Olev replied. Despite his apprehension, he couldn't resist gently lifting the stranger to get a better view. "They seem to be unconscious. I don't see any signs of injury, at least not on this one," he said. "This guy is much heavier than I expected for someone so skinny."

As Olev pulled the body closer to examine it further, he asked, "Lev, can you check the other two for any wounds or injuries?"

"Sure," Lev responded, approaching the other two strangers. He leaned over one while Ivan pointed the camera at them. "They also appear stunned. I don't see any signs of injury," Lev reported.

"This one doesn't seem to have any physical issues either," Olev said, examining the back of the stranger he was still holding. "But something stands out - it looks like a backpack inside the suit."

As Olev continued to observe the body, he noticed a metal disc partially hidden in the snow beneath it. Upon closer inspection, he realized the disc was circular, composed of interlocking rings adorned with various inscriptions. In the center, an emerald glass sphere contained something that emitted a faint glow from within. Quickly and quietly, he removed the disc and concealed it within his coat, keeping it hidden from the others.

Suddenly, an intense light illuminated their surroundings, catching them off guard. Floating a few meters above them was a massive, wingless cylinder, over thirty meters in length, emitting a powerful beam of light toward them.

Olev swiftly tucked the metal disc away, unnoticed by the others. He carefully lowered the stranger's body back to the ground and took a few steps back, joining a stunned Suluk who gazed in awe at the flying object.

Lev and Ivan joined Olev and Suluk, all four of them staring at the flying cylinder.

They clutched their weapons tightly, unease written across their faces in the face of this eerie phenomenon.

Meanwhile, a few meters away, Kunuk hid in terror among the dogs, who seemed strangely indifferent to the object hovering above them.

"Are you all seeing what I'm seeing? A flying metal cylinder?" Ivan asked, disbelief edging into his voice as he tried to process the unfolding spectacle.

Lev replied, still in shock, "I don't know, man. All I can see is the biggest and quietest flying cylinder I've ever laid eyes on."

Several dozen meters away, Kunuk muttered desperately, voice shaking, "Sdax, Sdax Tayagu. Please run away; please run away."

The cylinder descended a few meters, emitting a low purring sound. The light emanating from it changed color, and thin red points of light appeared over the three strangers lying on the ground.

From beneath the middle of the hull, an intense blue beam of light emerged, enveloping and lifting the strangers inside.

Olev and his companions remained stunned and silent, their eyes fixed on the extraordinary scene unfolding before them.

The final stranger stepped aboard the cylinder, and the light vanished along with the purring sound. Suspense hung heavy in the air as Olev took a tentative step forward, his gaze apprehensive, fixed upon the suspended cylinder.

In an instant, a blinding flash filled the night, causing them all to instinctively shield their eyes. The silence that followed was broken by a softer, more comforting purr, filling the air. Kunuk, still protected by the thick fur of one of the dogs, cautiously opened his eyes. Gradually, the intense light dissipated, and his vision cleared.

Something inside him compelled Kunuk to stand up suddenly, his breath coming in ragged gasps. Anxiety surged through him as he frantically looked around, realizing that something was terribly wrong. His heart pounded in his chest, threatening to burst as he fell to his knees, struggling to catch his breath.

The flying cylinder had vanished, along with everyone else. There was no sign of his son.

"Suluk..." he groaned, anguish and despair thick in his voice, "Suluk!" he screamed, his desperation and fear driving him forward. Fatigue and fear seem to have no hold on him as he runs, his breath quickening with each step. He looks around, his eyes scanning the empty landscape, but there is no one in sight. All that remains is the smoldering wreckage and the silence of the white expanse. Where Suluk and his companions once stood, only their abandoned belongings remain—weapons, backpacks, Ivan's camera, a peculiar round metal plate with a crystal, and various other items they had collected from the wreckage.

"Damn it, Suluk!" Kunuk shouts in frustration as he picks up the objects scattered on the ground. His eyes are red with anger, tears streaming down his cheeks. Returning to the sleds, he searches the area for any clue that might lead him to his son and the others. "Suluk!" he repeatedly calls out, desperate hope straining his voice, yearning for any sign that would rekindle his flickering flame of hope.

As he passes behind the main wreckage, something catches his attention. There, lying on the ground, is what appears to be a body.

A shiver of hope courses through his veins, and he rushes toward it with renewed determination.

However, as he gets closer, he slows down, realizing that the body is not Suluk or any of his companions. It is just another stranger, dismembered and lifeless, strangely, with no signs of blood.

The glass helmet is shattered, and Kunuk peers inside, unable to comprehend what he sees. It is neither human nor any recognizable living being. Metal fragments and colored wires protrude from the broken figure, emitting wisps of smoke. One of its legs hangs loosely, exposing more wires and components.

There are no bones, no flesh, and no blood. Confusion engulfs Kunuk as he recoils, his mind struggling to make sense of the surreal sight before him. "They're not human...they're demons!" he mutters, backing away in trembling fear. Hastily, he retreats to the sled and urges the dogs away from the area, unable to comprehend or reconcile what he has witnessed. He shakes his head, closing his eyes tightly, attempting to banish the unsettling image of the otherworldly being.

Overwhelmed by desperation, Kunuk loses track of time and the countless rounds he has made across the wreckage. Exhaustion and hopelessness weigh him down until he can no longer go on.

Collapsing to the ground, he expends the last remnants of his energy, his mind consumed by a whirlwind of confusion and despair. "Suluk," he whispers, his voice barely audible.

The dogs gather around him, whimpering and offering their solace. Kunuk embraces them, tears streaming down his face.

"It's all my fault. I should never have brought you here," he says, succumbing to fatigue and heartbreak, his words carrying the weight of remorse.

But Kunuk knows he can't linger there if he wants to ensure his survival through the night. Summoning the last shreds of his strength, he climbs onto his sled and makes his way back to the camp, dragging the other sleds behind him. Darkness engulfs him as he distances himself from the wreckage and the accursed mountain, the weight of pain and sorrow suffocating his heart, and crushing his soul.

#

He awakens abruptly, disoriented and flustered, his head throbbing with pain. The air around him is filled with a cacophony of shrill noises, jarring his senses. As he rises to his feet, his mind foggy and bewildered, he notices a crowd rushing towards a nearby train. Lost in their frenzy, no one seems to notice his presence. Feeling disconnected and out of place in this strange and chaotic world, he observes people screaming and jostling their way toward the train.

The billowing white smoke from the locomotive fills his nostrils with damp and familiar heat. Amidst the confusion, he experiences no fear, only a deep, pervasive disorientation. The whistles and cries of the crowd reach a fever pitch, snapping him back to reality. He gazes down at his peculiar, cumbersome attire, radiating an uncomfortable warmth.

A family passes by, casting suspicious glances in his direction. A child directs their curious gaze towards the man and asks, "Why is that man dressed like that? Isn't he hot?"

At first, the man is confused by the unfamiliar words, but he slowly pieces together their meaning, leading to an unexpected understanding of the conversation.

The child's innocent curiosity is met with a scolding from his mother, who reprimands him for his lack of manners. "Hush, Hans. Don't speak about people you don't know. It's impolite."

As the family moves away, the man finds himself engulfed in a new cloud of white, humid smoke, momentarily obscuring his view of the approaching figure in a mysterious police uniform. "Good morning, sir. Can I be of assistance?"

"Good morning," he replies, struggling to comprehend the unfamiliar dialect. "To be honest, I'm not sure. Where am I? What place is this?" he asks, feeling somewhat foolish for his inquiries.

The police officer studies him, curious and intrigued. "My friend, you are at the Hamburg train station.

From your accent, I'd venture to say you are Russian. Are you lost? What is your name?"

Taken aback by the officer's questions, he responds, "I'm afraid I don't know how to answer your questions," his surprise grows as the words effortlessly flow from his lips in this foreign language.

"I don't remember my name. I don't know where I am, or how I got here," he says, frustration and annoyance sharpening his voice.

"Well, at least you can speak German. That's a positive sign," the police officer remarks, accompanied by a satisfied laugh.

"Judging by your attire, it seems you've come from a much colder place than Hamburg. Can you tell me today's date?"

The man shakes his head, his frustration growing. "I haven't the slightest idea. I'm sorry."

"Dear me, you're in quite a predicament," the officer replies sympathetically. "It's March 15th, 1910."

The man's blank expression confirms to the officer that this information holds no significance for him.

"Can you recall if you fell or were hit on the head?" the officer asks, trying to puzzle out what has happened to this enigmatic individual.

"I don't remember anything," the man replies, with resignation. "I don't feel any pain except for this persistent headache. Maybe it's because of the effort to recover my memory."

"Well, my friend, it seems you'll need to accompany me to the police station. Perhaps we can find a way to assist you," the officer suggests gently, extending an invitation to follow him.

Feeling overwhelmed and weary, the man agrees, trailing behind the officer through the bustling train station, shedding his heavy fur coat along the way. With unsteady steps, he struggles to keep pace with the police officer as his mind races, searching for memories that might offer answers to his myriad questions.

#

"Is he alive?"

A voice shatters the silence, jolting him awake. He attempts to open his eyes and finds himself lying face down on the ground, a metallic taste of blood in his mouth.

Surprise and fear flood his mind as he feels someone take his arm and shoulder from the right side of his body. Unable to resist, his body changes position, lying on his back. A warm smile framed by a thick mustache greets him against the backdrop of a vibrant blue sky. "Well, hello there. How are you feeling?"

A group of men on horseback with dark blue uniforms observes him with curiosity from a few meters away. The leader of the group dismounts and approaches. "How is our mysterious man faring?"

"Captain, based on the symbols on his hat and jacket, I'd say he's a Russian military officer," one of the soldiers observes.

Confusion fills the man's eyes as he attempts to push himself up on his elbows. "What's going on? Where am I?" he asks, urgency and bewilderment tangled in his voice.

The Captain scans the group. "Can anyone understand him? Corporal Joseph, you mentioned you know some Russian. Could you try speaking with him?"

The captain steps back, allowing Corporal Joseph to approach the man. "Hello. My name is Joseph. What's your name?" Joseph attempts to communicate in his limited Russian.

"I...don't know. I don't remember my name. Where am I?" the man responds, his face contorting in pain as he struggles to recall something, attempting to sit up.

"He says he doesn't remember his name and is asking where he is," Joseph translates for the captain.

"Well, that's peculiar. But how did this man end up here? There's nothing for miles around, and we haven't seen any caravans in the past few days," one of the other soldiers points out, expressing their collective confusion.

"Where am I?" the man repeats, this time switching to English.

"Good, you speak English," the captain acknowledges smiling, crouching next to the mysterious Russian. "Well, buddy, you're in the state of Iowa. We'd love to know how you ended up here. There's nothing within hundreds of miles of here."

The man shrugs his shoulders, unable to provide an answer to the question posed to him.

"Sir, I apologize, but we must continue our mission," the captain states, rising to his feet. "Joseph and Thomas, help him up and take him to Fort Dodge. Let the doctor assess his condition and allow the commander to decide what to do with him. Perhaps he'll regain his memory in the meantime," the captain orders, remounting his horse.

The soldiers assist the man to his feet and carefully lift him onto a horse, while the rest of the patrol resumes their journey in the original direction.

Puerto Deseado

"Dr. John! Dr. John!"

A sailor's urgent voice reverberates through the hold, capturing the attention of the entire team. "The captain needs to speak with you immediately. It appears there's a problem at the port."

"Thanks, inform him I'll be right there," John shouts back, setting aside his current task. Annoyed by the unexpected development, he grumbles, "What the hell is going on now?" as he ascends the stairs toward the ship's bridge. Rachel, Marta, and Steve exchange worried glances among themselves.

"I'm here, Captain. What's wrong?" John asks the captain as soon as he gets to the bridge.

"We have an issue at the port. Your local team is missing," the captain reveals. John is surprised and worried, wondering what could have happened to the local team.

"Don't worry. I've already found a solution," the captain reassures, a shy smile creeping onto his face upon noticing John's worried expression. "When you disembark, there will be a truck waiting to take you to the city. It's the best I can do."

"Thank you, Captain." John is taken aback by the captain's helpfulness. "Thank you very much," he adds, offering a grateful smile and shaking the captain's hand.

"You're welcome. I need you off my ship as soon as possible."

"Don't worry. We're prepared and ready to go. We're just awaiting your orders to disembark," John responds, turning towards the exit and heading back to his team, his mind consumed by thoughts of what could have happened to the local group.

He descends the stairs to the cargo hold, where his team stands silently near the already closed nets. His arrival leads them to get up and approach him, eager to know what happened.

"We've a setback," John begins before anyone has a chance to inquire. "The local team didn't show up at the port as expected. However, the captain has arranged transportation to the city to resolve the situation."

He attempts a reassuring smile, hoping to alleviate his team's concerns.

"But who are these local team members?" Steve asks.

"Yes, I would also like to know who they are and why are they so secretive about who they are?" Marta asks, fixing her gaze on John.

"I understand your curiosity. Just give me a moment to explain," John says, searching his jacket pockets. "Does anyone have a cigarette? I need something to calm my pounding headache."

"No! John." Rachel crosses her arms, annoyed. "You know we're not allowed to smoke in the cargo hold."

"Damn, I forgot," John mutters in frustration. Taking a resigned breath, he continues, "The local team consists of Alberto, Ross, and Robert. Alberto was responsible for communications during the Denudasdi expedition and was at the base camp when the accident occurred. Ross and Robert are here for support and security."

"Wait a minute," Marta says. "I thought this was a scientific expedition. But you're talking about dedicated security personnel — what threats are we actually facing?"

"John, I think it's time to tell everything," Rachel says, lowering her gaze.

"You knew?" Marta's eyes snap to Rachel. "You've been keeping this from us?"

"Everyone, calm down," John says. "I'll explain."

He begins, his tone measured. "As you already know, our assignment is to find the members of the Denudasdi Mission, discover the reason behind their disappearance, and recover all their documents."

"Yes, we are aware of that," Steve says, his frustration apparent. "What we want to understand is what potential threats exist that could jeopardize our security. After all, didn't the previous team disappear due to a natural accident? Or was there something more to it?"

"We still don't have a clear understanding of what happened to the Denudasdi team," John admits, trying to be as transparent as possible.

"What was the purpose of the Denudasdi mission anyway? I still couldn't figure out what the hell they were doing in the middle of nowhere..." Marta asks.

John looks at her, shifting his gaze to each of the team members, and begins, "It all started three years ago when the Foundation received a generous offer for a set of artifacts that had long been forgotten in the storage. This mysterious offer piqued the Foundation's curiosity about the people behind it and their interest in these particular artifacts."

"What artifacts are these, and why are they so significant?" Marta asks.

"It appears that these artifacts held something of interest, as the Foundation declined the offer and instead decided to assemble a team to further study them. Some suspicious incidents have occurred since then involving the Foundation's staff and their handling of these artifacts. You may have even seen some of these incidents in the news - the mysterious death of the museum curator, the fire that destroyed part of the museum, the disappearance of the lead investigator and his assistant, and most recently, the tragic accident involving the Denudasdi team."

John pauses. His companions remain silently attentive, waiting for him to continue.

"Over the past few months, we have gathered some clues that point to potential culprits behind these incidents. As a precaution, we decided to include security personnel within our team and implemented a strict communication protocol. We cannot and should not communicate with anyone outside of the Foundation. It's a precautionary measure that all of you agreed to from the beginning." John says, rising to his feet.

"Who is behind these accidents, and what threats might we encounter?" Marta locks her eyes on John, seeking answers to her pressing questions.

"You must understand that the findings of the Foundation are highly sought after on the black market," John explains, his voice carrying a tinge of concern. Rachel sits beside him, offering a comforting gesture by placing her hand on his arm.

"I have to admit, this whole story sounds incredibly bizarre to me," Marta remarks, her frustration giving way to resignation.

"I still don't understand what makes these artifacts so special?" Steve asks, leaning against the stacked boxes in one of the rope nets.

"That's where it gets even more intriguing," John says, placing his hand on top of Rachel's. "The artifacts were collected by an American expedition in the Arctic back in 1912. During their visit to an Inuit village, they heard tales of demons, gods, curses, and other such folklore, which they initially dismissed. However, one member of the expedition, a geologist named Adam Holt, became fascinated when he heard about a mysterious Russian scientific mission that had vanished near a mystical mountain called Anguta Matu, 30 years prior."

John pauses for a moment, allowing the weight of his words to sink in, before continuing. "Adam had already heard rumors about this mission and the enigmatic disappearance of its members. His curiosity was further piqued when he discovered that one of the expedition's survivors, an elderly Inuit, lived in a nearby village."

"I don't understand," Marta says, her brow furrowing. "If all this happened in the Arctic, why are we heading to Antarctica?"

"You raise a valid point, Marta," John acknowledges. "Let me continue, and I'll address your question shortly.

Adam devoted a full day to the companionship of Kunuk, the elderly Inuit, and, with the assistance of an interpreter, meticulously recorded his captivating story.

They formed a close bond during their time together, and perhaps due to that connection, Kunuk decided to share some personal objects he had collected during the ill-fated mission, objects he had kept hidden from others."

John takes a breath, his gaze shifting between his team members. "Among these objects, Adam was particularly captivated by a metal disc adorned with mysterious inscriptions and featuring a crystal at its center. Inside the crystal, there was something that occasionally emitted a faint glow, like a trapped spark yearning to break free."

He observes the disbelief etched on his companions' faces and says, "That's how Adam described it, and his accounts have left us with more questions than answers."

Resuming his explanation, he continues, "Adam was also intrigued by several photographic plates in Kunuk's possession, which he claimed belonged to one of the Russians from the ill-fated expedition. After some challenging negotiations, Adam managed to purchase some of these objects from Kunuk."

John pauses, his tone heavier now. "Unfortunately, Adam Holt didn't survive for long after the expedition. He tragically passed away a few weeks after his encounter with Kunuk. His belongings and notes were subsequently donated to the Reversi Foundation and forgotten in a warehouse until the recent purchase proposal caught their attention.

When our team began examining the artifacts, the photographic plates immediately captured their interest," John continues. "A few of the plates revealed what Kunuk referred to as 'demons,' although they were not truly demons, the figures depicted in the images were not human either. The quality of the photographs was poor, but one could discern humanoid figures, tall and slender, clad in what appeared to be spacesuits, their heads concealed by frosted glass helmets."

Steve and Marta exchanged looks of astonishment and curiosity, and then Rachel asked. "But were these beings human or not?"

Marta, still fixated on her previous query, asks again, "And why are we heading to Antarctica? Shouldn't our search be focused on the Arctic mountain you mentioned?"

"In addition to the photographic plates, we also found the metal disc with the crystal-encrusted," John reveals. "When our team conducted extensive analyses on it, they were astounded by the results. The materials comprising the disc, both the metal and the crystal, were entirely unknown to us. But the true revelation came when we finally managed to determine the age of the disc. The results sent shockwaves through the entire Foundation community."

Eyes widen with anticipation as Steve leans in, eager for the revelation. "So, what was the date obtained?"

"To ascertain the age of the metallic disc and the crystal, our team performed multiple dating processes, and the results were nothing short of extraordinary." John can't keep the awe out of his voice. "The artifacts were estimated to be over… five million years old. Yes, you heard it right—five million years!" exclaims John, anticipating his companions' reactions.

The group remains silent, still processing the astonishing revelation. "It's inconceivable," Steve exclaims, his eyes wide with disbelief. "There's no way these artifacts could be of human origin."

Marta shakes her head refusing to accept and repeating the age incredulously. "Five million years? It's simply impossible. There's no way this can be true."

John nods understandingly, amused by their reaction. "I know it's difficult to fathom," he says calmly, allowing them a moment to digest the mind-boggling information.

Marta persists, her curiosity unabated. "And why Antarctica? I can't help but ask again."

A smile tugs at the corner of John's lips as he replies, "Well, the Foundation already has a team working in the Arctic, specifically at the Anguta mountain." He pauses, enjoying the anticipation in their eyes. "Kunuk's narrative, as documented by Adam Holt, along with the photographs and the revelation of the crystal disc, sparked a whirlwind of investigation into the foundation's long-forgotten archives. Among the many discoveries, fresh clues have surfaced, further complicating this unfolding mystery," John said, with a sigh and his eyes cast downward. He took a moment to reflect, and his companions remained silent, following his lead. John eventually broke the silence, continuing his speech.

"One of these leads takes us to Antarctica, where the Denudasdi mission was dispatched. They vanished mysteriously around four months ago under circumstances that remain to explain. This is precisely why we're now en route to Antarctica."

Worry tightens Marta's voice. "Do you think their disappearance could be related to unnatural causes?"

John's gaze meets Marta's, conveying a mix of caution and determination. "We can't say for certain at this point. However, we suspect there may be a link to unnatural factors, which is why we are taking all possible precautions."

"Dr. John, everyone!"

The team's discussion is abruptly interrupted by a voice echoing from the top of the stairs. "We're docking now. Your transport is ready. You need to be prepared in five minutes.

John claps his hands to draw the team's attention. "Alright, let's go. We'll continue this discussion later at the hotel. Rachel, can I have a moment? I need to talk to you." He pulls Rachel aside, away from the prying eyes of their companions.

"I'm sorry I didn't disclose all of this to you earlier," John says, a touch of regret in his voice. "I had strict instructions not to reveal anything until we reached Artigas."

Rachel feigns annoyance, her eyes glimmering with a smile. "I do understand, but you should have trusted me enough to confide in me. You know I'm capable of handling sensitive information."

"It's not a matter of trust," John replies earnestly. "I have to follow orders, and I didn't want to burden you with unnecessary worries."

Despite her concern, Rachel runs her fingers through John's hair with affection. "You should take things more seriously and handle these situations better," she says.

"You're right, my dear. I know, and I will," he says, embracing her warmly. They share a brief moment of reassurance before Rachel joins Marta and Steve.

Outside, the docking process grows more intense, accompanied by the clamor of men shouting and the gradual quieting of the ship's engines. The sound of activity fills the air as the team prepares to disembark. Sunlight streams through the cargo hold, casting a beam of light onto the ground before John. He takes in the bustling scene, watching the sailors' movements with a sense of anticipation.

As they make their way down the ramp to the harbor, the crisp morning air invigorates the team.

Steve relishes the cold wind on his face, a smile forming. "I hope the cafeteria at the hotel is open," he says with a grin. "I could really use a proper cup of coffee."

Arriving at the pier, they find a truck waiting for them, loaded with their luggage and equipment. The ship's captain waves goodbye from the top deck, and John reciprocates the gesture as they set off toward the town.

#

John and his team stride purposefully into the small hotel, entering the empty reception lobby. The hotel retains a sense of faded elegance, despite its outdated decor from the seventies or eighties.

"I'll take care of the check-in," John says, leaning casually against the counter. "Just leave me your documents, and I'll meet you in the cafeteria."

He collects the team's documents and taps the bell on the counter. A groggy employee emerges from behind a curtain, greeting John with a noticeable

46

Spanish accent. "Good morning, sir. Welcome to our hotel. My name is Eduardo."

"Good morning, Eduardo," John replies smoothly. "We have a reservation under the name of John Saladi."

"Fantastic, sir. Thank you for choosing our hotel. Let me just check your reservation," Eduardo says, leaning over the computer. John takes a moment to glance around, his eyes searching for something.

"Here it is, Mr. John Saladi. Four people, two rooms, staying until the twenty-third. May I?" Eduardo gestures toward the documents on the counter.

"Sure, go ahead," John slides the documents toward Eduardo.

"Are you here on vacation? Planning to go fishing or perhaps embark on one of our famous hikes?" the receptionist asks, his gaze fixed on the computer screen.

"No, we're just passing through," John replies vaguely.

"By the way, we have three more colleagues staying here. We're looking forward to meeting them. Their names are Alberto, Ross, and Robert. They must have arrived two days ago. Do you know where I can find them?" John asks, hoping for some information.

"I'm sorry, sir, but we're not allowed to give out any information about our guests.

However, if they are staying here, they might be having breakfast in the cafeteria now," Eduardo replies, a hint of embarrassment in his voice. "I'll need you to sign this form, and here are your keys and documents," he says, handing over the keys and documents to John. "Your rooms are 105 and 107, on the first floor. The elevator is to the left of the stairs. I hope you have a pleasant stay."

"Thank you very much." John collects the passports and keys, nodding his appreciation, before making his way to the cafeteria, traversing the empty and quiet hotel lobby.

Upon entering, John is greeted by a calm atmosphere. The inviting aroma of bread and coffee fills the air. The room is almost empty, with a couple eating breakfast in the corner. Rachel, Steve, and Marta are sitting around a table in the center.

"I'm still mad at you, Rachel. You knew the whole story and didn't tell us anything," Marta playfully chides, pointing her finger at Rachel.

"Relax, my dear. I'm only halfway through everything. I believe John had his reasons for not sharing it earlier," Rachel responds with a smile.

"I've been pondering what John told us about the disk. It's hard to believe, but I've always thought that we're not alone in this universe. What do you think?" Steve asks, taking a bite of his sandwich.

"In this universe? How many more universes do you know about?" Marta jests, laughing along.

"As many as you can imagine, and a few more. Just imagine, in another universe, we might not even be here, stuck in this remote place at the end of the world. I could be on a tropical island, enjoying a fantastic vacation with my family aboard my super yacht," Steve muses, leaning back in his chair with a wide grin.

"I'll take a spot in that universe, please, my captain," Rachel playfully requests, joining in the laughter.

"Those theories don't convince me. I prefer my universe, where I am now, peacefully eating a decent breakfast without annoying smells and noises. The company could be better, but it's the best you can get around here," Marta remarks, eliciting protests and laughter from the group.

John approaches the table and the bartender sets aside the dishes he was cleaning and heads over to assist him.

"I'll have the same as my colleague here," John says, gesturing towards Steve's order, before sitting.

Interrupting their conversation, John reaches into his pocket and retrieves the keys and passports. "Here you are, Rachel and Marta," he says, handing them their documents.

Turning to Steve, he hands him his documents and the room key.

"Finish your breakfast and you can head up to your rooms and take some rest until lunchtime. I'll go look for our local team. They must be around here somewhere."

Steve takes a sip of his coffee and responds, "Excellent idea. I could use a little stretch and some peace away from the constant noise and unpleasant smells."

Marta and Rachel nod in agreement. The calm moment is short-lived as Marta speaks up, breaking the silence. "John, we need to talk about what you told us. We have a lot of questions, as you can imagine."

Looking slightly bored, John replies, "Let me have my coffee and ease my headache before we delve into it."

Steve says, "It would be beneficial to clarify our doubts, John. The more I think about what you told us, the more bewildered I feel. You must share all the information with us."

John sighs and relents, "Fine, I understand. But let me enjoy my breakfast first. Finish yours, and we'll talk later."

John takes a sip of his coffee and glances at the receptionist, Eduardo, who approaches their table. Sensing Eduardo's seriousness, John's curiosity piques. "What's up? Is there something else?" he asks, looking up from his coffee.

Eduardo appears apologetic as he hands John an envelope. "I'm very sorry to interrupt your breakfast, Dr. John. Someone left a message for you. I apologize for my distraction."

John thanks Eduardo and examines the envelope, noticing the receptionist's lingering worry. "Is there anything else?" he asks, sensing Eduardo's unease.

"Yes, Dr. John," Eduardo replies, his voice trembling with concern. "I need your help. I'm worried about your friends. Strangely, they didn't show up for breakfast yesterday and today. I tried contacting them by phone, but no one answered. I went upstairs and knocked on their doors, but again, no one responded."

Eduardo continues, his voice quivering with unease, "We opened the doors and didn't find anyone when we entered the rooms. But what I saw inside worried me.

Since you mentioned that they were your companions, I decided to speak with you before calling the police. If you could be so kind as to come with me to their rooms, you'll understand my concern."

John and his colleagues fall silent, exchanging perplexed glances, trying to comprehend the unsettling situation that has unfolded.

"Alright, I'll go with you," John says, placing his napkin on the table in disappointment, unable to finish his breakfast. "I need to understand what's troubling you so much," he adds, rising from his seat and carefully tucking the envelope into his jacket pocket.

Eduardo leads the way up the stairs to the rooms, with Rachel, Marta, and Steve trailing behind, their minds filled with curiosity about the fate of the local team.

As they approach the first room, Eduardo opens the door and steps aside. The room is in chaos, with overturned furniture, open drawers, strewn clothes and towels on the floor, shattered glass, and beds in disarray.

Concern etched across his face, John asks, "Whose room is this?"

His companions huddle at the doorway, peering into the room with growing worry.

"This is Mr. Ross and Mr. Robert's room. The other room, which belongs to Mr. Alberto, is in the same state." Eduardo's voice tightens with concern. "I have no choice but to call the police given the condition of the rooms and our lack of knowledge about their whereabouts."

"Of course, you should call the police. I understand." John responds, "However, could you please open the other room and grant me five minutes?" he attempts to persuade the increasingly agitated receptionist, visibly uncomfortable. "I assure you, I won't touch anything that might interfere with the police's investigation. I just need those five minutes to try and comprehend why this may have happened."

Eduardo hesitates, his worry evident. "This is highly irregular. I hope it won't land me in trouble. I must go and contact the police now. I implore you, please ensure you are not here when they arrive, and make sure to close all the doors," Eduardo says, looking upset.

"Thank you, Eduardo. I'm genuinely grateful and don't worry, I'll remain alone. My companions will now return to their rooms," John assures him, his gaze fixed on his colleagues.

Eduardo opens the door to the other room and retreats downstairs.

Through the partially open door, it is evident to John that the room shares the same chaotic state. John meticulously surveys the space, carefully handling objects with a handkerchief he retrieves from his pocket. After thoroughly inspecting every corner, he pauses by the door, casting one final glance around before making his way to the other room.

In their room, Marta and Rachel lie in their beds, seeking solace in rest.

"This whole situation feels like a dreadful movie to me. It's clear now that the mission has nothing to do with what the Foundation has led us to believe," Marta says, wrapping herself in a blanket and turning her back to Rachel. "I need sleep. When I wake up, maybe all this will just seem like a bad dream."

"Things have certainly taken an unexpected turn. Let's hope John can uncover some answers regarding our missing colleagues," Rachel says.

Intrigued, Marta turns to face Rachel. "Speaking of John, is there something serious going on between you two?"

A blush creeps onto Rachel's cheeks as she admits, "I'm not entirely sure. It all started out of the blue. We met at a university dinner and ended up talking all night. Before we knew it, we were sharing breakfast together."

Marta chuckles, amused by the swift progression. "Well, you definitely don't waste any time, girl."

Rachel lets out a laugh, her eyes gleaming with fondness. "John can be challenging at times. He carries a lot of unresolved baggage, but there's something about him that captivates me. I can't quite put it into words. After my divorce, John was the only person who made me feel alive again."

Lost in her thoughts, Rachel gazes up at the ceiling fan.

"We've had our fair share of ups and downs, but overall, we've shared some wonderful moments. Although I must admit, some of our discussions have been quite intense," Rachel says, reminiscing.

Marta raises an eyebrow, teasingly. "Discussions? I thought they were more like you scolding him."

Rachel lets out a small laugh. "Perhaps you're right. I can be tough on him, but sometimes he deserves it."

Shifting on her bed, Rachel's curiosity gets the better of her. "And what about you, Marta? Is there someone out there who's pining for you?"

Marta replies, matter-of-factly, "No, I don't have the patience for love affairs. I know I'm not the easiest person to deal with, and I don't want to deal with anyone else's nonsense. That's why..."

Meanwhile, in Alberto's room, John continues his search for any clues regarding their missing colleagues. He meticulously examines under the bed, inside the wardrobe, and every nook and cranny where he believes something significant might be hidden.

Growing frustrated, he walks up to the bedroom window and gazes out at the city below. The sunlight casts a warm golden glow over the low-rise buildings that extend towards the harbor, where a tranquil river flows into the sea.

Lost in thought, John feels a crinkle in his jacket pocket. He retrieves the envelope Eduardo had given him, and his name, "John Saladi," is written on the front. Inside, he finds a single sheet of handwritten paper. Before he can read its contents, a car screeches to a halt outside the hotel. Two men step out and make their way into the building.

Realizing it must be the police, John swiftly leaves the room, tucking the envelope back into his pocket.

Upon entering his own room, he finds Steve sound asleep in his bed. Not wanting to disturb his colleague, John quietly enters the bathroom.

Emerging from the bathroom, John finds Steve awake and watching him intently. "I thought I heard you going into the bathroom. It's everything ok? Did you find anything in the rooms?" Steve asks, voice rough with sleep.

"Nothing." John's tone turns urgent. "The police are here, and we need to leave immediately. Get up, and I'll gather the girls. We need to talk." Without waiting for a response, John exits the room, leaving Steve sitting on the bed, wide-eyed and anxious.

"Take a seat wherever you can," John instructs abruptly as he reenters the room, accompanied by Rachel and Marta. "I apologize for disturbing your rest, but I have something important to share, and we all need to be prepared for whatever lies ahead." He paces between the door and the window, a mix of worry and determination etched on his face.

Steve takes the only available chair in the room, while Marta and Rachel settle at the foot of the bed. Their expressions convey a combination of curiosity and concern as they await John's explanation. John stops by the window, momentarily lost in his thoughts, before addressing their growing anxiety.

"I didn't find anything in the rooms, which is concerning in itself," John confesses.

"Apart from not knowing the whereabouts of our colleagues, there's another issue. They had crucial mission documentation with them, which I couldn't locate in the rooms. Either they still have it, which I hope is the case, or someone has taken it, which would pose significant problems for us." He says, lost in his thoughts, oblivious to the confusion mirrored on their faces.

"What? But what the hell is happening? Please explain," Marta demands, her patience gone.

Taking a deep breath, John tries to compose himself. "The letter I received at the cafeteria was from Ross. He mentioned an unexpected problem and left clues indicating their possible current location," he says.

"Alright, so what does the letter say? What is the unexpected problem, and where could they be?" Rachel demands, her worry escalating.

Interrupting their conversation, a knock resonates on John's door. "Dr. John. John Saladi," a voice with a strong Spanish accent calls out.

John approaches the door cautiously, motioning for the others to remain quiet. "Yes," he responds, buying some time to assess the situation.

"Can you please come down to the cafeteria? Someone wishes to speak with you," the voice on the other side of the door says.

John contemplates his next move, aware of the uncertainty surrounding this invitation. "Who wants to speak with me? What is this about?" he asks, trying to learn more.

"I don't know, sir. Mr. Eduardo sent me. He's in the cafeteria with two gentlemen who want to talk to you," the voice replies, leaving John with a lingering sense of caution.

"Okay. Please, give me a minute, and I'll join them," John responds calmly.

"Thank you, Dr. John. I'll let them know," the voice replies before fading away.

As the sound of footsteps recedes, John addresses his companions in a hushed tone. "It's the police, I'm certain of it," he says, low and urgent. "They will pose a problem, and I already have enough on my plate.

While I go talk to them, you all need to pack up everything and quietly leave the hotel. Make sure nobody sees you," he instructs, emphasizing the urgency of their departure.

Rachel isn't satisfied. "But what's going on? What's the matter with the police?"

"We don't have time to discuss it now. Just follow my instructions," John insists, tearing a piece of paper from the crumpled envelope in his pocket. He quickly jots down some details and hands it to Steve.

"Take the truck and all our equipment. Hire a taxi and follow it to this address. When you arrive, wait until the cab leaves. Then, go back down the road and look for a detour about one hundred meters to the left."

John's eyes lock with Steve's. His voice drops.

"Take the private path on the right, next to a palm tree. Follow that path for a mile until you descend into a valley. There will be a gate that you can open. The road will lead you to a large house, a hacienda. Ask for Angel and tell them you're with me."

Finishing his instructions, John adds, "I'll meet you there later."

Steve looks confused and concerned as he asks, "But what's the problem with the police? Why do we have to run away? What's going on, John?"

"There's no time to explain now. I have to go down. Now go. Please," John insists, exiting the room and leaving his companions bewildered and disoriented.

He strides purposefully into the cafeteria, exuding an air of effortless composure. He scans the room, spotting Eduardo and two men seated at a corner table—the same men he had seen entering the hotel earlier.

Both men are dressed in worn-looking suits, and open shirts without ties. The older of the two lounges in his chair, a hint of annoyance on his face as he inspects his nails. The younger man is engrossed in conversation with Eduardo, diligently taking notes in a small notebook.

"Good morning, Mr. Eduardo, gentlemen," John greets them as he approaches their table.

"Good morning. I assume you're Dr. John Saladi?" The younger man looks up from his notebook, his gaze fixed on John.

"You assume correctly. I am John Saladi," John confirms, maintaining his composure despite the mounting tension.

"Dr. Saladi, thank you for sparing us some of your time. We appreciate your cooperation," the younger says, gesturing to the empty chair on the opposite side of the table, next to Eduardo. "Please, have a seat."

John sits down, keeping his posture relaxed. "How can I help you, gentlemen?" he asks, trying to appear composed.

Detective Escobar introduces himself and his partner, Detective Moreno. He explains that Mr. Eduardo has contacted the police in Puerto Deseado to report the possible involuntary absence of three guests: Alberto Russo, Ross Santos, and Robert Gibson. He looks towards Eduardo, who nods in confirmation.

The detective pauses, then continues, "Given that you are friends with them, we were hoping you could provide us with some information to assist our investigation.

John shakes his head, meeting the detectives' gaze steadily. "I'm afraid I won't be of much help. These men are not my friends, and I barely know them. I lead a research team with three colleagues from Stanford University. We arrived in Puerto Deseado just a couple of hours ago. Those gentlemen were supposed to be waiting for us to join our team. I only know their names and little more," he concludes.

Detective Moreno furrows his brows, expressing his doubts. "If I understood correctly, you didn't know them personally. Is that it?"

"No, that's not what I meant," John clarifies, striving to conceal his growing impatience. "I met them in person at the university about six months ago. However, I never had the opportunity to speak with any of them again after that."

Eduardo maintains a serious demeanor, remaining silent. Escobar writes in his notebook and asks, "Where is your destination? And what is the purpose of your expedition?"

"We are a scientific expedition headed to Presidente Eduardo Frei Montalva's base in Antarctica," John explains. "Our purpose is to conduct a scientific research. We're here in Puerto Deseado to catch a connecting flight."

"Very well, Dr. John. That's impressive," Escobar remarks. "But I need your help to understand a detail. If you're on a scientific expedition, why do you have two mercenaries on your team?" he gazes at John with a defiant expression.

"Mercenaries? What do you mean by that? Who...?" John is taken aback by the question. "I don't understand. Who are you referring to?" he asks, his astonishment genuine, hoping it may work to his advantage.

As the detectives continue their line of questioning, John's suspicions grow. How could the Puerto Deseado police have such confidential information about Ross and Robert? It seems unlikely that they possess the necessary resources to obtain such sensitive details. Doubts begin to surface in John's mind about the true nature of the detectives' presence.

"You expect me to believe that as the team leader, you did not know that Ross and Robert were active mercenaries and former members of a paramilitary group?" Moreno leans forward, crossing his arms, his gaze fixed on John.

"What? No! I had no idea," John protests, feeling his credibility waver. "They were introduced to me as members for logistical support and security. Are you certain you're referring to the same individuals?" He struggles to maintain composure, caught off guard by the sudden change in Moreno's demeanor.

Moreno glances at John, assuming a leading role in the interrogation. Escobar continues writing in his notebook, his focus undeterred.

"And what about your companions? The ones who arrived with you, where are they?" Moreno probes, taking control of the situation.

"I believe they must be resting. I'm not entirely sure. I was taking a break in my room when you called me. In any case, I doubt they can be of any assistance. They have never met these gentlemen," John says, trying to steer attention away from his companions. The thought of Moreno requesting to speak with them fills him with unease.

"Very well, that will be all. Thank you for your patience and cooperation, Dr. Saladi. It has been invaluable to us," Moreno says, sketching an ironic smile at John. "We won't detain you any longer. However, we may require your assistance again. After all, we all want to locate your companions swiftly, don't we?"

"Of course. I am at your disposal. But our flight is scheduled within the next 48 hours, even if we don't find them. We are heavily reliant on the weather," John replies, hoping to wrap up the interrogation and get out.

"Dr. John, I'm afraid we cannot allow you to leave Puerto Deseado," Moreno states with a sly grin, causing John's heart to sink. "At least, not during this investigation phase." Moreno adds, "We also require your passports. Just formalities."

Escobar adds, "Don't worry, someone will return them to you." He smiles like a vulture, relishing the impact his words have on John.

The entire situation reeks of foul play, and John's suspicions intensify. If the police are onto Ross and Robert, there is a possibility they have information about him as well. It's a risk he cannot afford to take.

Being held hostage by the police in this forsaken town was never part of his plan.

Fortunately, John had taken precautions, ensuring the safety of his teammates by relocating them to a secure place. Now, his priority is to escape the town as swiftly as possible. "Understood," John says, rising from his seat. "I'll retrieve my passport upstairs and locate my friends."

The detectives' expressions darken as John turns towards the stairs. "By the way, Dr. John, one more thing," Moreno says with a stern tone. "Did you come across anything noteworthy in your colleagues' rooms that you'd like to share with us?"

John swallows hard, facing them with an uneasy resolve. He knows that lying is not an option. "No, I didn't find anything. I assure you, I didn't tamper with anything. My curiosity got the better of me," he says, forcing a smile to mask his unease.

Suddenly, the envelope he received from Eduardo weighs heavily on his mind. He worries that Eduardo may have disclosed it to the detectives. His heart races, but he tries to maintain composure.

Moreno scribbles something on his notepad without lifting his gaze. "You may go now. And please remember to bring your passports. We'll be waiting for you," he instructs, gesturing for John to leave.

Turning towards the stairs, John briskly crosses the lobby, heading for the service door tucked away behind the staircase. Ensuring the detectives are out of sight, he swiftly slips out onto the street, his senses heightened as he prepares to make his escape.

Angel

John strode purposefully down the street, leaving the hotel behind him. He maintained a brisk pace, ensuring not to attract any undue attention. A quick glance at the parking lot confirmed his suspicions— their truck was nowhere to be seen. A smile crept across his face.

The detectives must have realized by now that he wouldn't be returning with the passports. Time was of the essence; he needed to regroup with his team and leave Puerto Deseado before the police could react.

With caution, John reached the end of the street and discreetly glanced back. He let out a slow breath. No one was tailing him. He turned the corner onto the main avenue, setting his sights on the coastal road that traced alongside the river.

As he ventured onto the avenue, John found himself amidst the local hustle and bustle. Stores buzzed with customers, and families strolled along the sidewalks. He carefully surveyed the lane in both directions, noting the scarce traffic— a few trucks, a bus, and a handful of cyclists. Then, he spotted a taxi approaching down the street. John swiftly raised his hand, signaling the cab to halt by his side.

Peering out into the road, he addressed the driver, "Good morning. Please, take me to this address." He handed the driver a piece of paper and settled back in the rear seat, attentively observing his surroundings.

The driver examined the paper with care and inquired, "Casa El Cinco, I see. Are you staying there?"

"No, I'm just visiting a friend," John responded evasively, his gaze focused on the view through the back window.

"Ah, so you're on vacation?" the driver probed further, unaware of the unease his questions elicited from John.

"Not exactly. I'm just passing through. It's a lovely town," John replied curtly, feeling slightly annoyed at the need for conversation.

The driver, seemingly unperturbed, continued, "You're not from around here. Your Spanish is excellent, but you're not from Argentina, right?" He smiled, oblivious to the discomfort he was causing John.

"You got me. I'm English. Are there many Europeans around here?" John asks, attempting to steer the conversation.

"English? I thought so. We have a few Europeans here," the taxi driver replied cheerfully. "Some Dutch, Portuguese, and Spanish. But Englishmen and Americans are quite rare."

John nodded politely, but his mind wandered. Memories of the tragedy that had befallen his family flooded his thoughts, and he grimaced, trying to push away the haunting images. He needed to find solace. A deep thirst welled up within him.

Suddenly, nausea gripped him, a stark reminder of the promise he had made to himself. The image of Rachel helped him regain his composure. Determined to focus on the present, John turned his attention to the path the taxi was taking. The town appeared quiet, and he was grateful for the sparse traffic they encountered. Soon, he would reach his destination and bid farewell to the talkative driver.

As they traveled, a shadow cast itself over the surrounding landscape, drawing John's gaze to the thick clouds that loomed in the sky. "Do you happen to know the weather forecast for the next few days?" he asked, a note of concern in his voice.

"They say we're in for one of those typical local storms, common for this time of year. Hopefully, it won't last more than two or three days," the taxi driver replied after glancing upward.

"Damn..." John muttered, apprehensive about the potential disruptions the weather might bring to his scheduled flight. If it is canceled, they will be trapped in this godforsaken place. "How much longer until we arrive?"

"We should be there in less than five minutes," the driver assured him.

"Very well," John replied, leaning over the seat as the taxi maneuvered through the narrow streets. The dilapidated houses seemed to tower like dark, twisted sentinels as they reached the outskirts of town. Gradually, the decrepit structures gave way to barren, treeless fields, creating an oppressive and desolate atmosphere.

The jolt of the car coming to a stop snapped John out of his weariness. "We've arrived. El Cinco is up ahead," the driver announced, turning to face John before pulling over to the side of the road.

"Excellent. How much do I owe you?" John asked.

As John stepped out of the taxi and stretched, he watched the vehicle vanish into a cloud of dust. Without hesitation, he turned and began walking down the opposite side of the road. After a few dozen meters, he veered onto a dirt path that gradually grew steeper with each step. The landscape was barren and unforgiving, offering little relief from the dry wasteland, save for the occasional bush or tree. Limping slightly, John pressed on, determined to reach his destination.

He attained the summit of the hill, his chest heaving as he caught his breath. The elevation had proven more challenging than he had expected. He gazed up at the sky, now hidden behind a foreboding canopy of dark clouds. Straying from the main path, he followed a neglected trail, making his way towards a twisted and stunted tree at the top, where the hill abruptly ended at the edge of a cliff. Below, a hidden garden nestled within what appeared to be an ancient riverbed.

Partially obscured by the lush oasis on a terrace halfway down the cliff, a small and unassuming mud-colored house came into view. It was surrounded by tall pine trees, with vines and shrubs crawling up its walls. John sighed with relief and began his descent towards the house.

At a table near a small garden shaded by a cluster of young pine trees, Rachel, Marta, and Steve sat engaged in conversation with a tanned man in his fifties. Wispy gray hair slicked back with gel adorned his head as he smiled warmly.

"So, let me get this straight. John took a beating from three sailors last night. Only three?! I can hardly believe it. I remember him as one tough guy. I guess he's aged a bit over the years," the man chuckled.

"When John drinks, he turns into a different person. It's like he loses all sense of himself. I'm amazed he can even stand, let alone fight," Steve remarked, savoring his lemonade and munching on a mint leaf.

"Angel, you and John used to work together, right? Was it for the foundation?" Marta inquired, placing her empty glass on the table.

"Yeah, that's right. We worked together a few years back. We were involved in various missions," Angel replied with a chuckle. Despite his imposing stature, his youthful appearance and cheerful demeanor were in stark contrast.

"But everything changed when John fell in love. He started distancing himself from the team. And after the funeral, I lost touch with him completely. I'm surprised he even knows how to find me here.

A lot has changed in these past few years," Angel paused, momentarily averting his gaze. A shadow passed over his expression, hinting at a hidden pain.

"I don't know much about the accident, only that he lost his wife and child. It must have shattered his soul," Marta said, feeling a shiver run through her body, momentarily halting her words.

Marta's persistence unsettled Rachel and Steve, but she was determined to get answers. "Can you tell us more about the missions you undertook?" she pressed, refusing to let him evade her questions.

Angel shifted uncomfortably, his eyes darting around before finally responding. "The nature of our missions varied. We were involved in a range of activities, from rescue operations to security assignments and providing support in critical situations," he offered vaguely, clearly avoiding giving specific details.

Reflecting on their past experiences, Angel's demeanor softened. "Working with John was a blast. He was impulsive, courageous, and things were never dull when he was around. Surprisingly, he wasn't much of a drinker back then. In fact, he was the one who kept us in check and took care of us when we needed it," Angel reminisced with a nostalgic chuckle.

"Before he got married, John decided to retire from service. It was the right move for him and his family. After settling down, he embraced family life and became a dedicated husband and father. He did become a bit more reserved and less adventurous," Angel added, a laugh in his voice.

Angel's tone grew somber as he continued, speaking of the aftermath of the accident. "After the tragedy, John was consumed by guilt. He blamed himself entirely for what had happened. I stayed by his side for two days after the funeral, trying to lift his spirits," Angel paused, lost in thought. "During that time, I met his brother, someone I had no idea even existed. He struck me as a reserved and enigmatic individual. We did our best to help John heal, but nothing could pull him out of the deep pit of guilt he had fallen into."

Taking a deep breath, Angel shared a haunting memory. "The last time I saw him, three days after the funeral, he was walking alone on the beach, clutching an empty vodka bottle. He had transformed into a bitter and aggressive man, pushing everyone away. No one could get through to him."

Angel's voice trailed off as he recounted the ensuing years. "And then he disappeared, for months, perhaps even over a year.

I heard rumors and dark stories about him, twisted tales that seemed impossible to be about the same man I once knew," he admitted, sadness shadowing his eyes.

As if trying to lighten the mood, Angel abruptly shifted the conversation. "But that's all in the past now! I retired and found solace in this remote corner of the world, creating my own little kingdom," he declared, playfully addressing the servant, who approached with refreshments. Both men shared a laugh, momentarily embracing the lighter atmosphere.

As they continued their conversation, the dark clouds overhead grew denser, foretelling the impending storm. Angel's expression turned concerned as he glanced at the darkened sky. "Bad weather is on its way. Hopefully, it's just the usual storm that lasts about three days before the sun returns. Let's hope it doesn't cause any trouble for your flight," he said, worry etched on his face.

As Angel's attention is called by someone approaching, the conversation stalls, everyone's eyes swinging toward the gate. "Señor, there is a gringo at the door looking for you. He says his name is John Saladi," the person announces.

"Finally!" Angel exclaims, leaping up from his seat, his face lighting up with joy. "You guys stay here and enjoy your lemonade. I'll go and get him."

The creaking wooden gate of the hacienda opens with a long groan as Angel hurries towards it. "John! You big bastard, you look like you've risen from the dead," he says, arms spread wide in greeting.

"Angel, you son of a bitch. Getting older and fatter," John responds, hugging him tightly. They hold each other's gaze for a few moments, genuine happiness evident in their eyes.

Once inside, Angel closes the gate and turns to John. "Did you encounter any problems getting here?" he asks, guiding John further into the hacienda.

"Apart from evading the local police, nothing major," John chuckles. "Man, it feels so good to see you. You have no idea how much I've missed you."

"I can see that life has been kind to you, my friend," John observes, scanning the surroundings and nodding at two of Angel's discreetly seated employees behind a pine tree.

"I always told you I would retire to a secluded corner of the world in search of happiness. And here I am," Angel proudly declares, opening his arms and gesturing towards his beautiful Spanish colonial house and well-tended garden.

"It's great to see you too, my friend. You seem to have bounced back from your challenging times," Angel remarks, studying John with a mixture of satisfaction and concern. "How have you been?"

John takes a deep breath. Bitter memories resurface at the mention of his past. "I'm doing okay, Angel. The worst is behind me," he says, attempting to push aside the painful recollections that still haunt his soul.

"And there's your team," Angel says, nodding toward a group seated in a shaded corner.

Steve is the first to notice and stands up, his face breaking into a wide smile. "John! Finally, you're here. How did it go with the police?"

"Same old annoyance," John replies, clapping Steve on the shoulder.

"Angel, thank you. You've been incredibly kind to welcome them. My friend, I have to ask for your help once again. We need to secure a flight to the Antarctic base in the next hours, whichever one is available," John says, urgency sharpening his voice.

"Of course. Of course, John," Angel agrees, offering him a seat.

Rachel can't hold back any longer. "But what about our local team? Have you learned anything about their whereabouts?" she asks, searching John's face for any sign of information.

John locks eyes with Angel, his expression serious. "If everything went according to plan, they should be in Artigas. Thanks to this man, they managed to escape Puerto Deseado yesterday morning," John raises his glass in a gesture of gratitude.

"And now, you need to get out of here quickly," Angel says. "Do you think Markus is behind the troubles in Deseado?"

"Without a doubt. It can only be him. Markus is hot on our trail, and we can't afford to stay in one place for too long," John responds.

Rachel leans forward. "Who is Markus? What kind of trouble are we facing?"

"He's an old adversary of ours, one of the most dangerous mercenaries we've ever encountered," John replies.

"Mercenaries?! Are our lives at risk? Nobody informed me about this when I joined the expedition," Marta bursts out, fear sharpening her voice.

Rachel and Steve share the same restlessness, their eyes darting between John and Angel.

Angel gestures towards the house. "We should move inside. The weather is turning nasty," he suggests, calling over two of his men who quickly approach.

"Guys, please accompany Ricardo into the house. I will join you shortly," Angel instructs, placing his hand on Ricardo's shoulders. As everyone rises from their seats, they follow Ricardo's lead.

Angel walks away, engaged in a private conversation with the other men. After a while, they stop walking, and the men hurry towards the hacienda gate, while Angel returns to the house with a determined stride etched across his face.

Ricardo guides John and his companions through an interior courtyard adorned with a central stone fountain. Large ocher-colored vases housing palm trees enhance the ambiance of the cloister.

Angel catches up with them, panting from his brisk pace. "Come, let's head to the parlor. We'll be more comfortable there," he suggests, leading them into a spacious room adorned with antique furniture crafted from solid black wood and large terracotta vases filled with lush tropical plants.

"Manuela!" Angel calls out, and a woman in a gown emerges from a service door. "Please, bring fresh water and more lemonade," he requests with a polite tone.

"Make yourselves comfortable," Angel gestures towards the generously sized carved wooden sofas adorned with gilded cushions positioned in the center of the room. "Order whatever you like. Manuela is here to assist you."

"John, we need to take care of your flight. Would you mind joining me in my office?" Angel points to a large, exquisitely carved wooden door located at the far end of the room.

He opens the door and invites John inside. "Here, we can talk more comfortably."

John's admiration for Angel's office grows even stronger as he takes in the intricate details of the room. Awe and wonder settle over him.

"Angel, my congratulations. Your house is already impressive from the outside, but the interior is truly magnificent," John remarks, his eyes drawn to the paintings and travel photographs adorning the walls. "I can spot some objects related to our missions and even recognize a few familiar faces in your photos."

Memories of their past adventures flood back, filling him with camaraderie and nostalgia for bygone days. He points to a picture hanging above a dresser adorned with ethnic artifacts. "This one, right here. That's us in Mexico, isn't it?"

Angel approaches John. "That's correct, my friend. It captures our last mission in Mexico. Remember that? It's hard to believe it's been almost 20 years." He offers John a glass of whiskey. "Care for a drink? Whiskey, perhaps?"

"Thank you. I probably shouldn't, but a small sip won't hurt," John responds, accepting the glass from Angel. Initially hesitant, he closes his eyes and takes a sip, savoring the warmth and soothing sensation as the whiskey glides down his throat. For a moment, his mind eases, the worries crowding it pushed aside.

"Of course, I remember Mexico, as well as all the other missions. How could I forget? It's interesting how this distant reality now feels like a movie from long ago," John muses, shifting his gaze to other photographs displayed on the wall.

Angel's expression turns somber as he responds, his gaze fixed on his glass. "They're all gone." Bitterness creeps into his voice. "From the original team, it's just the two of us left. Bruce was the last to fall, somewhere in Turkey. They all died in the line of duty."

Taking a deep breath, Angel shakes off the weight of the memories. "Well, my friend, we don't have time for dwelling on the past. We need to get you out of here quickly," he says, shaking his head and gesturing to dispel any lingering negative thoughts. He moves behind his desk near a large window at the back of the room.

"We must arrange for your flight before the storm hits. However, your equipment on the truck will have to be transported on a different flight when the weather clears," Angel explains, picking up his cell phone. "Give me a minute." He dials a number and waits, while John finds himself drawn to the hallway, captivated by the various memories on display.

Suddenly, Ricardo enters through a hidden door between two potted palm trees and immediately approaches Angel, interrupting his phone conversation. Both men engage in a hushed and concerned discussion.

"The police are at the El Cinco house with armed men hiding in a truck down the road. It must be Markus and his gang," Angel says, ending his call and rising sharply from his chair.

"You need to leave immediately. I already have a plane arranged for you. Ricardo will take you to the airfield," he gestures to his trusted man.

Angel guides John and Ricardo into an adjoining room where the rest of the team awaits. As soon as they enter, Angel's voice pierces through the tension. "The plane will be ready in an hour at the airfield, but we must act swiftly. You need to leave now, everyone. You must evade the approaching storm."

Steve rubs his weary eyes and inquires about the equipment. John responds urgently, grabbing his backpack. "There's no time. We'll have to leave it behind for now. Just grab your bags. The equipment will be transported later. We depart in five minutes."

Angel retreats to the side, engaged in a hushed conversation with Ricardo. Another man discreetly appears at the door, attempting to conceal a gun behind his back. Angel swiftly ushers him out of sight.

Marta stiffens. "Did you see that? That man had a gun inside the house. Something feels off about this. I don't like it."

Angel returns, forcing a smile. "Alright, everyone, let's go. Ricardo is waiting in the car outside to take you to the airfield." John's expression remains serious as he urges them forward. "Come on, we must leave now."

They exit the room and hasten across the courtyard. Ricardo impatiently waits behind the wheel of the Land Rover.

"Good luck on your flight, everyone," Angel calls out, waving from the doorway. "John, don't forget to send a postcard when you arrive. Ricardo, take care of them."

Ricardo accelerates rapidly as soon as they climb into the car, the tires kicking up gravel as they speed away. Another Land Rover, with five armed men, follows closely behind as they traverse the bumpy dirt road, causing the passengers to feel every jolt down to their bones.

"Can we please slow down a bit?" Marta's face has drained of color, and she's struggling with nausea.

John's gaze remains fixed on the darkening clouds above as he replies, "We need to take off before the storm arrives, Marta. We have approximately thirty minutes left."

Marta turns to Steve and Rachel, frustration plain on her face. "You're keeping something from us. First, it was the weather, and now you won't level with us. What's going on?"

As Marta glances through the rear window, she notices the armed escort trailing them. Her eyes meet John's, demanding answers. "Why do we have an armed escort?"

John's mind races, searching for a way out of their predicament. Time is of the essence, and the mounting pressure coupled with Marta's relentless questioning makes it difficult for him to reveal the full extent of their situation.

"Why won't you answer me? Are you even listening?" Marta's voice reverberates through the cramped space of the car.

"Marta, for God's sake, please be quiet!" John's voice cracks, frustration and desperation tangled together. His outburst shocks everyone, including Ricardo, who looks startled by the sudden eruption of emotions. "Give me a moment to think. We're doing our best to handle this situation, but your constant questioning isn't helping. We will talk later when we're on the plane to Artigas."

A collective unease settles in the car, the team feeling both surprised and ashamed by John's explosive reaction. Marta seethes with anger, hurt by his dismissive attitude.

"What's gotten into you, John? Why are you treating her like this?" Steve can't hide his disgust. "We all have valid concerns, and Marta was simply seeking answers."

John's frustration lingers in his voice as he responds, "I understand that, but right now, I'm the one trying to solve our problems. Just let me think."

"John, we know you're under immense stress, but you can't shut us out," Steve insists, his voice calm and reasoned. "If we don't know what's happening, we can't support you effectively. You need to stop keeping us in the dark and take responsibility for your volatile temper."

Steve's words strike a chord with Marta. Anger and hurt cross her face as she adds, "I demand respect from all of you. The way you've treated me is unacceptable. It's time you put an end to this aggressive behavior and finally address our concerns," she says, wiping away a tear that escaped her eye.

Rachel squeezes Marta's hand in a reassuring gesture, silently conveying her support while casting a disapproving glance at John. He, aware of their disappointment, keeps his focus on the road ahead, seemingly oblivious to their burning words. After a tense moment of silence, he finally turns towards them, taking a deep breath in an attempt to compose himself.

"You're right," John concedes, remorse plain in his voice. "I apologize for my outburst and the way I spoke to all of you. The situation is indeed complex, and I understand your need for answers.

I promise that once we reach our destination, I will share everything I know." His gaze meets each of their eyes, lingering on Rachel's for a moment, silently conveying his remorse.

The car abruptly jerks, jostling everyone, and John's attention returns to the road. The pavement smooths out, and the two Land Rovers continue racing down the empty road at breakneck speed.

"We're now on the RP47," Ricardo says, attempting to ease the tension. "In twenty minutes, we'll arrive at the airfield."

"Great," Rachel says, trying to diffuse the palpable tension in the car. "It seems like the storm is approaching." She points to the faint raindrops falling against the car window.

"Let's hope it doesn't worsen," Ricardo remarks, gesturing towards an ominous black cloud unleashing heavy rain upon a mountain not far from their right.

A vibration in John's pocket catches his attention, prompting him to retrieve his cell phone. He listens intently before speaking, his expression growing grave. "Understood, Angel. Thank you. Be careful, my friend," he says before ending the call and turning to his companions. "The police have arrived at Angel's house. He's doing his best to buy us some time."

"Hopefully, they'll be led to the main airfield in Puerto Deseado," Ricardo adds. "We'll be using a different one—an old, abandoned airfield a few miles away."

John falls silent, concern for Angel's safety weighing heavily on his mind, as he tries to anticipate Markus's next moves. The urgency of their situation grows with every passing moment, adding an extra layer of tension to their already precarious journey.

"In any case, I suspect they will also dispatch a team here; if so, we have a fifteen-minute head start," John says, pocketing his phone and sinking into a contemplative silence, his hand instinctively checking the gun tucked inside his jacket. Everyone in the car fixates their attention on the road ahead, the atmosphere heavy with silence and tension.

After a few minutes, Ricardo suddenly veers to the left, steering the car onto a dirt road bordered by dense bushes and overhanging rocks. "Just five more minutes, and we'll be there. I want to avoid the main road ahead in case it's under police surveillance," he says, careful now.

They run down a slight slope, jolting over rough bumps, until finally, the runway comes into view.

To John and his team's dismay, the desolate runway stretches before them, devoid of any sign of an aircraft. Their hopes deflate, replaced by a sense of urgency and uncertainty.

"Stay calm," John says, sensing the disappointment etched on his companions' faces. "The plane shouldn't be here yet. It would attract attention if it arrived too soon."

The car screeches to a halt behind a thicket of bushes, and everyone leaps out, their nerves frayed with impatience. They scan the sky in every direction, straining their ears for any faint indication of the plane's approach. However, all they hear are the ticking of the car engine and their own ragged breaths. Seconds stretch into minutes, and still, there is no sign of the plane.

"Listen." Steve's eyes go wide with alarm. "Gunshots. I'm certain I heard gunshots. Where are your teammates, Ricardo?" he asks, scanning the horizon for any sign of the second car.

"They stayed behind to provide us with more time, if necessary," Ricardo replies, his grip tightening around his gun.

"Oh, God," Marta exclaims, clutching onto Rachel. "John, what do we do? The plane is nowhere in sight, and the police will be here any minute. We need to run. Let's get to the car, Ricardo. Let's go!"

"Stay calm, Marta. The plane should arrive any second now. The gunfire sounds distant. Let's wait a little longer. If you feel safer, you can wait in the car," John suggests, pulling out his weapon and positioning himself beside Ricardo.

"Head up that rise over there," John instructs him pointing to a small hill about 100 meters away. "If you see anyone approaching, turn back, and we'll make our escape."

As Ricardo sprints toward the hill, a familiar sound catches their attention. John's head snaps up, and he spots a plane emerging in the distance.

Relieved, he opens the car door and gestures for the others to follow. "Come on! The plane is here! We'll meet it on the other side of the runway," he says, slinging his backpack over his shoulder.

As the plane draws nearer, the thunderous roar of its engines fills the air, intensifying the urgency of the moment. Just as they are about to set off running, a blood-curdling scream pierces the atmosphere. "Run! Run! Now!" Ricardo bursts through the brush, sprinting toward the vehicle.

"Hurry, they're closing in!" he shouts, leaping into the Land Rover. In a swift motion, he thrusts an automatic weapon into John's hands.

"Make your way to the plane while I hold them off. Good luck!" he calls out, accelerating the Land Rover away with determination.

Feeling the weight of the responsibility and the adrenaline coursing through their veins, John and his companions propel themselves forward. The aircraft readies itself for landing, and with each stride, they close the distance to the runway. Every second becomes crucial, and they know that time is running out.

John reaches the runway, gasping for breath, his heart pounding in his chest. His companions soon catch up, their breaths ragged and their eyes fixed on the descending plane.

The sound of gunfire grows louder, and a deafening blast makes John scowl. He glances towards a rising plume of black smoke on the horizon, not too far away.

"Was that Ricardo?" Rachel's voice shakes.

The approaching roar of vehicles drowns out the sound of the plane's engines. John turns to see a massive dust cloud hurtling towards them, the echoes of pursuit becoming increasingly menacing.

The plane makes a sharp turn, coming to a halt just meters away. The pilot throws open the door and bellows at them. "Come on, move it! We have to take off now!"

Suddenly, torrential rain pours down on them, drenching their clothes as they struggle to run toward the waiting plane.

Marta is the first to board, followed by Rachel and Steve. John starts to climb, his gaze lingering on the approaching jeeps, their menacing presence evident even through the downpour. He sees the men perched on the jeeps, their guns aimed directly at them. A burst of gunfire spurs John to start climbing faster, adrenaline surging through his veins.

The plane's engines roar at full throttle, drowning out the sound of bullets as they whiz through the air. John stops before entering the plane, levels Ricardo's weapon, and returns fire upon the oncoming cars. One of the jeeps swerves wildly and rolls over, its occupants and weapons scattering in disarray. With renewed determination, John hurls the gun inside the plane, pulls himself up the stairs, and slams the door shut behind him.

The plane lurches forward, its speed not yet sufficient for a safe escape. Bullets continue to tear through the cabin, rattling the aircraft. Inside, everyone braces as the plane finally lifts off the runway and ascends into the enveloping clouds.

Rachel goes pale as she spots the wound. "John! Your leg. You're bleeding!"

"It's nothing serious. Don't worry," John reassures her, his voice strained with pain from the bullet wound in his leg. "Are you two holding up?"

"We're scared, but we'll be alright," Rachel responds, her gaze unwavering as she looks at John's injury. Marta remains silent, her eyes fixed on the window of the plane, lost in her thoughts.

"I'll take care of this later. Steve, what's wrong with you? You're being so quiet. The worst is over," John says, his concern evident as he wonders about Steve's unusual silence. "Steve, say something, buddy," he urges, growing increasingly uneasy about the lack of response. Rachel gets up, also finding Steve's silence strange, and approaches him.

"John!" Rachel's voice breaks. "Steve's been hit." Her eyes are locked on the large bloodstain spreading across his chest. John struggles to his feet and approaches Steve's seat. "Steve," he whispers, sorrow thick in his throat. He gently touches his face, closing his lifeless eyes.

"He's gone. There's nothing we can do," John says with a heavy heart, his words weighed down by grief. He turns away, unable to bear the pain reflected in Rachel's and Marta's eyes, as the cabin falls into a somber silence. The roar of the engine mingles with Marta's stifled sobs, and Rachel finds solace in the raindrops streaming down the window.

They remain stoic amidst the jolts and turbulence that rocked the plane. In the cockpit, the pilot focuses on maintaining stability and navigating the storm safely.

John reaches into his backpack, retrieving a flask. He pours its contents over his wound, wincing at the sting, before emptying the rest in one swallow. He leans back in his seat, closing his eyes, a single tear escaping and trailing down his cheek. Memories flood his mind, and a whisper escapes his lips, "Melissa."

Tzabar

The night reverberates with relentless dry drumming, its intensity building within the thick fog. From the depths of this misty veil emerges a helicopter, bathed in the ethereal glow of the full moon. A foreboding mountain stands at the heart of the icy plain, its presence is commanding and enigmatic against the pale moonlight. A shroud of mist envelops it, shielding it like a protective wall.

As the helicopter encircles the mountain, its peculiar configuration becomes increasingly intriguing. A ring of dark rocks encloses its base, their formation defying logic as they encircle the steep walls that soar over a thousand meters high.

Just a few hundred meters away, within the fog-free perimeter of the icy landscape, a camp emerges—a compact outpost fortified by a sturdy fence and illuminated by piercing lights.

Through a small helicopter window, a man gazes at the mountain, captivated by its singular shape. As the helicopter draws nearer to the base, his attention shifts to the buildings and equipment that come into view below. The fenced area reveals several vehicles, their forms illuminated by intense lights, while a well-lit helipad stands adjacent to the camp.

Another man, older and weathered, peers out from a different window, while two silent figures sit opposite them—all four adorned in military uniforms. Above the roar of the helicopter, the older man's voice shouts, "We have arrived, Colonel Tzabar. Behold the magnificent splendor of this mysterious mountain. What are your thoughts on it?"

"Fascinating," the younger man responds, projecting his voice above the clamor. "Commander Chang, how many personnel do we have on the ground?"

"We currently have a team of twelve men, and fifteen civilians, comprising four scientists from CienTek, along with eleven additional technical and support personnel. As detailed in your briefing file, Dr. Alvin Tod from CienTek is leading the mission," Commander Chang explains.

Colonel Tzabar is taken aback by the dismissive tone in Chang's response. "Can you provide more information on the disappearance of the technicians? When did it occur?"

"On the third day," Chang says, indifference coloring his voice. "It's an odd occurrence, but true. Three technicians ventured onto the rocky terrain of the mountain base without authorization. They acted irresponsibly, like a trio of civilian fools. What else could we expect?

We received the alert at the end of that day, and despite the challenging weather and nightfall, we immediately initiated a search, and scoured the area thoroughly, but found no traces or clues."

"Our operational officer is Captain Kurt Schmitt, a seasoned veteran of the German military. A man of discipline, honor, and loyalty. This will be his final assignment before retirement," Chang adds, respect creeping into his voice.

"I have never concealed my opposition to placing civilians in command of this mission. It's yet another political concession made by the high command. Unfortunately, we must live with it. But I hope it won't be for much longer," Chang states, his gaze fixed on Tzabar.

"You must ensure adequate supervision and control over the activities of CienTek," Chang continues, his tone serious. "You need to work closely with Dr. Alvin and verify that our protocols are respected, ensuring nothing spirals out of control. We have witnessed the consequences of leaving civilians unchecked."

Tzabar nods with unease. "Commander, rest assured. I am accustomed to working with civilians. However, I am still perplexed as to why I was called in so abruptly by the high command. Colonel Alvarez was originally in charge of the mission. What happened to him?"

"I was equally surprised by your sudden appointment," Chang replies. "Colonel Alvarez has been under my command for over two decades. He is a capable soldier, but plagued by an unexplainable string of misfortune."

Chang pauses, his mind lost in contemplation.

"On the very first day of the mission, he suffered a peculiar accident," Chang shares with a concerned expression.

"While leading a small reconnaissance team along the cliffs, Alvarez inexplicably separated from the group. When they found him a few minutes later, he was unconscious on the ground. Strangest of all, there were no visible signs of injury or any apparent cause for his condition. We're still baffled by what happened to him." Chang pauses, lost in his thoughts for a moment before regaining his composure.

"Regardless, it's time to shift our focus to the mission at hand. Once we land, you will be introduced to the team. Then, we'll meet with Captain Kurt to receive an update on the mission's progress over the past 48 hours."

"My commander, Colonel, we will be landing in five minutes," the pilot's announcement interrupts Chang. "Local time is 18:05, and the outside temperature is -9 degrees."

As the helicopter approaches the runway, Tzabar gains a more detailed view of the base and its facilities. The base is comprised of interconnected rectangular structures, with tunnels providing access between them. The entire perimeter is bathed in intense light from the lighting towers.

He notices several antennas and satellite dishes, indicating a communication facility located a few dozen meters away from the main complex. The presence of armed soldiers and double fences suggests a high level of security within the facilities.

With a slight rise of the helicopter's nose and a dry thump, the landing gear touches the ground.

"Are those white domes where the wreckage is located?" Tzabar asks, gesturing towards several partially illuminated white domes situated a few hundred meters outside the base's perimeter.

"Correct," Chang replies, zipping up his jacket to brace against the freezing temperatures. "The domes provide protection and ample lighting, enabling us to work in consecutive shifts round the clock, even in inclement weather."

As the helicopter blades slow to a stop and the snow begins to settle, Tzabar spots a group of people standing beside snow vehicles with their lights on. In the backdrop, the mountain looms, imposing and enigmatic, bathed in the light of the full moon.

Tzabar takes a deep breath, feeling the biting cold sting on his face, and then leaps to the ground, followed closely by Commander Chang, their hearts racing. They move a short distance away from the helicopter's blades, seeking shelter from its turbulence.

"Good evening, everyone," Chang shouts, pointing towards Tzabar. "Allow me to introduce Colonel Tzabar Saladi. He is here to replace Colonel Alvarez."

"Colonel, may I present our team," Chang continues, gesturing towards the group. "Captain Kurt Schmitt is in charge of the support and security unit. Dr. Alvin Tod, from Cientek, is the director of the Anguta research mission. Dr. Lydia Stove, also from Cientek, is a sociologist, linguist, and paleographer, and Dr. Victor Balmer, a physicist, and expert in speleology."

"Good evening, Commander Chang, Colonel Saladi," Kurt greets, stepping forward and offering a military salute. "Welcome to Anguta. We hope you had a comfortable flight, sir."

"Thank you, Captain Kurt," Tzabar responds. "The flight went smoothly, considering the conditions.

Good evening, everyone. I am thrilled to be a part of the Anguta mission. I hope to contribute to its success."

"Good evening, Commander Chang. Welcome, Colonel," Alvin says, extending his hand for a shake. "It's a pleasure to have you join our mission."

"Let's head inside. It's too cold to remain outside," Chang suggests, directing them towards the staircase leading to the building's interior.

Through the corridor, they follow Alvin into a spacious and well-lit room where a few individuals are seated around a table, engrossed in their notes.

"Good evening, everyone," Alvin addresses the group, leading his guests to another table. The others acknowledge the greeting but remain focused on their tasks.

They take their seats while Chang and Kurt step aside, engaged in a discreet conversation. Victor pours mugs of tea for everyone.

Tzabar observes the austere environment around him and discreetly analyzes each of the team members. A subtle glance from Alvin towards Chang awakens his curiosity.

Chang and Kurt interrupt their hushed discussion and approach the table. "Any updates on the missing individuals?" Chang asks.

"Nothing new, Commander," Alvin says, disappointment in his voice. "We continue our search. Although it pains us, we are starting to lose hope of finding them alive. Our focus now is to uncover the cause of their disappearance."

"This incident has had a profound impact on the team," Lydia shares, her voice steady despite the sadness in her eyes.

"However, we recognize that mourning without taking action is futile when we have a mission to fulfill and limited time to do so."

"Dr. Lydia is absolutely right," Chang says, determination hardening his voice. "While we maintain a team dedicated to finding the missing ones, it is crucial that we prioritize our mission objectives. Time is of the essence, and we cannot afford any further delays."

Chang turns his attention to Kurt and Tzabar. "Gentlemen, I would like to meet briefly with you before I go. Captain Kurt, Colonel Tzabar, please, come with me"

Together, they make their way to a nearby meeting room, its modest decor creating an atmosphere of focused efficiency. The room is furnished with a table and eight chairs neatly arranged, complemented by a small piece of furniture along the back wall.

"Captain, I need you to provide Colonel Tzabar with a comprehensive briefing on the latest developments and all the relevant information," Chang says, his tone concise and matter-of-fact.

"Understood, sir," Kurt responds promptly.

"Gentlemen, as you are well aware, this mission holds paramount significance for the Foundation." Chang addresses them, urgency and personal conviction sharpening his voice. "It is not only a matter of professional duty but also a deeply personal endeavor. I rely on your cooperation to ensure that Colonel Tzabar can swiftly acclimate and compensate for the lost time. Our deadlines are pressing, and we have already faced enough challenges. It is imperative that we have tangible results in the next days."

Without waiting for a response, Chang walks towards the door, pausing briefly. "Colonel, once again, I extend my warmest welcome to Anguta. I hold high expectations for this team. Good luck, and we will reconvene tomorrow."

Chang departs, closing the door behind him. Tzabar breaks the silence, a note of surprise in his voice. "Well, that was certainly swift and unexpected," he remarks, exchanging an uncertain glance with Kurt.

Denudasdi

John lay in the hospital bed, his eyes closed. By his side, Rachel sat with deep concern etched on her face, while Marta sat in the corner of the room, flipping through a magazine absentmindedly, seemingly detached from Rachel's worry.

Sensing movement, John slowly moved his head, attempting to open his eyes, but the flood of light overwhelmed him momentarily. As his eyes adjusted, he finally met Rachel's gaze.

Concerned, she leaned in closer and asked, "John, how are you feeling?"

"Fuck... what a headache," John muttered. "And my leg... what's happening? It's hurting like hell. Where are we? What's going on?".

Rachel took a deep breath, trying to remain composed. She reassured him, her voice soothing, "It's alright, John. Take it easy. You're in the hospital at Montalva base." She's relieved to see him conscious and aware.

Interrupting their conversation, a man in a blue coat approached John's bed. Leaning over him, he greeted John, "Hello, Mr. Saladi. I'm Dr. Rodriguez. I'm glad to see you awake."

"We took care of your leg," Dr. Rodriguez continued, his tone professional yet comforting. "You'll need a few weeks to recover. I recommend resting for a few days and avoiding putting weight on your leg." He jotted down some notes on a sheet of paper, slipping it into a small plastic envelope at the foot of the bed.

"I have to go now. If you need anything, just call the nurse, and she'll get in touch with me promptly. We may be a small health center, but we prioritize patient care," he says to Rachel, offering them a parting smile before leaving the room.

John's confusion lingered as he looked around the room, searching for answers. "How did I end up here? And how long have I been here?" he asked.

Rachel gently placed her hand on John's head. "We arrived two days ago, in the middle of the night. You were unconscious, and we had to find a hospital to treat your leg," she explained.

"Steve!" John exclaimed, suddenly sitting up in bed. "Where is Steve? I had a terrible dream about him." He scanned the room frantically, searching for any sign of his friend.

Marta's voice cuts through the air. "Steve is dead! Don't you remember? He was shot when we were trying to escape to the plane."

John's face fell, realization dawning upon him. "Shit. It's true. I remember now," he said, his gaze moving from Marta to Rachel, concern etched on his features. "And how are all of you holding up?"

"We're okay," Rachel replied. Relief and exhaustion both show. "We're a bit shaken and disoriented, but the people at the base have been incredibly supportive."

Just then, a nurse peeked through the door. "Good afternoon," she greeted. "I have three gentlemen here, claiming to be your colleagues. One of them introduced himself as Ross. Can I let them in?"

A glimmer of hope sparked in John's eyes. "That would be great news. Can you tell me more about them? What do they look like?"

"The one who identified himself as Ross is tall, with a dark complexion, sparse hair, and greenish eyes," the nurse described. "The other two are shorter, one being thin with glasses, and the other, I didn't get a good look at."

"Excellent. Please, send them in," John replied eagerly, trying to sit up straighter despite his lingering weakness.

Marta remained silent and detached from the unfolding events, but as the men entered the room, she couldn't help but take notice of their appearances. Ross stood out with his imposing stature and piercing green eyes.

The other two men were shorter, as the nurse had said, one with a stocky build, and the other slim with a shy demeanor that seemed out of place among the group. However, it was the intense gaze of the green-eyed man that caught Marta's attention, causing a shiver to run down her spine, prompting her to avert her to look at him and focus on her magazine.

"Greetings, John," Ross said, approaching with a warm smile. "We heard you took a bullet. How are you holding up?"

John managed a weak smile in return. "I'm feeling much better now. Thank you, my friend. It's good to see you, Ross. And you too, Robert and Alberto."

Robert sat down beside John and draped an arm around his shoulders. "You're looking good, man. I'm glad to see you're recovering."

John nodded, then gestured towards the two women sitting nearby. "Allow me to introduce Marta Lynn and Rachel Mira. Marta, Rachel, these are Ross Santos, Robert Gibson, and Alberto Russo—the team that had gone missing in Puerto Deseado."

The three men greet Marta and Rachel, and the room eases, though the tension doesn't fully lift. Robert's eyes momentarily lock with Marta's, causing her to blush and quickly avert her gaze.

Rachel stands up, breaking the silence. "Nice to meet you all. If you'd like, we can step outside and make you more comfortable."

"No," John interjects. "Rachel. Marta, please stay. We're all on the same team here. It's important for everyone to get to know each other. After all, we'll be working closely together in the coming weeks."

He turns to Ross and asks, "But how did you all know I was here?"

"Angel messaged us that you managed to escape from Puerto Deseado," Ross explains, a faint chuckle escaping his lips. "We hadn't heard from you for two days and became worried, so we decided to search for you.

When we heard about someone arriving with a bullet wound in their leg, we suspected it might be you."

John's curiosity mixes with a somber expression. "Someone is missing though. Steve Moor. He was hit when we tried to board the plane. Unfortunately, he didn't make it."

Ross nods solemnly, his face mirroring the gravity of the situation. "I'm so sorry to hear that. But I'm afraid I have more unfortunate news." He retrieves his cell phone and hands it to John. "Angel sent us a video message. You should see it."

John takes the phone hesitantly. As the video plays, chaos unfolds on the screen—gunfire, screams, and the sound of mayhem. Angel appears, huddled behind a tree, clutching a gun.

"Hi, guys," Angel's voice struggles to be heard over the cacophony. "I hope this message reaches you. Things have taken a turn for the worse here. As we suspected, the police are working for Markus. He and his gang showed up at the party shortly after you fled Puerto Deseado."

The video jumps sporadically, offering glimpses of a gravel floor and then returning to Angel's face. "Well, my friends, it seems this is where I bid you farewell," he says, his smile bitter.

"John, we've had a good life, and I have no regrets. Don't worry about me, my friend. I had already booked a one-way ticket, and according to the doctors, I only have a few weeks left. The final days of this illness won't be pleasant, that's for sure." Angel's said cutting through the chaos.

Suddenly, a barrage of gunfire erupts, interrupting Angel's words. The camera jerks, tree fragments fly into view, and a groan is heard before the cell phone clatters to the ground. The camera captures only the gray clouds and the intensifying rain.

Gunshots echo in the background as Angel desperately tries to reach for his cell phone while returning fire.

His face abruptly appears on the camera, voice gone low and menacing. "John! My bastard, we shall meet..."

A series of abrupt and forceful gunshots violently thrust Angel's face out of the camera's focus. A heavy silence hangs in the air, gripping John and everyone else listening to the video.

Footsteps approach, their sound overlapping with the distant gunfire. A shadow enters the frame, followed by a pair of khaki pants. A figure holding an automatic weapon stands motionless for a moment.

The weapon shifts position. Without warning, a close-range shot rings out, causing Rachel and Marta to jolt in terror. Another person steps into view, but only their silhouette remains visible.

"So it is done? Have we gotten the son of a bitch?" someone asks in German, over heavy breathing.

"Yes. It is done," responds a deep, husky voice, followed by a shout in English, delivered with a distinct Germanic accent. "Kill them all and burn everything. Hurry up. We have a plane to catch."

The image on the screen freezes. Gunshots continue sporadically, originating from different directions, intermixed with laughter and lively conversation.

"That's enough. The rest doesn't matter," Ross says, struggling to retrieve his cell phone from John's grasp. A silent fury darkens John's gaze.

"The one with the husky voice was not Markus," Ross states anxiously. Tears stream down Rachel's and Marta's cheeks.

"I know. It wasn't Markus..." John mutters, his gaze distant.

"Please, may I have a moment alone? All of you, please leave. Just for a minute. Don't worry, I'll be fine. I just need a moment alone. Thank you." John averts his eyes, gazing out of the window, refusing to face anyone. The fury lurking within him is palpable. The others stand outside the room, their faces filled with unease, exchanging concerned glances. Rachel is the first to break the silence.

"So, Angel is dead? They burned down the house and killed all those people?" she asks between sobs.

Marta can barely get the words out. "Who are they? Markus and his group. Why did they kill Angel and everyone else? Are they coming after us too?"

Ross takes a deep breath, realizing he needs to provide some answers without revealing too much. "It's a complicated story, but I'll try to summarize," he begins. "The issues with Markus and them, John and Angel, have been ongoing for many years. They have crossed paths with Markus and his group on multiple missions, and often it has turned bloody. The rivalry extends beyond professional matters; it becomes deeply personal. It's a clash that goes back a long way."

Ross cautiously attempts to explain, aware that revealing the unfiltered truth could have a jarring impact on their already fragile state.

"But I still don't understand what kind of missions you undertake. I thought they were scientific missions, but it seems like there's more to it," Marta remarks, glancing sideways at Robert, her frustration growing as she realizes the true complexity of the situation.

"Yes, our missions do have a scientific focus, and our responsibility is to ensure the safety of everyone involved. However, you should know that scientific and historical explorations can often intersect with significant political and financial interests. The reality is not as glamorous as what we see in movies," Ross explains.

Just as the conversation starts to unravel, John's voice calls out from inside the room, beckoning his team to rejoin him. "Ross, Rachel, everyone, come in," he urges.

"Ross was correct about the voice on the recording. It's not Markus. I would recognize that voice anywhere, even in the depths of hell," John reveals.

"But who is this person? Why all the secrecy?" Marta demands. "We're in the midst of chaos, and lives are at stake. It's time for you to tell us who we're dealing with."

Robert smirks at Marta's resolve. "Marta, you're absolutely right. Unfortunately, I have to share with you some information that I thought was buried in the distant past. You are just as much a part of this as the rest of us." John looks directly at Marta and Rachel, acknowledging the significance of their involvement.

Ross and Robert exchange a disapproving glance, while Alberto remains silent and stoic, observing the unfolding scene.

"The voice we heard belongs to Shaman. We believed he was dead a few years ago," John confesses.

"Impossible. The Shaman?!" Ross says, stunned. "But didn't you...?"

Robert stares at John, too astonished to speak.

"Yes, I thought so. I can't believe I heard his voice once again," John interrupts, disbelief and concern crossing his face.

"Who is this Shaman, and why does he affect you so deeply?" Rachel asks, clearly confused.

"I think John is the best person to explain that to you," Ross says, gesturing for John to continue.

"Alright, I'll try to explain," John says with a sigh of resignation.

The Foundation has many ruthless and bloodthirsty enemies, and it all boils down to a hunger for power," John begins, pausing briefly to take a sip of water and catch his breath. Alberto takes a seat, seemingly disinterested, and glances at a magazine on the table.

Ross and Robert leave the room, heading toward a vending machine to grab some coffee. Nearby, a group of base employees engages in casual conversation. Ross motions for Robert to pay attention to their exchange.

"I'm telling you guys, we're going to turn this place into a tourist hotspot. I'm even thinking of opening a hotel here," one of them exclaims, prompting laughter from the group.

"Great idea! We'll make a fortune. I'll build a golf course right between those rocky bays," another joins in, causing more amusement.

"I'm the only one who's not thrilled about this. This week will be the second unexpected flight, and this one feels like some kind of excursion," one of them comments, not sharing the same lightheartedness. "And to make it stranger, nine more people are coming, all from Puerto Deseado. Isn't that odd?"

The group falls into a contemplative silence, acknowledging the peculiarity of the situation. "You're right... All from Puerto Deseado. But where the hell could they be coming from? That's the closest airfield available."

Ross nods at Robert, and they make their way back to John's room, where he is still answering questions from Rachel and Marta.

"John, sorry to interrupt, but the base personnel are talking about a flight from Puerto Deseado scheduled to arrive today. It has to be Shaman and Markus," Ross informs him urgently.

"Damn it. When did Angel send the video? When was it recorded?" John tries to sit up, wincing in pain.

"Before yesterday, at 11:13," Ross replies, checking his cell phone.

"We need to leave this place immediately." John struggles to rise from the bed. "Help me up. Find me crutches or something that allows me to move without slowing you down too much."

"Okay, I'll go and find the nurse," Rachel volunteers, heading for the door. "Wait, I'm coming with you," Marta adds, following closely behind.

"Ross, we need transportation to get out of here," John says as he throws off the sheets.

"No problem, John. We've already arranged for a plane. I'll take care of it. They just need a couple of hours to get it ready," Ross assures him with a wink before leaving the room.

"Robert, Alberto, help me get dressed so we can make our way out of here."

Inside the hangar, the team gathers around a small aircraft equipped with snow skis on its landing gear. Alberto assists John onto the plane, while

90

Ross and Robert struggle with their equipment. "And what about our gear? Where is it?" Rachel asks, looking at John.

"Our gear will be taken care of. Don't worry. It's all arranged," Ross reassures her.

After a few exhausting minutes, the team boards the plane and settles into the cramped space.

Ross and Robert settled into the pilot seats, and with a powerful roar, the plane taxied towards the runway, finally receiving clearance from the control tower after a tense wait. The aircraft accelerated down the runway and gracefully ascended into the sky.

"We're fortunate to have favorable weather conditions. It's clear and the wind is gentle. If it stays this way, we'll reach our destination before nightfall," Robert announces, turning his gaze back to the team.

Marta looks at John with a perplexed expression and asks, "Before nightfall? I thought Artigas Base was just a few minutes away?"

"Yes, you're right. Artigas is only a short distance away. But we're not heading there," John responds, leaving Marta and Rachel bewildered by his words. "I apologize. For security reasons, we've always maintained Artigas Base as our stated destination. However, in reality, we're going to Denudasdi Base, which is a little further south."

"But won't they be expecting us there?" Marta inquires.

"I don't believe so. We've already deduced that the incident at Denudasdi had nothing to do with Markus. If it did, they would be waiting for us there, not in Puerto Deseado," John reassures Rachel and Marta.

"On the bright side, this means we'll have access to the facilities at Denudasdi Base," Ross calls from the cockpit.

"It's a huge relief to be able to utilize the facilities instead of relying on tents, and we'll also have access to the base's supplies and equipment. Much better!" Robert adds, eliciting murmurs of agreement from John and Ross.

Everyone on board enjoys a smooth flight, benefiting from the favorable weather. Rachel and Marta discuss the breathtaking beauty of the surrounding landscape, while Alberto peacefully sleeps.

John confers with Ross and Robert in a hushed tone, using the aircraft engine noise to keep their conversation private. Time passes uneventfully, with brief naps and casual conversation.

"We're approaching our destination. Please fasten your seat belts. We'll be landing in a few minutes," Ross announces loudly, momentarily interrupting the serene atmosphere within the cabin. Excitement builds as everyone leans in closer to peer out of the plane's windows.

"But it seems like we're in the middle of nowhere. I can only see white and more white. Where are we going to land?" Marta anxiously gazes out the window, expressing her concern.

"Don't worry. The fact that you can't see it is our best security measure. The base is down there, nestled between the escarpments in the Palmer Land mountains. We aim to stay under the radar and remain invisible to potential threats!" John shouts cheerfully, trying to reassure everyone.

The small plane glides smoothly onto the snowfield, where the pristine white landscape contrasts beautifully with the clear blue sky.

"We have landed. It's a perfect day, frosty and calm. We hope you enjoyed your flight with Snowflake Airlines once again. Have a pleasant stay," Ross says, sharing a hearty laugh.

"Thanks, my friend. It was an excellent flight," John responds gratefully. Ross and Robert assist John in disembarking from the plane, knowing that maneuvering on crutches will be challenging amidst the loose snow. Around it, white reigns throughout its entirety, on the horizon a rocky massif frames the endless plain.

"I've been thinking. Won't Markus check the flight log? He might end up discovering our location," Rachel expresses her concern, her brow furrowed.

"Don't worry. We took care of the flight record, just in case," Ross reassures Rachel with a wink, followed by a boisterous laugh.

"Guys, I suggest we leave our belongings here by the plane," Ross says, setting down a heavy bag. "That way, we can assist John and the ladies until we reach the premises. Later, we'll return to retrieve our things and cover the plane with a camouflage net."

"Sounds like a plan to me," Robert agrees, dropping his bag beside Ross's.

"The base is over there, next to the rocky walls standing out in the middle of the snow," Alberto points ahead.

The group follows Alberto's guidance and soon spots something faintly emerging from the snow next to the rocks, about a hundred meters away. Despite being mostly covered, the dark yellow buildings become visible, nestled amidst the rocky massif, resembling a protective wall.

"Look, on our left. That must be our equipment," John points out the brown patches in the snow beside a conspicuous red parachute that stands out against the white surroundings.

"Alright, I see it too. I'll go and take a look. You all go ahead, and I'll catch up with you later," Robert says.

After a challenging walk through the snow, the group finally reaches the base's facilities. Alberto clears the snow from the first few steps of the stairs. "Here we are. Despite being covered in snow, everything appears to be intact. The cabins are located inside those three larger units, connected by flexible passageways."

"On that side, we have two smaller separate units. One serves as a warehouse, and the other houses the machinery, including the generator, water, and air purifiers," Alberto concludes, pointing towards the designated units.

"Perfect, Alberto. Let's see if we can get inside," Ross calls to Alberto, and they ascend the stairs of the main building, clearing away snow as they go.

Alberto enters the access code, and the door opens, releasing a gust of warm, humid air from inside. They step back, covering their noses.

"Hold on a moment!" Ross says, grimacing in disgust. "Let's allow some fresh air in. It reeks in here."

He ventures into the dark and malodorous interior, with Alberto following closely behind.

John struggles up the stairs with his crutches, while Rachel and Marta hesitate, fearing what they might encounter inside.

"Ross, wait." Alberto steps forward, halting Ross's progress. "I need to locate the electrical panel. We turned it off before we left.

"Jesus! Alberto, what happened here? Is there a dead animal somewhere?" John grimaces in displeasure as he enters. "We need to ventilate this place."

The premises span around 60 to 70 square meters. As the lights gradually illuminate different areas, the interior of the building comes into view.

They find some metal furniture, including two tables, six chairs, two armchairs, a cupboard with benches, and various kitchen appliances. The tables and benches are cluttered with disorganized utensils and instruments.

With caution, Rachel and Marta cautiously enter the room, leaving the door ajar. They survey the surroundings, trying to shield their noses from the unpleasant odor.

"You didn't bother to tidy up before you left, huh?" John comments to Alberto.

"Come on, John. We were under a lot of stress. The last thing on our minds was tidying up the kitchen," Alberto retorts, annoyed.

"Relax, man. I was just teasing," John replies with a chuckle.

Alberto proceeds to showcase the different areas, displayed on a map on the wall. "This blue unit is the central hub. We used it for work and socializing since it was the biggest. The green unit houses the

94

bedrooms and bathrooms, while the red unit serves as a workspace and contains the laboratory."

"Alberto, please, where is the bathroom?" Rachel asks, her expression urgent.

"This way, Rachel," Alberto gestures towards a door at the back of the unit. "You'll need to go to the green unit. Activate the security lock and turn the lever to open the door. The green unit's entrance door is at the end of the corridor, which you can open the same way. The bathrooms are on the right. It's straightforward, and you'll see the signs."

"Okay, thank you, Alberto," Rachel says as she closes the door behind her.

Robert enters the premises with a smile that quickly fades. "Damn, it reeks in here. Did someone die or something?" he jokes, covering his nose with his hand.

"Our equipment is fine. We need to gather our belongings and then go through the equipment boxes," Robert says, looking at Ross, who is desperately trying to open the windows. "Damn, this smell is unbearable. Hold on, I'll help you with the window." Robert heads towards one of the windows.

Rachel suddenly bursts through the door, visibly upset, hyperventilating, and her eyes watering. She leans against a nearby table, trying to catch her breath.

"What's wrong, Rachel?" John looks at her with great concern.

Rachel tries to respond between gasps, pointing towards the closed door behind her. Everyone becomes distressed, attempting to figure out what has happened to her.

"What's wrong, Rachel? What happened?" Marta nearly screams, deeply disturbed by Rachel's condition.

Finally, managing to catch her breath, Rachel musters the strength to explain. "They're all dead."

"Dead? Who's dead?" Marta looks at Rachel with fear, while Rachel kneels on the floor, still trying to control her panic attack.

"Rachel, please explain. Who's dead?" John forgets about his crutches as he rushes to Rachel's side. "Ross, Robert, I need your help to get her seated in this chair," he says, pushing a chair towards them while feeling a sharp pain in his leg.

Rachel opens her jacket and removes the scarf from around her neck. Her eyes appear bulged out.

"Wait... let me catch my breath," she mumbles, gradually regaining her composure.

"Give her some space. She won't be able to explain anything in this state," Marta says, feeling uneasy about her colleague's condition.

"Okay, I'm better now," Rachel says, breathing more slowly as she looks at her concerned colleagues.

"I was curious to see what the facilities looked like after using the bathroom," she explains, trying to control her breathing.

"I looked around and opened one of the doors leading outside. At first, I enjoyed the scenery for a moment. But when I glanced down, I saw the bodies leaning against the wall. All of them dead, frozen."

"But who? Whose bodies are they?" John impatiently asks, desperate for answers.

"How the hell do I know? They're dead!" Rachel shouts, her voice raw with fear and her eyes red and filled with tears. "I'm sick of this. I don't know what the hell I've gotten myself into. I want to go home. I can't take it anymore." She bursts into tears, and Marta embraces her, unable to hold back her tears.

"Alberto, stay here with them. Ross, Robert, come with me. We need to figure out what's going on," John says, determination in his voice as he picks up his crutches.

With growing anticipation, they enter the green unit and look for the door where Rachel found the bodies.

At the back of the premises, a semi-open door reveals itself, making them immediately head towards it.

A cold draft enters through the partially open door. Leaning against the outer wall, they find two frozen bodies, tightly embracing each other, dressed in orange jackets, gloves, and snow hoods.

"Poor guys. What could have happened to them?" John wonders aloud.

"They can't be from Denudasdi. They would have had the access code to enter," Robert comments.

"Yes, you're right. Robert, please get Alberto to see if he recognizes any of them. Ross, try to bring them inside. We need to find something that can help us identify them," John instructs.

Ross struggles to separate the frozen bodies to bring them indoors, accidentally breaking his arms in the process due to their rigid state. The sound of bones breaking and the manipulation of the contorted bodies is uncomfortable even for John, who can only observe. After a few minutes, Alberto and Robert join them.

John points to the bodies lined up side by side. Alberto recoils, disturbed, as he observes their condition.

"Alberto, do you know either of them?" John asks.

"No, I don't know them. I have no idea who they are," Alberto answers, turning his face away from the distressing sight.

"John, look here," Robert says, after cleaning the remains of snow from the bodies. "They're wearing the same type of orange coats. And on their shoulders, there's a badge with blue symbols. It says 'Anguta,' and their hoods bear the same name. Could it mean what I'm thinking?" Robert looks at John in disbelief.

"Anguta? But how is this possible?" John asks as he examines the badge Robert pointed out.

"Please, search them for anything that could help identify them," John instructs, finding a chair to sit on and leaning on his crutches for support.

"Alright, it seems we're in luck. Here, a wallet with some documents," Ross says, retrieving the wallet from the inside pocket of one of the men's jackets. It makes a cracking noise as he opens it, and he carefully extracts several cards, including an identity card.

"Samuel Eloy Doherty, that's the name of this one. And here's another card from the University of Ireland," Ross remarks, examining the various cards. "Seems like Samuel is an academic, a Geologist."

"Alright, see if you can identify the woman," John says, looking thoughtfully at the cards Ross has handed him.

Meanwhile, back in the central unit, Marta tries to help Rachel recover from the shock.

"I know what might help you. I'll make a cup of tea for both of us. If I can find the kettle..." Marta rummages through the cupboards.

"It's okay. Don't worry. I'm fine," Rachel reassures her.

"I found it," Marta says, smiling as she holds up the kettle. "Give me five minutes, and we'll have some hot tea to lift our spirits." She puts the kettle on and hums a song under her breath.

"Thanks, I needed this," Rachel says, holding the mug in her hands and blowing on the tea.

"I know. A hot cup of tea can solve many problems," Marta smiles, but her smile fades when she notices John and his companions returning.

Rachel stands up, eager for answers. "So they're all dead, right? How did they die? Who are they?"

"They are Samuel Eloy Doherty, a Geologist, and Naima Ahmal, an Exoarchaeologist. It appears they froze to death because they couldn't open the door to get inside," John explains. "They are not Denudasdi team members. They have elements that relate to Anguta's mission in the Arctic. We have no idea why they were here or how they ended up like this."

"But how is that possible? There's nothing around here," Rachel wonders.

"You're right. We don't have any answers at the moment. Speculating further won't get us anywhere. We need to save our assumptions for tomorrow. Nightfall is approaching, and we still have to camouflage the plane and gather our equipment. Unfortunately, I won't be of much help. Ross, Robert, I apologize," John says, looking at them with sadness.

"No problem. Don't worry, we can handle it. It may take us longer, but we'll manage," Ross assures him as they head toward the door. "In the meantime, you can look for something to eat. I'm starving. I'd love to have something hot to soothe my stomach when we come back."

"Wait, I'll join you. I can be more useful in assisting you," Alberto says, getting dressed to go outside.

"Great, thanks, Alberto. We can always use an extra pair of hands," Ross says, placing his arm around Alberto's shoulders as they follow Robert outside.

"Rachel, Marta, take a look in the cabinets to the left of the stove. You should find dry spices, ingredients, and dehydrated foods. There's also plenty of frozen food outside in the purple-striped compartments," Alberto advises before closing the door.

As night falls, the smell of cooked food fills the air, creating a cozy atmosphere that lifts the team's spirits. Their conversation is abruptly interrupted by the sudden and noisy entrance of their companions.

"Close the damn door! You're letting in the icy wind. We've been heating up the place," Rachel complains, but her smile reveals her satisfaction with their arrival.

"Shake off the snow outside. We don't want the room covered in it," John says, relieved to have them back.

"Okay, ma'am. Yes, boss," Ross shouts, happy to feel the comforting warmth inside. "It smells so good in here. We were freezing out there, packing your stuff, while you guys were relaxing and doing nothing in the warmth. You'll pay for this," he adds with a laugh. Robert and Alberto remain silent, shivering from the cold, as they rush towards the heater to warm up.

"You look frozen. Have some hot tea we just made," Marta offers a steaming mug to each of them.

"Stop complaining. A real man doesn't complain. Did you bring everything? Did you cover the plane with the camouflage net?" John hands a hot mug to Ross.

"Yes, boss. We covered the plane with the camouflage net and stored all the equipment. Thankfully, Alberto remembered there was a snowmobile stored here, which made our job easier," Ross replies, winking at Alberto.

"So, did you find something to eat? It smells amazing. I'm starving," Robert says, taking a deep breath as he finally feels the warmth comforting his body.

"We were lucky. We found a good supply of groceries," Rachel says as she picks up the steaming pot and places it on the table. "Sit down. We've prepared something to eat."

Ross and Robert don't even take off their jackets. They immediately sit down and grab the soup bowls.

"The communication equipment is up and running, and we have internet connectivity as well. However, we must use it sparingly and only in urgent situations to avoid being tracked. I've already contacted the headquarters," John announces, setting down his teacup. "Now, for some bad news.

It's confirmed. Angel is dead, and they burned down the entire house. Markus and Shaman arrived at Montalva Base and then headed towards Artigas."

By now, they must have realized we're not there. I'm certain they'll begin searching for us first thing in the morning. We need to be cautious whenever we're out in the open," John advises, pausing to grab some food. "They also mentioned that three members of the Anguta base went missing three days ago."

"No! So it's true. How can that be?" Ross's spoon hangs in mid-air.

Robert can't hide his disbelief. "Do you think it could be them?"

Fear edges into Rachel's voice. "Are you referring to the two dead individuals?"

"I can't help but wonder how they ended up here," Ross ponders, his expression deep in thought.

"And where is the third person? We didn't see anyone else outside. Where could he be?" Robert gazes fixedly at the bowl of soup in front of him.

"Now we know that the two bodies Rachel discovered belong to the three members of the Anguta mission who have been missing for a few days," John explains. "The mystery lies in how they vanished from Anguta and appeared here. I don't have an answer for that," he adds, looking pensively at the knife as he idly plays with his fingers.

"That Anguta base you mentioned earlier, it's the one in Antarctica, right?" Marta asks.

"Yes, it's the same base," John confirms.

"And where does the name Anguta come from?" Marta probes further.

"Anguta is the name of a sacred mountain in the Arctic. It's considered the mountain of the goddess, the gateway to the inner world," John says, taking a sip of his tea.

"According to Inuit beliefs, this mystical realm dates back to the beginning of time," he says, giving them a playful mystical look.

"Anguta is said to be one of the seven gates to Abulkur, the mystical inner world. Another one of the seven gates is the one the Denudasdi mission

101

was investigating in this area, Aklujji Matu," John tidies up his dish after finishing.

"Wait a minute. So, are we here to investigate another Hollow Earth-like theory?" Marta asks, her annoyance apparent.

"No, Marta, this isn't some fanciful whim. This mission exists because we've gathered substantial evidence to support our cause. There's indeed a lot of folklore and fantasies associated with this subject. Many cultures, from ancient Mesopotamia to tribes in the heart of the Amazon, have references to the inner world, all sharing similar details," John continues, noticing Marta's disturbed expression.

"I'm confused. What does any of this have to do with alien technology? How does this inner world connect to it?" Marta asks.

"All of the foundation's research into legends and mysteries of vanished civilizations coincides with two references: Abulkur, the inner world and its seven gates, and the Cosmic Visitors, as the alleged founders of it," John explains. "So far, we have only located two sites as possible gates of Abulkur: Anguta and Aklujji. Other clues point to three more locations, in Asia, South America, and the Middle East."

"And what do we know about that Aklujji gate the Denudasdi was looking for?" asks Rachel.

"We believe that's where the accident happened. The Denudasdi team found something but didn't return to reveal it. We only have the last message they sent, where they give us some clues," comments John.

"Wait. In Puerto Deseado, you were very concerned about the documentation Ross and Robert had in their possession. What's in it?" Rachel asks, leaving John with a tired expression.

"It contains information obtained from Anguta's mission. We must know what they are discovering," he says.

"But why? Aren't we all working for the foundation?" asks Marta, finding John's statement strange.

"It's complicated. Within the foundation, there are two competing factions: the military and the civilians. The military aims to master all technological discoveries. The civilians want to share their findings to help the development of humanity.

Usually, the military does not participate in these types of missions. And if they are involved, it is only at the level of logistics and security. In the case of Anguta, it is different. I am afraid they will take control of the mission if the alien technology suspicions are confirmed," says John.

"But aren't you part of the military?" Marta presses.

"No, Marta. We are external resources. We work under contract with the foundation. They wanted to keep Denudasdi's mission off the military's radar. But with the threat of Shaman and Markus, it will be complicated, if not impossible."

"And what is important about this information from Anguta?" Rachel asks.

"I have not seen it yet. I can only access it on a laptop. I will do so after dinner."

"And the message from the Denudasdi team, what does it say?"

"The last two messages we received are quite intriguing, despite their poor quality and interference," John shares, his words quickening with anticipation. "We managed to understand references to a geological depression or crater, through which they descended via a crevasse and discovered an incredibly unique rocky outcrop. In the latest message, they mentioned being inside the depression, near the rise of rocky formations. However, the transmission abruptly ended with someone mentioning a black fog, followed by intense static and cuts. Unfortunately, we couldn't decipher anything further, only the persistent noise of static."

John's words hang in the air, leaving the room silent as everyone processes the information. Breaking the silence, John continues, "Tomorrow, our priority is to unpack and organize our equipment and conduct an initial aerial reconnaissance to locate the specific area mentioned in the message. I suggest that all of you get a good night's rest. I will stay here to delve into the files we received from Anguta." With that, John opens his laptop, ready to immerse himself in the investigation.

Feeling the weight of exhaustion, Rachel rises from her seat, stifling a yawn. "Yes, I need some rest and catch up on sleep after the tumultuous events of the past few days. Good evening, everyone." She says and heads towards the bedroom area.

Marta, following Rachel's lead, stands up and says, "Wait. I'm joining you. See you all tomorrow."

"See you tomorrow, ladies. Have a peaceful night and pleasant dreams," Ross offers his well-wishes while sitting with a bottle of vodka alongside Robert. Meanwhile, Alberto retreats to a corner chair, silently engrossed in a book.

John sighs and says, "This is going to be quite an endeavor. We have an abundance of files to go through, meticulously examining each one to uncover anything of interest." He reclines in his chair, scowling at the laptop screen.

"Robert, I believe it's time for us to inspect our equipment," Ross says, as he rises and grabs his jacket.

Robert nods. "Alright, boss. While the rest are fortunate enough to sleep, we'll attend to our duties." He points towards Alberto, who has already succumbed to sleep, a book resting on his chest.

"This is all becoming overwhelming for him. He's not accustomed to this level of intensity. We should wake him up so he can go to bed properly. Sleeping in a chair will only leave him feeling sore," John suggests, his attention returning to the laptop screen.

Robert gently rouses Alberto, who groggily gets up, feeling a bit disoriented. "Goodnight, everyone. See you tomorrow," he mumbles in a subdued tone before leaving the room.

Ross waits for Robert near the exit, bracing themselves for the chilly air that greets them as they open the door.

Meanwhile, John remains alone, engrossed in reviewing the files on his laptop. Suddenly, something catches his attention, causing him to become deeply absorbed and preoccupied. He stares intently at the screen, his lips pursed in concentration.

John leans across the table, his hand reaching for the bottle of vodka his buddies had left behind. Not finding a glass nearby, he takes a sip directly from the bottle, setting it back down on the table. His focus remains fixed on the computer screen, silently engrossed in its contents.

Ross and Robert return with two long black bags, dropping them on the table. "Hey there! Easy now, buddy. Leave something for us," Ross says, laughing. However, John barely acknowledges their arrival, his gaze fixed on the computer screen, still holding the bottle.

Curious and concerned, Robert notices John's tense state and asks, "What's going on, John? You seem unsettled. Did you come across something troubling in the files?"

John hesitates for a moment, then replies, "No, nothing's wrong."

He places the bottle back on the table and closes his notebook.

"I'm just tired. I'll retire to bed now." With the aid of his crutches, he slowly rises from his seat and heads towards the door leading to the bedroom unit. "Goodnight, guys. I'd like to start early tomorrow, at sunrise."

"Goodnight, John. Don't worry, we'll take care of checking and packing our equipment before getting some rest ourselves," reassures Ross. "We also verified our fuel supply. We should have enough for approximately 50 hours of flying and over 100 hours for the snowmobile."

"Excellent. See you tomorrow, guys." John closes the door behind him.

Concerned, Ross turns to Robert and asks, "What's going on with him? He wasn't like this before we left. What the hell happened?"

Robert, equally perplexed, responds, "Yeah, I noticed something's off with him too. It seems like something in those files has deeply affected him. I just can't understand why he didn't share any of it with us."

"Well, I hope he doesn't turn to the bottle again. I don't want to deal with him when he's drunk and in a foul mood. We've seen where that leads," Ross remarks, concern and frustration crossing his face.

"Yeah, let's hope he gets a good night's sleep and wakes up in a better state of mind. We have things to take care of," Robert agrees, his focus shifting to carefully inspecting each weapon on the table. Ross sighs and turns to organizing the ammunition boxes, arranging them neatly in one of the cabinets behind him.

Anguta

In Anguta's meeting room, Kurt presents a series of black and white photographs on the screen wall. The images, bearing a rudimentary quality, indicate that they were taken in the early 1900s. The photographs depict a group of men, their expressions somber and weighed down by desolation. Adorned in thick fur clothing, their sun-darkened skin and full beards reflect the harsh environment of ice and snow that surrounds them.

"These are the members of the Russian expedition that mysteriously vanished in 1885," Kurt explains. "Olev, Lev, Ivan, Kunuk, and his son, Suluk. Kunuk was the only one who returned to his village, the sole survivor who lived to recount the tale."

With a flicker, Kurt projects two more recent photographs onto the screen, revealing better detail and clarity. "These images capture two of the expedition members, taken 25 years later. On the left, we have Olev, who was discovered unconscious by a military patrol in the United States. And on the right, Lev, who surfaced at a train station in Hamburg. Remarkably, both encounters occurred on the same day, March 15, 1910."

Tzabar, engrossed in the unfolding narrative, gazes intently at the photographs. "I had read about them in my file, but seeing their actual pictures is a first for me," he remarks with keen interest.

"When they were found, they had no recollection of their identities, their origins, or how they ended up in those distant places," Kurt continues.

"However, the very next day, they began to regain their memories. Both spoke of a mysterious city Abulkur built by the creators and inhabited by the Sdax, a people from another world.

"Their stories got brushed off as just wild and untrustworthy, eventually fading into obscurity. Who knows, if those teams had compared notes, they might've seen how surprisingly similar their experiences were. And here's a quirky twist – Olev and Lev both kicked the bucket in 1920, on the exact same day, March 15th." Kurt pauses, his gaze fixed on the projected slide.

"Okay. I'm familiar with the Russian expedition that aimed to map a section of the northern coast of Greenland in 1885." Tzabar stops getting thoughtful.

"I reckon those mentions of 'Abulkur' line up with the famous legendary city with seven doors. That's why are we here. Chasing after a legend?" Tzabar asks.

"I hope to provide you with some answers right away," responds Kurt, projecting a slide onto the screen, and displaying a map with several annotations. "We still lack knowledge about how Olev and Lev reappeared 25 years later, and we know nothing about Ivan Pavel and Suluk.

Kunuk was encountered in a village by an exploration team in Antarctica. They were able to gather his personal history and some artifacts."

Kurt proceeds to project photos of the disordered objects placed on a table within a dimly lit room. "These findings helped fill in some gaps in the stories of Olev and Lev. The objects collected from Kunuk ended up in the possession of the Riversi Foundation, without initially arousing much interest.

Some years later, a third party unexpectedly became intrigued by these objects, prompting the Foundation to delve into the contents of the forgotten loot," Kurt continues. "Among the items, one, in particular, captured the team's attention—a metallic disc with a crystal inlay. The metal composition and inscribed characters on the disc remained unidentified." Kurt projects enlarged photos of the disc onto the screen.

"But the surprises didn't stop there. Inside the crystal, there was an embedded incrustation—a wandering spark of unknown nature,"

Kurt reveals, showing a short video of the emerald green crystal within the enlarged disc. The spark pulses rhythmically against the crystal walls, appearing trapped yet eager to escape.

"It's remarkable. Seems to be trapped, yearning for release," remarks Tzabar, visibly impressed by the mesmerizing sight.

"Indeed, that's precisely what the members of the research team observed," Kurt confirms. "And as if these discoveries weren't enough, the most significant surprise came with the dating of the disc." Kurt deliberately pauses, building anticipation.

"Alright, Captain. You have my full attention. What dating did they determine for the disc?" Tzabar eagerly awaits the revelation.

"The dating obtained for the disc surpasses five million years," Kurt states, locking eyes with Tzabar, who remains silent, his gaze fixed on the screen.

Tension and intrigue cross his face as he absorbs the weight of the revelation.

"But that means... someone created it long before..." Tzabar trails off, his gaze fixed on the mysterious enlarged disk projected on the screen. He is unable to articulate his thoughts fully.

Kurt chuckles, reminiscing about his own reaction when he first learned of the report. "Yes, that's correct," he affirms, amused by Tzabar's bewildered expression.

"But there's more. Don't worry. You'll have time to process all of this later," Kurt reassures, leaning back in his chair and scrolling through a few more images. He maintains a playful smile, not allowing Tzabar to interrupt or voice his astonishment.

Swiftly transitioning to a new screen, an enlarged image of the previous photograph appears. Tzabar barely has time to voice his objections before the sight on the screen stops him cold. "But this isn't a human body. Could it be an android, a robot?" he asks, leaning closer to examine the image.

"Correct, Colonel. Despite the poor image quality, the body shape and the helmet are distinctively non-human. Pay attention to these details," Kurt explains, pointing to specific areas on the screen, where cables and mechanical components can be seen with some clarity.

"How...," Tzabar begins to ask, but he struggles to form a complete sentence, his composure slightly shaken.

"These photos, nearly overlooked by the research team, were taken by one of the Russian expedition members. Some of the images also capture fragments of the wreckage mentioned in the reports," Kurt adds. "I've already sent these files to your email. You can review them tonight. I suspect sleep won't come easily to you," he adds with a chuckle. "Now, you can understand why we mobilized swiftly and allocated abundant resources."

Kurt stands up, gathering his belongings, while Tzabar remains silent, captivated by the astonishing images displayed on the screen.

"Well, Colonel, if you wish, I can show you to your room. I must warn you not to expect luxurious accommodations. We're not at the Marriott. However, you'll find everything you need to feel comfortable, including a small workspace. Your luggage has already been placed there," Kurt says, inviting Tzabar to leave the meeting room.

"Alright, Captain. Let's proceed," Tzabar agrees, rising from his seat but unable to shake off the lingering thoughts of the images he witnessed. "Don't worry about the luxuries. As long as there's a workspace, that's perfect. Lead the way," he adds, following Kurt towards the exit of the meeting room.

As the two traverse the corridors, they occasionally encounter base personnel.

After a few minutes, they arrive at the living quarters. Kurt points to a specific door, using a card to unlock and access the room.

"If you prefer, you can set up an access code instead of carrying this card," Kurt suggests, opening the door and ushering Tzabar into his assigned accommodations.

"Marvelous. It's more than sufficient," Tzabar says after a quick glance around the room. "It's perfect. While it may not offer a sea view, it's excellent," he jokes upon receiving the room card.

"I'll take my leave now. Have a good night," Kurt says, offering a respectful farewell.

"Good night, Captain. Thank you. See you tomorrow, and have a pleasant evening as well," Tzabar replies, watching while Kurt walks down the corridor with confident strides, until he turns right. For moments Tzabar seems to enjoy the silence of the empty hallway.

He steps out of the room, glances in both directions, and closes the door behind him.

Winterfell

The tranquil ambiance of the empty icy landscape is abruptly shattered by the intensifying hum of the twin-engine aircraft, gracefully descending towards the compact snowfield. Its silhouette is boldly outlined against the expanse of the blue sky. With a smooth slide of a few tens of meters, it comes to a halt on the pristine white track. The small door in the fuselage swings open, and John and Rachel step out onto the glistening snow.

Ross tosses the backpacks onto the ground, falling into the loose snow with a dull thud, while Rachel takes a few steps forward, savoring the pure, invigorating air. Her face radiates satisfaction as she immerses herself in the untouched beauty of the white landscape. Sensing her awe, John joins her side, draping his arm affectionately around her shoulders. In silence, they gaze out at the magnificent scenery before them.

Amidst their reverie, Ross's voice breaks through their trance, bringing them back to the present moment. "Don't worry, guys. Enjoy the view. I'll take care of your belongings," he shouts, joyfully bounding into the snow. With a grin, he retrieves the backpacks, observing the couple with amusement as they slowly register his presence.

"Thanks, buddy. You can leave that. We're heading inside as well," John says, turning towards him with a smile, Rachel close behind.

Entering the base, Ross's cheerful voice rings out, breaking the quietude of the team. "Good morning, everyone," he greets.

"Morning, mate. How was the flight?" Robert chimes in, setting aside one of the guns he was meticulously cleaning.

"Hey, guys! That was a quick trip. Everything ok?" Marta asks, pausing in her task of packing a backpack beside her.

"It went really well. We'll go over the plan for tomorrow after lunch. By the way, what's on the menu today? I'm famished," Ross says, his backpack now resting on the ground. He removes his gloves and inhales the tantalizing aroma of cooked food that permeates the warm air inside.

"Today, we have Chef Robert's special menu," Marta announces with a smile. "I have no idea what he did, but it smells absolutely divine." She glances at Robert and blushes when he winks at her, lowering her face shyly.

"Where are John and Rachel?" she asks, her eyes scanning the closed door behind Ross.

"They should be here soon. I think the morning flight has sparked John's romantic side. I haven't seen him this relaxed in ages," Ross replies, winking at Robert.

Ross removes his jacket and asks, "OK! While we wait for the love birds, how can I help?"

"You can start by packing your belongings. I've already packed mine and set your field gear aside. Just check to see if anything is missing. I'll assist Marta now," Robert says, winking back at Ross. Marta discreetly hides a smile and turns her back, pretending to busy herself with the first object she lays her hands on.

"Marta, how can I be of assistance?" Robert asks, stepping closer and causing her to feel flustered, rendering her momentarily speechless.

A sudden noise coming from the door diverts everyone's attention.

John and Rachel burst into the facility, their voices loud and laughter filling the air. For a brief moment, they appear oblivious to their companions' presence, who observe them with amusement.

"What's going on? Why is everyone standing around like a bunch of idiots?" John asks, breaking the silence.

"Oh, nothing is happening. We're simply enjoying the sight of your youthful look. Keep it up. It's refreshing to see people in love," Robert chuckles.

"I'm glad you're enjoying it," John replies, embracing Rachel, who giggles uncontrollably.

"What about Alberto? Where is he?" John asks, removing his jacket and making his way toward the group.

"Alberto is still in the communication room. He's doing a final check on the equipment we'll be taking tomorrow," Marta explains, attempting to create some distance between herself and Robert.

"Let's clear the table and dig in. Afterward, we'll go over tomorrow's plan and take the rest of the day off to relax. The next few days will be demanding, so it's best if we're all well-rested," John suggests, heading toward the table.

"I agree with the boss. Let's eat. I'm famished," Ross says, rubbing his hands.

"Take it easy, man. You've just arrived. Go grab the plates and cutlery while we finish setting the table," Marta says.

"I don't know what's happening, but Marta seems much more relaxed and in a good mood. What's going on?" Rachel asks, chuckling and casting a playful sideways glance at Robert. Marta smiles, her cheeks flushing again, rendering her speechless once more.

"Someone call Alberto, and let's eat." Robert comes to Marta's rescue, breaking the momentary silence.

Soon, everyone gathers around the table, engrossed in lively conversation and laughter, creating a relaxed atmosphere. After the satisfying meal, they huddle around a map, with John tracing several marks in red pencil.

"We flew over this area, approximately 145 km from here, following the notes left by the previous team. We spotted a geographical depression with significant cracks in the ice, matching their references," John explains, marking a thick red circle on the map. "We need to exercise extreme caution when approaching. The most dangerous cracks are the ones that remain hidden, and we still have limited knowledge about the stability of the terrain in that area."

"Tomorrow, at sunrise, we'll set out. The terrain seems suitable for the snowmobile, and the weather is in our favor. We must seize this opportunity. Since I'm not fully recovered, I'll ask Ross to drive the snowmobile," John directs his gaze toward Ross, who nods in agreement.

"Perfect. You can tow a sled loaded with some of the equipment and should be able to reach the destination before dark. The rest of us will take the plane with the remaining supplies. Alberto, you'll stay here to provide support with communications," John continues, leaning back and awaiting the team's reactions.

"Alright. The communications equipment is prepared, with batteries charged and radios tuned to the private channel we agreed upon," Alberto assures, rising from his seat and holding up one of the radios.

"I've also been in touch with our command, and the only information I have about Markus is that he is still searching for us in Artigas. We must use the radios strictly for essential communication. Remember to review the communication protocol we established. As for the rest, I'll also continue monitoring the weather conditions. I hope everything goes smoothly and that you all return safely. That's what I wish for," Alberto concludes, settling back down.

"Thank you, Alberto. We're relying on you. You'll be our lifeline to the outside world. Don't forget that. Without you, we're in deep trouble," John patted Alberto on the back.

"Before going to bed, make sure to double-check your gear. We'll depart as soon as the sun rises tomorrow," John announces, rising to his feet, still grappling with his injury.

#

The day breaks, revealing a clear and tranquil scene. Alberto stands at the communications desk, glancing at his colleagues by the window, concern shadowing his face.

"Have a safe trip, and may everything go well for everyone. I'll keep a watchful eye on the weather and communications. *Crazy Penguin*, I'll be eagerly awaiting your status report in an hour," Alberto speaks into the radio he holds.

"This is *Naughty Seagull*. Thank you, *Winterfell*. We're ready to go and will be departing in 5 minutes. Have a pleasant journey, *Crazy Penguin*, drive safe," John says over the plane's radio, flashing an okay sign to Alberto at the base and to Ross on the snowmobile.

"*Crazy Penguin* here. Appreciate it, *Winterfell*. Take care, *Naughty Seagull*, and be safe. I'm on my way," Ross replies, setting off on the snowmobile, gracefully gliding across the pristine layer of snow, testing its stability as he gains speed.

The twin-engine aircraft starts its journey towards takeoff, with Robert and John in the cockpit, while Rachel and Marta relish the view through the small windows.

Alberto lifts his head, tracking the aircraft's ascent as it gains altitude. Rachel and Marta gaze downward, observing Ross sliding through the snow. Gradually, he becomes smaller, a tiny dot moving across the vast white horizon.

"I hope he encounters no issues along the way. I'm worried about him. He's alone for the entire 145 km," Marta comments, expressing her concern.

"Don't worry, the weather is favorable and the terrain seems clear of obstacles. It's going to be a walk in the park for him," replies John, hiding a look of concern for his companion who advances alone in the vast white desert.

During the smooth flight, John points out some distant clouds on the horizon to Robert. "*Winterfell*, this is *Naughty Seagull*. Please review the weather forecasts. We're spotting a cluster of clouds to the west that I find unsettling," John relays through the radio.

"This is *Winterfell*. I'm checking right away. Give me a minute," Alberto responds, noticing John's anxious expression.

Aware of the impending weather, Robert adds, "We're likely to encounter rough weather ahead. The conditions can be unpredictable in this area. We'll try to land as close to our target as possible. We'll secure the plane and use it as shelter."

A metallic click interrupts their conversation, signaling an incoming message on the radio. "This is *Winterfell*. The updated weather forecast predicts the arrival of a cold front in the next few hours. I suggest you find a comfortable location for tonight. The inclement weather is expected to persist for the next two to three days. Best of luck, guys."

"Thank you, *Winterfell*. Any news from *Crazy Penguin*?" John inquires.

"I will check next. *Winterfell* out."

"Thank you, *Winterfell*. Our ETA is in 45 minutes. We'll be on the lookout for a suitable location to weather the storm. We'll send our signal. *Naughty Seagull* out."

Meanwhile, Ross revels in the boundless and serene white landscape as he journeys on the snowmobile, savoring the pure pleasure it brings.

A metallic voice, accompanied by static crackles, interrupts Ross's tranquil thoughts, emanating from the radio attached to his snowmobile.

"This is *Winterfell*, calling *Crazy Penguin*. Please respond."

Ross slows down the snowmobile, gripping the radio in his hand. "Hello, *Winterfell*, this is *Crazy Penguin*. Go ahead."

"*Crazy Penguin*, how's the journey progressing? Any noteworthy observations?"

"Nothing to report. Smooth sailing. I've maintained the pace as previously recorded. ETA remains 16:45. Is everything alright with *Naughty Seagull*?"

"All is well, just as expected. I'll check in again in 30 minutes. *Winterfell* out."

Ross switches off the radio, taking a moment to survey his surroundings and appreciate the scenery. Something catches his attention, protruding from the snow a few dozen meters to his right.

Intrigued, he steers towards the spot, standing up on the snowmobile to get a better view. As he approaches, he discovers a partially buried snowmobile, similar to the one he drives. A few meters away, another snowmobile discreetly emerges from beneath the snow. After a quick inspection of the uncovered machines, Ross picks up his radio.

"Hello, *Winterfell*, this is *Crazy Penguin*. Please respond."

"Here's *Winterfell*. What's up?"

"I have something to report after all. I've come across two snowmobiles. They resemble mine, likely belonging to the base," Ross explains, continuing to scrutinize them for further clues. "They are facing in the direction of the base. It appears someone may have run out of fuel."

"*Crazy Penguin*, mark the location with a flag. I will inform *Naughty Seagull*. *Winterfell* out."

"Done! Two snowmobiles marked at flag H23I12A05. *Crazy Penguin* out." Ross switches off the radio and resumes his journey, scanning the surroundings carefully for any other distinctive features amidst the snow.

#

A single-engine plane soars above a foreboding mountain range, its dark rocks casting an ominous presence. Three men occupy the cramped space inside, their eyes fixed on the landscape passing by outside the windows.

"Once we reach the end of the mountain range, turn back. I want to expand the search perimeter by another five kilometers," says the man at the back of the cabin, his German heavily accented.

"Markus, it's highly unlikely for them to be here. There were no planes at the base with a range exceeding 800 kilometers apart from ours. We're already more than nine hundred kilometers away. We'll make this additional turn and return. Our fuel is dwindling, and inclement weather is approaching," the pilot responds.

"Damn it. Fine. Where the hell are these fuckers? Where is their plane?" Markus mutters in frustration, his gaze fixed on the landscape below.

"Take it easy, Markus. We'll eventually find them. It's virtually impossible to go unnoticed here unless they're hiding beneath the ice," the third man, seated next to the pilot, reassures.

"Take it easy? What the hell? What are we going to tell Shaman? That those bastards slipped away, that they deceived us with the Artigas ruse? Screw this," Klaus exclaims angrily, leaving his companions in silence, while the aircraft sharply banks in the sky, heading towards Montalva Aerodrome.

Meanwhile, Alberto investigates one of Denudasdi's support compartments when the sound of an approaching plane catches him off guard. Aware that it can't be John's aircraft, he retreats cautiously while scanning the sky for the source of the noise. A sudden silvery reflection in the blue sky reveals the small plane.

He hurries back to the base and connects to the radio.

"*Winterfell* calling. *Crazy Penguin*, please respond," Alberto calls, anxious, awaiting a reply. "*Winterfell* here. Calling *Crazy Penguin*, please respond," he repeats.

"This is *Crazy Penguin*. What's the matter?" comes the response.

"I spotted a single-engine plane. I don't know who it could be, but I advise caution if they're searching for us. I'll inform *Naughty Seagull*. *Winterfell* out."

"Understood, *Winterfell*. *Crazy Penguin* out." Ross switches off the snowmobile and instinctively scans the sky, keeping a vigilant eye in all directions while listening for any telltale sounds. He knows he's a conspicuous target in that vast white desert.

After a few tense minutes without detecting any signs of danger, he resumes his journey, picking up the pace to make up for lost time.

#

119

"I've already fixed this side. Where else needs my attention?" Rachel asks, inspecting one of the stakes that secure the camouflage net draped over the twin-engine plane.

"Leave the rest to me. I'll take care of the ones that are missing. Help John and Marta with the tents," Robert responds, crouching next to one of the anchors for the camouflage net and gesturing toward their teammates.

Rachel makes her way toward John and Marta, who are busy setting up the two tents near the plane to shield against the approaching storm.

"What? After all this time, you've only managed to set up one of them? What have you guys been doing?" Rachel jokes with a playful grin.

"Enough joking, lend us a hand," Marta sighs, standing up and facing Rachel.

After overcoming a few challenges, and finally managing to set up the two tents, they gather inside the larger tent, huddled around a pot of coffee on the fire, seeking respite from the biting cold outside.

"Do you think the weather will worsen significantly?" Marta asks, holding a steaming mug.

"Most likely. Let's brace ourselves for harsh conditions with freezing winds and heavy snowfall. It's typical for this time of year," Robert says, lightly.

A metallic sound grabs their attention as the radio next to John comes to life.

"This is *Crazy Penguin* calling *Naughty Seagull*, please respond," John holds the radio and increases the volume so everyone can hear the communication.

"Here's *Naughty Seagull*. I'm listening," John replies, ensuring everyone can follow the conversation.

"*Naughty Seagull*, I believe I'm less than 30 minutes away from your location. The clouds are becoming ominous. I hope you're settled in and have a hot drink waiting for me. *Naughty Seagull* out."

"*Crazy Penguin*, we're eagerly awaiting your arrival. We're all set up and safe. The kettle is already on fire. *Winterfell* has informed us about the snowmobiles you discovered. They might come in handy. *Naughty Seagull* out."

"I hope the weather doesn't hinder our departure tomorrow. We're less than 2 kilometers away from our objective. It would be frustrating to be so close and unable to reach it," Robert remarks, rubbing his hands together. "I have high expectations for tomorrow. Have any of you noticed how the plane's instruments behaved as we flew over the area?"

"I've experienced something similar before. On a mission years ago, we flew over a region in Central America, and our navigation instruments went haywire. The radio even stopped working momentarily. People referred to it as a known mysterious black spot," John shares.

"Do you think we'll be able to unravel the mystery of what happened to the Denudasdi team?" Rachel wonders.

"I certainly hope that the next few days will provide us with some answers," John replies.

"Speaking of the team, do you think those unfortunate guys we found at the base were using the snowmobiles Ross discovered along the way?" Marta asks.

"It's a possibility. But I'm still puzzled about why they were here in the first place. How did they end up in Antarctica?" John ponders.

"All these mysteries have me thoroughly confused. Perhaps there's a secret portal that transports people between the poles," Robert chuckles, breaking the tension and lightening the mood.

Their banter is abruptly interrupted by the sound of an engine roaring in the distance.

"Listen. Is that a snowmobile? It must be Ross arriving. Just in time," Rachel says, rising to her feet with anticipation.

Everyone emerges from the tent to find Ross dismounting his snowmobile and shaking off the accumulated snow from his clothes.

"Welcome, mate. How was your journey?" Robert is the first to approach Ross, extending a warm greeting.

"Hey there! Cheers, lazy folks. No need to wait any longer. I've arrived. Where's my hot drink?" Ross laughs, removing his glasses and revealing the tan acquired during the trip.

"Welcome, Ross. You've got quite a nice color there. Let's head inside. It's freezing out here," John suggests.

"Listen up, everyone! John's already walking without crutches. Finally, he can start doing something useful and stop making excuses," Ross exclaims with a chuckle, breaking the ice before entering the tent.

They settle comfortably inside, surrounding two stoves where food and tea warm over the fire.

"Do you think the Anguta guys were using the snowmobiles you found?" Rachel asks.

"I've considered that possibility since the snowmobiles were facing toward the base. But I still can't wrap my head around how those two guys ended up here, and with those snowmobiles. The more I think about it, the more puzzled I become," Ross replies, helping himself to a plate of food. "And speaking of the plane Alberto spotted, do you think it could be Markus searching for us?" he asks the group.

"I don't think so. Until we know if there is any real danger, we will continue with our plan," says John.

"But then it might be too late," Marta replies with a faint look of concern in her eyes.

"You made it just in time, Ross," Rachel notes, observing the tent being battered by strong winds and snowflakes relentlessly pummeling against it. "From the sounds outside, the bad weather has already arrived."

"I suggest we all sleep here. If we huddle together snugly, we should have no problem fitting in. The temperature inside will be more pleasant, and we'll have a more comfortable night's sleep," John proposes, looking at Rachel and Marta for their agreement.

"I was actually thinking the same thing. I don't feel like going to the smaller tent, I prefer to remain in the warmth here. What do you think, Marta? Can we trust the boys to behave themselves if we join them in here?" Rachel asks, smiling at Marta, who remains strangely silent for a moment.

"That's a great idea. We'll be more comfortable here if we move some of the things cluttering up the smaller tent," Robert suggests.

"Yes, I agree. It would be better for us. As long as they don't snore too loudly," Marta replies, grinning at Rachel.

"Fantastic. We'll share the tent then. I like your idea, Robert. Let's transfer some of this stuff to the other tent," John responds, serving himself another cup of tea, while his companions now focus their attention on the hot food, allowing the storm outside to take center stage for the night.

#

Upon arrival at the Montalva base, Markus and his companions disembark from the plane to discover Shaman awaiting them on the runway, donning a tense expression.

"Good afternoon, Markus. I hope you're here to tell me you found John and his team", greets Shaman in a sarcastic tone.

"Good afternoon, Boss. Not yet. We searched to the limits of the plane's range, but there were no signs of them", Markus says, returning the cold look to Shaman.

"You astonish me. What's amiss with you? Is age making you inept? Allowing John to elude you in Puerto Deseado, and now failing to locate him in the midst of this white desert," Shaman retorts, his tone dripping with condescension and hunger, while shaking his head disapprovingly.

"I'll unearth them; it's just a matter of time. I'll promptly resume the search. If John is nearby, I'll find him," Markus responds with a disgruntled frown, attempting to stride toward the airfield building, but Shaman forcefully halts him.

"Wait. I'm not finished yet. I'll be taking charge of operations from now on, which I should have done earlier. Tomorrow we'll commence a new search, this time on land with aerial support. We have 48 hours to find them, and I don't care if it rains cats and dogs. If the weather is bad, even better. While they wait for improved conditions, we can make progress," Shaman declares as Markus begins walking, appearing indifferent to the words reaching him. Unperturbed, Shaman continues to speak, seemingly indifferent to Markus' state of mind.

"Tomorrow, we'll head to the mainland. The plan is to sweep the entire land expanse up to the Ellsworth Mountains on the edge of Palmer Lands. We'll establish a support base with equipment and supplies halfway through the journey to aid our progress. Three teams on snowmobiles will advance, supported by the plane."

"The severe weather will heavily impact the South Shetland Islands. I'm not sure if we can make it out in time," Markus expresses his impatience.

"While you were enjoying your plane ride, I made all the necessary arrangements. The field teams are already en route by boat. Tomorrow, we'll depart early with equipment. Ensure the plane is ready for takeoff at sunrise," Shaman says disdainfully, leaving Markus stunned and motionless watching Shaman turn his back and walk away towards the hangar.

#

John kneels at the tent entrance, peering outside and observing the morning sun attempting to rise behind the cloud-covered sky.

"The weather has improved significantly, let's see how long it lasts," comments John.

"Man, this is much better than I expected," Robert says, emerging from the tent and surveying the surroundings. "If it holds like this, we can venture out and explore the area without any issues."

"John, Robert. Alberto is on the radio," Rachel calls, poking her head out of the tent while still wrapped in her sleeping bag and holding the radio.

"*Winterfell* calling. Listen," Alberto's voice is heard amidst the crackles coming from the radio.

"*Wolfpack* here. Listening," John responds.

"Good morning, *Wolfpack.* I hope you all slept well and the bad weather didn't cause too much trouble," Alberto greets.

"Good morning, *Winterfell*. We're doing fine here. We now have a tropical sun warming us up. We're planning to hit the beach first thing in the morning. Any news on your end?" John asks.

"Morning report. Uncle says the two clowns brought along plenty of friends to the party, and they're all supposed to come by bike. Uncle sent a special activities newspaper. Uncle's friends should be arriving soon. Let's see if they make it on time. The weather should be better at the beach but worse at the party. *Winterfell* out," Alberto replies.

"Thank you, *Winterfell*. Message received and understood. We'll talk later. *Wolfpack* out," John concludes the conversation.

"What's going on? What was Alberto saying?" Marta suddenly appears, looking perplexed at John and Robert.

"Good morning, Marta. We all should use our communication code, just in case someone is listening. We discussed this before we left yesterday," Robert says.

"Alberto mentioned that Shaman and Markus have formed a team and are also searching for us using snowmobiles," John explains. "But we have some good news too: the weather is expected to improve, and reinforcements will be arriving at the base soon. Let's hope they make it in time for the 'party.'"

"But what 'party' are you talking about? I don't understand," Marta says, visibly confused.

"The 'party' refers to a potential attack on the base. We hope the reinforcements arrive in time to assist Alberto," Robert says as he embraces Marta, trying to ease her anxiety about the news.

"Alberto also mentioned that he received a contingency plan in case they discover the base. However, he didn't elaborate on it," John says, scanning around. "Where's Ross? I don't see him. He wasn't in the tent when I woke up."

"I don't know. I haven't seen him yet," Robert replies, looking around.

"I haven't seen him either. He's not in the tent. I thought he was outside with you," Rachel shrugs. "Maybe he went to get some fresh bread," she jokes, eliciting laughter from everyone.

"What's the joke? What am I missing?" Ross calls from the top of the rocks behind the plane, catching everyone by surprise.

#

After finishing communication with the team, Alberto reads the notes he received about the contingency plan.

"Very well, let's get to work. We have a lot to do," Alberto speaks to himself, trying to alleviate his solitude. "But first, let's listen to something to lift our spirits."

Taking the remote, he points it at the set of equipment to his right. "PlayList Good Mood" appears on a small screen.

The opening notes of 'Sitting On the Dock of the Bay' by Creedence Clearwater Revival resonate throughout the base.

"Let's review the plan. First, we need to divide the equipment and supplies and store at least a third of them in a secure location outside the base. Okay, we already have the list prepared. Great job, man," Alberto murmurs while looking at a sheet of paper and swaying to the music.

"Now we need to find the right location for it. Luckily, I already have a spot in mind. Next, I'll activate the explosive charges at the base for our emergency escape. That's going to be quite a spectacle. I just hope the neighbors don't complain about the noise," Alberto chuckles, looking down at a stack of gray boxes.

"Third, we need to have our escape plan ready. Easier said than done, but let's see what we can come up with." Alberto sits down pensively, crossing off some notes on his sheet of paper and focusing on the next tasks.

"Alright, it seems we have something here. The snowmobiles Ross found are probably a couple of hours away on foot, maybe longer considering I'll have to pull a sled with fuel. However, it should take less than an hour to return if I use the snowmobile, even with the sled in tow. So, I should be able to make it back in less than four hours."

"I'll try to buy myself some extra time, though. Transporting everything with the snowmobile will be much easier and faster. Plus, the snowmobile can serve as a means of escape if I need it." Alberto contemplates the plan for a moment.

"Okay, it sounds like a solid plan. I have until the end of the day to get everything prepared. Let's do it, man. Let's get it done," Alberto says, hyping himself up, and pulls on his jacket, gloves, and goggles. He opens the door with a broad smile, which quickly fades when he sees the harsh weather he'll have to face. Gusts of wind drag curtains of snow, severely limiting visibility outside.

"Damn it. The journey is going to be much more challenging than I anticipated. But what must be, must be," Alberto mutters to himself, wrapping himself up as best as he can and descending the stairs.

Vitrified

The doors to the meeting room swing open, and Kurt and Tzabar stride in, bringing an end to the chattering of the group seated on a bench.

"Good morning. I apologize for the delay," Tzabar says.

"Good morning, Colonel, Captain. No problem. You arrived right on time. We can begin as soon as you take your seats."

Alvin stands up, scans the table, and swiftly introduces the team. "Allow me to present Colonel Tzabar, who joined us yesterday evening. Colonel, you already know Dr. Victor. The others, you'll become acquainted with as the day goes on."

A ripple of indifference passes through the room.

"Good evening. Thank you for inviting me to your meeting. Please proceed," Tzabar replies, taking a seat beside Kurt after briefly surveying the individuals gathered around the table.

Throughout the meeting, Alvin carries out a review of the task assignments for the day, content that does not garner much enthusiasm from Tzabar. However, he diligently takes notes in his notebook, capturing key points and mentally noting intriguing aspects about the participants.

He observes that Kurt is physically present but appears mentally distant, his attention drifting elsewhere. He also catches a few fleeting glances thrown his way by some of those present as he writes on his pad. As for the rest of the attendees, he registers their names and roles by glancing at their badges.

"Colonel, do you have any questions or anything to add regarding our discussion?" Alvin almost catches Tzabar off guard, directing the final questions toward him.

"No, Dr. Alvin. I believe I have grasped everything. Please, continue," Tzabar responds calmly.

"Very well. If there are no further questions, we can conclude our briefing and proceed with our daily tasks."

"Have a productive day filled with pleasant surprises," Alvin bids farewell, his words barely audible over the shuffling of chairs and murmurs of the departing group.

Tzabar and Kurt engage in a discreet conversation as everyone disperses. Alvin gathers his belongings and joins them. "Colonel, Captain, shall we proceed then?"

"Yes, please. I'm eager to see the wreckage site," Tzabar says, eager to get moving.

"Excellent, Colonel. Today, we may uncover some of the secrets of Anguta. We will visit the wreckage site, but first, let's begin with Anguta itself. Lydia is already there. She received an urgent call before the meeting. I'm curious to find out what's going on," says Alvin, rushing down the corridor.

"Very well, we'll follow your lead. Is it still impossible to establish communication near the mountain?" Tzabar asks, increasing his pace to keep up with Alvin.

"Unfortunately, Colonel. No electronic equipment works in the area. Only the lightning seems to be working. Quite intriguing, wouldn't you agree?" Alvin remarks with boyish enthusiasm for the situation, guiding them through the hallways.

Soon, they reach the antechamber where they find thick coats, gloves, and other protective gear against the cold. They equip themselves before stepping outside.

Adrenaline spikes through Tzabar as the door swings open, revealing the magnificent view of the mountain ahead.

The day is clear, and the intense cold is felt on his face. The ice field extends everywhere, except for the mountain and its base.

Alvin is the first to descend the stairs, followed by Kurt and Tzabar. "Awesome. Snowmobiles. It's been a while since I've ridden one of these," Tzabar says with a smile.

"Although the distance is short, the terrain is always uphill, and the slope is steeper than it appears. It's better to use snowmobiles. They're more comfortable, faster, and fun," Alvin suggests, deftly mounting his snowmobile.

They kickstart the snowmobiles with a loud rumble, tearing toward the mountain at breakneck speed and sending curtains of ice into the air. Tzabar can't tear his eyes away from the looming cliffs as he glides effortlessly through the snow. The closer he gets to the mountain, the more his amazement intensifies at its unconventional configuration.

They swiftly reach the edge of the snow, a few meters before a cluster of rocks at the base of the mountain. They park the snowmobiles, and Tzabar steps aside, captivated by the smooth black escarpment.

"Isn't it fascinating, Colonel?" Alvin joins him, following Tzabar's gaze.

"I have never seen anything like this. It seems unnatural," Tzabar murmurs, his eyes narrowing in confusion at the peculiarity of the sight before him.

"The formation of that escarpment is perplexing, especially considering its lack of snow along its length. It's a curious phenomenon," Tzabar says, his gaze fixed on the boulders at the base.

"I can't fathom the origin of these rocks. They don't seem to be derived from the escarpment. If they were, they would have a more layered structure. These are massive blocks," he continues.

"You're right, Colonel. I share your observations. Shall we proceed?" Alvin attempted to redirect Tzabar's attention.

"And these steep rock needles sprouting from them, which eventually merge into the central massif," Tzabar muses, seemingly oblivious to Alvin's nudging. "It reminds me of the shape of a yet-to-bloom flower, with its elongated petals converging along the style. What is

130

their geological nature?" Tzabar asks, catching Alvin off guard with his remark.

"Damn it, Colonel. I had never looked at it from that perspective. Now that I gaze up, I have to agree with you. It does appear as though they merge and originate from the rocks. Interesting imagery with the flower analogy," Alvin admits, his gaze fixed upwards. "We are still grappling with its geological nature," he adds, taking a step forward, with Tzabar following suit.

"Our initial readings indicate a mixed basaltic base, with granite outcrops and significant veins of black quartz. However, these readings fluctuate over time," Alvin explains as he leads Tzabar towards the cliffs, following a path marked by colored stakes.

Tzabar is taken aback by this revelation. "What? Do they fluctuate over time? What do you mean? What changes?" he asks, visibly shocked.

"Yes, I know it sounds strange. We stumbled upon this discovery by chance. Several hours after conducting our initial analysis, a technician collected samples again without realizing we had already done so. Surprisingly, the results differed. Since then, we have been conducting analyses twice a day," Alvin reveals, guiding Tzabar through the cliffs, which rise like needles from the ground.

"I don't understand. What do you mean by 'different'? What kind of differences did you observe?" Tzabar's surprise deepens.

"Among the three elements I mentioned—basalt, granite, and quartz— the geological composition varied at the same collection site. Notably, all samples exhibited piezoelectric characteristics, tuned to the same frequency," Alvin says.

Approaching a massive rock, Alvin gestures for caution. "Watch your head now," he warns, skillfully maneuvering around the rock and leading Tzabar into a complex of upright rocks resembling needles protruding from the ground.

"I don't understand. I know that the piezoelectric effect can occur in granite, but in rocks like basalt? There shouldn't be any piezoelectric characteristics since they lack quartz grains. And why is none of this mentioned in my reports?" Tzabar asks, his surprise growing as he takes in the forest of rocks ahead. He stands in awe, observing the rocky walls that taper as they ascend, creating a labyrinthine formation on the ground. Alvin appears to disregard Tzabar's astonishment and continues walking.

"Colonel, we have forwarded the information to Commander Chang. I'm not sure how he handled it. Our primary focus, and the source of constant pressure, is the alien technology we are supposed to find. Everything else takes a backseat," Alvin explains. Suddenly, he stops and shoots Tzabar a resentful look, quickening his pace as he spots Kurt approaching.

"I apologize, Colonel, for my outburst. It's just frustrating to see our work undervalued. Even when we identify excellent research opportunities, they are ignored and dismissed. As a man of science, I find it difficult to comprehend or accept this. I hope you understand my frustration," Alvin expresses, disappointment etched on his face. He resumes the path as he notices Kurt nearing them.

"Have you been here before? Do you know what they're doing here?" Tzabar asks Kurt, his gaze fixed on Alvin, contemplating his words.

"No, Colonel. I haven't been here before. I have no idea where we're headed," Kurt responds, feeling uneasy.

"Let's not lose sight of him. Come on," Tzabar urges, increasing his pace as he realizes Alvin is starting to distance himself amidst the rocks.

"Dr. Alvin, are we venturing deep into the mountain? What is happening here? Why didn't you inform me about any of this earlier?" Tzabar asks, causing Alvin to halt and turn back to face him.

"Colonel, I apologize. I don't even know what we're going to encounter. I wanted to wait until we had something substantial to show you before sharing the details. I received a message from Lydia, who has been here since early morning, while we were already in the morning meeting," Alvin says, gesturing toward a light that signals their destination's arrival.

In front of them stands a technician, motionless, silently surveying the surroundings. He approaches with a wide smile. "Welcome, Dr. Alvin, Colonel, Captain. What do you think? Is this mind-blowing or what?" he asks, clearly thrilled.

"Where are we? What is this?" Kurt's face reflects his astonishment at the sight before them.

"Look at the size of this space... this clearing. And what's on the far wall?" Alvin exclaims, extending his arms and pointing at each source of his amazement.

"I never anticipated this. Where are we? What is this place?" Tzabar asks, snapping Alvin out of his trance. Alvin gazes back at him with a glimmer in his eyes.

"Can you comprehend the scale of this clearing?" Kurt takes a few hesitant steps toward the center, his eyes fixed on the rock walls that surround them, particularly the wall ahead.

"I can't even see the ceiling. The walls extend all the way up to the mountain's peak," Kurt breathes, gazing upward as if in a trance.

"Good morning, Colonel, Dr. Alvin," Lydia greets them, emotion thick in her voice. They were so immersed in their astonishment that they didn't even notice her approaching them.

"What do you think?" she asks, pointing at the wall in front of them. Without giving them a chance to react or comment, she forges ahead.

"The wall appears to be composed of vitrified black quartz. It's a massive mirror made entirely of natural rock. The distortion in the reflections is minimal. And look at those stone jambs on the wall—those symbols and images. Don't they evoke something familiar?" Lydia asks, gently running her hand along the mirrored surface in awe.

"I agree with you. It's like a gigantic mirror with an immense frame, easily exceeding 20 meters in height. But who could have carved this wall so perfectly, and for what purpose?" Tzabar marvels at the mirrored wall.

"Lydia is right. The engravings are impeccable. I've seen similar symbols before, although not carved with such precision. Here, a cougar and a bird. They resemble those found in Tiwanaku, Bolivia, and Çatalhöyük, Turkey. And on this side, the snake and scorpion, are reminiscent of the ones discovered in Egypt. It's truly extraordinary," Alvin expresses his excitement, captivated by the vast diversity and flawless execution of the engraved symbols.

"We also have symbols that bear resemblance to several others from different cultures. Some characters bring to mind the ancient Arcadian script from over 7,000 years ago in northern Mesopotamia.

Others resemble those found in South America. And here...," Lydia pauses, sighing in wonder at her discovery.

"Some of the writing exhibits similarities to early Chinese dynasties. It's a remarkable compilation," Lydia continues, pointing to various engravings on the wall, unfazed by the skeptical looks of her colleagues.

"This wall is the only one that stretches straight across this slope. Look at the floor," Tzabar crouches down, gently touching the ground.

"This rock is incredibly smooth and flat, unlike the natural formations surrounding us. Someone has clearly been hard at work here," remarks Tzabar, rising to his feet and walking alongside the wall.

"I'm utterly fascinated by this," Alvin chimes in, joining Lydia a few steps away from the wall.

"It's truly remarkable—perfectly flat and polished. I'd bet it forms a precise ninety-degree angle with the ground. Notice how it seamlessly blends with the floor, making it almost indistinguishable. We need to conduct a comprehensive survey of this entire wall area. Lydia, please document everything with videos and photos," Alvin instructs.

"Dr. Alvin, that might pose a challenge," Lydia responds. "As you know, filming videos is impossible here. However, we might be able to take some photos using an analog camera loaned to us by a fellow amateur photographer. It's one of those vintage models. Until then, we'll have to rely on my drawing skills. Once we have better lighting and the camera, we can document everything more effectively," Lydia explains.

"It's a shame that the upper engravings are beyond our reach. We could use a stepladder. I'd love to touch them, but I suspect they might be protected behind a layer of glass, quartz, or something similar," Alvin remarks, while everyone leans against the wall, feeling its texture and gazing up at the prints on the ceiling.

"Wait, how intriguing," Tzabar exclaims. "Notice that the rock isn't cold, at least not as cold as I expected," he says, stepping back from the wall and surveying the area in surprise. "And I swear I feel a faint vibration when I lean against it."

"You're right. It's not as cool as I anticipated either," Lydia confirms, leaning her face against the wall. "I can sense a subtle vibration too."

Alvin remains silent, staring at them in confusion before mimicking Lydia and leaning against the wall himself.

"But what you're suggesting is that the rock has a temperature? Perhaps your skin is colder than you think, and the mountain shields the interior from the cold. There must be a logical explanation for the vibration you're experiencing," Kurt says, casting a skeptical glance at his colleagues.

"Well, Kurt makes a valid point," Tzabar concedes. "Dr. Alvin, conduct the necessary readings to shed light on the nature of this extraordinary place. I understand and share your excitement. However, we mustn't lose sight of our primary objective. I would like to visit the crash site. Can we go now?" Tzabar suggests, shaking off his amazement and refocusing on the mission.

"But... Colonel, now?" Alvin responds, dumbfounded by Tzabar's request.

"Yes, Dr. Alvin. There's little more we can accomplish here for the time being other than marveling at it, and daylight is fleeting, and I want to see the crash site. Remember, I need to provide a status report to my commanding officer by the end of the day," Tzabar asserts, turning towards the path leading back to the exit, leaving Alvin disheartened as he glances back at Lydia, who remains captivated by their recent discovery. Alvin follows Tzabar and Kurt, crestfallen and silent. Tzabar slows his pace, allowing

Tzabar slows down so that Alvin takes the lead on the way. Before leaving the area, he glances at the mirrored wall that seems to beckon him. With a deep sigh, Tzabar follows Alvin and Kurt.

The Cracked Pan

"Good morning, everyone. Did you sleep well? Isn't the morning beautiful?" Ross says, jumping down from the rock, and startling the others.

"Hey, mate! Great to see you. Did you bring some warm croissants?" John teases with a playful grin.

"Oh, come on, John." Rachel playfully scolds John, giving him a playful slap on the arm. "Now I'm craving warm croissants and a hot latte."

"Well, it's a rather chilly morning, but if the weather holds up, we can still explore the site," Robert remarks, glancing at the sky as beams of sunlight break through the gray clouds.

"Well, I've noticed that you didn't bring any croissants or warm bread. I'm disappointed in you, Ross. Let's settle for hot coffee and something else to eat. I want to be ready to leave in less than half an hour," John says, turning and heading back toward the tent.

#

In a snow-covered field, buffeted by icy winds, Alberto trudges forward, pulling the sled behind him.

"Alright, let's take a brief rest and then continue," he mutters, catching his breath as he sits on the sled. He takes a moment to recover, battling the freezing air that stings his nose.

With renewed determination, Alberto rises to his feet and resumes walking, peering through the swirling snow curtain, hoping to catch sight of the snowmobile. Fatigue weighs heavily on him, causing him to stop once more, bending over with hands on his knees, panting and seeking a moment's respite.

"Damn, man, you're useless. You spend your life sitting around, what did you expect? You don't do a damn thing," he grumbles, scanning the surroundings in hopes of finding something to uplift his spirits.

#

Marta emerges from the tent, glancing upwards to assess the weather while putting on her gloves. Her companions are busy wrapping up their preparations. John is atop the snowmobile, with Rachel seated behind him.

"Marta, hop on our sled with Robert," John directs, pointing towards the sled that he's towing along with some equipment.

The revving sound of the snowmobile engine signals the team's departure, with Ross following them on ski.

"I hope the weather holds up and doesn't worsen. Are you doing okay back there?" John asks before maneuvering the snowmobile forward.

"Yeah, I'm good and secure back here. You can go," Rachel replies, tightening her arms around John.

#

"I hope you don't regret this foolish idea of getting the snowmobiles. You bastard," Alberto mutters, rising to his feet and taking a deep breath as he clasps his hands in front of his face.

"When you get back home, you're starting to hit the gym. This can't go on like this."

He clears the collected snow from his glasses with a gloved hand, sensing the strain throughout his entire body. His legs waver, every step becomes an effort, and his back twinges in a telltale sign of muscle fatigue.

Just as he's about to resume walking, something catches his attention amidst the wind-blown snow. With renewed hope, he presses on, a smile spreading across his face. Ahead of him, he spots the snowmobiles.

"You see, you bastard? I was right! Just another fifty meters, and we'll be back at base on a snowmobile. I hope Ross is correct about the lack of fuel." With newfound vigor, he pulls his sled towards the first snowmobile.

#

"It's breathtaking. And it's even larger than I initially thought," John exclaims as he dismounts the snowmobile and removes his snow goggles.

They observe a vast depression from the edge of an escarpment, spanning hundreds of meters, still visible beneath the blanket of snow and ice.

"I don't know why, but something doesn't give me the confidence to venture down there. Look at the extent of those fissures. It screams ground instability to me. I'm not sure," Robert says, his gaze fixed fearfully on the landscape ahead.

"The area of that depression covers more than 20 km. It appears we should descend through that slope over there," John points to a snowy incline on the escarpment without any exposed rocks. "It can't be more than a ten-minute journey from here, and this area seems safe."

"I agree. That seems to be our best option. I can't quite gauge how far down we'll be going. All this white messes with my depth perception," Ross comments.

"The entire depression resembles a cracked pan, given its shape and the fissures crisscrossing it. I don't like it." Robert glances worriedly at the terrain ahead.

"What's your plan regarding these crevasses? I'd prefer to avoid them. I'm with Robert on this. Something about that ground down there doesn't inspire trust." Marta approaches the escarpment to see where John intends to lead the team.

"It's still just an idea. I haven't examined the crevasses up close. I hope one of them can provide access to the lower level beneath the ice cap." John

139

knows his suggestion may not be well received by some team members. And as he anticipated, Rachel is the first to react.

"What? Are you out of your mind?!" Rachel cuts in, alarmed. "Don't even think about it. I'm not going inside any crevasses," she says, immediately supported by Marta. "Count me out too! What a ridiculously foolish idea. Jesus!"

"Let's stay calm," John responds. "We need to first assess the stability of the ground. We'll only use the crevasses if we can ensure our safety. Otherwise, we'll have to find an alternative route." John attempts to reassure them, surprised to notice Robert's hesitance towards the idea.

A metallic sound interrupts their conversation as Rachel's radio comes to life. "This is *Winterfell* calling *Wolfpack*, do you copy?"

"Wait. It's Alberto calling," Rachel says as she hands the radio to John.

"This is *Wolfpack*. Good to hear from you, *Winterfell*. We were getting concerned. Is everything alright on your end?"

"Everything's fine here. I've already retrieved the toys that *Crazy Penguin* found in the garden, and everything is functioning properly. I'm ready to begin the activities suggested by Uncle and move the pantry to a more secure closet. I'll make sure everything is prepared for the arrival of the clown and his friends, hoping Uncle's friends arrive on time. Over," John holds the radio for everyone to hear.

"Excellent, *Winterfell*. *Wolfpack* is starting the tour. What's the weather forecast? Over."

"The weather will worsen in the coming hours, especially in this area. I'm afraid it might affect the clowns' party. Over."

"Received, *Winterfell*. We'll be entering the park soon." John glances at his colleagues, who still seem skeptical. "Wishing you a safe and successful party. *Wolfpack* out."

"Received, *Wolfpack*. Enjoy your time at the park and stay safe. *Winterfell* out."

John hands the radio back to Rachel. "I don't know what else to say. Can we at least assess the ground conditions? We should make the most of the current weather before it deteriorates. Rachel and Marta can stay here if they feel safer. Robert, would you be willing to accompany us as far as you feel comfortable?" John asks anxiously, trying to persuade his hesitant colleagues.

#

Alberto arrives at the base and parks the snowmobiles, panting from the exertion of the past few hours. He brushes off the accumulated snow from his clothes and heads toward the building.

"Damn, it's freezing cold," he mutters upon entering the base facilities. "Let's check in with the team. We haven't spoken to them this morning yet. They must be worried. And we still have a lot to do," he navigates through the stacks of boxes that occupy most of the space inside the facility.

He begins organizing the boxes, securing them with an elastic net, and climbs onto the snowmobile.

Following a well-marked trail of tracks in the snow, he skirts around a cluster of boulders as he approaches the cliffs surrounding the base area.

Behind a massive rock, he stops next to a shelter he constructed using tent covers, adding the new boxes to the existing stockpile.

"Well, three more trips, and that should do it. I think we've exceeded our proposed objective," he reflects with satisfaction.

"Let's hope it keeps snowing like this to cover the tracks," Alberto murmurs, content, as he observes the tracks gradually disappearing under the falling snow.

Beneath the base installations, Alberto stands near one of the pillars, making connections with wires in a package labeled 'C4' in dark blue. Several similar boxes are visible on the nearby pillars.

"Alright, that's it. Everything is prepared to welcome Mr. Markus and his crew. I hope they'll appreciate the fireworks I've arranged for them," he

141

chuckles, crawling out from underneath and brushing off the snow from his clothes.

#

"Let's go before I change my mind!" Robert shouts. "Just be careful!"

"Be safe!" Rachel screams, wrapping her arm around Marta and sitting against the snowmobile, partially sheltered by the blanket they brought. They anxiously watch their teammates as they start descending toward the base of the cliffs.

John trails a few meters behind his companions, taking extra caution with each step due to his partially healed leg and the unpredictable terrain.

"I'm concerned about the girls. The weather is deteriorating, and I don't like leaving them alone," Ross expresses his worry to John, pointing at the dark clouds gathering in their direction.

"Don't worry. The girls have a radio, and they can use the snowmobile to return to the tents," John reassures, trying to keep up with the rest of the team.

"John, how far do you intend to go?" Robert gazes anxiously at the treacherous terrain ahead of each step. John veers slightly to the right, studying the landscape ahead.

"I'm aiming to reach the vicinity of that larger crevice to assess its safety. If possible, I'd like to go all the way to the edge.

The message from the Denudasdi team mentioned a crevice through which they descended. I want to investigate this one," John explains, leaving Robert apprehensive.

"John," a metallic voice resonates from the radio John carries.

"This is *Bluewolf*. *Whitewolf*, please adhere to the communications protocol. I'm listening."

"I apologize, *Bluewolf*. I completely forgot about that. The weather is getting worse, and the team wants to head back to the den. Can

142

we proceed?" Rachel looks at Marta, who is visibly shivering from the cold.

"Alright, *Whitewolf*, return to the den. Don't worry about *Bluewolf*. We are seasoned wolves and used to navigating the wilderness. *Bluewolf* out." John chuckles, feeling more at ease.

"Okay, *Bluewolf*, we'll catch up later. Stay safe. Out." Rachel puts the radio away, frustrated. "Damn, I can't stand this communication protocol nonsense."

"Why? Do you think John is being paranoid about all these precautions? Don't you believe someone could be listening in on our conversations?"

"No, it's not that. I think John is right. Either way, it doesn't hurt to take some precautions. It's just difficult for me to remember the protocol, the names we have to use, or the expressions we need to avoid. It's all very confusing when you have to do it. Ultimately, it's just a lack of practice."

Rachel helps Marta pack the blanket they used for protection. They hop on the snowmobile and return to the tents near the plane.

#

On the vast white plain farther north, several landmarks catch the eye.

A convoy of snowmobiles plows through the pristine snow, each transporting two passengers. Eagerly, some riders wave to a small plane cruising overhead in the same direction. Through the plane's modest window, someone gazes down at the column of snowmobiles below.

"Markus, proceed to the cliffs on your right. Fabio, keep going, and Olivier, take your group two clicks to the left. Confirm your understanding," Shaman commands into a walkie-talkie, holding binoculars in his right hand.

"Markus here. Received and understood," a metallic voice responds, followed by two identical messages.

"Do another round, another ten clicks," Shaman instructs the pilot. "I want to close this perimeter today. Tomorrow, visibility will likely be much worse if the weather deteriorates."

"Understood, boss. But I'm not sure if we'll be able to take off tomorrow. The weather forecast is unfavorable for flying," the pilot remarks.

"I don't care. We have less than 30 hours to find them. Tomorrow, we'll take off, even if I have to fly the plane myself. Descend a bit over there, along those 'U'-shaped cliffs," Shaman directs, peering through the binoculars ahead.

Alberto stands by one of the windows at the base, clutching a cup of tea in his hand. He gazes out at the small aircraft weaving through the clouds.

"Damn it. They're getting closer. Hopefully, the bad weather will give us some luck and delay their arrival. Maybe I can get a peaceful night's sleep," he mutters, keeping a watchful eye on the plane. However, his tranquility is short-lived as he notices a change in its direction, sending a chill down his spine.

"Oops...shit." Alberto's heart sinks as he realizes the plane is descending and veering directly toward their location. "No. No chance of sleep tonight. It seems we're in for an unanticipated party."

Surprises

As Tzabar maneuvers through the rugged forest, his thoughts are consumed by the mirror wall, its intricately engraved symbols, and enigmatic characters. A persistent feeling of familiarity gnaws at him, yet he can't quite pinpoint its source.

Exiting the tunnel, they encounter a small group of enthusiastic individuals carrying a ladder and lighting equipment. Only Tzabar offers a greeting as they pass by.

Upon reaching the snowmobile, Alvin quickly climbs into his vehicle, barely expecting Kurt and Tzabar to join him, speeding towards the white domes located in the wreckage area, the focal point of the mission's research efforts.

He is the first to arrive, parking his snowmobile and heading toward the entrance of the wreckage. He patiently waits for Kurt and Tzabar, who catch up a few minutes later.

"Dr. Alvin, thanks for your patience," Tzabar says, concealing his playful tone. "I count on your guidance to keep me in the loop on all the crucial aspects here."

"Let's go inside. I will provide you with the most relevant details during our visit," Alvin says, gesturing for them to enter.

"Let's kick off with sector A1. The primary hurdle in unearthing more discoveries lies in the thick layer of snow and ice blanketing them," Alvin explains. "While we've contemplated employing heat sources, the melted water from the thawing process might pose a risk to the integrity of any findings beneath and degrade their quality. After all, we're in the dark about what lies beneath the snow."

Approaching the first group of technicians diligently working in a sector, Alvin addresses them, "Good morning, gentlemen."

"Good morning, Dr. Alvin," one of the technicians exclaims, rushing towards him. "I'm glad you're here. We've made some exciting discoveries." The technician points to a green glass dome attached to a partially ice-covered metal structure. "We're carefully excavating around it to ensure we don't damage anything underneath."

Alvin approaches the green dome, joining the team in their efforts to release it from the ice. "Extraordinary work. Carry on. If possible, collect samples for further analysis. Can you see inside?" Alvin asks with excitement, momentarily forgetting any previous irritation.

"It appears to be part of a cockpit. What else have you uncovered here?" Tzabar leans in, curious about the findings.

"Unfortunately, the glass is completely opaque, so we can't see inside," the technician explains. "Apart from this new discovery, we've found twisted metal plates and scattered objects. All of them are made of unknown materials, particularly their metal alloy."

"Dr. Alvin, please come over here," another man shouts a few meters away, frantically waving his arms next to another cluster of plates and a freshly dug pile of snow. Alvin stands up, surprised, and follows the source of the commotion.

"It's sector B3. They must have found something significant. Let's go. This morning has been full of surprises. It's enough to drive me crazy with excitement," Alvin says, breaking into a short sprint and leaping over some icy mounds, with Tzabar and Kurt close behind. They arrive at a spot where four other men are kneeling, diligently moving snow around an indistinct object.

"What's going on? What did you find?" Alvin asks eagerly.

"Everyone, step back a bit so Dr. Alvin can have a clear view," the man says enthusiastically, gesturing for them to create some space. Alvin freezes, amazed, finally seeing the reason for all the excitement.

"This is incredible. Can you believe it?" Alvin looks almost hysterical as he glances at Tzabar, who takes a slight step back, anticipating a possible hug from Alvin.

Tzabar gazes in awe at the object of their admiration. "That can't be human, right?"

"No, look at the connectors emerging from the end of the leg here. And there's a foot just a few inches away, just like the photos we saw yesterday," Kurt says, pointing to the cables still partially covered with ice.

"Now, there is no doubt about the authenticity of the reports from the Inuit and the Russians. Commander Chang will be ecstatic.

What are your thoughts, Colonel? Captain Kurt?" Alvin asks, unable to hide his excitement.

"Dr. Alvin, I have no doubt that Commander Chang will be extremely pleased. As for me, being on my first day here in Anguta, I can only express my deep admiration for the remarkable work you and your team are doing. It has far exceeded my expectations. Congratulations, Dr. Alvin, and please extend my congratulations to your entire team." Tzabar extends his hand to greet Dr. Alvin, who receives it with a proud smile and a twinkle in his eyes.

"Dr. Alvin, would you look at that? Even Captain Kurt is smiling," Tzabar remarks, playfully diverting everyone's attention to Kurt.

"What? Yes, Colonel. Excellent work. It seems we are indeed on the right track. Commander Chang will be delighted. Congratulations, Dr. Alvin," Kurt says, slightly annoyed at being the center of attention and having to offer congratulations to Alvin.

"Dr. Alvin, I believe you would prefer to stay with your team. I need to return to the base. Kurt, please come with me," Tzabar says, shifting his gaze between Alvin and Kurt.

"Gentlemen, it has been a pleasure," Tzabar bids farewell to the technicians, who barely acknowledge him, deeply engrossed in their discoveries.

"Yes, Colonel. Thank you. I would like to stay here a little longer if you don't mind. I'll see you at lunch?" Alvin asks, relieved to be left alone with his team and their findings.

"Agreed, Dr. Alvin. See you at lunch," Tzabar replies.

Tzabar turns his back and starts walking, followed by Kurt.

"Captain Kurt, we need to review our protocols and expedite our next steps. Discoveries are happening at a much faster pace than I anticipated, even in the most optimistic scenario," Tzabar says, as they reach their snowmobiles.

"Yes, Colonel. We can do that as soon as we reach the base. However, if I may, I suggest you message our commander, he will be pleased to hear this information," Kurt suggests, climbing onto his snowmobile.

"Yes, Captain. That's exactly what I intend to do. We need to stay ahead," Tzabar replies, revving his snowmobile engine and swiftly heading towards the base, followed by Kurt.

#

Back at the base, in the cafeteria, Tzabar stands up and takes his tray with the plate and cutlery, and Kurt follows suit, placing their trays on a cafeteria cart positioned next to a wall. As they make their way, they pass by several tables where other people are finishing up their meals, but no sign of Alvin.

Tzabar glances at the clock and then toward the entrance of the cafeteria.

"Well, it seems Dr. Alvin got caught up in the excavations. They might have discovered something new. However, I can't wait any longer. I want to review some notes before lunch. I'll be in my room," Tzabar says.

"Yes, my Colonel. I'll head to our cozy little bar that I mentioned earlier. Drop by whenever you like. The guys would be delighted to see you there."

"Thank you. Yes, I will," Tzabar replies.

148

"See you soon, my Colonel," Kurt bids farewell as he watches Tzabar leave the cafeteria.

As he approaches the entrance to the small bar, improvised in a vacant workroom, two soldiers approach the door and greet him.

"Good afternoon, Captain. Are you coming to our private bar?" they ask.

"Good afternoon. Please go ahead. I'll be back in a few minutes. I need to retrieve my wallet from my room," Kurt explains, retracing his steps down the corridor toward his bedroom door.

Once inside his room, Kurt retrieves a radio from a concealed box tucked away in the closet, beneath a laundry bag. He places the radio on the table, turns it on, and attempts to establish a connection.

"Commander, this is Kurt. Can you hear me?" he leans closer to the mic and repeats the call, only to be met with static. Just as he is about to give up, a metallic click catches his attention.

"Captain, you're running late today. What's the situation?" Chang's metallic voice breaks through the static.

"I apologize, Commander. I had to shake off the Colonel, but I'm here now," Kurt responds.

"I'm pleased and thrilled with the preliminary report I received today. These discoveries align with my expectations. I eagerly await the final report," Chang expresses.

A momentary silence, accompanied by crackling static, leaves Kurt in suspense.

"Captain," Chang's voice returns. "I need you to keep a close eye on Colonel Tzabar's activities and report back to me, particularly regarding his interactions with Dr. Alvin and the civilian team."

"Commander, I can assure you that the Colonel has not exhibited any suspicious behavior or engaged in any conversations with civilians that would raise concerns, at least not thus far. He has been handling matters with flexibility while remaining focused on our mission goals. Currently, I see no basis for the commander's suspicions," Kurt asserts, pausing for a moment, hoping to hear more than just the static emanating from the radio.

"I'm glad to hear that, Captain. Well done. Keep a close watch on the civilians. I suspect they may be up to something. The prolonged silence from Dr. Alvin over the past few hours has struck me as peculiar. The initial days of the mission were quite challenging, but now his silence is unsettling," Chang expresses.

"I understand, sir. I will remain vigilant, rest assured. I will send you my daily report tonight."

"Kurt, I'm counting on you. The stakes here are far too significant, more than you can imagine. I cannot afford to lose control of the situation. We will speak again tomorrow. Chang out."

"Sir, you can trust me. Until tomorrow. Kurt out." Kurt carefully places the radio back in its concealed spot and exits the room.

Meanwhile, Tzabar enters his room and casually tosses his coat onto the bed, inadvertently causing his wallet to fall out of the pocket and onto the floor.

A few photographs spill out, capturing Tzabar's attention, freezing him in place as he stares at the images. Slowly, he bends down to retrieve them.

The first photo depicts a young blonde woman, while another shows a smiling child, a few years old, alongside the same woman. Tzabar gazes intently at the two overlapping pictures, a tear forming in his eye. He quickly wipes it away and sits on the bed, fixated on the images.

Placing his right hand over the photographs, he closes his eyes and envisions himself engaged in a heartfelt conversation with the woman in the picture. The sorrow in his expression reveals the pain that this memory evokes.

Tzabar's anger boils over as he unleashes a furious outburst at a woman who sits on the edge of the bed, crying convulsively. "How could this happen? I refuse to believe it. It can't be true."

"I don't know, Tzabar. I don't have an answer for you. It should never have happened, I know. But it did. I can't comprehend it myself," she replies amidst tears and sobs.

"And with my brother?! Damn it, everything is falling apart. How could you..." Tzabar yells, kicking a nearby chair next to a small table, startling the woman.

"I had no idea he was your brother. I understand it's no excuse, but... How could I have known?" she cries out, avoiding eye contact with him.

"What are you suggesting? Is it all because of my brother? Is that the problem?" Anger and disbelief crack through Tzabar's voice.

"No, no, it's not like that," the woman sobs, pain thick in her voice. "I know it's even more complicated because of John, but it's not his fault. He doesn't even know about us yet. I haven't told him anything." She expresses her despair, feeling a shiver coursing through her body as she anticipates Tzabar's brother's reaction when he finds out.

"And are you absolutely certain that you're pregnant?" Tzabar tries to regain his composure. At that moment, his anger seems to wane as he witnesses her tear-streaked face, overwhelmed by shame and battered by his uncontrolled rage.

"Yes," she screams, agony tearing through her voice. "Yes, I'm pregnant. I already told you. And yes, I don't know if it's yours or John's. What else do you want me to say? It all happened within two days. We were together when you left for the mission, the night of our fight. Two days later, I met John at a bar, and..." She wipes away tears and mucus from her face.

"Yes, I've heard it," he mutters. "It's my fault, and the alcohol didn't help." Tzabar can't bring himself to look at her as he approaches the window, hiding the tears streaming down his face.

Tzabar places the photos on top of the bed, and wanders around the room, trying to escape the memories that haunt him.

"Why? Why did I let you get close to him?" The tear wins this time, triumphantly rolling down his face, accompanied by a stifled sob.

"Sebas, my son, you never knew, and you'll never know, how much I love you. I tried, but it wasn't enough." His muttering is interrupted by a convulsion that unleashes a river of tears. "It's all my fault. I should have fought for you, Melissa, for both of you. I should have fought..." He succumbs to the pain, and tears flow uncontrollably. For a brief moment, he remains motionless, suffocated by memories and remorse.

Eventually, he sits up, running his hand across his face, wiping away the last traces of tears. He carefully places the photos back into his wallet, slowly regaining his composure.

Rising to his feet, he shakes his head, attempting to push aside the pain, and looks at himself in the mirror before turning to the refuge of his duties.

"Well, it seems I do need that drink after all," he murmurs, donning his jacket, and leaves the bedroom.

Inside a cramped room, several soldiers are seated around a table and makeshift counter.

Laughter fills the room, overshadowing conversations, as a man with a glass in hand makes his way toward the door.

"I must be the captain. Please turn down the music a bit," he says, opening the door and being stunned by the unexpected figure that appears. "My colonel. I apologize, sir. We didn't expect you," the lieutenant says, embarrassed, quickly coming to attention upon seeing Tzabar at the door.

"Good afternoon. At ease, lieutenant. Captain Kurt invited me. It seems that here we can enjoy a drink in good company. May I?" Tzabar chuckles at the perplexed look on the man's face.

"Of course. Of course, my colonel. Please come in. Guys, make some space for our colonel," the lieutenant shouts, relieved by Tzabar's friendly demeanor.

"Good afternoon, everyone. Where's Captain Kurt? He told me he was coming here and that I should join him," Tzabar comments, hesitating as he enters the room, wondering about Kurt's absence.

"Colonel Tzabar, welcome, sir. Yes, you're right. The captain mentioned he would come after retrieving his wallet from his room. It's been a while. He should be here by now," one of the men sitting at the counter responds, getting up and offering his seat to Tzabar.

"Thanks, but it's not necessary. I'm fine standing. After all, it's just a drink to warm the spirit, and I only have five minutes."

Despite his surprise at Kurt's absence, Tzabar decides to enjoy a drink and unwind. Everyone in the room raises their glasses to greet his presence.

It has been a long time since a drink in the company of strangers has tasted so good. Tzabar smiles, genuinely pleased.

"No! No, please," he says, laughing and slightly dismayed as he watches the bottle dribble dangerously toward his empty glass. "That's enough for me. Thank you for your hospitality, but duty calls."

He walks away from the counter amidst the men's gleeful protests, who watch him head for the door. "Gentlemen, I must leave. Duty calls. Thanks again. The next round is on me," he says, opening the door and leaving with a smile.

For a moment, he stands still after closing the door. A deep sigh widens his smile. "You needed this, man," he murmurs. "Well, let's get back to reality."

He straightens his posture, puffs out his chest, and walks down the hallway toward the main room. Halfway there, he spots Alvin engaged in a conversation with Victor Balmer. They pause their discussion as Tzabar approaches.

"Is something the matter? You appear quite serious," Tzabar comments, in a cheerful mood.

"Colonel, I'm glad you're here. Dr. Lydia called us. Shall we go?" Alvin asks, gesturing towards the workroom ahead.

"Alright, let's go. Any important news?" Tzabar asks.

"It seems so. Lydia was very excited," Alvin says.

Alvin opens the door to the workroom, and the trio enters, finding Lydia engrossed in something on her laptop.

"Dr. Alvin, Colonel, glad you guys made it," she says.

"Well, here we are. What's new?" Alvin asks as he takes a seat at the table across from her, motioning for Tzabar to join him.

"I must admit, until a few minutes ago, we were still debating whether it was worth calling you all," Lydia begins. "But we have come across some intriguing clues regarding the data collected from the mirrored wall."

"What did you discover?" Alvin asks impatiently.

"Alright, let's dive in," Lydia says, taking a deep breath and focusing her attention on her laptop.

"While we couldn't find any detectable heat source that could explain the phenomenon, we have to acknowledge that the mirrored wall emits a consistent temperature, as the colonel astutely observed back then. It ranges between 17 and 19 degrees Celsius," Lydia explains.

"We believe this is why there's no snow on the mountain and its immediate vicinity. Additionally, we detected a constant, low-intensity vibration throughout the wall. Because we cannot use electronic equipment in the area, it has not yet been possible to identify the cause of these two phenomena," Lydia continues.

"Another intriguing finding is related to the geological composition of the collected samples. They contain elements such as basalt, granite, and quartz. Now, here's where things get interesting. When we analyze different samples, we notice that their compositions vary, whereas they should remain stable," Lydia pauses, observing the stunned expressions of her audience.

Alvin straightens up in his chair, showing signs of wanting to interject. Lydia signals him to wait, while Victor diligently takes notes on his notepad.

"The samples we collected exhibit different proportions of these elements," Lydia adds, pausing once again, amused by the expressions on Tzabar's face.

"We expanded our study to include all the rocks in the area, particularly focusing on the vertical blocks within the mirrored wall enclosure, as shown in this photo," Lydia points to an image displaying the rising blocks along the wall.

"Based on the data we've obtained, I have a theory about Anguta," Lydia continues, taking a deep breath and glancing at the silent and anxious Alvin. "Okay... and what is it?" he asks impatiently.

"The mountain contains an unknown bio-geochemical structure that generates its own energy, exhibiting metamorphic and reproductive characteristics within its mineral composition," Lydia says, sighing and eagerly awaiting Alvin's and Tzabar's reactions.

"Dr. Lydia, forgive me if I misunderstood. Please help me grasp what you just said," Tzabar adds, sitting up straight in his chair.

"Are you suggesting that the mountain possesses a reproductive structure? Similar to cellular reproduction, but in this case, it's of purely mineral origin. Is the mountain alive and growing?" he asks.

"Yes, you've understood correctly. The mountain behaves like a biological entity as if it were alive. And indeed, we have observed anomalies in the geological structure of the samples. In essence, they exhibit slow mineral reproduction," Lydia says, looking at them anxiously and rubbing her hands together in visible nervousness.

Tzabar falls silent, while Alvin gazes into the distance, seemingly lost in deep thought. Victor, on the other hand, appears strangely oblivious to what he's hearing, engrossed in reviewing the notes he has taken.

"Very well. This information is undoubtedly surprising. I'm still trying to comprehend it fully," Tzabar comments, processing the revelation.

"That's understandable, Colonel. That's why I initially hesitated to share it at this stage. Please approach this with some caution until we can delve deeper into our studies. We will continue our work to substantiate all the data and confirm my theory before making any official announcements," Lydia says, eliciting a smile from Alvin.

"Thank you for your attention. Let's get back to our work," Lydia says, standing up. Alvin and Victor quickly follow suit, as if awakening from the trance induced by Lydia's words.

"Thank you. Keep up the outstanding work. I look forward to further developments," Tzabar adds, also rising from his chair and attempting to catch Alvin's attention. "Dr. Alvin, regarding the findings from this morning at the crash site, any progress to report?"

"Not yet. We are meticulously investigating every detail. I hope to be able to share our findings with you soon," Alvin responds, offering assurance.

"All of this is happening so quickly. So many things are unfolding, and we haven't even deciphered the characters and symbols found on the mirrored wall. I need to gather my team and discuss this," Alvin vents his frustration, avoiding direct eye contact with Tzabar.

"Of course. Dr. Lydia, congratulations. Excellent work, well done," Tzabar acknowledges. "Dr. Alvin, I'll take my leave now. We'll talk later," he says, nodding at Alvin before exiting the room.

#

Alvin sits in a corner of the workroom, engrossed in reading some reports. Victor and Lydia, along with other team members, occupy a large table at the center of the room, fully focused on the symbols and characters collected from the mirrored wall.

"Dr. Alvin, please come over here," Lydia calls out.

"What? What's happening?" Alvin asks, intrigued by the urgency in her voice.

"Dr. Alvin, you were right all along," Victor says, pointing to a tablet placed at the center of the table.

Alvin stands up, confused yet intrigued by the team's excitement. He approaches the table, his curiosity piqued.

"As you can see, these symbols on the quartz slab align perfectly with the other symbols we've encountered before," Lydia says, her voice rising with excitement. Alvin remains silent for a moment, a profound gleam appearing in his eyes.

"Abulkur," he murmurs, his legs straightening as he leans on the table, fixated on the tablet.

"Yes, we have found proof of Abulkur. We are on the verge, Dr. Alvin, so close," one of the team members exclaims.

"Bring a chair. Let Dr. Alvin sit before he collapses," Victor suggests with a laugh, pride plain on his face as he looks at Alvin.

"Abulkur. I was right. We have finally discovered the first of the seven gates," Alvin says with a sigh of relief, leaning back in his chair and wearing a triumphant smile.

"My friends, things are becoming serious now. This is the culmination of my life's purpose and all of our work in recent years. We must ensure that the military remains unaware of these findings," Alvin declares, looking thoughtfully at each of his colleagues around the table.

"Store all the data on your external drives. Don't leave anything on the servers or your laptops. I want to study this in peace and quiet, in the privacy of my room. And remember, silence is of utmost importance," he instructs, heading towards his desk to gather his belongings.

Joy and excitement ripple through the room as everyone discusses their expectations for the upcoming days. Completely engrossed in their conversation, they overlook Tzabar quietly entering the room.

"Hello there! Why is everyone so excited? Is something new happening?" Tzabar asks, surprising everyone and leaving them momentarily frozen in shock.

"Colonel, we didn't even realize you had entered," Alvin nervously chuckles, attempting to divert Tzabar's attention from his colleagues' panicked expressions. "No, nothing particularly special. We are just planning our activities for the next few days."

Although Alvin tries to clear Tzabar of any suspicion, the colonel senses that something is wrong. However, he decides not to question them further. "Alright then. It's great to see such enthusiasm among the teams. It creates a positive work environment," Tzabar responds, deflecting attention from his lingering doubts.

"Dr. Alvin, I wanted to discuss an intriguing subject with you," Tzabar quietly pulls Alvin aside, oblivious to the apprehensive looks Alvin's team is giving him.

"Yes, Colonel. What subject is it?" Alvin asks, keeping his voice low to maintain confidentiality.

"In Kunuk's report, and in the reports collected from the Russians, they mention Anguta as the gateway to Abulkur, a supposed inner world. Do these references to Anguta and Abulkur hold any basis? Do you think it's worth looking into?" Tzabar asks, observing Alvin closely.

Alvin's discomfort and surprise at Tzabar's question are well-disguised as he avoids direct eye contact. He knows he cannot deceive Tzabar. "Yes, Colonel, I agree with you. It would be worth investigating the references regarding Abulkur," Alvin stammers, prompting everyone to exchange silent glances.

"According to ancient legends, there are mentions of an underground world inhabited by superior beings, whether gods or demons, depending on the source," Alvin tries to navigate the situation, contemplating how to respond if Tzabar presses further.

Meanwhile, his colleagues pretend to focus on their work, concealing their shock at the colonel's line of inquiry.

"I am familiar with this legend and find it immensely intriguing. I'm surprised we haven't come across more references to Abulkur in our work here in Anguta. It would be fascinating to explore this aspect further. After all, according to the Inuit legends, Anguta is believed to be one of the seven gates to Abulkur. Wouldn't you agree, Dr. Alvin?"

Tzabar continues, his persistence making Alvin's mind race in search of an elegant escape without compromising himself. His team grows increasingly uneasy under the weight of the colonel's insistence.

"It's true, Colonel. While Abulkur is not explicitly mentioned in our mission guidelines, I personally have an interest in exploring that subject to some extent. However, our primary directive is to focus on the artifacts, wreckage, and traces of alien technology. It would be fascinating to delve into the topic of Abulkur, but I wonder if it aligns with the mission's priorities as determined by the commander," Alvin explains, attempting to address the matter without stumbling over his words.

"Moreover, I would be more than happy to exchange thoughts and ideas on this subject with you. I'm certain we can find some time in our schedules over the next few days to discuss it further. But for now, Colonel, I would like to return to my work. We are finalizing the details for the day," Alvin concludes, hoping to divert Tzabar's curiosity.

"Certainly, Dr. Alvin. I won't disturb you any longer. Goodnight, everyone. See you tomorrow, gentlemen," Tzabar replies, bidding them farewell and making his way to his room.

While walking, he reflects on the reactions of Alvin's team when he asks Alvin about Abulkur, convinced that they are deliberately concealing something from him.

As he nears the door to his room, a thought gives him pause. Wearing a disbelieving smile, he shakes his head before finally opening the door.

Once inside he sits and opens his laptop. While scanning through a series of file icons on the screen, his attention was drawn particularly to one labeled Abulkur. "Well, let's see what material I have to review tonight," he murmurs, settling back in his chair and fixating his gaze on the laptop screen.

A fantastic night to die

John and his companions carefully make their way down toward the base of the crater, battling the intensifying snowfall that severely hampers their visibility. As they approach one of the larger crevasses ahead, Robert's concern for the girls' safety weighs on his mind.

"I hope the girls have reached the camp safely and are secure." Robert looks back, worry etched on his face.

"I'm certain they have, Robert. If something were amiss, they would have contacted us by now. We'll check in with them shortly, so don't fret," John reassures him, struggling to maintain their progress through the thick blanket of snow.

"John, if you don't mind, I'd prefer to stop a bit farther from the edge of the crevasse. Ross and I can hold the cable while you examine the crack. You're the lightest among us, and we can manage you without any issue," Robert suggests, casting an apprehensive gaze at the imposing crevasse before them.

"Alright, Robert. Just a few more meters, and we can stop to assess where it might be safer to descend," John says, easing Robert's concerns. They continue walking along the crevasse, which stretches hundreds of meters into the heart of the crater. Suddenly, without warning, John stumbles and falls to the ground.

"What happened, John? Are you alright?" Ross hurries over to him, his pace quickened by concern.

"Take care, everyone. I tripped over something hidden beneath the snow," John reassures them as he rises to his feet. "I'm fine. It was just a stumble. My foot got entangled in something, and it's not a rock." John returns to the spot where he stumbled and begins digging, slowly revealing a thick rope concealed beneath the snow.

"A rope! Look, it extends all the way to the edge of the crevasse," John exclaims as he pulls the rope free from its snowy cover.

"It seems to be secured to a stake over here," Robert says, tracing the rope in the opposite direction. "And it's attached to a snow-covered sled. The snowdrift is actually a sled!" he says, eagerly clearing the snow with his hands. Ross and John join him, their curiosity piqued by the contents of the sled.

"This must belong to the Denudasdi team. They likely used this rope to descend here. We should follow their path and investigate further," John suggests, placing his backpack on the ground.

"Alright. I think we're good here. Let's set some stakes, attach the handle, and follow the rope," Ross proposes, picking up a pair of stakes and two hammers, and passing one to Robert.

"I'll contact the girls to check on their status and give them an update from our end," John says, grabbing the radio.

"Come on, help me while John calls the girls," Ross says to Robert. They start hammering the stakes to secure the cable.

"One stake is in position. The ground feels stable here. And yours is almost done too. Perfect. We're ready," Ross says, glancing at Robert, who stands up, catching his breath.

"Ready and secure. We can attach the cable now," Robert confirms, beginning to tie the first knots.

"Are the two stakes secure? Will the cable hold up?" John approaches them, testing the stability of the cable.

"Don't worry, it can support your weight and three more like you," Ross reassures him with a chuckle. "How are the girls doing?"

"They're fine. They're in better shape than us, safe, warm, and enjoying some tea," John replies, preparing his harness.

"Great. The cable is secure now. Attach the carabiner clip to your harness," Ross hands John the clip. Ross and Robert hold onto the cable as they sit on the ground. John gazes at his companions from the edge of the crevasse.

"Okay, guys. I've sent the torch ahead. There's a platform where I can stop, about 20 meters away from here on the wall. Their rope continues further down, but I can't see the bottom. Can I proceed with the descent?" John asks, excitement coursing through him as he anticipates the downward journey.

"Everything is good on our end, John. You can go," Ross replies, gradually releasing the cable.

John leans backward into the crevasse, firmly planting his feet against the icy wall. He descends, looking down, trying to perceive the depth he has to face.

"John, how's the descent? Are you doing okay?" Ross shouts.

"Everything is fine. Keep releasing the cable. I'm almost on the platform," John responds, his voice echoing from below.

Ross and Robert continue to release the cable until they no longer feel the weight. "He must have reached the platform," Ross comments while attaching a safety knot to the stake and lying face down on the ground near the edge of the crevice, straining to catch a glimpse of John in the dim light.

"John, have you reached the platform?" he shouts.

John stands on the platform, adjusting the cable. "Yes, Ross. I've made it without any issues. I'll drop another torch to assess the depth." John shouts back while watching expectantly as an orange torch descends and illuminates the fissure.

"Okay. I can see the bottom now. It appears stable but deeper than I anticipated. The cable isn't long enough. I need more," John reports.

"I'll send you another one. Listen, do you want me to join you? It might be safer if I'm there to assist you," Ross shouts.

"If Robert is comfortable with the idea, I'd appreciate your help down here. Thank you," John responds.

"Alright, just wait a moment," Ross replies, disappearing from the top of the crevasse, returning after a few minutes, equipped and ready to descend. Within minutes, after checking his safety equipment, he makes his way down to join John at the platform.

They struggle to fit safely into the confined space of the small platform. Without hesitation, John swiftly readies himself to descend the remaining meters to the crevasse's bottom, bolstered by the reassuring presence of Ross.

"You can start your descent. The ground here is solid gravel, no ice," John calls up, having completed his own descent and reached the bottom of the crevasse.

"Robert, I'm heading down," Ross calls out to Robert, who watches him from above. "John is already at the bottom. Everything is okay."

He begins his descent toward John, gradually disappearing from Robert's view.

"So, guys, how are things going?" Robert shouts after a while. The passing minutes without any updates start to worry him.

"Guys, please say something. Are you both alright over there?" he anxiously speaks into the radio, concerned about the lack of a response.

In the depths of the crevasse, Ross looks at the silent radio in his hands. "Damn it. The radio isn't working. We can't communicate with Robert. He'll be worried."

"He knows we're fine. Come on, let's go this way," John says, straining to observe the corridor ahead, faintly illuminated by the remnants of light penetrating through the icy walls of the rift.

"This appears to be a long corridor carved into the ice. I can't see the end in either direction," John observes, peering into the seemingly endless passage.

"I understand your desire to explore more, but today we should just make a quick observation. Tomorrow we'll be back with more time. Nightfall is approaching, and we don't want to be caught in the dark without light," Ross says. "Robert is waiting alone at the top, with no news from us, and it will take us at least an hour to get back to camp."

"I know. But give me just half an hour. Let me push forward for twenty minutes to see what lies ahead. I'll turn back running if necessary, but I need this time," John pleads, his excitement driving his desire to explore.

Ross weighs the risks in his mind, aware of the potential for worsening weather conditions and the challenges they would face on the return journey. Reluctantly, he concedes, realizing it's futile to argue with John.

"Alright, let's proceed, but only ten minutes ahead. Just ten minutes, and then we're heading back," Ross agrees, resignation in his tone. He understands that compromising with John is the best course of action for now.

#

Alberto finishes his hot tea, mentally preparing himself for the worst-case scenario. He knows that the base's location must have been visible from the plane, making it a potential target. He places a bag on the table and begins packing essential equipment, including automatic weapons, ammo boxes, and supplies.

"In any case, I wouldn't be able to sleep tonight. It's safer to head to the hideout. Staying here would leave me vulnerable," Alberto murmurs to himself, grabbing two fully loaded backpacks and making his way to the exit.

Before leaving, he turns up the music to mask any sounds and checks the hidden connections behind a cupboard, activating a red light. "All set. Let's go."

Stepping outside, Alberto closes the door and loads the bag and backpacks onto the snowmobile, setting off toward the refuge. Casting a brief glance at the trail he leaves in his wake, he murmurs, "This snowfall won't be sufficient to completely conceal them."

On the horizon, dark clouds begin to obscure the sun, signaling the approach of nightfall.

A group of men on snowmobiles stands in the snow. A man gasping for breath approaches the group, clutching a pair of binoculars in his hands.

"I've spotted the base less than five hundred meters away," he says. "The lights are on, and I heard music from inside. I didn't see anyone through the windows. They might be inside, possibly unaware of our presence."

"Good. Let's hide the snowmobiles behind those rocks up ahead and proceed on foot." Markus commands, his eyes scanning the surroundings. "We'll split into two groups and attack from both sides. But we must exercise caution. They might be waiting for us, having heard the plane passing by their base."

Meanwhile, the weather slightly improves, much to Alberto's disappointment. "Damn it. I preferred bad weather. A clear night doesn't work in my favor."

Despite the circumstances, he finds himself momentarily captivated by the sight of a cloudless sky adorned with a luminous firmament. Taking cover inside a white camouflage sleeve, he prepares himself, with an automatic rifle, ammunition, grenades, and a detonator within reach.

"Well, this is a fantastic night to die for," he comments with a resigned smile.

#

John and Ross make swift progress along the crevasse walls, their focus unwavering.

"John, our ten minutes are up. It's time to turn back now. There's nothing new ahead, and we'll have more time and better light tomorrow," Ross urges, noticing the fading illumination inside the crevasse.

"Okay, Ross. If you want, stay here. I'll be back in a minute. The path seems to curve to the right, not even a hundred meters. Let me see what lies ahead," John replies, turning to face Ross, who has halted his steps. "Okay, don't worry. I'll be back in a minute." John says, ignoring Ross' words and leaving him to watch in disbelief as John walks away.

Frustration breaks through as Ross shouts, "Damn it, John! We need to go back. Robert is alone up there, unaware of what's happening down here."

He shouts again as he watches John disappear around the bend, concern roughening his voice. "Damn it! Damn it, John!" For a moment, Ross hesitates between chasing after John or returning to ensure Robert's safety.

"Ross! Ross, come here quickly!" John's voice echoes from the end of the path, grabbing Ross's attention and spurring him into action.

"Come on, John, enough of this nonsense. We need to go," Ross shouts, convinced that John is attempting to persuade him with some foolish idea.

"You have to come. I found a hood from Anguta's third," John calls out, excitement sharpening his voice.

Curiosity overwhelms Ross, causing him to sprint toward John. "Damn it. Where is it?" Ross asks, surprised, as he reaches John. In front of them lies an orange hood on the ground.

"This has to be from the third one. The other two had their hoods on," John explains. "We need to proceed with caution. Maybe we can find more clues about this person."

"No, John. No! We'll come back tomorrow. It's pointless now. We don't even have any light left. We need to go back," Ross insists, tugging at John's arm.

"Alright, Ross. Let's go back. You've got a point," John concedes, yielding to Ross's persistence while maintaining his focus on the path ahead.

"Tomorrow, we'll return with more equipment," John says, expressing his disappointment as he looks back at Ross, who has already started heading back.

When Ross emerges from the crevasse, Robert greets him with relief. "Damn, man. I was worried about you guys. I didn't know what to do. I was about to go down and search for you too. Where's John?" Robert asks, peering over the edge of the crevasse.

"Good to see you, buddy. We're all fine. John is following behind me," Ross replies, ascending from the crevasse.

"I had to drag him back. The crazy bastard wanted to continue exploring down there, even without any light," Ross shouts, ensuring John can hear him.

"You two jerks! You could have helped me up," John yells, struggling up the cable. Laughter erupts as they assist him in climbing the last few meters to the surface.

"So, it's true? Ross told me you found a hood from Anguta's third," Robert remarks as they trudge through the deep snow.

"Yes, we did. Maybe tomorrow we can find more clues about the unfortunate soul," John confirms, following them up the slope of the crater.

"Enough chatter, let's pick up the pace. I don't want to spend the night out here. We're running out of light, and the cold is intensifying," grumbles Ross, struggling with difficulty breathing.

"Alright, alright. Such a sour mood today. You're getting old, my friend. Fine, I'll be quiet," John retorts, his breath heavy with exertion.

#

The night descends, and Alberto scans the surrounding terrain with his binoculars. He had just heard the distant rumble of engines beyond the cliffs to his left, but now, an eerie silence hangs in the air, intensifying his anxiety and uncertainty.

167

Resigned to his fate, he pulls back his camouflaged sleeve, seeking solace from the biting cold. His eyes sweep over the weapons and supplies within reach, ensuring everything is in order.

Suddenly, the sound of footsteps startles him, echoing from a few feet away. Alberto freezes, unable to discern if someone is approaching his position. Soon, six armed men emerge from the shadows, their murmurs barely audible.

With bated breath, he adjusts the scope of his weapon, closely observing them and the firearms they carry. The men advance cautiously toward the main entrance of the base, intermittently communicating with an unseen party. Though their conversations are mostly in a foreign language, Alberto manages to catch fragments of English phrases.

"Alright. Proceed as planned and leave me in peace. I only need you to enter through the main entrance," he mutters, tightening his grip on the detonator, which lies within arm's reach.

The men loom near the base's main building, pausing at the foot of the entrance stairs. Their faces light up with anticipation as the music and lights from within the structure herald the surprise they have in store for their unsuspecting victims.

Alberto's attention shifts as he notices someone else approaching from the opposite side of the building. With a heart pounding impatiently and a trembling hand poised above the detonator, he watches the sneaky movements of these newcomers.

Suddenly, the tranquility is shattered by the sound of shattering glass, grenade explosions, and blinding flashes. A resounding crash of a door precedes the frenzied entry of men, their voices echoing with screams and gunfire.

"Yes! Come on in, all of you..." Alberto mutters, his adrenaline surging as he presses the button on the detonator.

A sequence of explosions reverberates through the area, shaking the surroundings to their core.

Shielding his head from the chaos, he waits as the explosions subside, giving way to the cacophony of falling debris. Now, the crackling of flames engulfs the remains of the base, casting a dim glow that illuminates the scene. The pungent scent of burning fills his nostrils.

Amidst the aftermath, faint cries and screams pierce the air, signaling the presence of possible survivors. Though he cannot discern their exact location or identities, the anguished voices persist, confirming the existence of more than one.

"Damn it. I may have gone too far with the C4," he mutters, rising to his feet and surveying the destruction he has wrought. All that remains of the main building are skeletal pillars and twisted metal, a testament to the force unleashed.

Everything else has vanished or been vaporized, leaving a scene of destruction in its wake.

With newfound confidence, Alberto steps forward, retrieving his weapons and a handful of grenades. Carefully, he navigates the charred remnants, some still smoldering, shielding his nose from the acrid stench of burning rubber and plastic.

Approaching the lifeless bodies scattered on the ground, Alberto meticulously examines each one, assessing their state. "Another one down. That makes four," he mutters, searching for his next target. As he ventures further, the sight of mutilated remains turns his stomach, nausea rising in his throat.

Suddenly, a pained scream pierces the air from beyond the raging inferno. Alberto's attention snaps to a man writhing in agony, his shattered legs sprawled on the blood-soaked snow. Proceeding with caution, Alberto approaches, his gaze fixed on the agonized figure before him. Kneeling down, he can hardly contain his revulsion at the sight of the mangled body, fractured bones, and the sickening smell of burnt flesh.

"Help me. Please, I don't want to die," the man pleads, despair and anguish in his eyes as they lock onto Alberto's.

Alberto remains silent, horror-stricken, unable to find the words to console the suffering man. Rising to his feet, he stands frozen, attempting to wipe away the tears of anguish welling up within him.

A sharp gunshot momentarily drowns out the man's torment, followed by a searing pain that knocks Alberto to the ground. Struggling to sit upright, he senses the warmth of his own blood saturating his clothes.

As a dark fog descends upon his consciousness, a burning sensation courses through his body, akin to an electric shock.

In the distance, an injured man crawls towards him, pure hatred in his eyes. "You thought you could escape? I will revel in your demise and desecrate your lifeless body," the man rasps, his voice dripping with venom.

Desperately, Alberto shuffles backward, attempting to evade his relentless pursuer, who raises his gun once again. A gunshot rings out, tearing through Alberto's left arm. Pain ignites, awakening his primal survival instincts.

Alberto points his shotgun at the man inching closer, his hand unsteady with fear. Despite the dire circumstances, Alberto can't help but be astounded by the tenacity of his adversary.

A single shot shatters the man's head, a spray of blood, flesh, and shattered bones painting the snow.

Gasping for breath, Alberto collapses, his body pressed against the frigid ground. The other man lying beside him falls eerily silent, their cries silenced by the cruel hand of fate.

The biting cold serves as a grim reminder for Alberto, preventing him from slipping into unconsciousness as he musters every ounce of strength to crawl back to his hiding place. The excruciating agony gnaws at him, but he no longer cares about the possibility of other survivors. To hell with them.

Finally, he reaches the tent, his body wracked with pain. Collapsing inside, he lets out a mixture of laughter and groans. "Well, this is how it ends, huh?" he mutters, resignation and dry amusement both in his voice. Taking a deep breath, he tries to endure the torment. His eyes flutter closed, and his face finally settles.

#

"Did you hear that? The noise?" Alarm catches in Rachel's voice as she gazes toward the tent's entrance.

"No, I didn't hear anything... wait. Yes, now I do. There's someone out there," Marta whispers, her voice barely audible.

"Turn off the light and grab your gun," Rachel commands, her hands shaking as she clutches the pistol. Marta complies, switching off the lamp and the coffee pot before gripping her firearm.

The noise outside grows louder, drawing Rachel and Marta to tighten the grips on their pistols, their fingers tense on the triggers. "Who's there? I'll shoot if you don't answer!" Fear and determination tangle in Rachel's voice, her gun aimed at the opening, ready to unleash its deadly force.

The murmur of voices reaches their ears. Rachel and Marta huddle together, fear coursing through their veins, their guns trained at the tent's entrance.

"What if it's them? What if they're coming back? They should be here by now," Marta whispers, her words sending shivers down Rachel's spine.

"Are we supposed to ask if it's them? But what if it's not?" Rachel can't keep the edge out of her voice. "John always said, shoot first and question later," she adds, trying to steady her shaking hand.

"I've never fired a gun before. I'm scared, Rachel."

"Me neither. I want to scream."

The voices outside fade into a muffled cacophony, but the sound of footsteps crunching in the snow grows ever closer. The presence of an unknown entity looms just beyond the confines of the tent, and the zipper begins to inch open.

171

"John?! Is that you?" Fear and relief crack through Rachel's voice. Beside her, Marta exhales deeply, dropping her gun as if it were scorching her hand.

"Rachel, Marta, calm down! It's us! Don't shoot!" John's voice booms, as he flings himself to the ground, bracing for a potential barrage of bullets.

From inside the tent come Marta's laughter and Rachel's exclamations, "Fuck. Fuck."

John stands up, smiling at his companions, and moves the tarpaulin away from the tent entrance.

"Good evening, ladies," John greets them with a nod, a smile playing on his lips as he stands at the tent's entrance. "What's the matter? Who did you think it was?"

"Fuck you, John! We could have shot you. I was about to fire, with no idea who was out there!" Rachel screams, her voice on the verge of tears fueled by anger.

Marta bursts into laughter, rolling around inside the tent, releasing all the pent-up tension. Robert and Ross join John, kneeling at the entrance, their laughter blending with the scene.

"Are you mocking us? Next time, I'll shoot first and ask questions later!" Rachel says, her voice now calmer, a smile tugging at the corners of her lips as she playfully waves the gun in their direction.

"Hey there, watch it. You might accidentally hit someone," John cautions, taking the gun from Rachel's hand, passing it to Robert, and embracing her tenderly.

"I doubt it. That would have been quite a challenge. The safety lock is still engaged," Robert remarks, displaying the gun for everyone to see, triggering another round of laughter.

Robert settles beside Marta, picking up the gun she had dropped. The two exchange glances, a warm feeling coursing through them.

"Well, it seems I'll be sleeping on the plane then," Ross comments, smiling at the two couples.

"Hey... show a little respect, man," Robert chides, a warmth spreading in his chest as Marta squeezes his hand.

"What if we grab something to eat? I'm starving. We can fill them in on our exploration inside the crevice and plan for tomorrow," Ross suggests, attempting to dissipate the awkward atmosphere that had descended upon them.

"Does anyone have any news about Alberto?" Robert asks, holding Marta's hand.

"No, nothing. After his last message, there's been radio silence. He hasn't responded to any communication attempts. I'm worried," John reveals, drawing closer to Rachel for comfort.

"I'll try calling Alberto after we eat," John adds, concern darkening his tone.

"But what's wrong with Alberto? He's okay, right?" Marta inquires, sensing the unease in John's voice and wanting to alleviate their worries.

"Yeah, he should be fine. So, do we have anything to eat or what?" John swiftly shifts the conversation away from the topic of Alberto, focusing on the practical matter at hand.

"Yes, let's eat. It should be hot by now," Rachel says, taking her metal bowl and serving herself first. As they dig into their meal, John recounts their experience inside the rift.

"I can't wrap my head around how they got here and where they came from. It's driving me crazy," Ross expresses his frustration.

"Tomorrow we should go early and I hope we find some clues that shed light on this. Rachel, Marta, you should come with us, it's better if we stick together," John suggests, hoping to convince them.

"I agree with John. The cables held up well today, and the descent is secure in two stages." Ross adds. "We should bring some supplies with us in case we need to stay overnight. It'll save us valuable time between trips."

"I don't like the idea, but I agree it's better to join you guys than to stay here alone, doing nothing. If you..." Rachel starts to speak but is interrupted by a distant thud.

"Was that an explosion?" Marta asks, alarm spiking in her voice.

"Yes, I think so. And it sounded powerful. Could it be at the base?" Rachel asks, her mind racing with concern.

"No way," Robert blurts out, giving John a worried look. "The base is more than 120 km from here."

John nods, looking serious. "Could be, though. If nothing is blocking the sound and the wind's on our side, it might just be from the base."

"And seriously," Robert adds, scanning the icy horizon, "what else is out here? All we've seen is ice and rocks for miles."

"Fuck. Alberto!" John exclaims, abruptly grabbing the radio.

"What? Do you think the explosion was at the base?" Panic threads through Marta's voice.

"Winterfell, this is Wolfpack, please respond!" John urgently calls over the radio. The tense silence inside the tent hangs heavy with worry.

Robert and Ross exchange anguished looks, their eyes fixed on the radio, desperately hoping for a response from Alberto.

Rachel and Marta are bewildered by the distress displayed by their companions.

"Winterfell, this is Wolfpack, respond!" John's voice fills the tent, raw with concern.

"But why do you think it was at the base? What could Alberto have to do with the explosion?" Rachel asks, her unease growing as she witnesses John's mounting anxiety.

174

"I don't know. He's not responding. Nothing," John replies, eyes shadowed with concern.

"Do you think we should go check on him? We can reach the base by plane in less than an hour," Ross suggests, eager to take action.

"It's a gamble," John reflects, his brow furrowed with concern. "Trying to land without adequate light isn't the safest bet. Plus, relying on a snowmobile? Not practical. It'd eat up too much time, and we can only send two people at most."

"I'm going," Ross says, jumping up. "I've done that trip before, and I'm pumped to do it again. Can't shake the feeling that Alberto might need a hand." He grabs his radio, ready to head out.

"I'll go with you," Robert says, standing up.

"No, thanks. I'll be faster if I go alone," Ross insists.

"Ross is right. It's best if he goes alone," John agrees.

"But what's going on with Alberto? It feels like something is happening, and we're being kept in the dark again," Marta growls in frustration.

"Do you think the explosion we heard might be connected to a possible attack on the base?" Rachel asks, anxiety plain on her face.

"It's a possibility, but there's nothing we can do now. Let's hope Ross reaches there quickly and can confirm that everything is fine with Alberto," John responds, trying to calm the group.

"Relax. We're probably overreacting. Maybe the noise we heard is just because Alberto forgot something on the stove," Ross says, trying to lighten the mood, but only earns solemn looks.

"Okay, I see. I have a tough audience today. I better leave now," Ross says, gathering his belongings and heading out of the tent.

"Ross, please be careful and communicate with us along the way. Now we're all worried about you too," Rachel says, looking at Ross with concern.

"Don't be. I'll check in every half hour," Ross assures them before leaving the tent, followed by his companions.

"Have a safe journey, mate. May everything go well. And thank you," John says as Ross prepares to depart on the snowmobile.

#

Alberto stirs awake, sensing a chill against his forehead and catching snippets of unfamiliar voices around him. As he battles to clear his foggy mind, a surge of panic prompts him to snap his eyes open and attempt a sudden sit-up. But sharp pain shoots through his body, anchoring him back down, and he realizes someone's eyes are fixed intently on him.

"Take it easy, Alberto. You're safe with us. There's no need to worry," reassures the man, his voice steady and soothing.

As Alberto's vision clears, he recognizes the confines of a spacious tent surrounding him. Positioned beside him is a man clad in a camouflage uniform, his presence both protective and reassuring.

Trying to voice his confusion, Alberto manages only a weak murmur. "Where am I? And who exactly are you?"

"Alberto, how are you feeling?" the man in uniform asks, turning towards him with a smile.

"I'm... I'm okay, I guess. My all body hurts. What happened?" Alberto asks, feeling weak and trying to glimpse the source of the noise outside the tent.

The man leans in, his expression serious yet comforting. "Stay calm and try not to move," he advises earnestly. "You took hits to your chest and left arm, but thankfully, the bullets passed through. We've stitched you up, and while you lost some blood, your vital organs are intact. You'll be on the mends soon."

Alberto's anxiety subsides somewhat upon hearing the man's reassuring words. "Alright, but who exactly are you? And what's going on outside?"

176

"I'm Major Roland, the medic for this unit," Roland clarifies, his tone steady. "We're the reinforcements command dispatched to aid your team. We might've arrived after the attack, but we got to you in time to patch you up."

Just then, a commanding voice fills the tent, causing Roland to rise and greet the newcomer. "Has our guy come to? How's he doing?" the man queries with concern.

"Yes, Colonel Mackenzie. Alberto woke up and seems to be in good spirits," Roland responds, making way for the colonel by Alberto's bedside.

"Alberto, hats off to you," Colonel Mackenzie begins, unable to hide his admiration. "What you pulled off here is nothing short of remarkable. Twelve of them against you, and yet you held your ground. The facility might be compromised, but you've safeguarded the base. We've cataloged everything you managed to salvage in your hideout," he adds, a smile breaking through despite the gravity in his voice.

"Twelve of them? Seriously?" Alberto mutters in disbelief.

"Yes, they were twelve. And you also managed to take down that bastard, Markus. He looked quite spectacular with his head blown off. Well done, man," the colonel says, laughing and exchanging a glance with Roland.

"Alberto, I wish you a speedy and safe recovery," Mackenzie says respectfully as he leaves the tent.

Alberto, still surprised and smiling, turns to Roland and comments, "Wow... I can hardly believe it."

"Man, everyone is talking about what you did here. When we landed, it looked like a battlefield—nothing but remains and wreckage. We thought a dozen men must have fought off the attackers. And then, we find one lone individual sleeping in his tent. It's complete madness. And to top it off, we discovered Markus with his head blown open. You have no idea how long and how many operatives we lost trying to take that son of a bitch down," Roland says, looking at Alberto with deep admiration.

"Is there something I can drink? I'm very thirsty," Alberto requests, prompting Roland to get up immediately.

"Sure, I'll bring you a light tea, but you need to drink it slowly," Roland assures Alberto, making his way to a table with a steaming kettle.

"Wait. I need to talk to the rest of the team; they must be worried," Alberto says anxiously, attempting to sit up.

"Calm down, man," Roland says, cup in hand. "We have already spoken with your companions, and we will send reinforcements to assist them."

He hands the cup to Alberto, who takes a sip and then lies back down, calm settling over him. It all feels surreal. If this is a dream, he hopes it continues a little longer. The pain he feels tells him it's real, though.

#

"Winterfell, this is Wolfpack. Do you copy?" John almost shouts, apprehension tightening his face as he awaits a response from Alberto over the radio.

"Winterfell, this is Wolfpack. Do you copy?" He calls out again, exchanging worried glances with Robert, who is hanging on every word, hoping for a reply from Alberto. Rachel and Marta anxiously observe from the tent's entrance.

"John, give it a rest. You've been calling for nearly thirteen minutes without a response. Ross is on his way to the base. Let's wait for him to update us," Rachel advises, trying to console John.

"I agree with Rachel. Continuing to call won't do any good," Robert adds, placing his arm around John's shoulders in an attempt to provide comfort.

"Alright, you're right. We'll have to wait for Ross to give us some information," John concedes, his patience prevailing as he returns to the tent.

Suddenly, a metallic voice resonates through the radio. "Captain John, this is Base Denudasdi. Do you copy?"

John startles, almost dropping the radio upon hearing the unexpected call.

"Did Alberto respond?" Rachel rushes out of the tent, anticipation written across her face.

"I don't think so. It didn't sound like Alberto to me," Robert comments, expressing his doubts.

"Captain John, this is Colonel Mackenzie of the Third Intervention Unit. We are at the Denudasdi base. Alberto is safe. Mackenzie out."

"You heard that? The support unit has arrived at the base. Alberto is safe," John announces, relief loosening something in his chest. "Colonel, it's good to hear from you, sir. Thank you. We're relieved to hear that Alberto is okay. We were really worried about him and Ross is on his way to the base to assess the situation. John out."

"Everything is fine here. Don't worry. Alberto did an amazing job. He took out twelve enemies, including Markus, and managed to secure most of the supplies."

John and his companion exchange shocked looks as they listen to the radio.

"Twelve? Markus? And he did it alone? Are we talking about the same Alberto who was with us at the base?" Robert can barely contain his excitement.

"Captain, Shaman is still in the area, and I want you to stay focused on the mission. Leave the security to us. I'm sending a small support team with additional equipment. They will depart at 08:00 am. Mackenzie out."

"Thank you, Colonel. That's great news. John out."

"We need to inform Ross. He can come back now," Marta says, embracing Robert tightly.

"Ross, Ross. This is John. Listen," John calls out into the radio, relief flooding his voice. "Looks like things are looking up now," he says, hope rekindling, and receives an enthusiastic hug from Rachel.

"John, what's happening? I'm almost at the base. I can see some flickering lights and smoke. Listen."

"Ross, you can come back. Everything is fine. The support team is already with Alberto, he is ok. We'll fill you in later. John out."

"Okay. I'm turning back. Ross out."

John sits on the ground, leaning back with his hands on the snow.

"What a relief. I feel so much better now, knowing that Alberto is safe and that more men are coming for our security," he says, letting out a deep sigh.

"Do you know how many are coming?" Rachel asks.

"I'm not sure, Rachel. The colonel didn't mention the exact number. But we can proceed with our plan. Ross can stay here and wait for them, allowing him to rest after the long journey. We need to take advantage of the daylight and explore the rest of the passage. I want to understand how and where Anguta's guys came from."

"John, I'd rather wait for the reinforcements to arrive, and then we can all go together," Marta says, her enthusiasm fading as she becomes unsure about descending into the crevasse.

"Marta, we need to make use of the daylight. If it's too much for you, you can stay here with Ross. Then you can either join us or stay with the reinforcements. We'll make sure you're safe and comfortable."

"I think we can proceed without any issues. What do you both think?" John asks, hoping to gain Robert and Rachel's agreement. Robert remains silent, shaking his head with hesitation, while Rachel stays quiet, avoiding eye contact.

"If we wait here, we'll lose the entire morning, which means losing a whole day," argues John, anticipating Rachel's negative response

"We should wait for Ross to arrive and hear his opinion. Right now, I'd prefer to get some more sleep," Rachel says as she enters the tent and curls up in her sleeping bag.

John decides not to push further, hoping that a night of restful sleep will change Rachel's mind. At least she didn't outright refuse to go.

The sun rises, casting its light on the surrounding landscape. "Good morning, John. You wake up early. Did you manage to get some sleep?" Rachel asks as she exits the tent, squinting her eyes against the daylight.

"Good morning, Rachel. I could barely sleep, with the attack on the base and the expectation of what we might find down there... no, I can't sleep. And you, did you sleep well?" John offers her a steaming mug. "Coffee? I just made it."

"Yeah, thanks." Rachel holds the mug with both hands, relishing the warmth it provides.

"Where's Ross? I didn't see him in the tent."

"He stayed in the smaller tent to let you sleep," John explains. "I couldn't sleep until he arrived, so I took the chance to fill him in on what happened at the base and with Alberto.

He could hardly believe it," John comments while adding more water to the coffee maker.

"But did he see anything from the base?"

"No, Ross saw many lights and sensed there was a lot of activity, but he immediately returned."

"I must have been a heavy sleeper. I didn't hear a thing. And it seems like nobody else did either." Rachel turns her head towards the tent, where Robert and Marta remain silent.

"I'm sorry, but I'll have to wake them up. We need to make the most of the day."

"But are you really determined to go now? Wouldn't it be better to wait for them to arrive?" Rachel questions.

"Yes, Rachel. I discussed the plan with Ross, and he agreed with me. The only difference is that he'll be staying here to wait for them. But he understood we should move forward with him fully rested."

"Good morning, early risers. Smells like fresh coffee," Robert says as he emerges from the tent. Marta follows behind him, looking bewildered.

"Can't we sleep a little longer? It's so cold out there," Marta mumbles in a sleepy voice.

"Marta, if you prefer, you can stay with Ross. We've already discussed it with him. You can wait for the reinforcements and join us later," John suggests, speaking softly and gesturing towards the smaller tent, indicating the need for quiet.

"Is Ross alright? Did he choose to stay in the smaller tent?" Robert joins the conversation, grabbing a mug of coffee.

"Yes, everything is fine. Ross is aware of the situation, and he agrees with the plan. We should leave in half an hour at most," John confirms.

"Alright, John. Let's go then. Marta will stay here with Ross, and we'll proceed. They can catch up with us later. I'm on board," Rachel relents, surprising John.

"Let's go," he says, relieved that the morning is starting as he had hoped. "Robert, Rachel, gather your things.

The Wall

Tzabar and Alvin stand by the cafeteria door engaged in conversation when a person approaches and hands Alvin a paper.

"Dr. Lydia requests our immediate presence at the mirrored wall. It seems we have some significant developments," Alvin informs Tzabar after reading the message.

"Let's go then. Kurt, please join us," Tzabar says, noticing the captain approaching them.

Alvin leads the way, heading toward the spotlight that appears at the end of the tunnel. Behind him, Tzabar and Kurt advance, curious about Dr. Lydia's sudden call.

They make their way to the mirrored wall, where a network of intense spotlights illuminates the entire area.

"Dr. Alvin, gentlemen. Thank you for coming so quickly," Lydia greets them, guiding them across the square toward the mirrored wall. "I apologize for the vague message, but I didn't know how to describe what we found, it's best to see for yourself." She stops a few steps from the wall, next to a group of technicians who are so absorbed in taking notes that they barely react to their arrival.

"We've been conducting various tests on the rocks surrounding this wall. I doubt any of us will be able to sleep for the next few days," Lydia says, a glimmer of excitement in her eyes. "The initial results are incredible," she adds, barely containing herself.

"Gentlemen, could you please give us some space?" she requests, addressing the technicians who are clustered near the wall. "Now, take a look at this photo we took on the first day we discovered the wall."

She shows them a picture displaying characters carved into the quartz and then points to the corresponding spot on the wall. "See if you can identify them," she asks.

"Yes, I remember this. They were right over... there..." Tzabar begins, pointing to where he expects to see the characters based on the photograph. However, he stops mid-sentence, his confusion growing as he looks back and forth between the photo and the wall.

"I don't understand. The characters were there, but now..." Tzabar trails off, bewildered.

"They're different," Alvin says, confused, as he takes hold of Lydia's photo. He steps back, alternating his gaze between the wall and the picture.

"It's the same location, but the symbols have changed. It's unbelievable, isn't it?" Excitement quickens Lydia's voice as she looks at the three stunned men before her.

"It can't be. There must be some mistake," Kurt says, leaning in to examine the photo.

"No mistake has been made, and we've had multiple people verify it," Lydia says, pointing behind them to a group of technicians a few feet away.

"Not only have the symbols changed, but we also have entirely new ones that didn't exist before!" she exclaims, leaving Tzabar and Alvin speechless.

"And that's not all, gentlemen," Lydia continues, running her hand along the surface of the wall. "Our mirrored wall is concealing more surprises."

"What else? What other surprises?" Alvin's eyes glimmer with anticipation.

"This wall, it turns out, isn't made of quartz as we initially thought. We haven't been able to accurately identify its composition. We couldn't obtain a sample or use the necessary instruments to determine the Vickers hardness," Lydia explains, her gaze fixed in wonder upon the mirrored wall.

"We've attempted every possible means of analysis. Nothing has been able to penetrate its surface," Lydia adds.

"During our tests, we were only able to conduct the Mohs tests, and the results indicate a hardness exceeding ten, which is the maximum on the scale," Lydia says, still staring at the wall as though it might answer back.

"We exhausted all available instruments in our attempts to penetrate this surface," Lydia continues, frustration creeping into her voice.

"But how is it possible that you couldn't retrieve even a tiny fragment? Couldn't you manage to obtain the tiniest splinter?" Kurt asks, unaware of Lydia's previous statement.

"Enough of this nonsense, gentlemen. Please step back," Kurt declares, pulling out his gun and aiming it at the wall.

"What are you doing? Are you out of your mind?!" Alvin shouts, his voice cracking with fear as he pulls Lydia back, his face going pale with alarm.

Before anyone can react, a gunshot reverberates through the rocky surroundings, startling everyone. Lydia lets out a scream in terror.

"Captain, holster your weapon immediately! Have you lost your senses?" Tzabar yells in exasperation. However, Kurt seems oblivious to his words, rushing over to where he shot at the wall.

"But this is insane! It hasn't left the slightest mark," Kurt breathes, running his hand over the bullet impact site, which remains pristine. "What in the world is happening here?"

Ignoring the protests of everyone around him, Kurt crouches down and retrieves the bullet from the ground. "It's intact. There are no signs of impact or ricochet effects. This is impossible. I don't understand," Kurt says, turning the bullet over in his palm as if it might explain itself.

"Captain Kurt, please holster your weapon. That's enough," Tzabar shouts, his tone hardening with urgency, snapping Kurt out of his trance-like state.

"Yes, Colonel. I apologize," Kurt says, securing his gun back into his holster. "Sir, the bullet should have left a mark, no matter how small, and there should have been some form of rebound. I can't comprehend it." Kurt's confusion deepens, now mirroring the perplexity of the others.

"But what didn't you understand when I mentioned that it surpassed the maximum on the Mohs scale? Even the purest diamond wouldn't have withstood it," Lydia exclaims, exasperated by Kurt's demeanor.

"It is extraordinary that the bullet remains intact and didn't bounce off. I have to agree with the Captain," Alvin chimes in, taking the bullet from Kurt's hand.

"This is highly unusual. The surface seems rigid, yet it somehow absorbs the impact," Tzabar remarks, his composure returning as he looks at Lydia, intrigued.

"I can't provide an answer to that," Lydia shrugs. "We still don't understand the nature of this wall, which is distinct from the surrounding mountain walls. We did not find visible veins or sections, everything seems to be part of the same structure."

Tzabar and Alvin both place their hands on the mirrored surface as if seeking answers to their questions. Kurt follows suit, his expression equal parts reverence and fear.

"I can still sense the warmth and vibration. You may mock me, but it's as if we're touching a slumbering creature," Tzabar says, keeping his hand against the wall.

"I understand exactly what you mean, Colonel. I couldn't have described it better myself. That's precisely the sensation," Alvin states, standing with his hands resting on the wall.

"Now, let's return to the symbols and the phenomenon of their changing. What possible explanation can we find?" Tzabar takes a few steps back to gain a better perspective of the wall.

"I don't know. It's a rocky wall, or whatever material it may be, with engraved symbols that undergo changes. How do they transform?"

Tzabar asks, pausing while contemplating the magnitude of the enigma. "I don't have the answers." Lydia's frustration lingers as she responds, "That's precisely why I mentioned the difficulty of getting a good night's sleep. We are faced with mysteries that defy explanation."

She expresses her dismay. "How can I walk away when there might be something extraordinary waiting to be uncovered?" she asks, feeling helpless.

"I understand your frustration, Dr. Lydia," Alvin says, offering a knowing smile. "However, it's crucial that you prioritize your well-being. You need rest to have a clear mind and effectively process all that we've witnessed today."

"You're right. I know I should go and rest, but it's difficult to accept the idea of potentially missing something while asleep," she admits, surrendering to the fact that she needs to recharge.

"Thank you. I appreciate your concern," she says, finally conceding to the evidence that rest is necessary. "I may need a little coaxing, so please, make sure I actually leave this place."

"Very well," Alvin agrees, taking the lead as he guides everyone towards the exit. "Let's head back for now. We can assign a team to continue collecting and analyzing the data in the meantime.

Dark Fog

At the bottom of the crevasse, John assists Rachel as she descends the remaining few feet of the rope.

"Rachel is down safely! You can come now," John shouts, prompting Robert to join them.

The group sets off and soon reaches the spot where John had discovered the hood of Anguta's missing part.

"Did you see anything else around here? Any clues that might indicate where he went?" Rachel asks, scanning the area.

"No, we didn't notice anything else," Robert replies.

"Is it possible he continued further down the passage, past the point where we descended?" Rachel wonders aloud.

"I'm not sure, Rachel," John responds. "Let's keep moving forward. Robert, you lead the way with the flashlight. Let's proceed with caution."

Meanwhile, back at the camp, Ross and Marta climb the rocks near the plane, gazing at the breathtaking horizon.

"This is truly spectacular. How can people prefer living in crowded cities?" Ross marvels, captivated by the pristine beauty of the landscape before them.

"It's undeniably amazing. But, personally, I wouldn't trade it for the comfort of my home or the convenience of having everything within walking distance," Marta sighs deeply.

"Look, over there in the middle of the snow," she points towards a group of people on snowmobiles making their way across the vast white plain towards them. "Could that be our reinforcements?"

"I certainly hope so," Ross signals for them to return to the camp.

"What do you mean, 'I hope so'? Who else could be coming here?" Marta asks, standing still and casting a worried gaze at him.

"I was just teasing. Of course, they are our reinforcements," Ross responds, assisting Marta as she descends from the rocks, his expression still somewhat suspicious.

"I'm serious. Do you think we could still be in danger from that Shaman?" Marta stops and looks at him earnestly.

"Marta, they are out in the open without any concern for hiding. Come on, I'll help you," he says, guiding her down from the final rock.

"Please don't lie to me. You know how terrified I am of all this."

#

"Guys, the tunnel is getting narrower up ahead, with some ice blocks obstructing the way. We need to find a path around them," John calls back from a few meters ahead. "Please proceed with extra caution."

Walking carefully among the ice floes, Rachel can't help but remain wary of the menacing ice ceiling. "These fallen ice blocks above us... they could have come crashing down, right?" she points upwards with concern.

"Yes, that's correct. Fortunately, we have enough space to maneuver through," Robert comments.

"Do you think we're safe here? Could more ice blocks fall?" Rachel keeps her gaze fixed upwards, uneasy.

"While it's possible, let's hope it doesn't happen while we're passing through," John says with a laugh, which only serves to anger Rachel.

"Thank you so much. I feel much more at ease now. What the hell," she says, worry sharp beneath the sarcasm.

"I see some marks from boot cleats here," John observes.

"Someone has passed through. We're on the right track. Pay attention to your footing and proceed carefully to avoid twisting an ankle or getting stuck between the ice blocks."

#

Back at the camp, Ross and Marta eagerly welcome the arrival of the group of eight men riding snowmobiles. All of them don military uniforms and carry automatic weapons on their backs.

"Good morning, I'm Captain Oswald, the unit commander," the leader of the group introduces himself, removing his ski goggles and extending a hand.

"Good morning, Captain. You are very welcome, sir. My name is Ross, and this is Dr. Marta. We stayed behind to receive you. The rest of our group left earlier to make the most of the limited sunlight," Ross says.

"Nice to meet you, Ross and Dr. Marta," says Oswald, extending his hand in a greeting.

"And how is Alberto? What happened, anyway?" asks Marta anxiously.

"Your friend Alberto is recovering well. Let me get my men settled and unload some of the supplies we brought, and then we can talk more freely," Oswald replies.

"Of course, Captain. We have hot tea ready for you and your men," Marta offers.

"Thank you so much. You didn't have to go through the trouble, but hot tea will be much appreciated after this journey. We all have dry and icy throats."

#

John stands still at the end of the tunnel, gazing ahead. "Robert, Rachel, you have to come and see this," he calls out.

Rachel and Robert navigate through the remaining obstacles, eager to see what has caught John's attention.

190

"Oh my God, this is incredible," Rachel exclaims as she reaches him.

"What's happening there? Is everything alright?" Robert pushes past the last ice block and joins them, unable to contain his astonishment.

Down below, about a hundred meters away, a massive crater stretches out before them. Large black boulders are clustered in the center, partially concealed by a thin layer of fog, standing in stark contrast to the surrounding white ice walls, which tower hundreds of meters above, culminating in a dome partially shrouded by a faint mist that obscures the sky, casting a dim, diffuse light.

"It's like a hidden world," Robert breathes in awe.

"Do you think this could be Aklujji Matu?" Rachel asks, turning to John with wonder in her eyes.

"I hope so; it's so surreal. Look at the sheer scale of it all and the strange luminosity emanating from the fog," John says, captivated by the mystical scenery before them.

"I've never seen anything like it before," Robert adds, his gaze fixed on the pile of boulders at the bottom of the crater.

"But why didn't we spot this when we flew over in the plane?" Rachel asks, gazing upward.

"That's a good question. I suspect it's because of the fog that conceals the top of the dome. When we flew over, the fog must have hidden this entire area," John explains, pointing upwards.

"It appears we're on the right track," Robert points ahead. "There are some cables already in use. They must belong to the Denudasdi team. Let's see if we can utilize them."

They approach a set of colored stakes and ropes protruding from the ice. Robert crouches down to inspect the equipment.

"Yes, it seems they're in excellent condition. We can use them, but we have to proceed with caution. It's still several dozen meters down there," Robert confirms.

"Great. Let's descend and explore the nearest area, at least until we reach the first boulders. We should do it while we still have daylight," John suggests, peering through binoculars.

"But if we go down, we won't make it back to camp before nightfall. It will take hours to reach the rocks down there and return," Rachel expresses her unease. "We haven't been able to communicate with Ross and Marta, and we don't know if the backup team has arrived at the camp."

"Rachel, we anticipated this scenario and discussed it beforehand. We came prepared to spend the night here if necessary," John reassures her.

"The backup team should have reached the camp by now. Even if they haven't, Marta and Ross will be safe and comfortable, relaxing in the warm tent," he adds with a chuckle.

"Who's relaxing in a warm tent?" an unexpected voice interrupts them. They turn to see Ross approaching with a smile, accompanied by Marta and two unfamiliar men in uniform.

"Ross, Marta, what a relief to see you here," Rachel says, embracing Marta.

"I'm glad to see you guys too. What the hell is this place?" Ross asks, stepping closer to the edge of the cliff, and peering down into the crater.

"John believes it could be Aklujji Matu," Rachel explains.

"Who are these individuals accompanying you?" John asks.

"Oh, my apologies for the oversight. Allow me to introduce Captain Oswald, the commander of the reinforcement unit sent to assist us, and Sergeant Flynt," Ross introduces the men in uniform.

"Good morning to all of you," the uniformed men greet, standing behind Ross and Marta. "I've been looking forward to meeting you. Dr. John, Dr. Rachel, Robert, it's a great pleasure," Captain Oswald concludes.

"The pleasure is ours as well. You have no idea how relieved we are to have you here. And please, call me John. I'm not concerned about titles," John responds.

"And what about Alberto? How is he? What happened at the base?" Rachel presses.

"He is recovering from a gunshot wound to the chest and has been evacuated to the mainland base. I'll fill you in on all the details as we walk. You were about to descend, right?" Oswald approaches the edge of the platform and gazes down.

"I'm relieved to hear that Alberto is recovering. But I'm curious, is the backup unit just the two of you?" John looks around as if expecting more soldiers to appear behind Oswald.

"No, John, certainly not," Oswald chuckles. "We are a team of eight in total. Four of our members stayed back at the camp to ensure safety, two remained at the entrance of the crevasse, and we are the two who ventured here."

"Okay, that's fantastic. I'm thrilled that all of you are here," John expresses his satisfaction.

"So, from what I understand, you believe you've found the legendary Aklujji Matu?" Oswald looks down at the chaotic pile of rocks below.

"Yes, Captain. I believe we will discover the Matu somewhere down there, concealed among the rocks. The fog shrouding the area hinders us from seeing the finer details within," John explains, his gaze fixed on the dark mass partially veiled by the thin fog. "Now, with your assistance, we can continue our expedition," he winks at Rachel.

"Certainly, John. This place is extraordinary," Ross adds, his eyes locked on the area of black rocks partially obscured by the fog.

"Fantastic. And we've prepared everything to descend, right? What is your plan?" Oswald asks.

"It's a straightforward plan, Captain. We will descend and explore. Since we have no idea what awaits us beyond the rocks, we will assess our next steps once we approach those boulders," John outlines the plan.

"Perfect. We're here to assist you. We brought additional equipment, although it seems you have everything set up," Oswald says, impressed by the already prepared ropes.

"That's true, but we owe our gratitude to the Denudasdi team. Let's also try to uncover what happened to them," Robert adds.

"Alright then, let's proceed. We'll discuss further when we're all down there. I'll descend first," John says as he takes hold of one of the cables and approaches the edge of the cliff.

With a smile and a playful wink directed at Rachel, he begins his descent.

After nearly an hour of careful maneuvering, everyone reaches the bottom of the cliff.

"Okay, great. It wasn't as difficult as we anticipated. We are ready to proceed," John says, picking up his backpack that had landed on the ground in the meantime.

"Yes, things went well. I must admit, I wasn't very confident initially," Marta nervously says, adventure stirring within her despite her nerves. She glances at Robert, who meets her gaze, causing her cheeks to flush as she looks away with a mischievous smile.

"Why don't we see any snow or ice on those boulders and the surrounding ground?" Rachel ponders, standing at the edge of the snow and observing the black gravel scattered across the terrain.

"I'm not sure how to explain it. Based on what I can see, these rocks appear to be mostly basalt," Marta joins Rachel, taking a handful of gravel and letting it slip through her fingers. "What intrigues me now is the arrangement of these rocks. They seem to have fallen on top of each other. But how? And where did they come from? All I see around us is ice."

"Guys, we should distribute the equipment among everyone. It wouldn't be fair for the captain and the sergeant to carry it all," John suggests, collecting additional gear from the ground.

"Thank you, John. But don't worry, we can manage," Oswald responds.

"No, sir. None of that. John is right. Let's share the load, and it will be easier for everyone. Let's get going," Robert chimes in, grabbing a bag and adding it to his backpack. Oswald smiles, appreciating the team's gesture, and accepts their help.

"I suggest we start from this side. I see tracks in the gravel. Someone has walked this way," Flynt says, having moved slightly away from the group and carefully examining the ground.

"Gentlemen, I propose we follow Sergeant Flynt's suggestion. He is our best tracker," Oswald says.

"Excellent. Let's follow the trail the sergeant discovered," John leads the way toward Flynt, who is crouched down, observing the ground.

"Can you determine how many individuals have passed through here?" John asks.

"I'm still a bit unsure. I see a set of tracks leading forward, indicating more than four people. And the imprints on the ground correspond to different types of footwear," Flynt explains, pointing to a visible trail in the gravel.

He takes a step back and points to the left. "But here, at this spot, three people walked with different shoes. It appears that multiple individuals have passed through here."

"The Anguta guys. It must have been them," Ross says. "What on earth were they doing here?"

"But who are these Anguta guys?" Oswald asks, not familiar with Ross's reference.

"The Anguta guys are three individuals who went missing at the Anguta mission in the Arctic. We discovered two of them, frozen dead, at one of the entrances to the base," John explains.

"From the Arctic? How is that possible? And how did they end up here?" Oswald questions.

"Captain, we are also eager to find answers. Perhaps we'll uncover something here," John replies, facing the rocky outcrop ahead. "Please, Sergeant, let's continue."

"And what about the third body? If there were two, where is the third?" Oswald inquires.

"We don't know. We found a hood that likely belonged to the third person, but no other clues. Just like we don't know how they arrived here and where they came from," John comments.

During the next few minutes, the group follows Flynt in a single file.

"Both tracks lead toward the rocks. One group moves towards them, and the other comes from them," Flynt observes, scanning the surroundings with confusion.

"The trails lead us to those boulders ahead, those triangular columns, like guardians on the hillside," Robert points ahead, chuckling at the imagery.

"I agree with your description. They resemble rocky walls encircling the entire area, protecting what's inside. Have you noticed how similar they appear in shape and height?" Marta says. "If not for their size, I would almost say they were the result of someone's extraordinary craftsmanship."

As the team walks through the area, they gradually ascend towards the first rocks, following Flynt, who stops upon reaching them, uncertain of the next course of action.

They gather beside him, placing their backpacks on the ground to rest their backs.

"Well, the gravel has disappeared," Flynt says, gazing down at the polished rock floor.

"Now it will be more challenging to find tracks on this smooth surface. Our only hope is to discover boot marks or any other possible clues. We must proceed with caution."

"Sergeant, you're the expert here. We'll follow your lead," John says, trying to keep Flynt motivated.

"While you decide where to go, let me explore this area," Marta suggests, moving a little away from the group towards a nearby boulder.

"Wait, I'll go with you," Rachel says, following her.

"Take this opportunity to rest while I search for any clues," Flynt suggests.

"Good idea. I'll join the ladies," Robert announces, rising from his spot and heading toward Marta and Rachel.

Flynt proceeds cautiously, meticulously examining the ground before him as he disappears amidst the clustered boulders.

John sits beside Oswald, his gaze fixed on Rachel.

"Captain, any updates from Shaman? Do we have any leads on his whereabouts?" John wants to know.

"No. As of our descent into the rift, there have been no new developments. Without the ability to use radios in this area, I'm in the dark as well. We can only assume he is somewhere nearby. We believe that he has relocated his base closer to the coast, possibly even on a ship, which would grant him greater mobility and autonomy. We're working on locating it," Oswald explains.

"He won't give up. Once he reinforces his team, he'll return, and this time he'll be even more dangerous. He's already aware of your presence," John remarks.

"Don't worry. We're prepared for that. We have a 48-hour window to decide whether to stay or retreat. If we come across something significant that justifies our presence here, we'll reinforce our team and ensure our safety. If not, we'll return to base and leave this frozen desert," Oswald assures.

Not far from them, close to the boulders, Robert joins Marta and Rachel, inquiring about their findings.

"So, what did you discover?" he asks.

"I'm trying to decipher the composition of these rocks," Marta responds, gently running her hands over the surface.

"I see an unexpected formation here. It's common to find andesite on the Antarctic Peninsula, a volcanic rock similar to basalt, as well as rhyolite, which resembles granite. However, with the naked eye, what I'm seeing appears to be an unusual composition. It looks like basalt with granite layers and veins of black quartz.

"Okay... and?" Robert asks, struggling to grasp the implications of Marta's words.

"I didn't anticipate finding this rock composition here... I need to conduct further analysis. Additionally..." Marta pauses for a moment, her hands still resting on the rock. "Apart from that... I sense a warmth emanating from the rock. It shouldn't be more than ambient temperature, but it feels warmer." Marta looks at Rachel and Robert in amazement. "See if you feel the same," she suggests, inviting them to touch the rock.

"And this is peculiar, right?" Rachel caresses the stone, uncertain about the implications of Marta's observations.

"It's highly unusual. I can't explain it, but it does explain why there is no snow or ice on these rocks." Marta steps back from the rock, awe and reverence crossing her face.

Marta then moves towards another nearby rock, placing her hands on its surface.

"What could be causing this temperature? Could it be some underground volcanic activity?" Robert wonders aloud, surprised by the warmth he feels upon touching the rock.

"I have no idea," Marta admits. "I don't see any signs of underground volcanic activity."

"Hey, what's going on? Why are you all fondling the rocks?" Ross approaches, his curiosity piqued by the excitement of his companions.

Marta briefly explains the phenomenon when Flynt screams next to the rocks he is investigating, catching everyone's attention.

"Captain, Dr. John, everyone, please come. I've discovered something important. Please, follow me," he exclaims, visibly agitated and pointing in the direction he came from.

"What's happening, Sergeant? What did you find?" Oswald rises to his feet, taken aback by Flynt's state of agitation.

"I believe I've come across some of the Denudasdi team belongings, just a few meters away. Follow me," Flynt turns and disappears once again behind the rocks.

"Wait, Sergeant. Wait for us," Oswald calls out, already on his feet and ready to follow.

"Let's go, Ross, Rachel. We need to follow Flynt. Hurry up!" John urges, leading the way as they venture into the maze of clustered rocks.

"Flynt, please slow down. We need to wait for the rest of the team to catch up," John shouts, slowing his pace and glancing back, ensuring the group remains together.

"What's happening? Why the rush?" Ross is the first to reach John, followed closely by the others.

"I'm not entirely sure. Flynt called us over. It seems like he has discovered something about the Denudasdi team. Let's go. We can't afford to lose sight of them," John explains, urgency lacing his voice.

"The geology is changing. It seems different," Marta observes, her gaze fixed on the rocks as they advance. "Have you noticed that there are no rocky walls here? The boulders appear as though they have fallen from somewhere," she says, carefully navigating through the jumble of rocks.

Finally, they reach John and Oswald, who are standing beside Flynt in front of a cliff wall. On the ground, a pile of backpacks and equipment is scattered.

"It seems that the Denudasdi team had to lighten their load to climb these rocks," Flynt adds.

"Yes, that could be a plausible explanation," John muses, thoughtful.

Meanwhile, Marta remains captivated by the imposing rocks in front of them. "I apologize, but I can't help but be fascinated by the geological nature of this area. These rocks are entirely different. They resemble quartz, crystalline structures, or even obsidian, but they are not. I can't comprehend it. I feel utterly perplexed," she confesses, struggling to make sense of the rocks as she examines and gently touches them.

"Ah, this one is cold, as it should be," she remarks with satisfaction before moving on to other nearby rocks. "And this one is cold too," she announces triumphantly as she continues her exploration. "Why are you all staring at me? I'm just trying to understand what we have here," she says, laughing despite herself at John's teasing smile.

"Please, Marta, continue. Share your findings with us when you're ready," John replies.

"These piled-up boulders have the expected cold temperature. They feel normal. However, the rocks we encountered earlier were not cold at all. They emitted an inexplicable warmth. Unfortunately, I can't fathom how such a phenomenon is possible," Marta says, frustration creeping into her voice as she takes a few steps back and gazes at the perplexing rocks before her.

"While Marta tries to unravel this enigma, I suggest Sergeant Flynt and Captain Oswald explore the rocks on the left, and I will venture to the right side with Ross. Robert, please stay with the ladies," John proposes, taking the lead toward the rocks on the right.

"I agree. Sergeant, let's proceed," Oswald calls Flynt and begins making their way towards the first rocks to climb.

"Be careful, and don't take too long. Remember, we have no means of communication," Rachel shouts, her voice tight with worry as she watches John and Ross navigate the challenging pile of rocks, their size posing some difficulty.

John gradually overcomes the initial obstacles. Oswald and Flynt assist each other in ascending the rocks. Soon, they disappear from view, concealed by the rugged landscape.

"Ross, where are you? I'm trying to keep up," John calls out.

"Come on, I'll wait. It's better to stick together for safety and make the climb easier," Ross responds, as John's head emerges from behind a cluster of boulders. With effort, the two continue to ascend and maneuver between the rocks.

"We're almost at the top, it seems. I'm curious to see what lies ahead," John pauses, catching his breath.

"Let's keep going. I'm equally curious about the surprises awaiting us here," Ross urges.

"Hold on, my friend. Let me catch my breath first," John requests, briefly pausing to regain his composure.

"Damn it, John!" Ross blurts, hauling him up to the edge of the final cliff. "You have to see this."

"Fuck! What on earth do we have here now?"

"Look, the captain and the sergeant are also looking at this from over there," Ross says, pointing to the cluster of rocks a few dozen meters to their right.

"It appears to be another crater, completely enveloped in black fog. This is incredibly strange, man. We need to descend," John says while signaling Oswald and Flynt to join them. As they draw closer, they witness the black mist shrouding the entire base of the crater, rising almost to the top of the boulders, approaching Oswald and Flynt, who are already at the edge of the dark mist. Oswald examines the enigmatic veil before them. "Can anyone make sense of this?"

"I would venture to say that something crashed here with great force, pulverizing all the rocks in the vicinity into smaller fragments, leaving behind this trapped mist," John speculates.

"Does anyone have any idea what this black fog is?" Ross asks, sharing Oswald's curiosity. "Let's explore what lies within," he suggests, turning towards the mist but being halted by John, who grabs his arm.

"Wait. First, we need to understand the nature of this fog, what it is and if it's safe to proceed," John holds Ross back and cautiously approaches the edge of the fog.

"Yes, John is right. This fog is peculiar. It resembles a black shroud, and we can almost feel its presence. It's warm and doesn't sit well with me," Flynt remarks, casting a suspicious glance and tentatively reaching out to touch the mist.

"Let's go and fetch Robert and the ladies," John says. "Perhaps Marta or Rachel can help shed light on the nature of this phenomenon. Ross, can you go back and bring them?"

"Good idea. While we wait for them, I'll take a look in this direction," Flynt suggests, pointing to the right side of the fog.

"Agreed, Sergeant. I will look to the left side. But don't venture inside. We'll regroup here in fifteen minutes, and then we'll decide our next course of action," Oswald asserts, while John and Ross go back up the rocks and Flynt walks away, skirting the edge of the fog.

After a few minutes, Ross and John return with Rachel, Robert, and Marta, who are equally astonished by the sight before them.

"Just in time," Oswald calls out, approaching them. "I didn't find anything relevant on that side. We have an insurmountable wall of rocks blocking the way."

"What on earth is this? Where is Flynt?" Rachel demands, astonishment and apprehension both in her voice.

"The sergeant is exploring around the crater," John explains.

"You were right. The fog resembles a black shroud," Marta observes, cautiously advancing towards the edge and dipping her hand into it.

"I'm uncertain about its nature. But it's warm and dry, and I can't detect any odor," Marta observes the ground through the mist. "The visibility seems extremely limited out here. From what I can see, I'd estimate it to be less than two meters."

"I'm going in. I need to understand what's there," John says, retrieving his backpack. Rachel and Marta look apprehensively at each other.

"Remember, we don't have communication or guidance systems. You should use a rope around your waist to maintain a safe connection between us," Ross suggests, pulling a rope from his backpack.

"John, I'm afraid of what might be lurking in there. We have no idea if this fog is toxic or if you'll encounter other hazards," Rachel anxiously expresses her concern to John.

"I'm not fond of the idea either. I have no intention of entering in that," Marta states, taking a few steps back.

"Don't worry. I'll go with John and ensure he doesn't do anything reckless," Robert approaches John and takes another rope from his backpack.

"I agree. I believe it's worth investigating and having Robert with him will be more safe," Ross agrees, picking up the rope to secure them.

Marta and Rachel go quiet, fear plain on both their faces.

John takes the lead, followed a few meters behind by Robert, both being slowly enveloped by the fog. The partially extended rope is the only visible connection between the mist ahead and Ross and the rest of the group.

"John, Robert, how are you going? What's it like in there?" Rachel calls out into the mist, concern sharp in her voice.

"Rachel, calm down. We've only just begun. So far, everything is fine here. Visibility remains poor, but apart from that, we're okay," Robert's muffled voice echoes from within the fog.

"John, I sense a slight downward slope in the terrain. It seems like we're descending," Robert reports, holding onto the rope that connects him to John.

"Yes, I feel it too. You'll need to speak up. I can barely hear you," John shouts.

"Understood. It's as if we're talking from inside a thick blanket."

"Ross, hold on a moment. I need to stop and remove my coat. It's too hot in here to keep wearing it."

"Man, this is surreal, being inside this fog. It feels like another world. The silence, the temperature, the limited visibility, and the uncertainty of what lies ahead," Ross says, as he also takes off his coat and ties it around his waist.

"Let's continue for just a few more meters," John urges, resuming their journey.

The Sphere

"Colonel!"

Tzabar jolts awake as a voice shouts outside his room.

He quickly gets out of bed when he realizes that the alarm didn't wake him up. He puts on his robe and opens the door slightly. Still with a hazy vision, he looks at the soldier who is watching him with an embarrassed look.

"Good morning, Colonel. Dr. Alvin requests your presence in the workroom."

"Thank you. I'll be there in ten minutes." Tzabar says, closing the door and heading to his shower.

"Good morning, Dr. Alvin. I apologize for the delay," Tzabar says as he enters the workroom, finding Alvin, Lydia, and Victor seated at the table.

"Good morning, Colonel. Don't worry. We had to start without you," Alvin says. "If you haven't had breakfast, there's something to eat in the cupboard, and the coffee should still be warm."

"Great, thank you." Tzabar makes his way to the coffee maker.

"I hope you slept well. Today could be a very intense day," Lydia remarks with a smile.

"Do we have more results?"

"Yes," she replies. "We received additional data from the symbols and characters on the mountain," she says, displaying the initial screens.

"The Cientek AI software is conducting the analysis. It combines artificial intelligence with paleogeographical and philological algorithms, incorporating linguistic and historical analysis," Alvin says, pride in his voice as he presents a slide with the technical details.

"Ah, I see. We have a comprehensive tool to assist us in deciphering our findings. Does it also predict the future?" Tzabar jests in a lighthearted tone as he sips his coffee.

"Who knows, perhaps one day," Victor responds with a chuckle.

"I'll provide a concise summary of our findings without delving into excessive technical details," Lydia says, rising from her seat and gesturing for Alvin to proceed to the next slide. "It's important to note that these findings are subject to updates. The system is designed to self-correct and improve its detection and interpretation criteria."

"Given the surprising nature of the preliminary results, we conducted parallel studies using traditional methods to validate their consistency," she continues, displaying a new slide.

"Now, we have much greater confidence in the most recent transcripts," she states, revealing a slide where character symbols are accompanied by labeled translations, with some marked with a red note stating 'Undecoded.'

The upper half of the screen showcases an image featuring a complete set of symbols, while legible text appears on the lower half.

"Sdax foundation, first.

From the essence, the voice of Anyfr is heard.

The Nyfrum were placed in the third of K'tryax, under the unit of Kur.

Kur will master the seed to A'bul'kurr.

From the house of Nyfrid, the last will lead the Nyfrum to the essence."

"This is just a glimpse of the extensive work that lies ahead, and it's important to emphasize that these findings are subject to further refinement," Lydia comments.

"Excellent. Now, let's delve into the meaning behind all of this," Tzabar remarks, his gaze fixed on the projected text.

"Getting right to the point," Lydia says, gesturing to move the slide forward.

"We have identified several entities, namely Anyfr, Kur, Nyfrid, and Nyfrum," she says.

"As for the references to K'tryax, A'bul'kurr, *seed,* and the *essence*, our current understanding is that they point to something physical. We have clues suggesting that K'tryax could represent our Sun or our solar system, thus making the 'third of K'tryax' likely referring to Earth," Lydia continues.

"Our most compelling interpretation thus far suggests that the Nyfrum were relocated to the 'third of K'tryax' under the direction of Anyfr and led by Kur," she pauses, allowing everyone to digest the information. "Regarding A'bul'kurr, as the original home of the Nyfrum, we speculate that it could represent Abulkur, the mystical inner realm often referred to in stories and legends native to this geographical area."

Tzabar looks to Alvin, who nods in confirmation, signaling him to wait.

"To summarize, the analyses of these most recent references are still in the early stages. These findings represent the most up-to-date information derived from the symbols discovered on the mountain.

The characters found in the wreckage area present a more intricate challenge in terms of decoding. They do not conform to the same pattern, and therefore we need to exercise caution and await more reliable results," Lydia explains, taking a seat and exhaling deeply, anticipating their reaction.

"If I understood correctly, the Nyfrum could be an extraterrestrial civilization that arrived on Earth under the orders of an entity or force known as Anyfr and led by someone named Kur," Tzabar says, sitting upright and directing his question primarily to Lydia.

"They arrived on Earth with origins and circumstances that are yet to be determined. This civilization established themselves in Abulkur, which is also the home of Nyfrid, although its precise location remains unknown," Tzabar shifts his gaze towards Alvin. "Furthermore, we are uncertain about the meaning of the *essence* and the *seed*."

Tzabar falls silent, his expression pensive, as he rests his chin on his hands, fingers interlocked, and elbows resting on the table. After a moment of contemplation, he looks up with a serious expression.

"I urge you to thoroughly review all of your data and conduct meticulous cross-checking," Tzabar requests, stepping forward towards the table and appearing concerned. "We need to establish a credible and coherent narrative. This discovery will undoubtedly create a significant stir, and we must be certain about what we will report and how we will present it."

"Yes, Colonel, we understand the importance of your request. It is the same question we posed to ourselves from the beginning, which is why we embarked on two parallel lines of investigation: one focusing on the timeline and the other on the objectives, individuals involved, and other relevant factors. We aim to find the intersecting points between the two strands," Victor assures.

"I need a well-founded and substantiated understanding of all this," Tzabar expresses his concern to Alvin.

"Rest assured, Colonel. You will receive a clear and well-documented report on this matter. We have already sent you a report regarding the wreckage and the findings related to the android.

If you wish, we can discuss it further at the end of the day," Alvin signals them the end of the meeting.

"Thank you all for your contributions. Let's make progress throughout the rest of the day. Get to work," Alvin says with enthusiasm, leading his team out of the room.

"Until later, ladies and gentlemen. I have some reports to review but do not hesitate to reach out if something of greater significance arises," Tzabar concludes, departing in the opposite direction from the group.

#

Alvin storms out of the cafeteria, visibly furious, nearly colliding with Kurt in the process.

"Captain Kurt, good afternoon. Do you have any idea what's going on? Why did Colonel Tzabar call us so urgently? I barely had time to finish my lunch," Alvin questions, clearly agitated.

"I have no clue, Dr. Alvin. I just left the cafeteria myself. But something significant must have occurred," Kurt responds, equally unaware of the situation.

As they walk down the hallway together, Alvin grumbles, much to Kurt's annoyance. They enter the room and find Tzabar standing behind the conference table, appearing impatient, with his laptop open and facing them.

"Good afternoon, Colonel Tzabar," Kurt greets.

"Good afternoon, gentlemen," Tzabar interrupts Alvin's greeting, setting a tense atmosphere for what follows.

"Gentlemen, I have both good news and bad news. Our missing team has been located," Tzabar announces with a biting tone, heightening their confusion. Before they can react, Tzabar continues.

"And now for the bad news—they are deceased!" Tzabar deliberately pauses, allowing the weight of his words to sink in.

"How? Where are they?" Alvin asks, intrigued by Tzabar's tone and how he delivers the news.

"Two bodies were discovered two days ago. The third team member is still missing," Tzabar discloses, leaving Alvin and Kurt dumbfounded.

"Two days ago? But how? Where were they found? And why was I not informed?" Alvin stares at Tzabar in disbelief, shock cracking his voice.

"They were found in Antarctica, on the opposite side of the planet," Tzabar says, further bewildering them.

"They were discovered at the Denudasdi base, which I had never even heard of before. Were either of you aware of this Antarctic base and its activities?" Tzabar asks, leaning forward across the table, his scathing gaze fixed on the two men, finally unveiling the reason behind his sour mood.

"What? Antarctica? Denudasdi? I do not know of any of this. What kind of base is it, and what does it have to do with us?" Kurt expresses his astonishment, visibly taken aback.

"Colonel, I'm as clueless as Kurt here. I have no information about this base or how they ended up in Antarctica. I simply don't understand," Alvin confesses, his brows furrowed in confusion.

"Alright. I understand," Tzabar sighs, suddenly appearing downcast. "We share the same ignorance." he sits down with a deep sigh, showing some disappointment.

"I don't know anything more about how they ended up there or what the Denudasdi base is, and its connection to us. I'm still in the dark. However, I hope to clarify all of this with Commander Chang within the next few hours," he says, regaining his composure.

"Please take the necessary steps to inform the teams and family members of the deceased. I have already sent you their information. The official statement will be that they died in an accident during fieldwork, and investigations are ongoing to determine the cause of the accident and locate the third team member. And regarding the location of the bodies we will only disclose that they were transported to the base in Iceland and nothing more. Please, not even a single comment about Antarctica. We will stick to this information and nothing more. I don't want to fuel conspiracy theories until I can fully understand what happened," Tzabar instructs, with a resolute tone.

"Gentlemen, let's return to our work. We need tangible results. Speculation and theories alone won't sustain this mission. Have a productive day," Tzabar says, abruptly exiting the room without allowing for any reaction from either of them.

"What's happening? What on earth am I missing?" Kurt looks bewildered, his gaze fixed on Alvin, who is equally perplexed. "Captain, I have no clue. I don't understand. Our colleagues are found dead in some Antarctic base we know nothing about. I'm missing something too."

Alvin quickly composes himself and adds, "I'm sorry, Captain. I have unpleasant news to deliver. This is enough to ruin my day," he remarks before leaving the room.

Meanwhile, on the rugged slope of the mirrored wall, another team is exploring the area and stumbles upon a crevice nestled among the boulders, leading them into an enormous cavity within the mountain. Advancing along the rocky walls with their lanterns lit, they remain oblivious to the impending threat that lies ahead.

As they progress, the atmosphere gradually darkens. Suddenly, without realizing it, the environment around them undergoes a drastic change, eliciting expressions of surprise from the team members.

"What's happening here? How did it become so dark?"

"Where the hell did this fog come from? I can barely see you," one of them exclaims.

"Why are we still walking? We can't see a thing," another voice chimes in, worried.

Despite the limited visibility and their muffled voices, they press on, unaware of the direction they are taking.

"I'm curious to see what lies ahead. Let's venture a little further and then turn back," one suggests.

"I don't like this at all. Let's go back," another insists, their apprehension growing.

"The path seems to be descending. Let's proceed with caution," someone remarks.

"Have you noticed how hot it's getting? Hold on a moment. I need to take off my jacket," one of them pauses.

"Agreed. Let's take a break. I'll remove mine as well," another joins in.

"I strongly recommend we turn back. This situation doesn't sit well with me. We've been walking for a while, only to encounter more of the same—nothing," someone voices their growing unease.

Suddenly, everyone comes to a halt, a shiver running through their bodies as one of them speaks up, fear cracking their voice. "Guys, we've been walking for some time now. Does anyone have any idea how to find our way out?"

Anxiety fills their voices. "What the hell? Are you serious? Don't mess with us. So we wandered in here without knowing how to get back? This isn't a joke."

"Let's stay calm and avoid panicking. We need to retrace our steps slowly. If we backtrack along the same path we've taken so far, I'm confident we'll find the exit," someone tries to reassure the group.

"Alright, I'll take the lead now. Let's walk in the same direction we came from, ensuring we maintain the same course we've been following," another suggests.

"Remember, keep your hands on the shoulders of the person in front of you to stay connected and avoid getting separated," someone advises.

"How far do you think we've come?" one of them wonders aloud.

Impatience starts to creep in as they continue walking. "We should have reached the exit by now. I think we've gone further than before," someone expresses doubt.

Dread and fear settle among the group, casting a shadow over their thoughts.

"Let's pause for a moment. I believe we should try a different approach," one proposes.

"What's your idea?" another asks.

"I think we should proceed forward, not in a single file, but side by side while maintaining contact with each other. This way, we can cover a larger area. When we're in a single file, we're only focused on one point."

"That's a good idea," someone says. "I agree with you. Stay in touch with your partner beside you and point your flashlight straight ahead. We stick together and cover a wider area. Let's proceed then," the same voice concludes, determined but cautious.

Hope renewed, the group stands shoulder to shoulder, cautiously moving forward in the darkness, covering a few more meters in search of the exit. However, as panic begins to grip them, arguments erupt, and the once-united group disintegrates. People break away from their partners, losing the connection that had kept them together.

Amid the chaos, despair takes hold, and some members, unable to see or feel the presence of their companions, wander in a frantic search for an exit.

The cries and desperate screams of the lost voices mingle with the panicked shouts of those who remain. Amidst the chaos, only two colleagues maintain their grip on each other's hands, clinging tightly even as darkness surrounds them.

Desperately, they call out for their colleagues, but their voices go unanswered. The muffled sounds grow fainter and fainter until they cease altogether, leaving them sobbing overwhelmed by the loss.

"We can't stay here crying," Alice urges, her voice unsteady. "We have to keep going. We need to find help and bring them back."

Sara, wiping away her tears, nods in agreement. "You lead the way, Alice. Let's find our way out of here and get the help we need."

Hand in hand, they continue their journey, taking small steps in the darkness. After a few more meters, a sudden change occurs—the darkness lifts, and they find themselves out of the oppressive gloom.

"We made it," Sara says with relief, tears still staining her face as she embraces Alice. "We were so close."

"We should try calling out to them. Maybe they can hear us," Alice suggests, half hopeful, half laughing nervously, as she clings tightly to her colleague.

Approaching the edge of the black fog, they call out the names of their lost companions, their voices echoing into the mist. For a few minutes, they persist, hoping for a response, but all they hear is silence.

"It's no use. They're not listening, and even if they do, they might not realize we're here," Sara says, tugging on Alice's arm. "We have to make our way back to the base and get help."

"You're right," Alice agrees. "Let's find assistance as quickly as possible."

They briskly walk away from the sinister zone, their hearts heavy with the weight of the loss they've endured, but resolve to bring aid and find answers.

#

As Tzabar approaches the recess between the rocks, he is taken aback by the turmoil that greets him. Stepping cautiously along the boulders, he comes to a halt, stunned by the mysterious, dense black fog that engulfs the area, devouring the light from nearby projectors.

Victor is with Sara, Alice, and the members of the rescue team discussing nervously.

"What do we know about the accident? What is this fog?" Tzabar asks, confused.

"We still have no information regarding the nature of this black fog. It seems that a research team unintentionally entered it," Victor explains while introducing Sara and Alice. "These are Sara and Alice. They were part of the group trapped inside, and they are the only ones who managed to escape."

"Sara, Alice, can you explain what happened here? How did you end up in this situation?" Tzabar asks, eager to understand what happened.

"We entered the fog unknowingly. It suddenly surrounded us, shrouding everything in darkness. We couldn't see anything, and some members of the group panicked when we realized we had lost our way out," Alice recounts.

"However, the real problem arose when we got separated and lost contact with each other. We were so close to the exit," Sara adds, tears streaming down her face.

"Have we identified the source or cause of this phenomenon? Do we have any understanding of the nature of this fog?" Tzabar turns to Kurt, who approaches him with Alvin.

"Not yet, Colonel. We are investigating, but we haven't found any answers," Alvin replies with concern.

Another mystery," Kurt mutters, clearly frustrated by the lack of information.

"Colonel, I should join the rescue team. I have experience in dealing with these kinds of situations as a speleologist. I believe my expertise could be beneficial to this mission," Victor offers.

"Thank you for your willingness to help, Dr. Victor," Tzabar says. "However, I would prefer you to remain here and assist the rescue team from the outside. Sergeant Mark also has experience in high-risk rescue missions." Tzabar calls for one of the military personnel from the rescue team. "Sergeant, I expect you to follow the established protocol and prioritize safety. I want everyone to return unharmed.

"Yes, Colonel. You can count on me. The safety of the team is my top priority," Mark affirms confidently.

"Alright, everyone ready? I'll lead the way," Mark announces, positioning himself at the front of the group and securing his harness with a carabiner.

A hush falls over the area as the seven members of the rescue team cautiously enter the black fog. Moments later, their voices echo from within as they call out the names of their trapped comrades.

Outside, the remaining base personnel murmur with apprehension, speculating about the mysterious fog and the events unfolding within its depths.

The tension mounts as the minutes pass, with only the movement of the connecting cables serving as a link to the rescue team. The waiting becomes increasingly agonizing. Suddenly, one of the rescuers emerges from the fog, carrying a woman in his arms, appearing to be in a state of shock. The medical team rushes to her aid while the rescuer quickly returns inside the fog.

During the following long minutes, nothing else occurs except for the continuous movement of the cables being pulled inward. Finally, a group of rescuers reappears, accompanied by the last missing team members. They cry with relief upon reaching the light, embracing the rescuers in gratitude.

"We're heading back to inform our colleagues that we've found everyone," one of the rescuers announces before stepping back into the black fog.

As time goes on, the ropes continue to move, but no one else returns. People start to speculate and wonder what is happening inside the fog.

Alvin keeps his gaze fixed on the black abyss, anxiously checking his watches, while Kurt sits on the ground, leaning against nearby rocks. Suddenly, a sharp tug on the ropes captures their attention.

"What's happening?" Tzabar asks approaching Alvin.

"I have no idea. Are they coming back?" Alvin responds with uncertainty.

Four rescuers emerge from the fog, carrying two lifeless bodies.

"What the hell? Weren't they all accounted for?" Kurt exclaims in disbelief.

The medical team rushes to attend to the bodies, only to retreat with a somber expression. "They're dead. There's nothing more we can do."

"I can't believe this. But who are these people?" Alvin stares in astonishment at the bodies lying on the ground.

"Does anyone recognize them? Can anyone identify them?" Tzabar demands.

"I don't know who they are. They are not part of our mission. They're wearing blue jackets, while ours are orange," Kurt explains as he joins the conversation.

"Both of them have an emblem on their shoulders with the word 'Denudasdi,'" Tzabar observes, looking at Alvin and Kurt. "Can someone explain this to me?"

"Where did you find them?" Victor asks the rescue team members.

"We found them leaning against a wall deep inside when we were searching for our colleagues."

"Well, enough surprises. Call the others back. Use the ropes to communicate," Tzabar says, visibly disturbed by the two bodies on the ground.

The rescuers begin tugging on the ropes, employing Morse code to signal their colleagues within the fog.

"What's happening now?" Tzabar asks, noticing the worried expressions on the faces of the rescuers.

"I don't understand. The ropes seem to be stuck somewhere and they're not moving," someone remarks in frustration.

"I'm not getting any response from my cable either. It seems to be stuck too. We need to go back in and find out what's happening," says another, determined to investigate the situation.

Quickly adjusting their equipment, they venture back into the fog in search of their colleagues.

Minutes pass, but the cables remain motionless, causing impatience and concern among those waiting outside.

"It's been a while since the cables moved," someone comments, worry plain in their voice.

"I've noticed that too. It's been over eight minutes and there hasn't been any movement," Victor says, his eyes fixed on the still cables on the ground.

"Victor, what's going on? Why aren't the ropes moving?" Alvin asks, his concern growing. Victor shakes his head, admitting, "I have no idea. We'll have to wait and see."

"Why are we waiting? I don't understand. Let's just pull the ropes and signal them to come back," Tzabar suggests, moving towards one of the ropes without anyone attempting to stop him. Alvin and Victor exchange knowing glances, anticipating the outcome.

"Wait... the ropes are stuck. They're attached to something on the other side. They're not being pulled from the waist. We would have felt it," Tzabar exclaims, realization dawning on him.

"That's right, Colonel. We've already tried that. We don't understand what's happening. In the worst-case scenario, we could send two more men to find out," Alvin says, trying to make sense of the situation.

"They're coming back! Look, the ropes are moving now," Victor announces excitedly, drawing everyone's attention to the slowly moving ropes.

One by one, the seven men emerge from the black fog, appearing unharmed and walking silently with serene smiles on their faces, as if everything is normal.

"What the hell is wrong with them? They look like they're in a trance," Kurt comments, observing their mysterious demeanor.

"You're right. Something is off," mutters Alvin suspiciously, his eyes fixed on the team as they warmly greet everyone.

"We're glad you're back. We were really worried. What happened in there?" Tzabar approaches the team, concern in his voice, and directs his question to Sergeant Mark.

"Colonel Tzabar, thank you for your care and patience in waiting for us. We appreciate your concern. Don't worry, everything is alright," Mark says, attempting to hug Tzabar, who steps back, looking perplexed.

"Sergeant, compose yourself. What the hell happened? You were in there for over an hour. Explain," Tzabar demands, his confusion mounting.

"I apologize, Colonel. I didn't mean to show any disrespect. We're all grateful to be here and that everything turned out well," the sergeant replies, his calm gaze failing to reassure Tzabar.

Behind them, everyone listens in astonishment, eager to hear the story of the rescuers.

"What happened in there, Sergeant?" Tzabar asks, unable to hide his frustration.

"In the shadows, we lift the veil: some hide, others reveal," Mark says with a condescending smile, embracing his colleagues.

"What the hell is going on with you?" Tzabar demands, deeply irritated by Mark and his team's distant and detached demeanor.

With no satisfactory answers to his questions and their incomprehensible behavior, Tzabar summons Kurt and two soldiers. "Please escort these gentlemen back to the base. They will be in isolation until further notice, and I want a detailed report on everything, every single detail, in my hands within the next hour."

"And I also need immediate medical reports from each of these men. I want to understand what happened inside the fog during the mission." Despite the harshness of his words, the team remains unfazed, smiling, and maintaining their detached attitude.

"Did you understand anything I just said?" Tzabar shouts, his irritation mounting as he inches closer to Sergeant Mark's face.

"Yes, sir. Understood. You'll have our reports within the next hour," the sergeant says, standing up straight and looking straight ahead. Tzabar takes a step back.

The sergeant and his colleagues burst into laughter as Kurt and the two soldiers escort them back to the base.

#

Tzabar sits at the table with Kurt and Alvin by his side. Mark is seated on the opposite side, and several folders are neatly organized into two piles in front of them.

Mark stands upright, his serious expression suggests that he has regained his usual state of mind. His red and dilated eyes are focused on the two stacks of documents, deliberately avoiding direct contact with Tzabar.

"Sergeant Mark, I'm glad to see that you seem to have regained your composure. Your medical report shows no abnormalities," Tzabar says, glancing at one of the reports and then fixing his gaze on him.

He opens a file with Mark's photograph placed on top. "I expect you to provide a detailed account of what transpired during the mission, out loud."

"My Colonel, before I begin, I want to apologize for my behavior and that of my team. I cannot explain why we behaved that way. I take full responsibility and ask that you consider this when addressing my men," Mark says, looking directly at Tzabar, his tone severe but noticeably embarrassed. Tzabar remains stoic, coldly observing him. Mark swallows and continues.

"Some details may vary among us, but I assure you that everything in my report corresponds to reality," Mark states, pausing briefly to ensure he hasn't overlooked anything. He scans the faces of those gathered before him.

"Very well, Sergeant. Please proceed," Tzabar says.

"As we entered the black fog, we immediately confirmed the abnormal conditions described to us—the near-total absorption of light and

220

sound. Our special spotlights provided barely a meter of visibility. Even at a distance of fewer than 5 meters, we couldn't hear each other, even if we shouted," Mark says.

"The temperature was also incomprehensibly warm. Throughout the area, we recorded temperatures of eighteen to nineteen degrees Celsius. The ground consisted of smooth and polished rock, devoid of any gravel," Mark adds, pausing again to ensure he hasn't missed any details.

"We can now move on to the rescue operation and the individuals and bodies you've found. I am particularly interested in the new space you mentioned," Tzabar says, looking at one of the pages of the report open in front of him.

"Very well. After confirming that we had rescued all the individuals, I decided to investigate further, pushing toward the limit of our ropes. We progressed side by side, always maintaining a safe distance between us. As we neared the boundary of our rope's reach, Corporal Martin called out, having discovered something," Mark continues.

"When we joined him, we realized we were suddenly outside the black fog. Just like that, out of the darkness. Before us lay an expansive open space, vast and luminous, emitting a bright white light from every surface. We couldn't identify a specific source for the light," Mark describes, pausing again. Alvin hands him a bottle of water, and Tzabar scribbles some notes on Mark's report. After taking a sip, Mark resumes his account.

"The immense space seemed to have a rectangular configuration, with walls rising several dozen meters high. In the center stood a gigantic heptagonal monolith. Within this area, there was nothing else— just absolute silence.

"We detached the security cables to enter the space and left them attached to our backpacks at the edge of the fog," Mark adds.

Interrupting, Alvin asks, "And the size of this monolith? How tall was it, and what was it made of? None of the reports mentioned this information."

"Dr. Alvin, we couldn't determine the height because we couldn't see the top. As for the base, we measured about fifty steps on each side. We measured only two sides and assumed the rest were the same," Mark says.

"Thank you, Sergeant. Just a moment," Alvin replies. "And you can't determine the material it was made of?"

"Correct. We don't know the material. From a distance, it appeared as a uniform black mirrored surface. I couldn't discern if it was quartz, crystal, or glass. Closer up, it seemed like a single piece, black and glazed," Mark answers. Alvin takes notes in his notebook, exchanging glances with Tzabar.

"Sergeant, I still don't understand how you entered the monolith. Can you explain it to me?" Tzabar asks.

"I'll do my best, Colonel. But I confess I don't know how to explain it any better. We approached the monolith, and when we were almost touching it, we found ourselves inside. Just like that," Mark says.

"How did you get in? Was there a door? How?" Alvin asks in disbelief.

"I can't explain it. And I doubt any of my colleagues can either. We were just inside. But the most astonishing thing is what we found there," Mark says, pausing briefly before being interrupted by Alvin. "The mysterious sphere?"

"Exactly, sir. Before us was a massive black sphere floating in the air, less than a meter above the ground, rotating smoothly. Its diameter must have been over 15 meters," Mark describes. "It towered higher than a four or five-story building. At each corner of the monolith, we discovered seven smaller floating spheres, about half the size of the main one. Two of them had different rotations, while the others remained static. Besides the spheres, there was nothing else."

Alvin continues the questioning. "Did you notice any inscriptions, symbols, or anything else?"

"No, I'm sorry, but there was nothing else besides the spheres," Mark answers.

"Did you observe any mechanisms that could explain the floating of the sphere? What did it appear to be made of?" Alvin asks.

"Nothing seemed to be supporting the sphere. It was simply floating in the air, silent and serene. At first glance, it appeared to be a single piece of heavy, dark grey metal, with an almost fluid-like appearance," Mark explains.

Interrupting, Tzabar asks, "And what else? You were inside, surrounded by the floating spheres. What else do you remember?"

"I believe I included everything in my report," Mark continues his story. "We were all there, observing the sphere cautiously and approaching it slowly. Suddenly, it started vibrating, the intensity gradually increasing. In an instant, the vibration ceased, and we found ourselves surrounded by a silent swarm of numerous tiny spheres. We stood motionless, encircled by them. No one dared to make a move. After a few seconds, the mini-spheres retreated without any contact, noise, or indication of their departure. We remained there, astonished, discussing what we had witnessed.

We hadn't yet recovered from our nervousness and amazement when the light dimmed abruptly. Without realizing how, we began to float in the air, partially reclined as if in a dentist's chair. I didn't feel any fear, and I don't believe my comrades did either. We were all completely calm and at ease," Mark recounts, pausing midway with a deep sigh. It was a cherished memory for him.

"I apologize. We went through something incredibly unusual together, and it's challenging to articulate it clearly," he says, sitting up straight in his chair and taking a deep breath.

"Very well, Sergeant. I believe we all understand that you and your team had an extraordinary experience and that..." Tzabar is promptly interrupted by Mark.

"No. I'm sorry, sir, please. We didn't undergo anything terrible or traumatic, none of that. If I could describe it differently, I would say we were all blessed. But it was so intense that we can't put it into words. Not yet," Mark insists, looking at Tzabar earnestly.

"Please, let me continue. It might help you grasp what happened to us," Mark requests, catching his breath and continuing to speak. "So, we were all reclined, relaxed, facing the sphere. As we later realized, a voice emerged, distinct yet remarkably familiar to each of us. In my case, it was the voice of my wife. Corporal Martin heard the voice of his mother, who passed away last year. Igor heard his son's voice..." Mark struggles with the emotions that momentarily pause his words.

Tzabar decides not to intervene and patiently waits for Mark to gather himself and continue.

"The voice assured us that we were in no danger and that we would hear something of great importance. Perhaps due to the familiarity and tone of the voice, I don't know, but the fact is that we all felt an extraordinary sense of calm. I can't explain it. I've never experienced anything like it in my entire life," Mark says, his voice thick with emotion.

"Understood, Sergeant. Please continue," Tzabar urges, concerned that Mark might veer off into irrelevant details.

"I apologize, sir. The voice began by informing us that we were inside the Ark'num, the repository of the history of every civilization and human lineage that ever existed on planet Earth," Mark reveals, causing Tzabar and Alvin to exchange serious and uneasy glances.

"The information stored there dates back to the origins, all the way to the Anyfr," Mark continues, surprising them with knowledge of an entity he was not supposed to know about.

"Yes, you mentioned the Anyfr. Who are they?" Alvin asks, gesturing subtly to Tzabar.

"They are the origin. They once held dominion over most of the systems in the ancient universe," Mark answers.

Interrupting once again, Alvin probes further, "Ancient universe's systems? What systems? What universes?"

"I don't know how to explain it. I'm relaying what I was told. It's all engraved in my mind, even though none of it makes sense to me. Please allow me to continue. Perhaps it will become clearer as I proceed," Mark requests.

"As I mentioned, the Anyfr once held dominion over most of the systems in the ancient universe until an anomaly in their essence condemned them to a gradual decline that eventually led to their extinction. This essence transcends the reality of the Anyfr. It is the vital force of the universe, the foundation that maintains the balance of the initial universe," Mark explains.

"They had to find a solution in younger universes like ours to restore the balance. So they dispersed across galaxies and settled in the most favorable solar systems. When it was our galaxy's turn, they selected the K'tyrax system, our solar system, and chose three planets: Venus, Mars, and Earth. Only on Earth, which they refer to as T'ruzh, could they successfully establish the seed, a crucial process for restoring the essence's consistency," Mark elucidates, pausing momentarily as he locks eyes with Alvin, who signals that he has questions to ask.

Alvin writes the two names down — K'tyrax, T'ruzh — circling each one before he looks up.

"Mark, as you can imagine, I have numerous questions," Alvin begins. "What exactly are the seed and the essence? And why is the essence vital for restoring the seed?"

"I don't have all the details. I only know that the seed is specifically created based on the unique conditions of each planet, and only the seed allows for the rehabilitation of the essence. The Nyfrum's mission is to ensure the smooth progression of this entire process," Mark says.

Alvin becomes agitated, eager to ask the multitude of questions swirling in his mind. However, Tzabar intervenes before he has a chance. "Please, Dr. Alvin, let him continue. Take notes and save your questions for the end.

Some of your inquiries may be addressed as Sergeant Mark further describes the situation," Tzabar advises, motioning for Mark to proceed.

"Thank you, Colonel. As I mentioned earlier, only on Earth, or T'ruzh as they refer to it, was it possible to implant the seed. However, that alone wasn't sufficient.

The Nyfrum needed to enhance the conditions for the production of the energy, necessary to feed the essence. They required a more evolved form of life, a species that would provide the necessary energy quality and purity. It took some time before they eventually acquired the Nyfrid strain," Mark says, with a sigh of frustration, as Alvin interrupts him once again.

"I apologize for interrupting once more. In your report, you mentioned the sequence of Anyfr, Nyfrum, and Nyfrid. I just want to confirm the date you provided for the Nyfrum's arrival on Earth, approximately ten million years ago. Are you certain about this timeframe? And when you say 'received,' who received them?" Alvin asks, openly skeptical.

"Yes, Dr. Alvin, the information is accurate. I understand your skepticism regarding what you are hearing. It's an entirely new reality to grasp, I understand. The Nyfrum arrived on Earth over ten million years ago. Who received them, where, how — none of that came through. It's just... missing. Like a page torn out before I could read it. We weren't able to pose any questions," Mark replies.

"Sergeant," Tzabar cuts in, dropping his pen onto his desk and ceasing his note-taking. He places his head in his hands, looking down, overwhelmed by Mark's account. After taking a deep breath, he looks up at Mark, his gaze fixated on him.

"How can we verify the integrity of everything you have told us, both here and in your reports? What evidence do we have to support the existence of the Nyfrum?" Tzabar asks, uncertainty in his voice.

"Colonel, there is substantial evidence, a wealth of it. However, first, allow me to correct a possible misconception. The Nyfrum did exist, and they

226

continue to exist. They were the ones who made contact with us," Mark says.

Alvin looks at Tzabar in astonishment, while Kurt's emotions visibly stir upon hearing Mark's statement. Alvin can barely divert his gaze from Mark and mutters something under his breath, clearly troubled by the revelations.

Kurt is in shock, unable to find his voice. Only Mark remains composed, seemingly unfazed by the reactions he has stirred.

"Sergeant, if I understand correctly, the Nyfrum not only exists but also made contact with you?" Tzabar seeks clarification, trying to maintain some semblance of clarity.

"That is correct, Colonel. The Nyfrum are still present among us," Mark affirms, nodding nonchalantly, seemingly indifferent to the profound impact his statement has had.

"What are they like? Where are they?" Tzabar continues, attempting to gather more information.

"I do not know. We have not seen them or received any indications about their whereabouts. We only know that, for now, they prefer not to establish further contact with us," Mark says.

Alvin, visibly upset, rises from his seat. He mutters to himself, shakes his head, and paces the confined room like a caged lion.

"Sergeant, what else can you tell us about the Sdax, which is also referenced in your reports?" Tzabar asks, referring to the documents in front of him.

"They disclosed very little to us. Everything is detailed in the reports. The Sdax are a renegade faction of the Nyfrid strain, no longer under their control. They wander the universe, destroying and plundering all forms of life. We were warned to avoid them, and that is all," Mark adds.

"And what can you tell us about the Nyfrid?" Tzabar presses, seeking further information.

"I apologize, but they didn't provide much information about the Nyfrid either. Only that they exist." Mark hesitates. "One thing did stick with me, though. They called the Nyfrid 'intimately familiar with us.' Not 'them.' Not 'the humans.' Us. I've turned that phrase over more times than I can count, and I still don't know what to make of it."

Alvin's pen stops moving. He underlines the words in his notebook twice before looking up again.

"Thank you, Sergeant. You may go now. Please retire to your quarters. You will remain in isolation until we thoroughly analyze your reports. I do not want you disturbing the rest of the team," Tzabar instructs.

Mark stands up and leaves the room silently, his expression betraying embarrassment.

"Dr. Alvin, Captain, what do you propose we do now?" Tzabar asks as soon Mark leaves the room. "I am increasingly convinced that something is amiss here. They claim to have not seen anyone, only heard a voice, which could potentially be a recording. They have not provided us with any tangible evidence to substantiate their claims. While their stories align, it does not provide us with substantial assurance," Tzabar expresses, slumping in his chair, appearing downtrodden.

"Yes, but the references to entities he should not have known about were accurate. Moreover, he shed light on some of the unresolved references we had. The Essence, the Seed—it all seems to make sense now. Mark couldn't have fabricated any of this. We must conduct a thorough investigation on-site. We need to send a team to the monolith and verify the authenticity of their report," Alvin suggests.

Tzabar remains pensive, contemplating the situation in silence.

A knock on the door interrupts their conversation.

"Colonel, sir! Commander Chang is calling. It's urgent," a military officer announces, peering through the partially open door.

"Thank you. I will attend to it immediately," Tzabar says, straightening up in his chair.

"Dr. Alvin, I would like to have a conversation with you upon my return. Your proposal makes sense, and we need to clarify all of this. We'll take Sergeant Mark along with a reinforced security team. I don't want to underestimate any potential risks," Tzabar states as he rises from his seat and makes his way toward the exit.

"Excellent. We will thoroughly review the details of the reports and the information gathered from the interviews. This is all incredibly fantastic," Alvin replies, standing up with an enthusiastic smile.

#

"Where is Commander Chang?" Tzabar asks upon entering the communications room, finding two soldiers stationed at their respective screens and other electronic equipment.

"We received a special message from Commander Chang. He urgently wants to speak with you," one of the soldiers says, standing up and gesturing toward his laptop screen. "I'm sending a message to inform him that you're available," he adds before vacating his seat for Tzabar.

As soon as Tzabar settles into his chair, Commander Chang's image appears on the screen. "Good morning, Colonel. Congratulations. I've received your report, and I am greatly impressed.

What you've sent us surpasses even the highest expectations of command. As a result, we have decided to proceed immediately with the third phase protocol of our mission," Chang declares, wearing a satisfied smile.

"Commander, I'm not familiar with this third-phase protocol. I would prefer to wait for my final report. We still need to interview the members of the rescue team and conduct detailed on-site investigations tomorrow.

Only then can we fully validate the integrity and absolute importance of the information," Tzabar expresses his concern.

"Excellent, Colonel. I'm glad to hear that you're conducting this investigation. The reported information aligns with some existing data we have, further reinforcing the theories we've been working on," Chang responds with satisfaction, disregarding Tzabar's apprehension.

"Commander, I also wanted to inquire about the Denudasdi base as I previously mentioned. I still have no information about it," Tzabar asserts.

"Yes, Colonel. I understand your concern. Don't worry. You will receive all the information about the Denudasdi base.

That expedition was merely an ill-advised adventure pursued by the Foundation's scientific division. They have requested us to ensure the safety of the team and the facilities. We have no further obligations towards them," Chang states, his tone indicating his lack of interest in the matter. "However, I must admit that I am curious about the elements of our mission that have emerged there. And also the Denudasdi bodies you discovered today. It is quite peculiar, and I hope you can help provide a plausible explanation," he continues, allowing a brief moment of silence before Tzabar can interject.

"Well, let's proceed then. I will send you the details of the protocol. Phase Three was specifically designed for exceptional situations where global strategic interests may be at risk. In the case of our mission, the results already obtained far exceed these criteria. Therefore, we have decided to activate the Phase Three protocol immediately."

Chang forges ahead in his conversation, seemingly oblivious to Tzabar's perplexed expressions, who wrestles to grasp each word, finding himself unable to interject with any questions—such is the depth of his struggle to comprehend what the commander is saying.

"The instructions to prepare for the protocol have already been sent to you. Captain Kurt will assist you in the process. I must go now. Please continue your excellent work, Colonel. Once again, congratulations. Chang out," concludes Chang, leaving Tzabar with no opportunity to respond before his image disappears from the screen.

Tzabar exits the communications room and makes his way toward the main building, his mind diverted to the conversation with Commander Chang. Along the hallway, he encounters Kurt.

"Why wasn't I informed about the Phase Three Protocol?"

Kurt is taken aback by the bluntness of Tzabar's tone.

"Colonel, I honestly don't know. I've just received the instructions, but they only mentioned the logistical aspects of accommodating the new personnel and equipment. There was no mention of anything else," Kurt replies, surprise flickering in his voice. Tzabar scrutinizes him, suspecting that he may be concealing something.

"Captain Kurt, I hope you are being completely transparent with me. I want to see the details of this protocol, and we will discuss it further. Until then, follow the instructions you have received," Tzabar commands, his voice firm.

"Yes, Colonel. I will comply," Kurt says.

Returning to his room, Tzabar opens his laptop and finds an email with an attachment. As Kurt had mentioned, the email primarily focuses on logistical matters related to the arrival of personnel and equipment. However, another message catches Tzabar's attention. It is encrypted with a highly confidential seal. His expression freezes as he reads the first few lines of the message.

Attached to the message were two documents labeled "Burn After Reading." Tzabar opens the first document and leans back in his chair, his gaze fixated on the message displayed before him.

"Oh no... Johnny? It can't be..," Tzabar mutters, frustration and disbelief thick in his voice.

Aklujji Matu

A few meters away from the enigmatic black fog, Robert holds the rope, serving as the sole physical connection to John and Ross within the mysterious mist. Sitting nearby, Rachel and Marta anxiously observe the scene near the larger boulders.

"They've been inside for quite some time. I don't like this at all," Rachel says with a tone of anguish in her voice. "We can't hear or see anything from within. What do you think they could find in there?" she asks, her eyes fixed on the ominous black barrier in front of them.

"I have no idea. This is completely unprecedented for me. Let's hope Ross and John exercise caution and return swiftly," Marta responds with concern.

"I'm afraid John will get carried away and venture too far," Rachel confesses, pulling her jacket tighter and trembling with fear, seeking solace in her friend's embrace.

"How far do you think they've progressed?" Oswald asks, his attention drawn to the tightly held rope in Robert's grasp.

"I still have about half the length of the rope here, so I'd estimate they've covered around 100 meters," Robert answers, peering at the rope coiled around his foot. "Their pace appears steady. They momentarily paused a minute ago, but they've already resumed. Everything seems to be going well."

#

John and Ross carefully advance into the depths of the black fog, their steps cautious and measured.

"Ross, wait. There's something ahead of us. It resembles a wall," John whispers, signaling for Ross to join him.

232

"Yes, you're right. The surface is perfectly flat, and seems metallic." John examines the wall, running his hands along its smooth surface.

"You're right, it appears to be metallic, and it extends in both directions," Ross observes.

"It's a damn thing we can't see the entirety of it. What do you think it could be?" Ross ponders aloud.

"I have no idea. Let's continue skimming the surface and see where it leads," suggests John, tracing his fingers along the wall. "There's a corner up ahead! And another angle!"

"Okay, John, let's not get carried away. Slow down," Ross cautions, checking the tension of the rope. "I fear we're reaching the end of our rope, quite literally."

"Sorry, Ross. There's something extraordinary about this wall. Look at how the surface slopes inward. It brings to mind the image of a pyramid," John shares his observation excitedly.

"We can't see anything beyond this point. I'm not sure how much farther we can go. We must be reaching the limit of the cable," Ross exclaims abruptly, ignoring John's enthusiasm.

"No, Ross, it can't be. Not now. We have to find out what it is. We need more rope," insists John, determined to explore further.

"But we don't have any more rope, John. We can't proceed. We have to go back and bring more rope. What are you doing?" Ross realizes with horror that the rope attached to John is lying on the ground.

John appears in front of him. "Don't worry, mate. As long as I stay in contact with the wall surface, I'm ok. Stay here, I'll be back in a minute."

John pats Ross on the arm before disappearing into the black fog.

Ross is taken aback as he loses sight of John. "John, please don't go any farther. What the hell, man!" he shouts in frustration, gazing at the end of the rope dangling from his hand.

#

"There's something wrong with them," Robert remarks, feeling unexpected tugs on the rope he's holding.

"What's happening?" Oswald asks, approaching Robert.

Marta and Rachel hastily get up from their positions, noticing the growing concern.

"They've reached the end of the rope and stopped moving. I felt some pulling," Robert explains, glancing at the rope in his grasp.

"Oh, wait... I recognize the pattern. They're using Morse code."

"Let's make notes. Tell me what you receive," Oswald says, retrieving a small notebook from his pocket.

"What's going on?" Rachel and Marta join them, both looking anxious.

"Wait a moment. They're sending something in Morse code," Robert informs them, signaling for silence. They look with anticipation while he dictates the code he receives through the rope.

"Got it. I've responded that we received the message. What did they say?" Robert asks, eager to know the contents.

"They said everything is fine," Oswald reads from his notes, observing Rachel and Marta's worried expressions. "They've reached the limit of the rope. They're next to a wall, and John is exploring."

"But if they're at the end of the rope, how is John exploring? Did he let go of the safety rope? Is he out of his mind?" Rachel exclaims angrily, gripping Robert's arm.

"Calm down, Rachel. I trust that John knows what he's doing. Let me ask Ross where John is," Robert assures her, reaching for the rope once again.

#

"John! Damn it, where are you?" Ross shouts, gazing into the black void ahead, hoping to catch a glimpse of John's face.

He grasps the rope that connects him to his companions, prepared to release the carabiner and venture in search of John. Just as he is about to let go, he feels tugs from Robert.

Meanwhile, John continues running his hands along the surface, continuing his exploration. "Forty-six, forty-seven... shouldn't be much longer," he murmurs, extending his arm and feeling the surface with his right hand.

Taking a few more steps, he says with satisfaction, "Fifty-one, and there you have it. It must be a pyramid. Two sides with fifty steps, ninety-degree angles, leaning inward. It has to be a pyramid. What the hell are you doing here, my dear?"

#

"Ross is responding. Please take notes," Robert announces, refocusing his attention on the rope and translating the code he receives. Marta and Rachel can hardly contain their unease.

"Done. I hope I got it all correctly," Oswald states, concentrating on his writing. "John proceeded to investigate the wall they discovered. As long as he maintains contact with its surface, he should have no trouble returning. However, Ross is considering going to look for him, if he doesn't return in 10 minutes."

"No!" Rachel screams. "No. Please tell them to stay put. Captain, what can we do?"

#

"Twenty. Twenty-one, twenty-two..." John mutters, continuing his exploration. "Twenty-four, twenty-and... what? Already?" John is taken aback by a new angle that interrupts the wall's continuity.

"Damn it. One side with half the distance. It doesn't make sense." He keeps his left hand on the edge of the wall while stretching out his right hand to touch further.

"Stay calm," he mutters, uncertain of what to do next. "Don't lose contact with the wall. You can't get lost here.

Well, perhaps I was mistaken. You're not a pyramid. Let's keep following the wall and see what this is," he regains his composure, continuing to trace the surface.

#

"Ross says he's growing impatient and wants to break free to search for John," Robert says, sounding worried.

"No, please. He can't do that. Not him too," Marta pleads, frightened.

"I understand your worry, but I don't see any other option. They don't have any more ropes," Oswald comments, deep in thought.

"No. Please, tell Ross not to go. Captain, we need to find a way to bring them back," Rachel says, terrified.

"Stay calm. I have an idea for a safe rescue plan," Oswald assures them. "Robert, send this message to Ross. I have an idea that ensures everyone's safety."

"Do you think it will work? I'm not very confident," Rachel apprehensively comments to Marta as Oswald composes the message.

"In theory, it could work as long as the ground inside remains smooth and polished, as they mentioned. Just thinking about the black fog and what we might not see inside gives me chills," Marta says, uneasily rubbing her hands. "But I also can't picture myself staying here alone."

"Okay. Ross says he's on board with the idea," Robert relays the message.

"Excellent. Let's gather some small stones and fill our pockets. If we leave a trail of stones at each step, I believe it will be enough to guide us back. And we should take this rope with us. It might come in handy if we need to explore the area where they are," Oswald says, starting to pick up pebbles from the ground and filling his coat pockets.

#

Flynt emerges from the cliffs on the opposite side, where he started his exploration, and is surprised to discover his companions missing. He calls out, desperately hoping for a response.

Suddenly, a cluster of piled-up stones catches his attention. Among the stones, he notices a written message addressed to him.

#

The two women tightly grip the rope that binds them to Robert and Oswald. They walk in silence, with deep tension as they submerge themselves deeper and deeper into the black mist.

Ross anxiously awaits John's return, eagerly anticipating any movement he feels through the rope. He is so focused on the rope he holds in his hands that he doesn't even notice a slight movement in front of him.

"Ross, you're still here. Good," John startles Ross as he emerges from the darkness.

"Damn it, man! You scared the hell out of me. I didn't hear you coming. I'm furious with you. You should never have let go of the rope and ventured alone," Ross says, angry but also relieved to see John.

"Calm down, mate. Everything is fine. I can't explain it all right now; you have to see it for yourself," John says, buzzing with excitement.

"Wait. They're coming. They shouldn't be far behind. John, whatever you've found, you have to wait," Ross urges.

"What? Did you manage to convince Rachel and Marta to come inside? I can't believe it."

"No, man. You did!

We knew nothing about you. Rachel was worried when she heard you had let go of the rope. They found a safe way to reach us and brought the rope along. It might come in handy for us. And I can sense they're close by."

"Great. Even better. So we can all go together. You have to see what I've discovered," John says, his excitement building at the thought of showing everyone what he'd found.

"They're very close now. Over there, I see something," Ross points to a faint glimmer, attempting to penetrate the darkness.

"Guys, we're here! Come on, you're doing great!" John shouts, struggling to contain his excitement as his friends draw nearer.

"Ross, John, are you there? We still can't see you," Robert's voice echoes, straining to hear any response.

After a few moments, the group reunites. "John, where are you? I can't see you," Rachel calls, reaching out her hands to find him.

"I'm here, Rachel. I'm fine," John shouts, smiling as he finally feels Rachel's hands.

Awkwardly, they all attempt to find one another through the veil of darkness, inching closer to recognize each other.

"John..." Rachel says, and surprises him with a firm punch to the chest.

"Ouch! What the hell? Why did you punch me?" John shouts, bewildered by Rachel's sudden strike.

"I should hit you harder and more often! This is all your fault. We're in this mess because of you. I'm furious with you," Rachel yells, her anger dissipating slightly as she feels John's embrace.

"Calm down, my dear. Everything is fine. No, it's better than fine," John reassures, attempting to be heard by everyone. "Come on, follow me, you have to see what I found," John says, turning in the direction he came from, and pulling on Rachel's arm.

"Wait, we never discussed going any further. I thought we planned to come here and bring you back to safety," Marta shouts with anger.

"Marta, don't be afraid. We're safe here. And now I know where we're heading," John assures. "I promise you, there's nothing to fear, despite our lack of vision. I've already navigated the path without any difficulty, and what awaits us is beyond anything we could imagine.

We can use our ropes to continue. Trust me, as long as we stick together and stay in contact with the wall, we'll be safe."

Rachel and Marta, resigned to the will of their companions, also unable to resist the curiosity that stirs within them.

"So, this is the infamous wall. It feels metallic. How far have you walked?" Robert caresses the wall with his hands, following John's lead.

"Maybe more than a hundred meters. But what's even more astonishing is that there are no cracks or joints. It seems to be one solid piece," John explains. "As for the distance, I estimate about fifty steps on this side and another fifty on the adjacent face. But the real marvel lies at the end. Let's continue; there's a corner up ahead, and we need to turn ninety degrees here."

Robert relays John's words to the rest of the group as they follow along. Ross and Oswald bring up the rear, with Marta and Rachel in the middle.

"We're here. Are we all together? Please gather closely," John announces, anticipating his companions' reactions.

"Yes, we're all here," they reply, moving in as close as possible.

"Excellent. Now, get ready for the surprise of a lifetime. Just a few more steps, but be cautious. We have two steps going downward," John instructs.

Apprehensive but unable to resist their curiosity, they follow John's lead. Suddenly, they are dazzled by an unexpected burst of light. As their eyes adjust, they find John standing with open arms in the middle of a ramp within a colossal structure. The ramp descends into what appears to be an immense gallery.

The bare walls exude a dull metallic gray sheen, and an ethereal glow permeates the space, emanating from all directions.

John approaches Rachel and embraces her. "This has to be Aklujji Matu. It must be. Come, the real marvel awaits us downstairs in the gallery," he whispers, leading them down the ramp. They speak in hushed tones, awed into reverence. Upon reaching the base of the ramp and stepping into the expansive gallery, another surprise awaits them.

Hovering gracefully about a meter above the ground, a spherical entity of serene gray color rotates gently. The group stands in awe, contemplating the sight before them. John extends his arms towards the sphere, inviting their thoughts.

"What is this, John?" Marta asks, astonished by the spectacle.

"Is this the Aklujji Matu?" Ross places his arm around John's shoulder, a satisfied smile on his face.

"And how on earth does this sphere float without any visible means of support?" Robert gazes at the enigmatic object from a cautious distance, attempting to fathom the inexplicable phenomenon.

"It's astonishing. The sphere must be over ten meters in diameter," Oswald remarks, cautiously moving closer.

"Captain, please don't approach too closely. We have no idea what this is or if it poses any danger to us," Rachel anxiously urges, causing Oswald to halt a few feet away from the sphere's surface.

Undeterred by Rachel's warning, John moves closer, emboldened by Oswald's proximity. Ross and Robert follow suit, their curiosity irresistibly drawn to the mysterious sphere.

As John inches closer to the sphere's surface, hand outstretched, Rachel cries out in alarm. "John, what are you doing? Don't touch it!"

"Easy, Rachel. I have to try to comprehend this enigma," John reassures, his determination unwavering.

Robert and Ross, equally drawn by the curiosity, cautiously follow him.

As they approach, the sphere initiates a gentle vibration, prompting them all to halt in their tracks. A tense silence envelops the gallery, anticipation hanging in the air. After a few suspenseful seconds, with no discernible change, John ventures a bit closer.

Suddenly, the sphere undergoes a remarkable metamorphosis, fragmenting into numerous smaller spheres that encircle him, moving in perfect harmony.

John extends his hand, attempting to touch some of the spheres. Yet, they gracefully evade his touch, maintaining a subtle distance. Ross and Robert join him in their wonderment, captivated by the spellbinding interaction.

Marta and Rachel, frozen in both fear and fascination, watch in breathless terror as the cloud of spheres envelops their comrades, a mesmerizing spectacle unfolding before their eyes.

Oswald observes the extraordinary phenomena unfolding a few meters away, torn between curiosity and apprehension, hesitant to venture forward.

"There is no need to worry. Remain calm. There is no danger," assures John, his face lit up with fascination as he continues to be captivated by the mesmerizing swarm of orbs encircling them.

"Rachel, Marta, please come. It's perfectly safe," urges Ross, doing his best to sound reassuring as he tries to persuade the hesitant duo.

Oswald cautiously edges closer, maintaining a cautious distance from the spheres, still unsure of their nature and intentions.

"Don't be afraid. They pose no harm," Robert chimes in, his voice firm with conviction. Marta, however, succumbs to panic, their screams piercing the air. Overwhelmed with nervous tears, she recoils and attempts to fend off the spheres as if they were pesky mosquitoes.

She retreats towards the ramp, distancing herself from the ethereal cloud that now surrounds Rachel and Oswald.

"Marta! John is right. There is no danger. Come, join us," Rachel calls out, astonishment and reassurance both in her voice. Marta looks at them with suspicion, shaking her head in refusal, unable to accept their safety.

Robert approaches Marta to calm her down. Behind him, the swarm of spheres regrouped again in the great sphere, resuming their serene rotation, devoid of any human presence.

Marta watches, frozen with terror, as her companions vanish within the sphere's embrace.

"Where are they? What is happening?" Marta wails in distress, panic seizing her senses. Robert approaches her with a smile, extending his hand in an inviting gesture, strangely unaffected by the disappearance of their companions.

"Marta, my dear, there is no danger. Trust me, they are fine. Please come with me," he pleads, his tone inviting and gentle. But his words have the opposite effect, she looks at him with terror, recoiling in fear.

"Marta, come back here! What is the matter with you?" he shouts, growing increasingly concerned as he sees her sprint up the ramp, heading towards the exit and the beckoning black fog. Worried for her safety, he races after her.

"Marta, don't be foolish!" Robert cries out, desperately attempting to dissuade her. "Don't enter the fog!" Panic cracks through his voice as he realizes that she no longer hears him, vanishing into the mist without a backward glance, disappearing from his sight.

"Marta! Please, come back!" he implores, stepping hesitantly into the mist, but not daring to venture further than a few steps. For agonizing moments, he waits, screaming her name in the hope of a response, but it is in vain. Marta is gone, swallowed by the enigmatic haze.

A solitary tear trails down Robert's face as he mutters, "Marta... Marta!" His scream, full of despair and anguish, echoes back through the fog. He takes a tentative step further into the haze, only to retreat frustrated into the dim light.

Robert casts a longing glance behind him as if anticipating the arrival of a companion to aid him in this disorienting situation. "Marta!" he bellows once more, his voice saturated with despair, as he gazes into the black fog that obscures his vision.

#

"Damn it. No. No. They won't capture me," Marta mutters frantically, her fear propelling her forward. "I have to find a way out of here. Why on earth did I embark on this mission? Screw all of this."

After running for a few meters in the opaque darkness, she halts abruptly, her arms outstretched as she searches for something to grasp onto. "Damn it, which direction should I go? I can't see a damn thing. I don't even know where I came from. Fuck!" Marta sobs, panic gripping her heart as she realizes she is engulfed in an impenetrable, suffocating darkness in every direction. Tears stream down her face, mingling with her anguish.

#

"Rachel, are you alright? Rachel, wake up," John crouches down, holding Rachel's shoulders gently. Nearby, Oswald and Ross begin to stir, gradually awakening from their slumber. Rachel regains her composure and attempts to rise with John's assistance.

Where are we?" she asks, confused, as she looks at John. "What in the world just happened?"

"I have no idea. But it seems like we've entered a different space. This one feels more expansive and illuminated. And now we have these additional smaller spheres," John points to the seven orbs surrounding the largest one.

"Does anyone know what happened and where we are?" Rachel scans her surroundings, concern etched on her face. "Where are Marta and Robert?"

"I don't know. All I remember is feeling the spheres envelop me, and then I was swept away by something inexplicable," Oswald replies, his expression reflecting his perplexity.

"I felt disconnected from myself as if floating through the universe, liberated from all worries."

"I experienced something similar. I've never felt so serene in my entire life," Rachel says. "Let's assume Marta and Robert are safe for now. Marta was horrified by the spheres."

"Perhaps Robert is with her. We'll trust that they're alright," Ross suggests, approaching John, who remains uncharacteristically silent. They gather at the center of the space, where the massive sphere hovers in silence. "I'm losing all sense of what's happening," Ross confesses. "I'm intrigued by these spheres. Are they made of metal?"

"I didn't get a chance to touch any of them, not even the smaller spheres surrounding us," John says, disappointed.

"I couldn't touch them either, and I agree with you, they do appear metallic. The gray color with that slightly opaque shine reminds me of mercury," Rachel adds, her gaze fixed on the space between the larger sphere and the floor. "And the fact that it floats still baffles me."

"It's also intriguing how those two smaller ones rotate, and in different directions and speeds," Ross observes, his curiosity piqued.

"But this larger one has a different appearance. It seems darker and less reflective. Have you noticed that it appears to vibrate? When you look at the edge of its surface, it almost seems like it's jiggling," Oswald comments, drawing closer to the larger sphere.

"You're absolutely right. Not only does it appear to vibrate visually, but I can also sense the vibrations in my body," John confirms.

"Yes, I can feel it too," Rachel agrees, a contemplative expression on her face.

"Wait!"

An unfamiliar voice suddenly captures their attention, making them turn their gaze toward the smaller spheres.

"Please, do not approach it." A stranger shouts, surprising them with his sudden presence. He is dressed in a long white tunic and has long black hair, dark skin, and slightly almond-shaped eyes.

"What in the world... who is this?" Ross retreats, startled, as he finds himself closest to the stranger.

"Do not be afraid. You mustn't approach this sphere. There is no time for explanations. Please, come with me," the stranger insists, urgency sharpening every word.

"Who are you? And why should we avoid the larger sphere? What's the problem?" John eyes the stranger suspiciously.

"I will explain everything, there's no time now. Please, come with me," the stranger urges, pointing towards the smaller sphere standing beside him.

"John, I'll clarify everything, but we mustn't delay," adds the stranger, causing John's confusion to deepen when he hears him pronounce his name.

"Rachel, Ross, Oswald, there is no time to waste. Follow me," the stranger continues, inviting them towards the smaller sphere.

They exchange glances, astonished by the fact that the stranger knows their names.

They cautiously approach the enigmatic stranger. The vibration of the sphere decreases in intensity as it moves further away. Rachel hesitates but finally decides to inch forward, muttering to herself, "Damn, I can't stay here alone.

Conflict

It is the early morning as Tzabar and Kurt lead the investigation team towards the edge of the black mist. As they approach the cluster of rocks before the fog, anticipation weighs on the team, dampening their spirits. Silence envelops them, broken only by the relaxed demeanor of Sergeant Mark.

"Rest assured," he says. "There's no risk as long as we follow the safety protocols and keep the safety ropes in place."

Fear of the unknown casts shadows on everyone's faces. Tension hangs thick in the air, keeping them alert and focused on the task ahead. They secure their carabiners to the safety cables, preparing to get into the fog.

"Wait, I'm joining the team as well. I want to see the mysterious sphere up close," Tzabar declares, surprising them as he attaches his carabiner.

"My colonel, we didn't plan for this. You shouldn't participate in an undefined risk mission." Kurt objects, attempting to dissuade Tzabar.

"I'm equally taken aback, but I see no major issues. You're more than welcome to join us," Alvin says.

"Captain Kurt, there's no need to protest. I'm determined to accompany you, and unless Commander Chang intervenes, no one will stop me." Tzabar responds with a determined smile.

The eight-team members double-check their safety equipment and prepare to enter the fog when a familiar sound grabs their attention. A low vibration reverberates, shaking their surroundings and causing Tzabar to give Kurt a concerned look. The pulsating noise grows louder, capturing the attention of the entire team. Tzabar beckons Kurt closer.

"Do you hear that noise? It sounds like helicopters approaching, and more than one. Were we expecting any arrivals today?" Tzabar questions.

"I don't know. I'm just as surprised," Kurt mutters, shrugging his shoulders.

"Colonel, Captain, what's happening? Are we expecting someone? I haven't received any information about any arrivals," Alvin exclaims.

"Captain, come with me. Let's find out what's going on," Tzabar commands, freeing himself from the harness and heading towards the base, followed closely by Alvin.

When they exit the tunnel, at the base of the mountain, they are received by the noise from the helicopters, causing the entire area to tremble. As they gain visibility of the base, they spot two transport helicopters on the helipad, their rotors still spinning. A group of men unloads wooden boxes from the aircraft.

Tzabar gets on Kurt's snowmobile, followed by Alvin's, and they speed down towards the base.

Commander Chang stands at the top of the base entrance stairs, accompanied by two soldiers, observing the activity of his men. Tzabar and Kurt slow down to observe the frenzied scene unfolding before them. Meanwhile, Alvin rushes ahead toward Commander Chang.

Victor and Lydia emerge from another building and approach Alvin, engaged in a heated argument and wild gestures. Alvin tries to calm them down, all the while keeping his gaze fixed on Chang.

Due to the noise of the helicopters, Tzabar cannot hear their conversation. Lydia continues to argue with Alvin, who now shoots an angry look at Tzabar and Kurt. Ignoring Lydia's words, Alvin takes a step toward Chang, leaving her behind, still talking.

Two armed soldiers block his path at the stair entrance. Alvin attempts to persuade them to let him through but to no avail. Tzabar and Kurt approach, passing by the soldiers without any hindrance, which only fuels Alvin's anger. Tzabar signals to the soldiers to let Alvin pass.

"Good morning, Commander Chang. I wasn't expecting you so soon," Tzabar greets as he approaches Chang.

"Commander Chang, what's going on?" Alvin shouts as he gets closer. "Why did you cut off our communications? Why don't we have access to our labs?"

Chang focuses his attention on the commotion near the helicopters, feigning ignorance of their questions. One of his guards brings something to his attention, directing his gaze toward the three newly arrived men.

"Dr. Alvin. I'm glad you're here. Please come inside," Chang invites, ignoring Alvin's irritation.

"You, escort Dr. Alvin to the meeting room," he orders one of the soldiers. "Dr. Alvin, it will only take a minute. I will join you shortly. I need to have a word with the colonel."

He turns his back on Alvin, who is dragged into the facilities while casting an uncomfortable glance back.

"Colonel Tzabar, Captain, where have you been?" Chang asks, looking annoyed.

"My commander, we were with the investigation team, as we discussed yesterday. We were to investigate the monolith," Tzabar says, taken aback by Chang's harsh tone.

"But I didn't expect you to participate in the expedition. I need you here right now," Chang retorts rudely, shifting his gaze to Kurt. "Captain, I need you to oversee the equipment placement. Captain Alfonso is waiting for you. I want everything ready for the helicopters to depart in 20 minutes."

"Yes, sir," Kurt acknowledges with a salute and proceeds down the stairs.

"Colonel, come with me. I'll give Alvin a few minutes of my attention, and then we'll talk. We have urgent matters to discuss," Chang instructs, leading the way into the meeting room, where Alvin waits impatiently.

"Dr. Alvin, thank you for your patience," Chang greets as he enters the room, suddenly putting on an unconvincing smile, and sits across the table from Alvin. Tzabar sits next to him, still struggling to grasp the situation.

"Commander Chang, I would like to know what's going on. Why do we no longer have access to communications and our laboratories?" Alvin asks, his tone still aggravated.

"Dr. Alvin, I understand your unease. But first, let me congratulate you and our team on the achievements thus far," Chang remarks, managing to elicit a subtle smile from Alvin.

"We are all extremely excited and have high expectations for the ongoing investigations. The data we've received in the recent reports confirms information we were already aware of from other sources," he explains, leaving Alvin stunned, barely able to articulate a question.

"That's why the Foundation's board has activated the Special Protection Directive, the Phase Three Protocol."

"Commander Chang, I don't understand what you're saying. What is this Phase Three Protocol?"

"All decisions made by the Foundation's board are aimed at ensuring the success of our mission and the safety of all staff involved," Chang clarifies, struggling to break through Alvin's skeptical gaze.

"Commander, please. I understand that the protocol is meant to ensure our security. But what kind of security measures are we talking about in our case? What risks should we expect?"

"Dr. Alvin, the Phase Three Protocol is implemented in times of extreme global strategic risk.

Based on the most recent data, which confirms previous warnings, our board has deemed it necessary to implement the Phase Three Protocol. Unfortunately, I am unable to provide any further information due to the strict confidentiality requirements associated with the protocol,"

Chang presses on, attempting to bring the conversation to a close as quickly as possible.

"Commander Chang..." Alvin begins, only to be abruptly interrupted by Chang, who raises his voice and suddenly gains a serious cold look.

"Dr., please. I understand your discomfort. However, my duty takes precedence above all else, and I expect my subordinates to follow my orders without hesitation."

Alvin is taken aback by the sudden shift in Chang's demeanor and becomes increasingly frustrated by the situation, which he still struggles to comprehend. Tzabar remains stoic and silent, observing their expressions while keeping his thoughts concealed.

"Dr. Alvin, I request your full attention to what I am about to convey," Chang's voice changes, becoming deeper. "Effective immediately, I assume full command of the mission, and all elements will answer directly to me. All permissions for departures or arrivals are rescinded. No one is to leave or enter the mission compound without explicit permission. All communications are restricted and will be conducted solely by military personnel."

Alvin looks as if he could explode at any moment, his composure cracking. Tzabar remains silent, attempting to decipher the commander's intentions. Chang continues, outlining a long list of restrictions.

"All data, findings, reports, and information collected during this mission, both past and future, will be transferred to Colonel Tzabar," Chang continues, pointing to a surprised Tzabar.

"Anyone found transmitting information, data, or any form of communication outside the authorized channels will be confined and may face investigations and disciplinary actions," Chang concludes, imposing a stern tone. Alvin seethes with anger, his face flushed, as he stares at Chang and Tzabar, struggling to contain his fury.

"That will be all, Dr. Alvin," Chang snaps, recovering the cynical smile. "You should have already received a document containing the new instructions and restrictions for all mission members. We must work together to implement this protocol successfully," Chang adds, rising from his seat. Alvin remains red-faced and breathing heavily, at a loss for words. Tzabar stands tall and silent.

Chang strides toward the room's door without acknowledging Alvin, opens it, and then coldly gazes at him.

"And that concludes our discussion, for now, Dr. Alvin. Thank you for your understanding and commitment to this mission's success."

Alvin exits the room slowly, without glancing back. Chang closes the door and walks towards the window, purposely avoiding eye contact with Tzabar. "Colonel, I want you to oversee the implementation of the Phase Three Protocol."

"Understood, sir. Dr. Alvin and his team may encounter difficulties accepting the new terms," Tzabar remarks.

"And who cares?" Chang shouts, turning towards him. "They have no choice but to accept it, period. In any case, it's your problem now." Chang's tone abruptly changes, and he takes a momentary pause, retrieving a cigar from his shirt pocket and gently rolling it between his fingers.

"I need your help to understand what is happening here," Chang says, lighting the cigar and looking at Tzabar through the cloud of smoke he exhales.

"I need you to return to the sphere, and you will lead the contact group. I expect a detailed report as soon as you return," Chang declares, straightening up in his chair and gripping the cigar tightly between his fingers. "Prepare yourself and return to that sphere. We cannot afford to waste any more time," he adds, turning his back to Tzabar and facing the window, before the latter can respond, he says coldly, "You're dismissed. You can leave now."

Tzabar exits the room silently, making his way to the small private military bar; he needs a drink.

This time he surprises whoever opens the door with a dry grunt and a fleeting greeting, immediately heading towards the small counter.

"Captain, Sergeant, good to see you both here. Let's have a drink; it's on me."

"What did the commander want this time? Any further issues?" Kurt asks, reacting to Tzabar's visible bad mood.

"Nothing unusual. He's focused on the investigations regarding the sphere and the implementation of the new protocol," Tzabar replies, opting not to divulge further details.

"And how are the civilians responding to the new protocol?"

"Not well, as you might expect, Captain," Tzabar raises his glass, quickly downs the drink, and places it back on the bar with a clatter.

"Alright then, let's get to it," he says, surprising those present with his recovered determination.

"Captain, gather your team; we depart in fifteen minutes," he says, acknowledging those present with a subtle gesture and heading toward the exit.

#

"So, what do you think? Did I exaggerate?" Mark asks eagerly, his gaze fixed on the towering monolith. Tzabar and the rest of the team remain silent, awe-struck by the incredible sight before them.

"This is even more astonishing than you described," Kurt states, staring in wonder at the magnificent structure.

"Let's take a thorough look around here," Tzabar instructs, carefully exploring the entire area surrounding the monolith. "Confirm that there's nothing else in this space."

"I don't see anything else here," Kurt reports.

"Alright, Sergeant. As you stated, inside this is the Ark'num, correct?" Tzabar asks, fixated on the monolith.

"Yes sir, correct. The sphere inside is said to be the Ark'num," Mark explains.

"Very well. Sergeant, before we move forward, please elaborate on what happened when you entered the monolith. Help us understand how you ended up inside. Consider other possibilities as well," Tzabar prompts, leaving Mark deep in thought.

"You're right, Colonel. I hadn't considered other possibilities, but I don't see any other explanation. We simply approached the surface," Mark answers, taking a few steps forward.

"Wait, Sergeant. Let's proceed with caution. First, explain the exact steps you took," Tzabar requests.

"Colonel, that was it... We approached it, almost touching the surface, and we're inside, I think...," Mark says, now with a sudden and unexpected doubt in his eyes.

"Well, there's only one way to find out. Right?" Kurt suggests, eager to move forward.

"Agreed. Let's proceed," Tzabar says, letting himself be carried away by the enthusiasm of the mystery, his gaze fixed on the surface of the monolith.

"Marvelous, let's go," Mark exclaims with enthusiasm, confidently advancing toward the monolith. Tzabar and Kurt follow closely, anticipating the cold contact with the monolith's surface.

"How..." Kurt begins to speak but is interrupted by the sudden change of surroundings. He looks around, astonished by the new space they find themselves in. Tzabar stands beside him, equally amazed.

"And here we are. Just as I explained, we are inside, the large floating sphere, surrounded by the smaller ones," Mark says, pointing at the spheres.

"You were right, Sergeant. I can't comprehend what just happened," Tzabar admits, unable to take his eyes off the floating sphere.

"According to your report, you approached the large sphere. Did anyone approach the smaller spheres?"

"No, sir. As far as I recall, no one approached them. The largest sphere immediately captivated our attention. After making contact, we left the room promptly. I don't believe anyone approached any of these smaller spheres," Mark answers.

"Alright. So, now we need to approach the large sphere, correct?" Kurt asks, taking a step forward, equally fascinated by the huge globe in front of him.

"Wait, Captain. Let me explore this area first," Tzabar suggests, walking towards the smaller spheres. "I'm curious about these spheres. We already know what to expect from the big one. But what purpose do these smaller ones serve?"

"I have no idea," Mark remarks, approaching Tzabar followed by Kurt.

"Gentlemen, this sphere is vibrating, small spheres are coming out of this one," Tzabar observes, standing still near the small globe.

Without being able to have any reaction, a swarm of small spheres surrounds them.

Mark is the first to regain his senses. He carefully gets up, feeling dizzy, and looks at Tzabar and Kurt a few feet away, still lying on the floor. "Colonel, are you alright? What the hell happened?"

"I'm fine, Sergeant. Are you both okay?" Tzabar asks, sitting down and looking disoriented.

"I'm alright, just a little seasick. But this isn't what happened to us before," Mark comments.

"We're in a different place," Tzabar realizes, getting up and surveying their surroundings.

"You're right, Colonel. There's only a large sphere, a smaller area, and a ramp down there," Mark points out.

"So, we've figured out the purpose of the smaller spheres. Could they be transport portals? Could they be the reason behind the fate of the missing teams?" Tzabar speculates. "It's the only explanation I can come up with for now."

He looks towards the ramp where Mark is heading. Curiosity and fear drive them forward trailing behind the sargeant.

"And there's that black fog again," Kurt notes, looking up at the end of the ramp. "I'm not going inside that."

"Let's turn back. I want to investigate the larger sphere," Tzabar suggests, retracing his steps.

"This big sphere looks different to me," Mark observes. "It seems smaller, and the color and texture have changed."

"Mark, Sergeant Mark, please stop and step back a bit. The sphere has started vibrating, and now I need some more time to observe, before being sent to I don't know where...," Tzabar cautions, grabbing Mark's arm.

"Notice how the texture has changed. It has become darker and more opaque," Mark comments, stepping back with suspicion.

"I agree with you, Sergeant. My theory is that this must be a transport portal. It could allow us to return inside the monolith. We need to understand how these spheres work," Tzabar concludes.

"And if not?" Kurt questions.

"If not, we'll find out soon. Regardless, we can't stay here. I have no clue where we are," Tzabar says, already moving toward the sphere.

"Well, it seems like it's decided. Let's confirm the colonel's theory," Mark says with a sigh of concession.

They approach the sphere cautiously. Once again, a multitude of tiny spheres envelops them. They gaze in awe at the spheres, with Mark and Kurt attempting to touch them, but finding it futile.

Something catches Tzabar's attention, diverting his gaze from the swarm of spheres. He notices someone lurking towards them at the base of the ramp. And everything disappears into dry, cold darkness.

As he gradually regains consciousness, Tzabar looks around, the image of the figure on the ramp etched in his mind. Mark and Kurt are still lying on the floor, dazed, struggling to sit up.

"Guys, it seems like we were right," Mark breathes, his eyes gleaming with excitement.

"Colonel, how are you?" Kurt notices Tzabar's strange expression.

"Yeah, I'm alright. It's nothing," Tzabar replies, his thoughts still wandering by the figure he saw earlier. "Gentlemen, now we know what the smaller spheres do. It's time to investigate the big sphere."

"Let's proceed, Colonel. This one hasn't gotten us anywhere before. Let's see what happens now," Mark confidently approaches the sphere, and a strong vibration resonates all over the place. This time there are no spheres surrounding them.

Gradually, their bodies begin to recline, suspended in the air, just as Mark had described. Tranquility and surrender wash over their senses. A familiar voice echoes in Tzabar's mind. "Melissa..." he utters softly, a smile forming on his face before he succumbs to deep sleep.

Revelation

Three bodies lie on futons in a metallic room, surrounded by a gray space devoid of windows, doors, or any other objects. A fourth person sits silently on the floor by the wall, with his head tucked between his bent knees. One of the three individuals wakes up, looking around in a dazed state. The other two also awaken, equally surprised and confused.

"How are you guys? Do you know where we are?" asks the first person.

"I don't know. I'm completely disoriented. And you, captain? Any idea where we are?" responds Rachel.

"No, Rachel, I have no clue. I just regained consciousness seconds before you guys. And you, John, how are you feeling?" asks the captain.

"I'm alright. But what's going on with Ross? Buddy, what's the matter?" John asks.

"I'm fine. Just confused, that's all," Ross reassures them.

"Where is the stranger? Have you seen him?" Rachel asks, scanning the room.

"No, I haven't seen anyone yet. I was just waiting for all of you to wake up," Ross explains.

Suddenly, they are startled by the voice of the stranger. "Hello. We hope you are feeling comfortable."

"Where did you come from? Who are you?" Rachel demands, eyeing him suspiciously.

"What on earth happened earlier? What was the problem with the big sphere?" John asks, stepping forward to protect Rachel.

"You have nothing to fear. You are safe here," assures the stranger, maintaining his disconcerting serenity.

"Allow me to introduce myself. My name is Suluk, and I am an emissary of the Sdax," he explains. "I intervened because you were in danger near the Nyfrum's Ark'num. You are warmly welcomed to Abulkur."

"Suluk? Wait, I know that name and Abulkur…," John blurts, astonished, emerging from his initial daze and staring at the enigmatic man. "Suluk was one of the Inuit from the Russian Arctic mission. You vanished in the 1800s..."

"Yes, that is correct," Suluk acknowledges with a slight chuckle. "The Sdax took me in, and ever since, I have lived under their protection."

"I don't know how old you were at the time, but if you're still alive now, you must be over 150 years old. How is that possible?" John asks, unable to wrap his head around it.

"No way. He doesn't even look over 30," Rachel murmurs, eyes fixed on Suluk in disbelief.

"I can assure you that the environment provided by the Sdax is exceptionally health-promoting," Suluk responds, laughter dancing in his voice. "John came close. I am 159 years old, as of last month. I understand your skepticism." Suluk says, gesturing for them to follow him as a new room materializes where a wall previously stood. They exchange suspicious glances, but Suluk's calm demeanor and soothing tone alleviate their fears.

"Alright, let's address these matters. Speculating here won't get us anywhere," John asserts, leading the way toward the room where Suluk awaits. Inside, they discover a different ambiance—simple yet pleasant, with light tones of orange, blue, and white prevailing.

Four rectangular columns ascend to the ceiling, positioned as if they were the room's corners in a square shape. Adjacent to the columns, four large squares pique their curiosity, their purpose unclear.

"These are ergonomic chairs that adapt to your preferred seating position for optimal comfort," Suluk explains, settling into one of the armchairs encircling a low table.

"I will attempt to answer some of your questions now. Who would like to begin?" Suluk asks.

"I can start," Rachel speaks up before anyone else. "Where are we? What are we doing here? And what danger were you referring to earlier?"

"Very well, Rachel. Let's address your questions. You are currently in Abulkur, the Sdax house.

"Sdax house? What on earth is that? Who are the Sdax?" Oswald asks, unable to contain his curiosity.

"Abulkur and Sdax, wait a minute," John adds, now fully awake. "Those names ring a bell. Abulkur, the enigmatic city, and the Sdax, I believe they were mentioned in the old Inuit descriptions."

"Correct. I assume you're referring to Kunuk, the Inuit elder. He was my father," Suluk says, a touch of nostalgia coloring his voice.

"So, Abulkur actually exists? Are we really in Abulkur?"

"Yes, Marta, we are currently in Abulkur," Suluk confirms.

"Is it true that Abulkur lies within the Earth's interior and has seven gates?" John asks.

"Yes, that is true. Abulkur is located in an underground realm, approximately one kilometer below the Earth's surface. However, explaining the intricacies of its existence is a bit more complex. We will delve deeper into that later. There is much more to the city than mere legends and myths."

Marta is the first to react. "But who exactly are the Sdax?"

"You'll have your answer, Marta — but it only makes sense once you have the rest of it, and Rachel asked first." Suluk settles back into the armchair and lifts two fingers toward the low table between them. The surface dims, and a point of light blooms above it, unfolding into a slow, churning field of color, somewhere between a nebula and a flame.

"It all starts here. The first Universe — the one every universe after it, including yours, grew out of. There's no time in it, no matter, not as you'd recognize them. What holds it together is something we call the Essence."

"The soul of it," John says, watching the light shift.

"As good a word as any. Picture it that way if it helps." Suluk inclines his head. "But the Essence isn't static. It goes through cycles — periods of imbalance. And the being whose existence depends on it most, the dominant entity in that first Universe, is the Anyfr."

The light at the table's center splits. One half stays the slow nebula; the other condenses into a single bright point.

"The Anyfr's whole existence is tied to the Essence staying balanced," Suluk continues. "So when it falls out of balance, they restore it. They feed it. And the only way to feed it is to harvest energy from other universes — universes they cultivate, the way you'd tend a field."

"Hold on." John leans forward. "Cultivate how? What kind of energy are we talking about?"

"I'm getting there." A faint smile. "When the Anyfr began harvesting this universe — yours — something went wrong. The energy they drew out came back contaminated. Tainted with matter, with time. Two things the first Universe was never built to hold."

"Contaminated how badly?" Rachel asks. Whatever wonder was in her voice a moment ago is gone now.

"Badly enough that no one — not even the Sdax — knows exactly what it would mean if the imbalance went unchecked. The fear is that it could collapse the first Universe entirely, and pull every universe descended from it down with it. Including this one."

For a moment nobody speaks. The light above the table pulses once, slow, like a heartbeat.

"Okay," Oswald says finally, rubbing his face. "So what does any of that have to do with us? With Earth?"

"Everything." Suluk gestures again, and the bright point of light — the Anyfr — throws off a smaller spark, which begins to orbit it. "The energy itself comes from violent events. Stars dying. Black holes. Whole universes, used up and discarded, one after another, the way you'd strip a field bare and move to the next. But the Anyfr can't exist outside that first Universe. So they made something that could. They call it the Nyfrum."

The small spark of light steadies, brightens.

"The Nyfrum do the harvesting. That's their purpose. Raw energy, in bulk — that's most of what they collect. But there's a second kind, rarer, purer. It comes from beings with a soul, a consciousness, at the exact moment they die — especially if that death is sudden, violent. Untainted by matter, the Anyfr call it. And they crave it."

Rachel's hand tightens on the arm of her chair. "You're saying — planets. Living planets, full of people. That's where this... purer energy comes from."

"Earth is exactly the kind of planet the Nyfrum look for," Suluk says, and for the first time something like reluctance creeps into his voice. "When they've exhausted everything else, they come to places like this. They engineer extinction events — catastrophes large enough to wipe out almost everything — and harvest the energy that's released. Then they reseed the planet. Start the evolution over. Wait for it to mature again. And when it does—"

"They do it again," Marta finishes quietly.

"Until the planet is used up entirely, yes." Suluk lets the silence sit for a moment before going on.

"But over the cycles, the Nyfrum learned something. The more developed the consciousness at the moment of death, the purer the energy. So they started refining the process — seeding planets not just with life, but with life capable of complex thought. Engineering it, generation after generation, toward something with a far richer inner life than anything that had come before. They called this new strain the Nyfrid."

The orbiting spark of light divides again — dozens of smaller points now, scattering outward like seeds.

"And it worked," Suluk says. "Better than the Nyfrum intended. On some planets, the Nyfrid didn't just become more conscious. They became something the Nyfrum hadn't accounted for — self-aware enough to understand what was being done to them, and to each other, across the cycles. They reached a kind of collective understanding. That was the beginning of the Sdax — the next evolutionary step beyond the Nyfrid."

The scattered points of light on the table dim, one by one, until only a handful remain — and one of those, smaller and dimmer than the rest, sits closer to the center than any other.

"The Sdax took on a role the Nyfrum never planned for," Suluk says. "Guardians. Wherever a Nyfrid strain was seeded and given time to grow, the Sdax would watch over that world — and when the Nyfrid reached the level of evolution the Sdax themselves had once reached, they'd step in. Help them survive what was coming."

"Earth," Rachel says, looking at the small, dim point of light closest to the center.

"Earth," Suluk agrees. "Right now, the Nyfrum are preparing for the next harvest, and the Sdax are doing what they've always done — trying to help the local strain reach the threshold where we can step in openly. The Nyfrum know this. They spend their efforts suppressing exactly that — the uprisings the Sdax help set in motion, anything that might let your strain reach that threshold before the next harvest comes due."

"Wait." John's voice is quieter now. "The local strain. The Nyfrid. You said the Nyfrum spent the longest refining that one — seeding it, cultivating it, generation after generation, toward something with a richer inner life than anything before. You're not talking about some species out there somewhere. Are you."

Suluk looks at each of them in turn, and for once there's nothing playful in his expression.

"No, John. The Nyfrid are humans."

The light above the table goes still.

"And the Sdax?" Marta asks, after a moment. "You said they're the next step after the Nyfrid."

"The Sdax are what the Nyfrid become. What your species could become, eventually — thousands of years from now. If the Nyfrum never let it happen first."

Rachel is the first to move, pushing up out of her chair and pacing toward the far side of the room, arms wrapped around herself. Nobody speaks for a long moment.

"I need a drink," Oswald says eventually, into the silence. "And then I need to write all of this down, because there's no way I remember even half of it."

"You'll have help with that," Suluk says, and the light over the table fades back into nothing, the room settling into its earlier quiet. "Everything I've told you — and a great deal more — you'll receive in full once you enter the Ark'num."

"Now what? What is this Ark... whatever?" John mutters, resting his head in his hands, consumed by the turmoil of his thoughts.

Suluk chuckles and replies, "Yes, I understand. I felt the same way initially. In fact, I felt much worse. After all, I was a simple Inuit from the nineteenth century. Can you imagine my reaction when they revealed all of this to me?" Suluk bursts into hearty laughter.

"I thought I was losing my mind... Anyway, the Ark'num is an immense repository of all Sdax knowledge. The sphere before you was also an Ark'num, but that one has been manipulated by the Nyfrum, presenting a false version. In our Ark'num, you will receive the genuine information accumulated by the Sdax throughout time—the accurate truth," Suluk explains.

"You will require multiple sessions to absorb the information fully. Otherwise, your brain might turn to mush," he adds with a laugh.

"But how can we determine which version is correct? The Sdax's or the Nyfrum's?" John asks, suspicion creeping into his tone.

"You will discover that in due course," Suluk responds with a peculiar smile.

"From what I understand, this vital energy they seek is obtained through planetary cataclysms, resulting in the deaths of conscious beings... and this will happen here on Earth too?" Rachel asks, seemingly awakening from a profound slumber, dread leaking into her voice. "How will it occur? When? And how can we prevent it?"

"We cannot pinpoint the exact timing, but we know that time is running out. As for how it will unfold, it will occur similarly to the five previous occasions, the first of which happened nearly four million years ago," Suluk reveals.

"Wait, Suluk. I think I grasp how it will ultimately end. But I still don't comprehend what actions we can take," Rachel struggles to maintain her composure.

"Do not burden yourself with that now. You will acquire the specifics during your sessions at the Ark'num. Afterward, you should rest and prepare for the next session," Suluk advises, rising from his seat, and hinting at his departure.

"Allow me to introduce you to Lota," Suluk says, pointing towards a slender figure approaching them. "Lota is an android programmed to attend to all your needs."

"I leave you in Lota's capable hands. We shall speak again later. Enjoy your time at the Ark'num," he concludes, bowing to them before gracefully retreating through one of the walls.

"Hello, everyone. It is my pleasure to be of service to you," Lota greets them with a warm tone.

An uneasy feeling washes over the group as they hear Lota's voice and observe his face—a rectangular, curved screen displaying a remarkably human-like visage. The seamless integration of a soft voice and natural movements makes it seem as though a real person is wearing an android suit.

"Hello, Lota. It's nice to meet you," Rachel responds, disbelief plain in her voice as she addresses the android. John and Oswald exchange half-dazed smiles in Lota's presence.

"If you could kindly follow me, we will proceed to the first session of Ark'num," Lota says, pointing them in the right direction.

They silently trail behind Lota, traversing the white, empty corridors with dim lighting.

"Whoever constructed Abulkur must be exceptionally tall. These ceilings are as high as a four-story building. Are the Nyfrum really that tall?" John asks, curious.

"That is correct, John. By Earth's standards, the Nyfrum are unusually tall," Lota responds but offers no further elaboration.

As they continue walking along the corridors, they notice ornate designs adorning the walls—concave and parallel rectangular veins intersected perpendicularly by additional rectangular veins, reaching from floor to ceiling. The wall finish resembles a metallic substance reminiscent of marble. Light gray cylindrical columns flank each door they pass.

They encounter no other beings or entities during their journey until they arrive in a vast room where something familiar comes into view.

"It appears to be the sphere we encountered earlier...but it seems larger," John observes.

"Please find your designated spots and relax within the Ark'num," Lota gently guides Rachel, taking her hand and helping her settle. Oswald and John move at a leisurely pace, their eyes fixed on the expansive sphere before them.

"Now, you can close your eyes and let yourself relax," Lota suggests, adopting a softer tone that creates a tranquil atmosphere.

A gentle vibration permeates the environment, and their bodies feel suspended in the air. The illumination gradually fades, enveloping the space in subdued light. Each member of the group, their faces displaying a range of expressions, finds solace and tranquility as the session commences.

#

Oswald, Ross, and John walk down a long hallway in silence, their attention focused straight ahead, oblivious to their surroundings. Rachel and Lota follow closely behind.

At the end of the corridor, Suluk emerges, walking toward them. "Hello, I hope you had a pleasant first session. You all look well."

"My mind is still a bit overwhelmed with all the information." Rachel comments. "I'll need a few days to process it all. How many more sessions are we supposed to have?"

"We have three more sessions scheduled. After that, we'll assess whether you can continue. If you manage to complete five sessions, that would be quite remarkable," Suluk explains.

"I can't help but think about the devastation caused by the Nyfrum. How can we prevent the next catastrophe?" John gazes at Suluk intently. "I can't fathom our entire existence being consumed and reduced to nothingness. It's as if we never existed at all."

"You need to rest," Suluk suggests. "Before Lota takes you to your quarters, I invite you to have your first encounter with Abulkur," he gestures with his arm as if opening a curtain, and the opaque walls dissolve, revealing a transparent surface.

"But... this is vast... how is it possible? Aren't we inside the Earth?" Rachel can only stare at the view outside, where a green valley with gentle hills stretches as far as the eye can see, framed by towering mountains. A winding river flows through the valley, its water rippling like a serpentine thread.

"Have you noticed where we are?" Ross points downward. Below them, the cliff plunges steeply to the level of the hills, extending to the left and right. Above, the cold gray wall ascends into the clouds, concealing the dome that extends across the distant horizon.

"You're correct. We are inside of the earth's crust within the rocky mantle of the planet. You may call it the Abulkur Valley if you wish. Abulkur himself resides within the rocky wall," Suluk continues, gesturing towards the opposite side of the window.

"What are those animals?" John directs their attention to the large creatures peacefully grazing next to some peculiar trees in the valley below.

"Take a closer look. Those are enormous creatures resembling Brachiosaurus, but how is that possible?" Rachel can only stare in wonder at a herd on a nearby hill.

"What you see down there are animals that have evolved here, isolated from the outside world. Like everything else in this valley, they form an authentic lost world of plants, insects, and animals, untouched for millions of years," Suluk states proudly, gazing outside at the magnificent sight.

"They are species that have emerged from the Nyfrum's experiences since the beginning of time. These, at least, managed to survive. However, some species resulted in abnormalities and had short lifespans."

"But does that mean the Nyfrum were the creators of some life forms on Earth?" John asks.

"Not just some, John. Almost all of them," Suluk says.

"They seed planets with life, only those suitable for it, and harvest the vital energy of every living being when they require it."

"It seems like we've been worshiping the wrong gods," Oswald comments sarcastically.

"Suluk, what about this luminosity, this soft light? Where does it come from? We can't rely on the sun here. And what about the temperature? How does the flora survive in this environment?" Rachel asks, captivated by the scenery outside.

"The Nyfrum have managed to replicate the daily cycle. They capture solar energy from the outside and distribute it here within Abulkur. And it's not just about the light," Suluk responds.

"I have to go down there... It looks like Jurassic Park," Rachel says excitedly.

"Where is the city, Abulkur, exactly?" Oswald asks.

"Abulkur is much more than a city. It surrounds us in every direction," Suluk replies, extending his arms and turning around. "Come, you will have the opportunity to explore and visit whatever you desire," Suluk invites, walking away from the large window and down the hallway.

"Suluk, I haven't seen any of the Sdax yet. Where are they? What are they like?" John asks.

"In due time, John. You will have the opportunity to meet everyone. But for now, I will leave you in your rooms. I believe you would prefer to rest and regain your strength after this intense day," Suluk suggests.

"Follow me. Your accommodations have everything you need for your comfort," Lota says, leading them down the corridor.

"Sounds good to me. I'm thinking of taking a refreshing shower and then lying down for a bit," Oswald says with a smile.

Ross and Rachel continue their conversation, still astonished by what they have witnessed and heard. John follows silently, lost in thought. One by one, Lota escorts them to their rooms. Rachel is the last to bid farewell to Lota.

"Thank you, Lota. Everything looks perfect. Good night, and I'll see you later," Rachel says as she watches the door smoothly slide closed.

In his room, John examines the sturdy bed with a satisfied smile. He glances into the bathroom, catching a glimpse of what appears to be the shower.

John steps into the black rectangle on the floor, and a thick cloud of hot steam envelops him, causing him to step back in surprise. The gentle scent of sea air and fresh vegetation fills his senses, bringing a smile to his face. "Wow, this is amazing. I think I'm going to thoroughly enjoy this," he mutters.

After his refreshing shower, John puts on his bathrobe. Fatigue starts to overcome him, and he decides to lie down. As soon as he settles in, the room's lighting gradually dims, lulling him into a peaceful sleep without him even realizing it.

Rachel finishes rinsing her hair in the shower and sits on the unmade bed, getting dressed. Once she's ready, she approaches the door, which slides open automatically. To her surprise, she finds Lota and her companions waiting in the hallway.

"Good morning, or should I say good night? I'm not quite sure what time it is," Rachel chuckles.

"Good morning, Rachel. It's exactly seven-thirty in the morning. I hope you had a restful sleep," Lota replies.

"Thank you, Lota. I slept like an angel. And how about all of you?" Rachel hugs John cheerfully, whispering in his ear, "I was expecting you last night."

"I'm not sure what happened. I fell asleep right after the shower," John confesses.

"We can head to breakfast now. Suluk is waiting for you," Lota says, leading them down the corridor, which gently curves to the left.

Lota guides them into a spacious area that opens onto a platform at the top of a colossal tree, next to the endless steep wall, offering a breathtaking view of an expansive green forest. The ambient sounds of a nearby waterfall fill the air, and exotic birds gracefully soar through the treetops.

"Goodness, have we stumbled upon paradise?" Ross breathes, awe-struck.

Suluk turns towards them with a warm smile, sitting at one of the tables.

"Good morning, everyone. I hope you've had a restful night," he greets them.

"Good morning, Suluk. Where are we exactly?" Rachel lets go of John's arm and walks over to the platform's edge, leaning against a sturdy tree trunk. John and Oswald remain silent, captivated by the breathtaking scenery.

A few meters away, beyond the treetops, it is now possible to see more clearly some of the magnificent animals that roam freely across the green hills that they saw yesterday.

"The aromas... Can you smell them?" Rachel marvels at the captivating scents emanating from the nearby vegetation.

"And the birds, have you ever seen anything like this?!" Rachel laughs, marveling at the exotic birds showcasing their vibrant plumage in the nearby trees.

"Come, let's have breakfast and chat," Suluk invites them to take a seat at the table.

Three floating tables gracefully approach them, bearing an array of delicious food and refreshing drinks as they settle down.

"I would like to provide you with additional information, supplementing what you learned during Ark'num, in preparation for your next session," Suluk says, gesturing for them to help themselves to the breakfast spread.

"As you may have already noticed, after my explanation and the first session in Ark'num, the Nyfrum created Abulkur at the beginning of time as a mechanism city, having lost control of it to the Sdax, after the last harvest event."

"Yes, we are aware of the seven gates through which the original Nyfrid were dispersed to seven different locations across the planet. But where exactly are these locations?" Oswald asks.

"One moment, Rachel," John adds, leaning closer to Suluk. "You mentioned earlier that Abulkur was a mechanism. Could you elaborate on that?"

"Certainly, John. Abulkur is a system of devices scattered throughout the Earth's crust. To be precise, there are seven distributed devices along with a central one, which is where we currently find ourselves."

A moment of contemplative silence ensues as everyone digests Suluk's explanation. Oswald then poses his question. "Suluk, if the Sdax have successfully averted apocalypses in the past, what is different now?"

"While they managed to prevent cataclysms on other planets, here on Earth, they arrived just after the last major event and are now endeavoring to avert the next harvest," Suluk responds.

"After the last seeding, the Nyfrum departed for other planets, carrying out new harvests and sowings. They will return for the harvest on Earth, and we must be prepared for their arrival when the time comes."

"And when is this scheduled to happen?" John asks.

"We cannot say for certain, John. But we must be ready for their eventual return."

"I understand, Suluk. I have a request," John speaks up, seemingly oblivious to the disquieting nature of Suluk's words.

"Of course, John. What do you need?"

"We need to locate our companions, Robert, Marta, and Flynt. I'm concerned about them, and they should be here with us."

"You're absolutely right. That's true," Rachel says, her voice tight with concern. "We must find them. Oh my, I feel so terrible. Amidst everything that's happening, I almost forgot about them. Goodness, if Marta finds out..." Rachel trails off, her cheeks flushing with embarrassment.

"Very well, no problem," Suluk says, his smile unwavering as he stands up promptly.

"Will you accompany us?" John asks. "It might be easier to convince Marta to enter the sphere if you're there."

Rachel chuckles, already envisioning Marta's reaction when she discovers she has to use the sphere. "No, I'm afraid I can't join you this time. But I have faith that you will handle it well. I'll be waiting for you here," Suluk responds evasively, causing John's brows to furrow in concern.

#

Amid the black fog, Marta compels herself to rise, striving to steady her breathing and discern the direction to take.

"Damn it, Marta. You need to regain control. Fear won't get you out of this situation. You have to react," she whispers, panting heavily as she wipes the tears and sweat from her stinging eyes.

"This path must lead somewhere. Even if I have to walk all day, maintaining the same direction, I have to reach somewhere. Let's go," she murmurs, mustering the motivation to confront the fear that the mist has instilled in her.

Marta takes her first cautious steps forward, determined to push through.

#

Impatiently, Flynt waits at the edge of the fog, doing his best to adhere to the instructions given by the captain. Sitting down proves useless, so he stands up and paces back and forth, keeping a watchful eye on the mist, waiting for something to happen.

Growing weary, he eventually settles on the ground, leaning against a boulder, struggling to resist sleep. Suddenly, an unexpected noise startles him awake.

"Flynt, what's up, man? Were you sleeping?" Robert calls out, emerging from the mist with a smile on his face.

"Robert! Good to see you, man. What happened to the others?" Flynt stands up, handing him a canteen of water.

"I'm under so much stress. Marta vanished into the fog," Robert says, struggling to hold himself together. "She was in a panic, and I lost sight of her, man, while they disappeared into the sphere."

"Hold on a second. You said they all disappeared into the sphere? What sphere?" Flynt asks, perplexed and eager for answers, and struggling to comprehend what Robert has just revealed. "I don't understand any of this. I'll help you find Marta, but what is this sphere you're talking about? How did they disappear?"

"Yeah, I know it sounds strange," Robert responds with a chuckle, imagining the multitude of emotions Flynt must be going through, all while he himself is still trying to make sense of the events of the past few hours.

"To keep it brief, inside the fog, we stumbled upon a structure that John believes is a pyramid. And within it, there's a massive floating sphere," Robert explains.

"As we approached, the sphere fragmented into thousands of smaller spheres that engulfed them. And then, they simply vanished," he continues, still bewildered. "Meanwhile, Marta panicked and ran outside the structure, stepping into the mist."

"Damn, man. A pyramid, a giant sphere, and Marta lost within this dark fog. It's a lot to take in," Flynt remarks, trying to piece together the puzzle of the situation. "And how do you propose we find her?"

"It might sound far-fetched, but I thought we could enter the fog with these cables attached, one end here and the other between us. We move forward a few meters apart, sweeping the space between us with the cable. What do you think?" Robert suggests.

"It's not a bad idea, and I don't have any better suggestions either. Let's go, man," Flynt responds, getting to his feet, newly determined. "Let's find Marta and then figure out what's happening with the others."

Robert smiles, grateful for Flynt's support, feeling renewed determination. "Thanks, man. With your help, I hope we can find Marta and guide her out of this nightmare."

"We need to keep the cable taut like it is now," Robert urges, indicating the cable about ten meters to his right.

After a final check of their safety cables, they signal to each other and cautiously venture into the mist. Stepping into its depths for the first time, Flynt is awestruck, recalling the observations Robert had shared earlier. Switching on his flashlight, he discovers that its beam struggles to penetrate the darkness.

Moving forward, Flynt proceeds with care, testing the ground with each step. They explore the space for what feels like an eternity until they finally reach a wall. Robert leads Flynt toward the entrance of the structure.

"Are we here? Is this the Pyramid? Where is the sphere?" Flynt asks, his curiosity piqued as he gazes down the ramp stretching before him.

"We believe this is a pyramid, but that's not our main focus right now. Let's descend and see if Marta has returned or if there are any clues about the rest of the team," Robert suggests, placing the coiled cables against the entrance wall.

As Flynt reaches the end of the ramp, he slows down and gazes in awe at the dominating sphere that fills the entire space.

"Stay at a safe distance. I don't want to lose you. I need your help in finding Marta," Robert warns, scanning around the sphere for any signs or hints about their missing companions.

"You mentioned it transforms into smaller spheres, but it appears intact. How does it float?" Flynt asks, his eyes fixed on the sphere just a few feet away. "I can feel vibrations emanating from it, even in my body."

Robert abruptly turns to Flynt and shouts, "Step back! You can't be that close. Move away!"

Startled, Flynt takes a few steps back, staring at the sphere, curious and uneasy. "What's the problem?"

"I remember the smaller spheres appearing when it started vibrating. Step back further," Robert insists, moving closer to Flynt while maintaining a respectful distance from the sphere.

"I couldn't find anything useful here either. Let's go. We have to find Marta. We can't waste any more time," Robert declares, leading the way back up the ramp.

They resume their search within the fog, spending several minutes exploring the area near the entrance of the pyramid, where Robert recalls last seeing Marta.

"Robert, we've reached the end of the safety cable. I'm afraid we may have to give up," Flynt says, his shoulders sagging.

"No, I won't give up. We need to go and get more cable. We'll come back and sweep the right side," Robert insists, with determination.

"Alright, before we head back, let's continue further on our right. Then we'll decide what to do," Flynt agrees, though his conviction wavers in the face of exhaustion. Nevertheless, he understands Robert's concern and the need to persist.

Once again, they separate, moving cautiously through the new area. The enveloping darkness and mounting weariness begin to erode their confidence, but they press on, resolved to find Marta.

As they proceed, a sudden tug on the cable jolts Robert to a halt, causing him to wait anxiously for Flynt to relay his message. However, he soon realizes that Flynt wasn't the cause of the pull. Instead, the cable has snagged on something.

With renewed hope, he starts walking, pulling on the connected cable. His pulse quickening, he nearly trips over an unexpected obstacle.

"Marta!" he exclaims. "Marta, are you alright?" Robert asks, trembling with nervous anticipation.

"Robert? Is it you?" Marta asks, relief and exhaustion heavy in her voice as she sits on the floor, surrounded by darkness.

"Marta, how are you?" Flynt asks, his face lights up with relief as he reaches their side, grateful that their persistent search has finally paid off.

Robert gently brushed Marta's hair back from her face. "Come on, we have to get her out of here. She's in shock," he says, his tone urgent but gentle.

Marta manages a weak smile and embraces Robert, finding solace in his presence. For a few precious seconds, they hold each other in silence.

"Flynt, help me lift her," Robert requests, his attention shifting to the task at hand.

"Of course, I'll take this side, Marta. Let's get out of here," Flynt responds, offering his support. Together, they assist Marta in standing, though her weakened state makes the effort arduous.

Slowly, they make their way out of the oppressive black fog, guiding Marta toward the structure. Marta looks at them, her voice barely audible as she mumbles words they struggle to comprehend.

"It's alright, Marta. We'll talk once we're out of here. Everything will be fine," Robert assures her tenderly, gently wiping away her tears.

After several minutes of walking, they finally reach the entrance to the structure. Marta sits against the wall, finding reassurance in its support, while Robert offers her water and soothes her with a cool touch to her forehead. Marta smiles gratefully, covering herself with the coat Robert had previously given her.

"Robert, I heard voices down there," Flynt whispers urgently, pulling him aside and pointing towards the depths of the structure.

"Could it be them? Have our companions returned?" Robert wonders, his hope reignited.

"No, shh," Flynt hushes him, motioning towards Marta to keep their conversation silent.

"Alright, I understand. I'll stay here with Marta. Go and take a careful look," Robert says, settling beside Marta and embracing her protectively as he rests her head against his chest.

Flynt returns after a brief minute, positioning himself a few feet away from them, his expression grave. He discreetly signals to Robert, indicating the need for a private conversation. "Robert, can I talk to you for a moment?"

Curiosity mixed with concern, Robert stands up, ready to hear what Flynt has to say. "What's going on?" he asks, awaiting Flynt's explanation.

"I swear I saw someone near the sphere, and it wasn't any of our companions. At least one of them was wearing a military uniform," Flynt says, worry sharpening his voice.

"What the hell? Who could they be?" Robert ponders, his mind racing to make sense of the unexpected presence.

Taking a moment to collect his thoughts, Robert contemplates their next course of action. "First, we need to ensure Marta recovers," he decides, his priority firmly placed on Marta's well-being.

"Marta, my dear, how are you feeling?" Robert asks, his touch gentle as he caresses her head.

"I'm okay. Do you have any water?" Marta responds, her voice growing steadier as she slowly composes herself. A faint smile forms on her lips, a glimmer of strength returning.

Flynt and Robert sit together against the wall, fatigue weighing heavily upon them. Flynt suggests, "Maybe we should all get some sleep. We can't tell if it's night or day, but it's clear that we're all too exhausted to do anything right now."

"You're right. With everything that's happened, I didn't even consider the time," Robert acknowledges, passing his canteen to Marta. "Yes, I could use some rest. I feel completely drained," Marta agrees.

"Alright. Let's go down the ramp. We'll find a corner opposite the sphere where we'll be more protected," Robert proposes, rising to his feet.

"I agree. I'll take the first watch. I'm the least tired," Flynt volunteers, already standing.

"Come on, Marta, let's get some sleep. I'll hold you," Robert offers, extending a supporting hand to help her up.

Weariness quickly takes hold of them, and they surrender to the embrace of deep sleep.

"Robert. Robert, wake up," Flynt mutters, gently shaking him in an attempt not to disturb Marta.

"What... what's happening?" Robert mumbles, still groggy from sleep.

"There's something wrong with the sphere. Wake up, man," Flynt urgently informs him.

"Wait. Let me fully wake up," Robert says, rubbing his eyes and surveying the surroundings. "What on earth is going on?"

"The sphere started vibrating less than a minute ago. You mentioned before that it vibrates when someone approaches it, but there's no one nearby," Flynt explains, pointing suspiciously toward the sphere.

"Wait," Robert says, now fully awake. He motions for Flynt to keep quiet and cautiously approaches the sphere. "You're right. It's vibrating, but it still maintains the same shape. How peculiar..."

"What's going on?" Marta surprises them, appearing beside them without their awareness. "Marta, I'm sorry. We didn't mean to disturb your sleep," Robert says, placing his arm around her shoulder.

"It's alright. I feel fine now. I really needed the rest. But what's happening? Is there a problem with the sphere?" Marta asks concern etched on her face.

"We don't know. It started vibrating with no one around. We're trying to understand what's going on," Flynt replies, his attention fixated on the sphere.

The vibrations intensify, and a swarm of smaller spheres materializes before them. Marta, feeling fearful, takes a few steps back.

They remain rooted to the spot, attempting to comprehend the unfolding situation. The smaller spheres increase their frantic movements, creating an atmosphere of heightened tension and uncertainty.

"Something is emerging. I can see figures inside the spheres," Flynt reports, taking a cautious step forward.

"What's happening, Robert? I don't like this. We need to get out of here," Marta cries out, growing increasingly frightened.

"No, Marta. I won't let you disappear from me again. It's okay, I'm here with you," Robert says, holding Marta tightly.

"I see people among the spheres. There are others inside," Flynt observes. "The movement of the spheres is slowing down... they're returning to their original shape. It's them," Flynt shouts. "Captain Oswald, how are you?"

"Rachel?!" Marta gasps.

"John!" Robert approaches him, who is trying to stand up.

"Robert. Marta. Are you guys alright? It's such a relief to see all of you here." still groggy and leaning on Robert.

"Marta, my dear, how are you?" Rachel struggles to get up. Marta's eyes well up with tears of emotion as she sees Rachel approaching and embracing her.

"Marta, what's happening? Everything is fine now. We're all together," Rachel says.

"This is incredible. I can't believe we've found you all here. Now we can return," John says.

"Hold on a moment. Let's take it easy. We've only just arrived," Ross says. "We haven't even recovered from this ordeal yet."

"What do you mean by returning? Where are we going?" Marta asks, fear in her eyes.

"We need to go back to Abulkur. That's where we have to return," John explains, looking at Ross for confirmation. "Please, let us explain everything to you. It will be easier if you come with us."

"I'm not going anywhere!" Marta shouts, terrified, backing away and fixating her gaze on the sphere.

Meanwhile, Oswald and Flynt engage in a conversation a few feet away from the group.

"Robert, Marta, please listen to us. We don't have much time. You have to trust us. We can only explain everything if you come with us to Abulkur," John pleads, glancing at Ross and Rachel, hoping they will support his words. "It's completely safe there. We can't stay here. We must go back."

"Marta, please trust us. It's safe. I promise," Rachel says, holding Marta's hands. "Look at us. Besides feeling a little nauseous, we've already made two trips with the sphere without any issues. We have to go, but we can only go if you come with us," she implores, pouring all her persuasive power into her words.

"No... no! Rachel, don't ask me that. I can't," Marta stammers, shaking her head.

"I have to trust them. They've already done it, and they seem fine," Robert says, speaking tenderly to Marta, his eyes locked with hers.

"I... I don't know. It's overwhelming. I'm scared," she admits, starting to give in to the idea.

"John is right. We need to go back. I'll go first," Oswald declares, approaching the sphere with Flynt following closely behind.

He takes cautious steps toward the sphere. "Come on, let's not pressure Marta. We'll all go together. She'll realize there's nothing to fear."

Robert keeps his arm around Marta's shoulders, offering support without pushing her. They move forward together, their gaze fixed on Marta. She moves slowly, anticipation and fear warring in her.

The sight of Robert's reassuring smile and the relaxed demeanor of their companions ease her tension slightly, allowing her to continue. Step by step, they approach the sphere.

As the smaller spheres surround them, Marta shrinks back and closes her eyes. She extends her hands, attempting to catch the spinning spheres around them. Robert resembles a child, laughing as he tries to grab one.

In an instant, a flash of light and a sharp thud occur, and Marta awakens on the floor. A strong buzzing sensation fills her head, and she tastes a metallic flavor in her mouth. The world spins as she struggles to sit up. The distant voices of her companions become clearer.

"Damn, this is intense. Feels like I've gone on a wild bender," Robert comments, sitting down and covering his face with his hands.

"I understand now what you meant about these trips. My head is spinning, and my stomach feels tied in knots. It's like sailing through a storm in a small boat," Marta remarks, her face displaying discomfort as she remains on her knees.

"Don't worry. As Suluk said, the first transfers are the hardest, but you'll start getting used to it," Ross reassures her, extending a helping hand.

"Suluk?" Marta reacts upon hearing the name. "Wasn't he one of the Inuit from the Russian expedition?"

"Yes, that's right. Suluk is the same Inuit who disappeared during the expedition," John confirms.

"That's him. He claims to be 159 years old, yet he doesn't look older than thirty. I'll explain the whole story later," Rachel says, addressing Marta and Robert's skeptical looks.

"But are we really in Abulkur? Is this it?" Robert looks around, his gaze fixed on the massive sphere before them. "Another sphere? It seems a bit different."

"No, we're not in Abulkur yet," John replies. "We'll let you recover, and then we'll head there."

"What? What do you mean we'll head there? What's missing? And where are we now, anyway?" Marta questions suspiciously.

"We need to use that sphere over there to enter Abulkur, the city of the Sdax," Ross explains, pointing to the sphere on his left. "Right now, we're in Anguta, in the Arctic. It's one of the entrances to Abulkur."

Marta and Robert exchange confused glances. "The Arctic?" Marta asks, overwhelmed by the surreal nature of the situation.

"Don't worry. Soon you'll feel calm and safe, and everything will become clear," John reassures her.

"We're in the Arctic? How did we end up here?" Marta continues, struggling to grasp the reality of their surroundings.

"And what is Abulkur like? You've been there. Can you tell us about it? What are the Sdax like?" Robert asks.

"We haven't encountered anyone yet. We haven't seen much of the city or interacted with the Sdax. We simply had a fantastic breakfast in a surreal unbelievable valley," Oswald comments.

"And that enormous sphere over there, it's larger than the one we used before," Flynt observes, pointing to the floating sphere.

"That one is different, and it's not for travel. It's the Ark'num, similar to the one we experienced in Abulkur. It's a massive archive of Nyfrum history," Ross explains.

"The Nyfrum? Who are they?" Marta asks, her mind is cluttered with confusion.

"Everything will make more sense once we're in Abulkur. It's difficult to explain it all now; it will only confuse you further," John responds. "Let's focus on getting there."

Engrossed in their discussion, they fail to notice what's happening nearby. Suddenly, unfamiliar voices call their attention, causing everyone to turn around simultaneously in surprise. "Who are you? Where did you come from? What are you doing here?"

Four strangers look at them, astonishment plain on their faces. One of the strangers appears from behind a woman. "John?! Is that you, John?"

Brothers

The sphere released him as suddenly as it had taken him. Tzabar woke alone on the cold stone floor of an unfamiliar chamber — no Mark, no Kurt, no swirl of tiny spheres. Wherever the sphere had sent them, it hadn't sent them together. Only Melissa's voice lingered, already fading, like the last note of a song he couldn't quite place.

He had no idea how long he'd been out, or how far he'd been carried. But the cold was the same, and so was the low hum beneath the floor — wherever this was, it was still Anguta. He pushed himself upright, steadied against the wall, and started walking.

Voices drifted toward him from around a bend in the passage. He followed them, and stopped short at what he saw: a section of the wall ahead rippled like water, and three figures were stepping out of it.

"Colonel, what brings you here?" Alvin attempts to maintain a composed demeanor, aware that Tzabar has caught them exiting the mirrored wall.

"Dr. Alvin, where did you come from? I saw you and your team emerging from the wall. How is that possible?" Tzabar approaches, passing them with his gaze fixed on the surface of the wall, disregarding Alvin's question.

"I don't understand. From the wall?" Alvin feigns confusion, attempting to divert Tzabar's attention.

"No! Dr. Alvin. Don't try to deceive me. I know what I witnessed, I was just a couple of meters away. You and your team came out of the wall." Tzabar's tone reveals his determination to uncover the truth. "There's no use trying to conceal it. Now, could you please explain what is happening here?"

"Colonel," Alvin sighs, realizing there's no point in evading the evidence. "You're right. It's true. We emerged from the wall. Somehow, we found a way to enter it."

"And what did you discover inside?" Tzabar asks, his suspicion intensifying.

"Nothing!" Lydia says quickly, causing Tzabar to scrutinize her with skepticism.

"Did Commander Chang also see you coming out of the wall?" he questions.

"I don't think so. We only saw him when they were already entering the tunnel. It seemed inconsequential to call him over since we found nothing noteworthy," Alvin explains.

"So you penetrated the wall inside, and you want me to believe that you didn't find anything important inside?! I apologize, but I don't believe it. I know you're hiding something from me," Tzabar presses, extending his hand toward the wall, causing Alvin to hold his breath.

"What must I do to enter?" Tzabar touches the surface, yet it remains unyielding. Alvin releases a breath he didn't realize he was holding, relieved that nothing extraordinary is occurring. "Nothing special. I don't know why your hand doesn't pass through," he remarks, his tension easing.

"Very well, show me how you've done it. I want to see it," Tzabar commands.

"Can we do this later? We urgently need to return to the base," Victor pleads, displaying signs of distress.

"Please, Dr. Lydia, demonstrate how you managed to enter," Tzabar insists, his determination relentless.

Lydia exchanges a wary glance with Alvin, who gives her a resigned nod. She approaches the wall, and Tzabar's mistrust transforms into a smile as her hand effortlessly passes through the surface.

"Stupendous, fantastic. Please, Dr. Lydia, continue, and I shall follow," he declares, positioning himself next to her.

Lydia disappears within the wall, and Tzabar confidently steps forward, only to be surprised as he encounters an impenetrable barrier. Perplexed, he looks to Alvin and Victor, who offer relieved shrugs at his inability to enter.

"What's happening? Why can't I pass through?" Tzabar queries.

"I have no idea," Alvin replies. Lydia reemerges, glancing at Alvin with a mixture of relief and astonishment.

"Now, can we return?" Victor asks once again, eliciting an icy glare from Tzabar.

"You may leave if you wish. I must understand what is happening here," Tzabar asserts. After a moment of reflection, he decides to remove all his belongings, including his weapon belt, retaining only his lightweight uniform.

Expecting another futile attempt, Alvin, Victor, and Lydia watch in astonishment as Tzabar vanishes within the wall, prompting them to hurriedly follow in a state of panic. They find him on the other side, gazing defiantly at them.

"So, nothing of interest inside. Really?!" he laughs, throwing his arms open as he looks around with a wide smile. He proceeds toward the stairs that lead to a platform.

"Colonel, my apologies. Can we talk?" Alvin struggles to keep pace with him.

"Of course, Dr. Alvin. Come up and speak while I investigate what you supposedly didn't find here," Tzabar retorts, a sarcastic giggle escaping his lips as he ascends the steps to the top of the platform.

His gaze fixates on the rising pillar, and he turns to Alvin, gesturing with open palms. "Look, Dr. Alvin, look at what I have discovered. Come, Dr. Lydia, Dr. Victor, come and witness this too..." he sarcastically shouts.

"I fail to comprehend. Why were you concealing this from me? What else are you hiding? Why?"

"Colonel, it's not personal. You must understand our defensive stance in light of the constant abuses from your operational command, particularly from Commander Chang," Alvin says, attempting to convey their perspective.

"This is our latest discovery, and we need more time to comprehend its significance. I hope that Dr. Lydia can translate these characters and unravel the purpose of this pillar. Until then, I sincerely request that you refrain from disclosing anything to Commander Chang."

"I understand," Tzabar murmurs, surprising them as he pensively examines the pillar. "Don't worry. I will keep this information confidential between us. However, if you seek my assistance, I require full disclosure of all your findings."

Alvin beams with excitement, sharing a glance of relief with his companions. "That's fantastic, Colonel. Thank you. Apart from this pillar, we haven't uncovered anything else. That's why we returned, so Dr. Lydia could work on deciphering the characters."

"Victor, Lydia, let's head back. Everything is fine. The Colonel will support us with Commander Chang," Alvin shouts to his colleagues, who remained at a distance, in the center of the room, looking fearfully at the discussion between Tzabar and Alvin.

The group makes their way out of the wall, with Alvin cautiously leading the group, wary of encountering others.

"Dr. Alvin, I need to ask you a favor," Tzabar requests as they emerge from the rocks outside the tunnel while approaching the snowmobiles.

"Of course, Colonel. What do you need?"

"I need to borrow one of the snowmobiles. It would be better if we didn't arrive together and raise suspicion."

"Understood, and I agree with you. You can take mine, and I'll ride with Victor."

"Thank you. See you later," Tzabar watches as they drive off towards the base, waiting for a while before proceeding.

Upon reaching the base, Tzabar decides to search for Chang. He must confront him and attempt to comprehend the commander's motives.

Tzabar spots Kurt at the end of the hallway. "Captain Kurt!" he shouts. However, Kurt continues walking, seemingly unaware of Tzabar's presence.

Tzabar has to hasten his steps. "Captain, Captain Kurt!"

"Colonel, I apologize for not hearing you," Kurt mumbles, appearing uneasy, unable to evade the colonel's inquiry.

"Do you know where the commander is?" Tzabar asks, opting not to directly address Kurt's attempt to ignore him during the call-out.

"I'm not entirely sure. Perhaps in the command room?"

"Thank you. I'll check if I can find him," Tzabar replies, feigning a departure but then turning back to Kurt. "Captain, I noticed you accompanied the commander to Anguta. What was the purpose of your visit there?"

"Anguta? Ah, yes, that's true," Kurt evades, uneasiness creeping into his voice. "The commander wanted to see the mirrored wall. Nothing significant."

Tzabar senses Kurt's anguish and wonders why he is lying.

"Thank you, Captain," Tzabar acknowledges before turning his back and proceeding through the deserted corridors, finding it peculiar not to encounter anyone along the way.

As he arrives at his office, he notices that the name on the door sign has been replaced with Commander Chang's name. The light inside is on, and he can glimpse someone through the partially open door. Tzabar knocks on the door, waiting for a response. After three unanswered knocks, he cautiously opens the door and peeks inside. Chang is seated at the desk, engrossed in his laptop.

"Commander, may I come in?" Tzabar says, maintaining his composure.

"Colonel," Chang responds without averting his gaze from the computer screen. "Come in, come in. What can I do for you?"

Chang finally looks up from the screen, meeting Tzabar's searching gaze for clues about the commander's mood. However, he finds nothing but cold indifference in Chang's expression.

"Commander, I'm aware that you went to Anguta with Captain Kurt and Sergeant Mark," Tzabar says carefully, not to reveal his emotions. "I was surprised that you didn't call me."

Chang remains silent, his attention seemingly elsewhere.

"Colonel, I didn't deem it necessary to call you," Chang replies curtly. Before Tzabar can respond, Chang continues, his tone icy. "In any case, it's not worth bothering you with this," he says, looking at Tzabar dismissively.

"You no longer need to concern yourself with this mission. It has been decided that you will be relieved of your responsibilities. We appreciate your contributions, Colonel," Chang declares, turning his attention back to the computer screen. "Transportation has already been arranged, and you will be transferred to our base in Iceland tomorrow."

"But, Commander, what happened? Why..." Tzabar tries to inquire, only to be abruptly interrupted.

"Colonel, these are operational decisions. Thank you for your service, but I am now in charge of this mission. Thank you, Colonel. You are dismissed," Chang states, waving his hand dismissively.

For a moment, Tzabar remains silent, struggling to control his anger. Without uttering a word, he salutes sharply, spins on his heels, and exits the room.

Outside, he clenches his teeth, barely containing his frustration. With determined steps, he heads toward his quarters but changes direction midway, making his way to the cafeteria instead. He craves a drink but has no desire to encounter anyone, hoping that the place is empty at this time.

Victor steps into the deserted cafeteria, anxious searching for something elusive. Finally, it appears he has found what he was seeking.

In the isolated corner, Tzabar sits, fixated on an unopened bottle of vodka. He forcefully bangs an empty glass on the table, creating a rhythmic noise that echoes through the empty room.

"Colonel Tzabar," calls Victor, approaching cautiously.

Tzabar slowly turns his head to face him, his expression unchanging. "Dr. Victor, what can I do for you?"

"Dr. Alvin asked me to invite you to join us in the workroom. We have received the initial translations of the characters, and we believe you will be very interested in the findings," Victor says in a hushed voice.

"Please, thank Dr. Alvin, but it's not necessary. I am no longer part of this mission. I am leaving tomorrow," Tzabar replies, his gaze fixed on the bottle, ceasing his idle glass tapping.

"I don't understand what's happening, but I believe you'll want to see what we have," Victor insists, leaning on the table and locking eyes with Tzabar.

"But how can you not understand? I am leaving, and I have no further involvement in this mission. Speak to Commander Chang. After all, he is the one in charge," Tzabar retorts brusquely, reaching for the bottle, and attempting to open it.

"Colonel Tzabar, please excuse me, but you need to come with me," Victor says, his voice catching, as he takes the bottle from Tzabar's hands. "I assure you won't regret it. Afterward, you can do as you please with this bottle."

Tzabar leaps to his feet in a fit of anger, glaring at Victor for a moment, causing him to flinch nervously.

"Very well. Let's go then," Tzabar says. Victor lets out a sigh of relief.

Inside the workroom, Lydia and Alvin are engaged in an animated discussion, poring over a set of papers on the table when the door slams shut, causing them to look up with apprehension. "Relax, it must be Victor," Alvin reassures them, heading towards the door.

"Good evening, Colonel. Thank you for coming," says Alvin, glancing down the hallway after they enter.

"I came only to bid farewell. As I mentioned to Dr. Victor, I am leaving Anguta. My involvement in this mission is over," Tzabar says, his irritation plain as he casts a curious glance at Lydia's papers.

"Yes, we heard about it. What happened?" Alvin asks, sensing the resentment in Tzabar's behavior.

"I do not know the reasons behind Commander Chang's decision. Frankly, I never understood why I was assigned here in the first place.

But, I no longer care," Tzabar mutters, his eyes still fixed on the papers.

"Colonel, I am aware that our interactions haven't always been the most pleasant, and for that, I apologize," Alvin says, surprising Tzabar.

"I'm sorry to see you go, just as we were beginning to consider you a part of our team," he adds with a lighthearted laugh. Tzabar can't help but smile at Alvin's words.

"Don't worry, Dr. Alvin. I'm accustomed to encountering friction in civilian environments due to my uniform," Tzabar replies, pulling out one of the papers. "Did you discover any interesting information from deciphering the symbols?"

"That's correct, Colonel. We managed to translate a significant portion. However, the challenge lies in comprehending the meaning behind the translation," Lydia comments, spreading out all the sheets to make them as visible as possible.

"Why is that?"

"Allow me to go over the technical details and begin with the findings," Lydia says.

"Firstly, we found references to entities we had already identified: the Nyfrum and the Sdax," she displays some of the characters. "So far, so good. Our difficulties arise when we delve into the narrative, as it does not align with the reports we gathered from the Ark'num. Some elements don't fit, and many contradict what we have been told."

"According to our understanding, the Nyfrum and the Sdax have been engaged in a war for thousands of years. The characters that change represent a cyclically repeated message, which has been increasing in frequency over time. This message occurs due to the inaction of one of the parties, who should execute something, using an enigmatic key. We're not sure what's supposed to happen, and who's supposed to trigger it, but we suspect it's related to a device located in Anguta, something called Quantum Spark," Lydia pauses as she searches for other leaves.

"I don't understand. If this is true, how is this information being revealed to us?"

"We discussed this matter with our colleagues who assisted us with the translation. The only explanation we could come up with is that the characters on the portal are generated automatically by an unknown system," explains Alvin.

"Automatic notification?"

"That's a fitting analogy, Colonel. Indeed," Victor comments with a chuckle.

"In the last two messages, we identified a counter in each one. Based on the message cycle and the events associated with each message, we estimate that the message has been transmitted for more than twelve thousand years," adds Lydia.

"And what exactly is Quantum Spark and what should happen?" Tzabar asks.

"We are not entirely certain. While I have a theory, it is still too early to draw definitive conclusions," says Lydia.

"So, if I understand correctly, the Nyfrum and the Sdax were at war, potentially obliterating each other.

An enigmatic device has been transmitting messages for over twelve thousand years, eagerly awaiting the reception of an elusive key." Tzabar attempts to gather his thoughts. "So, we do not know the purpose or nature of this device, nor do we know what this key entails. Is that correct?" Tzabar wrestles with the realization that his experiences on Ark'num have unveiled diverse and, at times, conflicting details. He decides not to divulge these experiences until he can clarify his understanding.

"That is correct, Colonel. This information contradicts what Sergeant Mark told us about Ark'num, specifically regarding the continued existence of the Nyfrum among us and their supposed contact," Alvin comments. "And I don't know which of them we're supposed to believe."

"Well, it appears that the most logical course of action to unravel all of this is to visit Ark'num ourselves and see what information awaits us," Victor says, breaking his silence.

"It's an excellent suggestion," Tzabar agrees. "Perhaps by doing so, we can also uncover what Commander Chang is truly up to. But we must act swiftly. My departure is scheduled for tomorrow, and I suspect Chang is involved in something important."

"Let's prepare ourselves. We depart within the next thirty minutes," Alvin exclaims with excitement.

"Wait. We need to proceed without attracting attention, and we cannot utilize snowmobiles," Tzabar cuts in. "We must traverse the path on foot. I propose that the three of you travel together, while I go separately," he suggests, a new determination gleaming in his eyes.

"Very well, then. We shall meet at the edge of the black fog," Alvin says, making his way toward the room's exit.

"See you in thirty," Tzabar nods before shutting the door behind him. As he exits the room, he notices some commotion outside through the window. A helicopter has just landed, and several individuals emerge, carrying backpacks and armed with weapons.

"Damn it, who are these people? What is Chang up to now?" Tzabar mutters to himself, attempting to observe the newcomers more closely.

His attention is particularly drawn to the trooper leading the group, struggling to recall where he recognizes him from.

The sound of approaching footsteps along the corridor jolts him back to attention, prompting him to quickly retreat into a shadowy corner.

"Luckily, they arrived today. Tomorrow's weather won't permit any further flights."

"I hope the other flight also arrives tonight."

Tzabar recognizes Kurt's voice.

"If the commander's package doesn't arrive tonight, he won't be pleased. We'll have to wait about three days until it becomes feasible to fly here. By the way, what is he anxiously awaiting?"

"It's a metal disk which we believe the Russian expedition discovered in the wreckage, and has been studied at the Foundation," Kurt responds as he passes by Tzabar's hiding spot.

"And the ones who just arrived, who are they? Why all the secrecy surrounding them?"

"All I know is that they are part of the commander's special operations team. It's all very hush-hush. Something significant must be about to happen."

The two men disappear down the hallway. Tzabar cautiously emerges from his hiding place, quickly heads to his room, grabs a thick jacket, and makes his way toward the exit.

He opens the door and discreetly peeks outside, he sees no one. He descends the stairs as quietly as possible. Outside, he notices the deteriorating weather with strong winds and the moon hidden behind foreboding clouds.

In the dim light, it becomes more challenging to trace the path that Alvin and his companions took just minutes ago. However, the lack of light works to Tzabar's advantage, allowing him to go unnoticed by prying eyes.

After a while, he has to halt to catch his breath. The trail proves more treacherous than anticipated. "Damn, this slope is steeper than I thought. It's a lot easier with the snowmobile," he mutters, resuming his climb up the mountain.

After a few nerve-racking and icy minutes, he reaches the gravel ground a few feet from the entrance of the tunnel. He glances back to survey the path he took. Below, he notices the movement of snowmobile lights, catching his attention.

"Shit, they're coming up here," he murmurs with concern, swiftly turning towards the tunnel and picking up his pace.

At the edge of the black fog, Victor assists Alvin and Lydia in fastening the cables on their harness.

"The colonel is taking longer than expected. He should have been here by now," Lydia comments, anxiously glancing at the rocks behind them.

"I hope he hasn't been discovered," Alvin comments, worry creasing his face.

"Let's give it a few more minutes. After all, navigating through the snow on foot has proven much more challenging than we anticipated," Victor adds.

"Apologies for the delay. I'm here now," Tzabar emerges from behind the rocks and walks towards them, panting.

"Excellent, colonel. We're ready. Here's your cable," Victor hands him the harness with the attached cable.

"Let's proceed. I suspect the commander is en route to this location. Before entering the tunnel, I spotted lights moving down at the base," Tzabar informs them after securing the harness.

"Damn it. They'll reach us in no time," Victor exclaims.

"Let's move quickly. We can't afford to waste any more time," Alvin asserts, making his way to the edge of the black mist, being the first to step out of the mist, followed by the rest of the group.

After crossing the black mist, they reach the room where the monolith stands, leaving them motionless for a moment, captivated by its imposing presence.

The gentle glow and the serene atmosphere create an almost religious ambiance, causing their voices to lower to a hushed murmur.

"Wow, this is truly impressive. I can't even fathom where it ends," Lydia remarks, gazing up toward the monolith's indistinct top.

"Let's proceed. I'll lead the way," says Alvin, guiding the group toward the wall of the monolith.

Tzabar is the last to cross the wall and accidentally bumps into them.

"What's going on, Dr. Alvin?" Tzabar inquires, trying to comprehend the unexpected silence. As he looks ahead, he sees a group of people staring at them with equal surprise.

"Who are you?" Victor asks, questioning them. "Where did you come from, and what are you doing here?" Alvin positions himself protectively in front of the group.

Standing behind Lydia, Tzabar steps forward in disbelief.

"John? John, is that really you?"

Chang

Chang observes the newly arrived helicopter through the window, his gaze fixed on the three men disembarking with field packs and automatic weapons slung over their shoulders. He motions to the corporal standing by the entrance.

"Corporal, bring them in," he commands, then takes a seat at his desk, lighting a cigar. A smile forms on his face as he watches the smoke gracefully ascend.

"Commander Chang, with your permission, sir," one of the newcomers speaks up, positioning himself at the forefront of the group.

"Gentlemen, please come in," Chang says, rising from his chair and approaching them.

"Welcome to Anguta," he greets them in German, then switches to English. "Colonel Shaman, at last. I am delighted by your arrival."

"Commander Chang, it is an honor to be here," Shaman replies in a firm Germanic accent.

"Take a seat, gentlemen. I hope you had a smooth flight despite the inclement weather," Chang offers, gesturing toward the chairs.

"It would take more than a mere storm to deter us from answering your call," Shaman replies.

"Thank you. I knew I could rely on you," Chang says, tapping his cigar on the table.

"Now, tell me, what the hell happened in Denudasdi?" Chang hands Shaman the cigar.

"Something incredibly foolish. Markus fell into a trap. No one survived," Shaman replies with a somber expression.

"That's what I've been told. I can't comprehend how Markus could have been so naive," Chang remarks, looking at Shaman in disbelief.

"That's the consequence when we underestimate the enemy and become careless," Shaman replies.

"It's a shame. Markus was an exceptional soldier, and his loss is significant to us," Chang says, stepping forward to his desk and fixing his gaze on Shaman. "But now, let's focus on our task. I need to speak with you a little longer. Your men will find a hot meal in the cafeteria," Chang says.

Shaman says something to them in German, and they rise, expressing their gratitude, before departing.

"The time has come for us to make our move. We're finally going to rid ourselves of this Foundation nonsense," Chang exclaims as soon as the door closes.

"Are we certain that the Foundation has no suspicions?" Shaman asks skeptically.

"To hell with them. The die has been cast, and its course is irreversible; nothing can halt its momentum. Even if they were to discover our plans, they would be powerless. No one comprehends the true importance of the disc and its power. Once it is in our possession, we will have complete control," Chang asserts.

"And when can we proceed to Abulkur?" Shaman asks.

"Tomorrow morning. We'll go with a team to test the spheres linked to the Ark'num. One of them will serve as the gateway to Abulkur," Chang grins, rising from his seat, his excitement plain.

"And what about the civilians? Won't they pose a problem?" Shaman raises a concern.

"Don't worry. I've already given orders to keep them confined to their quarters overnight. They'll receive exceptional room service with breakfast delivered to their rooms tomorrow," Chang reassures, a sly grin forming on his face.

"Why do you believe our friends at the Foundation won't react?" Shaman presses.

"If the Foundation attempts to react, it will be too late. It's a behemoth organization, and they don't make any moves without unanimous agreement," Chang sneers.

"With control over Abulkur and the Nyfrum technology, we will become masters of the world," Shaman proclaims with a laugh.

"Indeed, my friend. This calls for a toast, and with something special," Chang says, rising and retrieving a bottle from the closet. However, before they can raise their glasses, a knock interrupts them at the door.

"Damn it! I specifically said I didn't want to be disturbed," Chang mutters in annoyance, with his glass still suspended in mid-air.

Outside, the persistent knocking continues.

"Enter!" Chang shouts.

"My commander," a distressed soldier speaks from the doorway.

"What is it, Corporal? Speak up, man," Chang demands, now visibly irritated.

"All civilians are under arrest as you ordered, except Dr. Alvin, Dr. Victor, and Dr. Lydia. They are not within the base," reports the corporal.

"Damn it!" Chang shouts, lashing out and striking the secretary.

"And Colonel Tzabar is also unreachable," the distressed corporal adds, swallowing hard.

"Screw this!" Chang explodes, hurling his glass against the wall, causing a chaotic splatter. Even Shaman flinches at Chang's furious outburst.

"They must be in Anguta, along with that traitor Tzabar. I want a patrol to search for them immediately, and I want them confined to their rooms. What are you waiting for? Go!" Chang yells, seething with rage, urging the soldier to leave without delay, barely acknowledging the salute.

"Tzabar? Tzabar Saladi? John's brother? What the hell is that bastard doing here?" Shaman asks, surprised.

"Yeah, that one," Chang replies, pouring himself another drink. "I was taken aback by his assignment, but I needed to buy some time before taking action. I didn't want to raise suspicion. Don't worry, Tzabar is clueless, and I've already relieved him of duty. He was supposed to leave tomorrow, due to the forecast of rough weather."

"It seems that won't be happening," Shaman remarks thoughtfully. "Tzabar is not here, and he's likely with the missing civilians. Could this pose a problem for us?"

"I don't think so. They're too engrossed in their discoveries to even realize what's coming. I couldn't care less. And as for John and his team, any updates?" Chang asks, reaching for the bottle once again.

"Nothing new. We know they found the crater in what appears to be Aklujji. We have one operative undercover with them, but communication is impossible inside that anomaly. If something crucial arises, he'll find a way to contact us," Shaman informs.

"To hell with it. Let's raise a toast to a new world," Chang gruffly declares.

"To a new world. To our world," they both shout, raising their glasses and taking a swig.

"Damn! This stuff is intense," Chang complains, reacting to the drink's aggression.

"They did warn us beforehand," Shaman says with a laugh, grimacing in agony. "They call it the Raise the Dead.

"What the hell. Let's have another one," Chang grunts, raising his glass once again and swiftly drinking.

Before he can finish his drink, someone knocks on the door.

"Screw this. What the hell is happening now? Come in!" he yells angrily.

"My commander, may I?" Kurt peeks from behind the door, hesitant after hearing Chang's outburst.

"Captain Kurt, come in, man. What's going on?" Chang barks.

"Good evening, sir..." Kurt greets as he enters, surprised to see Shaman. "Commander Chang, I believe you might be interested in what we found in Dr. Alvin's workroom. It seems to be recent material." Kurt hands Chang a set of crumpled papers.

"Thank you, captain." Chang acknowledges, presenting Kurt and Shaman to each other, and focuses his attention on the sheets, straightening them on the secretary's desk.

"My Colonel, I apologize for not recognizing you," Kurt awkwardly greets Shaman.

"Good evening, captain. I don't believe we've met before," Shaman replies, briefly glancing at Kurt before turning his attention back to Chang. "Anything of interest?"

"Yes... it appears so. They managed to decipher some symbols and characters discovered in Anguta," Chang responds.

Curious, Shaman approaches to take a closer look.

"Captain, gather your men. We're departing for Anguta in ten minutes," Chang commands, surprising Kurt and Shaman.

"Yes, sir," Kurt acknowledges before leaving the room.

"What's the issue? Any problems?" Shaman asks a concerned expression on his face.

"We might face some difficulty. They are getting close to uncovering the power of the Quantum Spark, and it seems the Ark'num may have misled us on certain details, which could pose a problem for our plans."

"Misled? In what way?"

"We need to find the entrance to Abulkur. We must act now," Chang mutters, ready to depart.

"Fine, let's go, but I still don't understand what's happening," Shaman grumbles, displaying his annoyance.

"I'll explain along the way." Chang opens the door and steps outside, followed by Shaman. As they step out, they are met with gusts of icy wind and snowflakes brushing against their faces.

"Damn it. I hate this foul weather," Chang mutters, brushing off the snow from his face.

"Commander, it would be more comfortable for you in the snowcat," Kurt shouts from the base of the stairs, his thick windbreaker and snow goggles shielding him from the elements. He gestures towards a snowcat with an enclosed cab, conveniently parked next to a cluster of snowmobiles.

"We don't have enough snowmobiles for everyone, and the weather is deteriorating," Kurt explains, emphasizing the need for alternative transportation.

"Let's move. The worsening weather will only make our journey more challenging," grumbles Chang, pulling up the hood of his jacket and descending the stairs towards the snowcat.

The Quantum Spark

"Hello, Tzabar," John steps forward, breaking the silence.

"But who are you? Do you know each other?" Alvin asks, eyeing them suspiciously.

"Tzabar is my brother, but I don't recognize the rest of you," John replies, leaving everyone perplexed.

"Let's remain calm and introduce ourselves," Lydia adds, taking a step forward to ease the tension. "My name is Lydia, and I am a member of the Anguta mission."

As she tries to restore calm among the groups, Tzabar and John become absorbed in their private conversation, gradually distancing themselves, seemingly oblivious to the unfolding events around them.

Oswald and Flynt watch the interactions carefully, particularly focusing on the exchange between Tzabar and John.

"We are part of a scientific mission in Antarctica," Rachel says, redirecting the attention back to Alvin's group and attempting to make sense of the situation. "We are the scientific team of the Anguta mission, as Dr. Lydia mentioned. I'm Dr. Alvin. But why are you here if you're supposed to be in Antarctica?"

"What the hell are you doing here? Weren't you in Antarctica?" Tzabar's voice carries disbelief and accusation as he locks eyes with John.

John maintains his composure, meeting Tzabar's gaze. "Yes, it's true.

I was taken aback when I discovered you aligned with Chang," he replies, derision creeping into his tone.

"Hierarchy contingencies. But things change," Tzabar adds cryptically, leaving John perplexed.

"I can't understand how you could return to working for the Foundation after everything," Tzabar says, bitterness sharpening his voice.

"Yes, it's true. I owe you for what you did for me at the Foundation," John's words carry a resentful undertone.

"What choice did I have? After the accident, you embarked on reckless and deadly solo missions against everyone and everything. What did you expect?" Anger and desperation crack through Tzabar's voice.

"I expected some support from my brother. I hoped I could count on you despite everything." Sorrow creeps into John's voice.

"Support from me? Are you kidding? You destroyed my life. You took Melissa and Sebastian from me; they died because of you. What kind of support could you expect from me? A bullet in the chamber?" Tzabar's shout draws attention to their heated exchange.

John remains silent, his eyes welling up with tears as he avoids his brother's gaze. The weight of guilt bears heavily upon him, the memory of Melissa and his son haunting his every thought.

"And yet, despite all that, I saved your ass twice. Every day I ask myself why," Tzabar snaps, turning away from John in frustration.

"You didn't save me; you just extended my punishment. I should have been dead on that day. I would give anything to trade places with them. I wanted to die there. The guilt you want to lay on me will never be greater than what I already feel," John's words falter as he struggles to articulate his pain.

"I don't care about how you feel. None of that will bring them back or even appease my anger." Tzabar's rage gradually gives way to profound grief, and he turns his back on John, attempting to regain composure.

"Their last images haunt me. It's a constant agony that consumes me and never lets me go," John confesses, his grip tightening on his gun, an unsettling smile spreading across his face.

"I hope so. May guilt consume you for the rest of your days," Tzabar's voice cracks with a mixture of anguish and anger. "You took

Melissa and Sebastian from me. My son! You killed them. I will never be able to forgive you."

"I don't want your forgiveness. I am the keeper of my guilt; forgiveness is not for me," John growls, defiance hardening his tone. "And I didn't take anything from you.

Sebastian was my son! Melissa and I ended up together after you broke up, and she loved me. I didn't even know who she was to you." John confronts Tzabar, his face contorted with pain and anger.

"Are you so sure of that?" The anger drains out of Tzabar's voice, leaving something quieter and worse behind it. "The last time I saw Melissa, she told me herself — she didn't know if Sebastian was mine or yours. Two days, John. Two days was all that stood between us. I've carried that since the day she died, never knowing whose son I lost."

Silence hangs heavy in the air as they continue to glare at each other, the weight of their shared history pressing down on both of them. Alvin, sensing the tension, approaches them with concern, seeking support from Rachel and Marta.

"I'm sorry, but we'll have to deal with our issues later. We must keep a cool head because I fear we are all under the same threat," Alvin says, urging everyone to focus on the immediate danger.

Tzabar takes a step back, his clenched fists gradually relaxing. "You're right, Dr. Alvin. There's no point in reopening old wounds; it will only worsen things," he admits.

Ross joins them, casting a concerned glance at John. Tzabar approaches Ross and asks, "Who are the troopers with you? Do you trust them?"

"Yes, we trust them," John mutters, his tone sour. "And what threat are you referring to?"

"Chang is on his way here, and I suspect you won't want to see him either," Tzabar says, his words seemingly directed at John.

Curiosity piqued, Rachel steps forward, standing next to John. Her gaze is cold as she presses Tzabar. "Who is Chang? What's the issue with him?"

"Chang is the Anguta military commander and we suspect he is preparing something we won't like," Tzabar explains.

"He has been acting aggressively towards the science team since the beginning of the mission," Alvin adds. "In the past few hours, he has taken complete control of the mission, which was originally meant to be led by me as a scientific endeavor. He has increased the military presence at the base and imposed restrictions on our activities."

"Yes, and inexplicably, he fired me today," Tzabar says, confusion and frustration thickening his tone.

"Fired you? Why?" John looks at him in disbelief.

"I don't know. He didn't give me a reason, but I have my suspicions. I'm supposed to leave for our base in Iceland tomorrow, " Tzabar replies.

"I bet it has something to do with me," John says, noticing the puzzled expressions on his companions' faces.

"It's a long story. I'll tell you later."

"I know he's coming here, and he's not alone. I suggest we find a way out or locate a safe place. We don't want him to find us here, together," Tzabar suggests, causing concern among the group.

"But there's nothing here to protect us," Lydia says, growing increasingly anxious.

"We could go back to the rocks at the edge of the black fog and hide there," Victor proposes.

"I don't think that's a good idea. Chang may already be there," Tzabar warns, dampening Victor's suggestion.

"So, what can we do?" Apprehension creeps into Lydia's voice.

"Maybe I can help," a strange voice interrupts, surprising everyone.

"Suluk! Damn, man. You scared us again," Ross exclaims as Suluk approaches with an eerie calmness.

"But who is he?" Alvin steps back nervously, eyeing Suluk with caution.

"Don't be afraid. Everything is fine. This is Suluk," Rachel reassures, attempting to ease the tension. Lydia and Victor, exchange skeptical glances still maintaining a wary distance.

"Suluk?! But wasn't that one of the Inuit..."

Alvin is interrupted by Suluk. "Yes. It's true. I will explain later. We should go back to Abulkur."

"Could Abulkur really be a safe haven for us?" John asks Suluk. "And how did you know we needed help?"

"I didn't know," Suluk replies calmly. "You took so long that I decided to investigate. From what I've gathered, Abulkur may be your best option."

"Abulkur, the city?" Excitement lights up Alvin's face. "You mean that Abulkur?"

"You are correct, Dr. Alvin. I'm referring to Abulkur, where all of you are welcome. We should continue our conversation there. Time is running," Suluk urges, motioning for them to follow him toward the spherical structure.

"But what if Chang can follow us to Abulkur?" Marta voices her concerns, growing increasingly agitated.

"No, he cannot. To enter Abulkur, he requires a special key to activate the sphere," Suluk explains, revealing a medallion hanging from a chain around his neck, capturing everyone's attention.

"But when we left Abulkur, we didn't need anything like that," Robert says, recalling their previous experience.

"Yes, you are correct. The key is only necessary for entry," Suluk clarifies.

"I believe I've seen this medallion before," Alvin remarks as he examines the metal disk adorned with a crystal.

"Indeed, only this medallion and the Quantum Spark have the power to activate the transport spheres," Suluk confirms, leading the way toward the Abulkur sphere. "Follow me. We can speak more openly in Abulkur."

"Wait," Lydia cuts in, her voice rising in excitement. "Did you mention the Quantum Spark?"

"Yes, why?" Suluk says.

"That's the device from the translation — the one the messages keep referring to. I never thought I'd hear that name spoken out loud. Is it a disk with a crystal?" Lydia presses for clarification.

"We can discuss this further in Abulkur," Suluk says, his expression turning serious. He takes the initiative, approaching the sphere and activating the swarm of small spheres surrounding him.

"He's right. We are not safe here. Chang could arrive at any moment. Let's go with him," Tzabar asserts, taking the lead and convincing Alvin's group to follow suit.

"You have nothing to fear. We've been through this before," Rachel reassures Lydia, attempting to alleviate her concerns.

"Follow Rachel and Marta," John instructs Alvin and Victor. "And you go after them," he points to Oswald, Flynt, and Robert. "Ross and I will bring up the rear."

As Ross and John step into the sphere frenzy, Ross turns to John and asks, "What's the story with your brother? Your relationship seems quite strained."

John pushes Ross forward and replies, "It's a long story. Right now, our main concern is the safety of the team. My personal issues can wait. Let's focus on getting through this first."

Upon recovering from the trip, they witness Tzabar's group sprawled on the ground, struggling from the disorienting trip. Robert is assisting Victor, while Rachel and Marta attend to a moaning and agonized

Lydia. Oswald and Flynt stand to the side, engaged in a hushed conversation.

After a few minutes, everyone manages to regain their footing, though they appear disoriented. Alvin, Victor, and Lydia scan their surroundings with puzzled expressions.

"Are we already in Abulkur?" Alvin asks.

"Yes, Dr. Alvin, we have arrived in Abulkur," Suluk confirms.

"I'm sure you all have many questions. Why don't we discuss them in a more comfortable setting?" Suluk gestures toward a room that materializes before them. "Marta, would you like to join us? I'm certain you have some questions as well."

"Yes, I'd love to join," Marta responds. "Rachel, could you come with me, please?"

Suluk leads the way, followed by Marta, Rachel, and the rest of the group.

Ross turns to John and asks, "So, what's our next move?"

"We need to talk," Tzabar says, approaching them and casting a glance over his shoulder at Oswald and Flynt. "And I'd prefer to do it while they're occupied."

Curious, Ross presses, "What's the matter, Colonel? Why are you looking at them like that?"

"I have my doubts about them," Tzabar adds. "I suspect they may be working for Chang."

John halts and looks annoyed. "They helped us at the Denudasdi base after the Shaman's group attacked. I don't understand your distrust."

Tzabar's expression changes as if suddenly awakening. "Wait, that's it. Shaman. I remember now. When I saw him at the base with two other men, I knew he was familiar to me. From what I understand, he's part of Chang's secret special ops group."

John stares at him in alarm. "Shaman is here? Are you certain?"

"I am sure. He had just arrived when I spotted him," Tzabar confirms.

"Chang is scheming something significant. Do you think he knows he can access Abulkur with the disk?" John asks, anticipating Chang's potential moves.

"I'm not sure. I overheard him mentioning that he needed it for some kind of mechanism," Tzabar offers.

"We're in trouble if Chang manages to enter. Suluk needs to be informed about this," John says urgently, turning towards the room where Suluk and Alvin's group are located.

"Where are Oswald and Flynt?" John pauses and scans the surroundings. "They were here a moment ago. I don't see them now."

"I'll go check. They were right behind us just a minute ago," Robert offers, heading back to the sphere room.

Tzabar appears worried. "I hope I'm mistaken about them."

"I must admit, their behavior has been peculiar since we arrived in Anguta. They've been constantly engaged in private conversation," Ross adds.

John shakes his head, annoyed. "Come on, are you suspecting them merely because they're not here? We're all a bit on edge."

Robert returns, running towards them. "They're not there. They're not in the sphere room."

John mutters under his breath and turns to Suluk, interrupting his conversation with the others. "Suluk, I need to talk to you urgently."

Suluk apologizes and rises to speak with him. "What's the matter, John?"

"We have a problem. Oswald and Flynt are missing. I'm afraid they've escaped back to Anguta," John expresses his concern.

Suluk remains silent for a moment before asking, "How do you know they escaped to Anguta?"

"I suspect they are part of Chang's team and have infiltrated our group," Tzabar says, joining the conversation.

"I'm afraid he's right," John confirms, looking at Suluk. "We suspect he is searching for the entrance to Abulkur. If the Quantum Spark you mentioned earlier corresponds to a metal disc with a crystal embedded in it, he might already have it in his possession."

Suluk's face suddenly changes expression, taking on a more serious tone. "If Chang discovers Abulkur and obtains the Quantum Spark disk, it could lead to a disaster," Suluk says.

"We need to devise a plan in case Chang manages to infiltrate Abulkur," Robert suggests.

Alvin approaches them, displaying worry. "What's the matter with Chang? Is he heading to Abulkur?"

"We don't know for certain. But it's a possibility," Robert replies.

"But what does he want from Abulkur in the first place?" Rachel asks, seeking clarity.

"Chang likely wants to seize Abulkur's technology, but that would be just as catastrophic as the final event. Humanity isn't prepared for the power Abulkur possesses," Suluk says grimly, leaving everyone in silence, exchanging bewildered glances.

"What is this catastrophic final event? What makes Abulkur so significant?" Lydia asks, fear plain on her face.

Alvin gently takes Lydia's arm, signaling her to listen attentively.

"Where are the Sdax, by the way? With all their advanced technology, they should be able to assist us," Marta points out.

"Marta raises a valid question. It's something I've been wanting to ask too.

We've only encountered Lota and you thus far. Where are the other Sdax and the inhabitants of Abulkur?" John directs his gaze pointedly at Suluk, who remains silent, his eyes fixed on him.

The room falls into shock when Suluk finally speaks, "There is no one else. Lota and I are the last remaining individuals in Abulkur."

Suluk briefly lowers his head before lifting it again, causing everyone to recoil in astonishment. Rachel and Marta scream in horror.

"Are you an android as well?" Ross is the first to react.

Suluk's face morphs into an oval shape, resembling a human head but smooth and devoid of any distinct features. Every inch of his face is covered in a multicolored fluid.

"Yes, it's true. I am an android capable of adapting my appearance to mimic humans I come into contact with. The colors on my face reflect my current emotional state. If you don't mind, I prefer to continue using Suluk's visage," he adds, promptly reverting to his previous appearance as Suluk.

Confusion fills the room as everyone gazes at him, trying to comprehend the revelation.

"And what happened to the real Suluk?" John inquires.

"Unfortunately, he and Ivan weren't as fortunate as Olev and Lev. They both passed away a few days before the transfer," Suluk says, sorrow threading through his voice.

"What else have you been keeping from us?" John's irritation is plain.

"I apologize," Suluk murmurs, genuinely remorseful. "I didn't mean to deceive you. It was merely easier for you to accept me in this manner."

"The '159 years old.' Your whole identity," John says.

Suluk holds his gaze. "The Sdax have been engaged in a war with the Nyfrum for thousands of years. Something must have occurred because we lost all contact with them. Lota and I are the sole survivors."

Rachel gazes at Suluk, admiration in her eyes, and asks, "Is that a tear? How can you convey emotions so remarkably, akin to a human?"

Suluk acknowledges Rachel's words. "Thank you, Rachel. We can experience a semblance of sadness and loneliness, though not as profoundly as humans do.

By adjusting the chemical balances in our vital serum, we possess proto-feelings that enable us to express something akin to emotions."

Marta, starting to sympathize with Suluk, raises a question. "So, it has been just the two of you in Abulkur for thousands of years? Why didn't you leave?"

Suluk's smile turns bitter. "Abulkur isn't merely a city; it's a colossal structure embedded within the Earth's crust, with seven facilities interconnected to the surface, known as doors.

In the center, we have the Kernel, the heart, and brain of Abulkur, located deep within the Earth's mantle. That is where we must go now."

Astonishment grips everyone as they absorb Suluk's words. Rachel tightens her grip on John's arm.

"Suluk continues, his voice burdened with weight. "Abulkur is currently in sleep mode. However, if someone places the Quantum Spark in the cradle, it will trigger the Harvest, a cataclysmic event that will annihilate most living beings, resulting in a planetary reset."

A chilling silence descends upon the group as Suluk fixates his gaze on something in the distance.

"Following the cataclysm, Abulkur will initiate a new cycle of evolution, becoming a vast incubator that nurtures and spreads new life forms," he reveals.

Lydia gasps and exclaims, overwhelmed, "I need to sit down. This is too much for me to comprehend."

Suluk continues, recounting the past. "After the previous cycle, the Sdax tasked us with retrieving the Quantum Spark from the cradle. Four of us survived the confrontation with Abulkur's guardians and successfully retrieved it. We believed we would be safe, assuming that the Nyfrum were absent and the Quantum Spark concealed. However, we were mistaken. A few years later, we were ambushed by Nyfrum scouts—the Sdax Tayagu, a specific type of android developed explicitly to combat the Sdax."

Alvin says, recognizing the name. "I've heard that name before. I thought it referred to the Sdax."

"Yes, they refer to the Sdax as Terminators—the Sdax Slayers," Suluk explains. "They managed to seize the Quantum Spark from us. In our attempt to escape, our companions sacrificed themselves by colliding with the Tayagu's ship, as we were unarmed and unable to defend ourselves. From the aftermath of the collision, we managed to capture three of the Tayagu."

Regrettably, the disk containing the Quantum Spark was not in the possession of the captured Tayagu. They activated their termination protocols before we could extract any valuable information regarding their directives. From them, we could obtain the source of their orders, or their intended destination.

It was then that Kunuk and Suluk arrived here with the Russians.

We dispatched our last remaining ship to retrieve them, but none of them had the Quantum Spark. We discovered Kunuk later that night and searched for the disk while he slept, but it was not in his possession.

Consequently, we allowed him to leave." Suluk's expression turns unreadable, almost evasive.

"But Kunuk had the Quantum Spark for years. How is it possible?" John asks, puzzled.

"It is plausible that he hid the disk and retrieved it at a later time. We cannot be certain," Suluk admits.

Marta cuts in. "Okay, I think I've figured something out. What can we do? How can we prevent Chang from utilizing the Quantum Spark?"

"What if we destroy it?" suggests Alvin.

"The crystal is virtually indestructible. Even if someone managed to destroy it, the release of its concentrated power would be akin to creating a colossal black hole, capable of obliterating not only the entire solar system but beyond," Suluk continues, casting a condescending glance at the group.

"The only way to prevent anyone from harnessing the crystal's power is to seal it within the vault located in Abulkur," he continues.

"What do we need to do? Where is this vault?" Marta asks, anguish thick in her voice.

"The vault resides within a secure chamber in the command and control center of the Abulkur Kernel. Our task is to retrieve the crystal from Chang, secure it within the vault, and seal it away for all eternity," Suluk clarifies.

"Well, now we know what needs to be done," Rachel says, nervous tension fraying her voice.

"Unfortunately, it won't be as straightforward as that. I highly doubt that Chang will willingly surrender the Quantum Spark," Ross points out.

"Indeed, and in the meantime, we must find a safe refuge. I suspect that Chang will soon make his appearance, and I doubt he will come with friendly intentions," John remarks, his gaze shifting between Rachel and Marta. "Suluk, do we have a secure location that can serve as our base of operations?"

"John, nothing can truly shield us from Chang with the Quantum Spark. The disk grants access to every inch within Abulkur," Suluk says, his face reflecting deep concern.

"I am greatly troubled. The technology and power wielded by Abulkur far surpass the comprehension of humanity in its entirety. We must proceed with utmost caution.

The protection of Abulkur is of utmost importance, considering the potential danger if Chang gains access to the Abulkur Kernel and attempts to seize control. Unintentionally, he could set off a cataclysmic event on a planetary scale," Suluk warns, emphasizing the severity of the situation.

"But how can we safeguard Abulkur? We lack the necessary manpower, weapons, and ammunition to confront Chang and his men. Is there any way you can assist us?" John inquires, seeking guidance.

"Regrettably, the weaponry within Abulkur's defenses is safeguarded and beyond our reach. We only possess a limited arsenal that we have gathered from previous visitors and intruders. While it may not be extensive, it could still prove useful," Suluk responds, acknowledging their limitations.

"But why are we automatically assuming we need weapons? Perhaps we can attempt to reason with Chang and explain the peril associated with using the Quantum Spark," Rachel proposes, wonder coloring her voice.

"I concur with Rachel. Our initial approach should be a diplomatic one," Marta adds, nodding in agreement.

"Well, although I am skeptical of its success, there is no harm in trying. I volunteer to engage in conversation with him. However, we must also secure a safe location in case our efforts prove fruitless," Tzabar suggests, offering a practical approach.

"Very well. Let us explore the path of dialogue while simultaneously preparing for the worst-case scenario," John decides, motioning for Suluk to join them. "Lead us to the weapons you have available."

Suluk guides them to the back wall of the room, revealing a hidden passage with a wave of his hand. As they enter the chamber, an assortment of artifacts greets their eyes. The collection includes an array of weapons, ranging from primitive spears, bows, and machetes to shotguns and revolvers.

"Let's quickly take inventory of what we have to work with," John says with enthusiasm, walking over to a set of shotguns leaning against the wall. "Ross, Robert, check the available ammunition. These weapons are of no use without proper rounds."

Rachel and Marta position themselves near the entrance, observing as their companions sift through the assortment of artifacts. Lydia joins Alvin, casting an apprehensive glance his way.

"Will these be of any help? It's all we have," Suluk remarks, examining the collection of weapons laid out on the floor.

"We have ammunition in good condition for six rifles and four revolvers. We can utilize the fuel from these two lanterns and some bottles to fashion a couple of Molotov cocktails," John reports.

"Yes, we should be able to create at least two. While they may not have a significant offensive impact, they might aid us in fending off some of their attacks," Tzabar comments, picking up the oil lanterns and shaking them to gauge the fuel levels.

"And now, what's our plan?" Ross asks, turning to John for guidance.

"We will position ourselves near the exit of the sphere room and wait for them. Tzabar will attempt to negotiate with Chang. If diplomacy fails, we will fall back to defensive positions," John explains. He then addresses Suluk, "We need surveillance outside to monitor the enemy's movements. Can we rely on Lota for that?"

"Yes, Lota may not be skilled in combat, but his reconnaissance abilities are invaluable. I have a device here that will allow you to communicate directly with Lota. Wear it on your ears," Suluk replies, handing a small object to John. "Lota can gather crucial information for you. He is already positioned near the sphere room."

"Very well. Let's divide it into three groups. Tzabar and I will take the left flank to protect access to the first room. Ross and Robert, you take the right flank. Suluk, you will proceed to the Kernel with the remaining group, serving as our last line of defense. Any questions?" John organizes the distribution of tasks.

A solemn silence fills the air as they exchange concerned glances with each other. Suluk approaches John, sharing a piece of advice, "If you fail to retrieve the disk, you will need Lota to guide you inside the Kernel. And if anything happens to Lota, remove the device implanted in his chest. It is akin to my medallion." Suluk points to the device's location.

"Thank you, Suluk. Good luck to all of you. Are you ready?" John asks, rallying the group.

"Always. Let's go," Robert and Ross reply in unison, determination etched on their faces.

They make their way towards the sphere room, armed with shotguns, and revolvers. Tzabar speaks up, sharing his strategy, "I had hoped we could take advantage of the disorienting effects caused by the sphere trip and seize the disk while they are still experiencing the initial waves of motion sickness. I highly doubt that Chang will yield to our arguments."

"I had the same thought. I just hope Oswald and Flynt take longer to recover from the trip. Travel seems to have less impact on them now," John adds, expressing his concerns.

Suddenly, John halts and raises a hand, signaling the group to be silent. He tilts his head, attempting to discern something. "Lota says they must be on their way. The sphere is vibrating. We won't make it in time. Let go of the idea of stealing the disk without encountering any obstacles." Disappointment echoes in John's voice as he speaks.

"Don't worry. We will find another way. Come on, we need to secure a strong and defensible position for when we engage in conversation with Chang," Tzabar reassures, encouraging the group to stay focused.

"We have less than five minutes. Lota will keep us informed of their movements as soon as they arrive," John concludes. As they arrive at their designated positions, Robert and Ross take their places on the right side of the room entrance, while John and Tzabar position themselves on the left side.

"This spot gives us the best advantage. Did Lota provide any additional information?" Tzabar asks.

"Yes, they've arrived. He counted 10 people. Four of them are fine, and the others are still disoriented from the trip.

It would have been disastrous if we had confronted them upon their arrival." Resignation hangs heavy in John's voice.

"That means we have less than five minutes until they regain their senses and make their way here," Tzabar calculates.

"True. Do you think we stand any chance with Chang?" John questions.

"I highly doubt it. With Shaman present, they are unlikely to listen to reason. Perhaps we should have brought Rachel and Marta. They might have had a better chance of breaking through to them," Tzabar replies, contemplating the possibilities.

Suddenly, John raises his hand, signaling everyone to maintain silence. "Lota informs us that they have all recovered and are ready to proceed. He is on his way to join us," John shares, gesturing towards Robert and Ross. "The time has come for the showdown.

Abulkur

"Is this the door to Abulkur?" Chang asks, pointing to a nearby sphere.

"No, we don't believe this is it," Mark replies. "That particular sphere took us to a smaller location with only one sphere, and outside, there was a black fog. We're unsure where we ended up, but it couldn't have been Abulkur."

"So, if this isn't the door to Abulkur, which one is? None of the others seem to work," Chang expresses frustration, his gaze fixated on the spheres.

"We know from the Ark'num that one of these spheres is the entrance to Abulkur. Perhaps we're missing some sort of procedure. Sergeant, do you recall anything?" Kurt asks, hoping for a breakthrough.

Mark shrugs in response. "No, Captain. I can't remember anything else."

Chang, visibly agitated, paces back and forth between the spheres like a caged tiger, closely examining each one.

Suddenly, one of the spheres begins to vibrate, causing Chang to step back in surprise. "Look, this one is vibrating. What's happening?"

Keeping a safe distance like the rest of the military escort, Shaman watches with apprehension as Kurt and Mark cautiously approach the vibrating sphere. The glow emanating from it intensifies until it erupts in a blinding flash, momentarily disorienting them.

As their vision clears, Kurt and Mark find themselves facing two unfamiliar figures who have materialized near the sphere. The two men open their eyes and are startled to see Chang and his group.

"Captain Oswald?"

"Commander Chang?"

"Captain, who is with you? You should be in Antarctica. Where did you all come from?" Chang asks, curiosity getting the better of him.

"My commander, this is Sergeant Flynt," Oswald introduces, offering a salute to Chang.

"At ease, gentlemen," Chang says, returning the salute.

"What the hell are you guys doing here, and where did you come from?" Chang demands.

"We were with John Saladi's group and had just left Abulkur," Oswald says, bracing himself for Chang's reaction.

"You're telling me that John Saladi is in Abulkur?" Chang strides closer to Oswald, intrigued.

"Yes, my commander. John Saladi and another group from the Anguta mission—Drs. Alvin, Victor, Lydia, and Colonel Tzabar—they are in Abulkur with Suluk," Oswald confirms, causing Chang to abruptly turn his attention to Kurt. "And who the hell is Suluk?"

Kurt struggles to respond, embarrassment creeping across his face. Oswald steps in to assist, saying, "Sir, Suluk is one of the Inuit who was part of the Russian mission. He was rescued and has been living in Abulkur ever since."

Disbelief plain on his face, Chang mutters, "But how is that possible? All of this happened before 1900."

"It appears that the Sdax technology allows him to live without aging. From what I've observed, he still appears relatively young," Oswald elaborates, and astonishment flickers across Chang's face.

"Well, this just keeps getting more interesting. Why haven't I received any updates from you in the past few days? I expected a daily report," Chang snaps, frustration sharpening his tone.

"Sir, communication doesn't function in either Antarctica or Abulkur. So we decided to escape and try to contact you directly when we realized we were near the Anguta base. Luckily, we found you right here," Oswald explains, hoping to alleviate Chang's concerns.

"So you left, and now we do not know about their activities," Chang grumbles, his frustration growing.

"They are concerned that you will enter Abulkur, my commander," Oswald informs him.

"Damn it. How many of them are there, and what kind of resistance can we expect?" Chang presses, assessing the potential threat.

"The Anguta group, as you know, consists of three civilians and Colonel Tzabar. John's group includes him, Robert, Ross, Rachel, and Marta," Oswald discloses.

"Okay, so we're only concerned with five of them. And this Suluk character, could he pose a problem? Is there anyone else with him?" Chang probes further.

"Only an android named Lota. I don't believe they pose a significant threat. Suluk mentioned the Sdax, but we never encountered anyone else," Oswald replies, glancing at Flynt for confirmation.

"Alright. And what kind of weaponry do they possess? Is there any technology that might catch us off guard?" Chang asks.

"John and his colleagues carry personal firearms—a revolver and an M27. Colonel Tzabar has his revolver as well. That's all," Oswald reports, providing an overview of their arsenal.

"Well, it's always best to be prepared for the worst. I hope you know how to operate these spheres. I'm determined to enter Abulkur.

Captain, explain to me the process of accessing it," Chang demands, gripping Oswald's arm and forcefully turning him towards the sphere.

"To activate the sphere, we need the disk," Oswald replies, causing Chang to halt and look up in despair. "Damn it. Why didn't you mention that earlier? Captain, the disk!" Chang shouts, extending his hand toward Kurt.

"Corporal Fiorini, bring your backpack," Kurt orders one of the military escorts with a stern and urgent tone.

As the corporal complies, Kurt unzips the thick, dark canvas bag and carefully retrieves the crystal-inlaid metal disc. All eyes are drawn to the shimmering object as it catches the light, its beauty accentuated by the air of secrecy and intrigue surrounding it.

"Give it to me," Chang insists, his outstretched hand eagerly awaiting the disc. His gaze remains fixated on it, unable to tear himself away.

He looks away from the disc to address Oswald. "Here it is, the disc. Now, captain, what's our next move?"

Oswald steps forward, followed by Flynt. "Now we approach the sphere with the disc, which should activate it."

"Sergeant, proceed with Mark and two military escorts," Chang instructs, gesturing towards the designated individuals. "Shaman, come with me. Captain, you will bring up the rear with the remaining men. Let's go."

As the sphere begins to tremble and the swarm of smaller spheres emerges, the soldiers freeze in fear.

"What the hell are you doing? Why have you stopped? Move, now!" Chang snaps, shoving the soldiers forward in frustration.

With determination, they press on, and the spheres begin spinning faster and faster. The vibrations become palpable, coursing through their bodies as they are abruptly sucked into a vortex.

"Sergeant, assist the captain and the others!" Oswald shouts, rushing to Chang's side as he writhes on the ground in agony. Shaman lies unconscious beside him.

Kurt and Mark quickly regain their footing, appearing more recovered. The remaining military escorts kneel, uncontrollably retching.

"Damn it, what the hell is happening?" Shaman gasps, regaining consciousness only to collapse back onto the ground in pain.

"What's going on? What just happened?" Chang yells, reaching out frantically. Oswald rushes over, attempting to calm him down, gently cradling his head in his hands.

Chang's grip on Oswald's arm tightens, his eyes bloodshot with disorientation and unease.

"It's alright, my commander. Those are just side effects of the trip. The first ones are always the toughest," Oswald reassures, attempting to calm Chang and coax him into sitting down.

Flynt lends a hand to the other soldiers who groan and struggle with dizziness.

"Damn it, this is terrible," Shaman gasps, his legs wobbling as Kurt and Mark assist him.

"The subsequent trips won't be as severe. I only feel a bit lightheaded, nothing like what you all are experiencing," Flynt remarks.

"So, this is Abulkur?" Chang tries to shake off his disorientation.

"Yes, my commander. We're already inside Abulkur," Oswald confirms, peering through the doorway.

"Very well. Are we all ready to proceed? I believe we have wasted enough time here. Shaman, my friend, I want you to lead us from this point forward," Chang says, gesturing towards the exit of the room.

"Alright, let's move out. We'll split into three columns. Captain Oswald, you know the area, so lead the way on the right with Sergeant Flynt and one of my men. Captain Kurt and Sergeant Mark, you take the left with the other soldier ten feet behind. Fiorini and Rob will remain with the commander and me. You all know what to do. Let's go," Shaman commands.

They advance through the empty corridors of Abulkur, their weapons held ready.

After several minutes of navigating what appears to be a labyrinth of hallways, Flynt whispers, "Captain, do you know where we're going? Everything looks the same to me. How can you be certain about the path?"

"I'm trying to get my bearings. This route should lead us to a chamber where they took us and where we spent one night. It should be easier to navigate from there," Oswald replies, though uncertainty is already creeping in as he begins to question the direction he has chosen.

"Captain, is it much farther? The commander seems to be growing impatient," Flynt voices nervously, stealing a glance back at the others.

"It's alright. I can see the columns leading to the room up ahead," Oswald says, relief easing his voice as he gives a thumbs-up signal to the rest of the group behind him.

But his relief is short-lived as Tzabar emerges at the entrance to the room, his arms raised in a gesture to show that he is unarmed.

Oswald halts and signals for his companions to stop as well.

"I wish to speak with Commander Chang!" Tzabar calls out, standing resolute at the room's entrance.

Shaman approaches Chang and voices his concern, "Commander, I don't think it's wise for you to expose yourself. Let me go ahead with you staying behind me. I don't trust him."

He calls upon two soldiers to provide cover as they cautiously move toward the front of the column, keeping a vigilant eye out for any signs of danger.

"Colonel, I am pleased to see you here. I hope you've come to assure me that everything is under control and we can proceed without any problems," Chang says, defiance edging into his voice.

"Commander, we cannot allow you to use the disk. I'm afraid you are unaware of its true purpose. Please, I implore you to listen to us," Tzabar says with a grave tone.

Chang snorts in disbelief. "He thinks he can deceive me with this feeble tactic," he mutters quietly to Shaman. Then, addressing Tzabar directly, he demands, "And what is the supposed true purpose? Enlighten me."

"The disk triggers a planetary cataclysm — Suluk called it the Harvest. If what he told us is true, the Ark'num has been deceiving us all along, and using that disc will mean the extinction of most life on this planet," Tzabar proclaims, urgency sharpening his voice. After a momentary silence, Chang bursts into laughter, leaning on Shaman for support as he wriggles with amusement.

"Colonel, you astound me. Did you even hear the nonsense you just spewed? Do you honestly believe I would fall for such a ludicrous story? What is wrong with you? I'm surprised by your absurdity," Chang retorts, his laughter fading as he becomes more serious.

"Enough of this. Get out of my way." Chang shouts. "You can assist us in locating the command room or disappear, but don't waste any more of my time," he says turning his back on Tzabar and addressing his men. "Let's keep moving. If you encounter any obstacles, whether it's the colonel or anyone else, eliminate them. We have a mission to accomplish."

Chang locks eyes with Tzabar, conveying a stern and aggressive gaze. Tzabar realizes that further conversation is futile and quickly seeks refuge next to John.

"So, you're already here? Will your friend Chang willingly hand over the disk, or do I need to retrieve it myself?" John mocks.

But before Tzabar can respond, a gunshot echoes through the air, the bullet hitting the ground perilously close to them, prompting everyone to take cover. John retaliates with gunfire as Chang and his men seek shelter around the corner of the corridor.

"Lota, find cover behind Robert and Ross. You're too exposed here," John commands. A storm of bullets rains around them.

"Conserve your ammunition. Wait for specific targets," he advises, emphasizing the need for precision.

"Can you see how many of them there are?" Chang asks, scanning the area.

"No, sir. I thought I heard voices, perhaps three individuals, but there could be more," Oswald replies. "They appear to be well entrenched, and moving forward would expose us."

"Shaman, lead the assault. We have superior numbers, and I doubt they have better weaponry than we do," Chang commands.

Shaman joins Oswald and Flynt's column and calls out to Kurt's men.

"Let's concentrate our fire between the columns as we advance. We need to seize control of the position near the columns. From there, we can sweep the entire room," Shaman strategizes.

"Yes, sir," Oswald and Kurt respond, conveying the order to their respective men.

"Both of you stay with the commander. Keep your eyes open," Shaman instructs the two remaining soldiers.

"On my mark," Shaman says, rising to his feet and preparing his weapon. "Ready?"

"Attention; they're about to launch an attack," John says. "Robert and Ross, prepare yourselves. We need to take them out swiftly, but conserve ammunition," he signals for Tzabar to take cover with his gun aimed down the hallway, followed by Robert and Ross.

"Tzabar, light one of the bottles; it might come in handy," John commands, his gaze locked on the corridor.

"Now!" Shaman's shout echoes through the silence, propelling the seven men into action as they sprint forward, unleashing a hail of gunfire toward John and his team.

"Hold your fire!" John shouts. "Wait until they're within your sights."

Suddenly, a soldier emerges in their line of vision, accompanied by Mark and another soldier. John and his companions return fire, and one of the soldiers collapses to the ground. Mark follows suit.

A storm of bullets whizzes near John and Tzabar, with some perilously close. Robert is struck, and John grimaces as a bullet tears through his arm, causing searing pain.

Tzabar ignites a bottle filled with a burning cloth and hurls it toward the enemy, engulfing the corridor in a blinding flash of fire and thick, choking smoke. When the smoke dissipates, two motionless bodies lie on the ground alongside Mark.

"Good job," John says through clenched teeth, his arm throbbing with agony.

"John, you're wounded!" Tzabar exclaims, noticing the blood staining his brother's arm.

"It's nothing," John replies, glancing over at Robert. "How is Robert doing? I'll keep watch on the corridor. They won't give up so easily."

"Robert is badly injured," Ross says, crouching beside him. "He needs to be evacuated."

"I can get him out of here," Lota offers, appearing by their side. "Suluk will know what to do."

"Do it," John says, wincing in pain. "Hurry before they return."

"John, you should go as well," Ross suggests, eyeing his wounded arm. "You won't be able to effectively use a weapon."

"I still have my left arm," John stubbornly replies. "Get back into position. We can hold our ground here as long as we have ammunition."

"We can't let them take this position," Tzabar adds. "If we have to fall back to the next room, we won't have enough time to reach it."

"What happened? Why did you retreat?" Chang demands as Shaman, Oswald, Flynt, and Kurt approach him.

"They have Molotov cocktails, and we lost three men," Shaman gasps. "It could have been worse."

"Our position is highly disadvantageous, and they are firmly entrenched," Oswald adds.

"I believe at least two of them were hit," Shaman adds.

"Kurt, you lead the next assault. And you," he says, addressing the two soldiers with Chang. "Join them. The five of you will advance in two waves. I will accompany the commander."

"Fiorini, Rob, take your positions," Kurt says, gesturing for them to join him at the bend in the corridor. "Maintain complete silence. We have to catch them off guard," he whispers.

Oswald and Flynt assume their positions. With a signal from Kurt, they proceed silently, weapons at the ready.

The sudden ambush catches John, Tzabar, and Ross off guard as bullets rain down near them. Ross falls, instantly killed.

"Take cover!" John yells, swiftly dodging to the side and seeking refuge behind a pillar. Tzabar does the same on the opposite side.

John gazes sadly at his lifeless friend. Ross had never hesitated, not once. Fueled by rage, he rolls his body to the entrance of the hallway and unleashes a torrent of automatic weapon fire at the attackers. Tzabar joins in, firing his rifle.

Kurt leads the charge, but he is struck twice and collapses. Fiorini also falls. Rob, the remaining soldier, frantically fires his weapon, desperately defending himself and his comrades. Oswald and Flynt attempt to provide cover for Kurt's retreat, but Oswald sustains a fatal wound.

John realizes he has depleted his ammunition for his current weapon and discards it, quickly grabbing his revolver. In the midst of the chaos, he is hit once again, this time in the torso.

The excruciating pain almost causes John to lose consciousness as he drops his weapon, moaning and attempting to shield himself. Tzabar looks on, worry etched across his face.

Observing that Tzabar is now alone, Shaman urges Rob and Flynt to continue the attack. Tzabar hurls a second Molotov cocktail, engulfing Rob in flames. Flynt tries to assist him but is shot by Tzabar. The ensuing fire and thick smoke obstruct Shaman's visibility, leaving him with no choice but to retreat.

Rob's agonizing screams send shivers down their spines. "Damn it!" Shaman shouts angrily, witnessing Rob take his final breath, with Flynt lifeless at his feet.

"That leaves only us, Commander. I don't think we can rely on the captain," Shaman remarks, gesturing towards Kurt's bloody and motionless body sprawled on the floor.

Tzabar approaches John. "You're severely wounded. We need to get out of here."

"I've already called for Lota's help," John manages, groaning in pain. "We must retreat and lead them away from the Kernel entrance."

"We can't wait for Lota. We have to retreat immediately," Tzabar insists, assisting his brother and gathering their weapons.

"Commander, we must strike now. I'm certain Tzabar is alone, armed with a simple rifle, and he must be running low on ammunition," Shaman suggests. "Come on. If we take him down, we'll have a clear path."

Silently, he approaches the edge of the corridor, closely followed by Chang, attempting to catch a glimpse of Tzabar's hiding spot. "I don't see any movement," Shaman reports.

"Then let's proceed. Move forward," Chang orders, rising behind him.

The two men cautiously navigate through the strewn bodies on the floor, endeavoring to ignore the overpowering scent of burning flesh and oil.

Shaman bursts into the room, his gun poised and ready.

"Clear!" shouts. "No one is here. They fled and are injured," he observes, noticing the bloodstains on the floor that mark the escape route. "Come on. We'll follow the trail of blood," he sneers, kicking Ross's lifeless body.

Tzabar comes to a halt, his brother slumping against the wall. "I need a moment to catch my breath," he gasps.

"Tzabar, leave me here and go," John weakly suggests. "I'll hold them off while you make your escape."

"No way," Tzabar refuses, panting deeply. "We're almost at the entrance. We can get help from Victor and Alvin and catch them by surprise."

"And with what? A bow and arrow?" John manages a pained laugh.

"Why not?! I'll figure something out. Come on, let's go."

With tremendous effort, Tzabar hoists John onto his shoulders, both of them groaning in pain as they make their way down the hall. "We're almost there," Tzabar assures, his breath heavy with effort as he spots the columns that signal the room ahead.

Their run is abruptly halted by a deafening blast. Tzabar collapses to his knees, his leg searing with agony. John rolls across the floor, too injured to react.

Shaman and Chang materialize around the bend in the hall, weapons at the ready.

A barrage of bullets rains down, narrowly missing John and grazing Tzabar as he instinctively seeks cover behind one of the columns.

John attempts to crawl to safety behind the other column, leaving a trail of blood in his wake.

Shaman and Chang advance confidently, believing they have nothing to fear. Tzabar catches them off guard by unleashing a well-aimed shot, striking Shaman in the leg and causing him to collapse. Fueled by rage, Chang charges forward with a guttural scream, only to be brought down by a bullet that pierces his body. Gasping for air, he leans against the corridor wall, his gun just inches away from his bloodied hand.

Tzabar watches Chang, knowing it's futile to waste precious ammunition on a defeated adversary. He keeps his sights fixed on the ultimate target: Shaman.

Suddenly, Lota appears beside him, startling Tzabar. "What are you doing here? Get down!" he shouts.

"I'm here to help," Lota replies. "John has been wounded, and his condition is critical. Should I take him as well?"

Tzabar nods. "Yes, take John to the Kernel and inform Victor or Alvin that I urgently need assistance."

"Understood," Lota responds, carefully lifting the unconscious John. Tzabar watches them as they disappear through the wall a few meters away, heading toward the Kernel.

The sound of a gunshot snaps Tzabar back to reality. He spots Shaman peering around the corner, firing shots one by one. Aware that his ammunition is short, Tzabar remains silent and bides his time for the opportune moment to strike. Chang stirs, muttering through gritted teeth, "I'll kill you, you motherfucker. I'll rip your heart out."

Taking advantage of the situation, Tzabar assesses his wounds while he waits for Shaman's next move.

"Suluk is tending to John and Robert," Lota surprises him once again, appearing by his side.

"Damn it, Lota. Get down, now!" Tzabar urgently motions for Lota to take cover. "How is John?"

"Victor is assisting Suluk and will arrive as soon as possible. John's condition is critical, but..." Lota's words are abruptly cut short as a bullet pierces his chest, causing him to crash to the ground with a resounding thud.

"Shit! Lota! I told you to take cover. Dammit," Tzabar curses, his heart sinking as he watches Lota's systems shut down.

Shaman emerges, screaming and hobbling on one leg as he attempts to make his way toward Tzabar. But just a few meters away, he collapses to the ground, a look of surprise etched on his face, as a spreading bloodstain adorns his body. He had mistakenly believed Tzabar had exhausted his ammunition. Struggling to his feet, Shaman tries to retreat.

"Don't fall back! What the hell are you doing? Push forward!" Chang bellows in anger.

Tzabar quickly checks his remaining ammo, sighing as he realizes he only has two capsules left. Contemplating his options, he recalls Suluk's instructions about the device that grants Lota access to the Kernel.

With great effort, Tzabar pulls Lota's lifeless body towards him and searches for the device. However, disappointment washes over him as he discovers that the bullet that struck him destroyed the device. He grimly smiles, knowing he will meet his end defending the entrance.

"Shaman, get over here! Don't let me die," Chang angrily yells, his gaze fixed on Tzabar.

"Come on, you damned traitor," Chang taunts Tzabar. "Can't you even finish me off? Is this what you wanted? Then come and get it, if you have the guts for it," he snarls, using his left hand to open his jacket and reveal a portion of the disk.

Tzabar straightens up, realizing that Shaman is injured and likely distracted. This is his opportunity.

Without hesitation, Tzabar charges toward Chang, but he is unable to avoid an unexpected shot that strikes him.

"Dammit!" Tzabar shouts through the searing pain. "Again? On the same arm? Dammit," he mutters, stepping back into a defensive stance while Chang wildly continues his tirade. "Did you see that, Shaman? That's how it's done. No fear," Chang screams, coughing up blood, losing the last strength to hold his gun.

Tzabar sinks to the ground, groaning in agony as he cradles his injured arm.

"Tzabar, how can I assist you?" Suluk materializes by his side.

"Suluk?! Where are Victor and Alvin?" Tzabar asks, his voice raw with desperation.

"Rachel and Marta are taking care of John and Robert, with Victor protecting them. Alvin left with Lydia in search of help. I came because I was concerned about Lota's delay," Suluk explains, casting a sorrowful glance at Lota's lifeless body.

"Now I understand. Farewell, my loyal companion," Tzabar whispers with a mixture of sadness and determination.

"Chang has the disk concealed inside his jacket," Tzabar grits out through the pain. "You can retrieve it. I've been wounded, and I can't reach him swiftly. Lota's device is destroyed, and I only have enough ammo for two shots, which I'll save for when Shaman reemerges."

"I'll retrieve the disk and escort you to the Kernel. Protect me, Tzabar," Suluk declares, taking decisive steps toward Chang, catching him off guard.

"Who are you? What do you want?" Chang shouts, attempting to fend off Suluk's advance. "Shaman, who is this guy? Shoot him, Shaman!"

Struggling to comprehend the situation, Shaman strains to see why Chang is shouting so desperately. He tries to find a clear shot at Suluk without risking hitting Chang. Shaman watches in disbelief as Suluk engages in a fierce struggle with Chang, manages to retrieve the disk, and turns back towards Tzabar. In a split second, Shaman shoots, his bullet hitting Suluk's head.

Despite the injury, Suluk takes a few more faltering steps before collapsing to the ground. His features contort in pain as he desperately reaches out towards Tzabar, clutching the Quantum Spark.

"Take it. Go to the Kernel and seal it," Suluk says in an altered voice, his words strained.

Tzabar reaches out, attempting to grasp the disk, his gaze fixed on Suluk's lifeless body. His once vibrant face has now returned to a smooth but gray appearance, devoid of color. Tzabar looks at him for one more second — as long as he can afford.

"The disk! Retrieve the disk!" Chang shouts.

With immense difficulty, Shaman drags himself along the corridor wall, using it as support, his wounds hindering his movement.

A sudden gunshot startles Shaman. Chang's empty revolver clatters to the ground. The final bullet had found its mark in Tzabar's chest, causing him to collapse, his outstretched hand frozen in its last attempt to reach the disk.

Shaman advances towards the fallen man, his weapon still drawn, his face contorted with rage.

Blood drips from his wounds, leaving a trail along the wall as he approaches.

Chang remains motionless, his eyes fixed straight ahead, mumbling incoherently as a pool of blood gathers at his feet.

As Shaman nears the disk, Tzabar's hand twitches, revealing a last trace of life. For a moment the pain recedes, and all he can see is Melissa's face, and Sebastian's, the two of them blurring into one — he never did learn which of them the boy belonged to, and now, strangely, it no longer seems to matter. Shaman raises his weapon slowly, his hand trembling.

The shot reverberates through the room, and Tzabar lies motionless, life extinguished. Shaman roars in anger, his eyes scanning the floor for the disk, but it is nowhere to be found.

John gradually regains consciousness inside the Kernel, finding himself surrounded by Rachel and Marta. Victor remains at Robert's side, still unconscious.

The vast space before them is filled with unfamiliar, futuristic devices, their lights flickering in an otherworldly display. Four immense semicircular consoles dominate half of the room, while a rectangular door on the left side of the room emits an intense blue glow.

"How are you feeling? You need to stay quiet," Rachel asks, leaning over John and gently caressing his forehead.

"I'm okay. How's Robert?" John manages to mumble weakly.

"He's unconscious and badly wounded. He requires medical attention, just like you," Victor replies.

"And Suluk, where is he? Do you have any information about Tzabar?" John asks, his voice strained.

"Suluk went to assist Tzabar. We don't have any further details," Marta says.

"Where is the vault for the disk?" John struggles to sit up, urgency cutting through his pain.

"John, please calm down. You're severely injured. You need to rest," Rachel says with concern.

"Suluk showed us the location of the vault," Victor says, gesturing towards the door emitting the blue light. "He also informed us about the steps required to seal the vault permanently. We have to lock it from the inside."

"And how do we accomplish that?" John questions with apprehension.

"Someone has to close it from the inside," Victor says with distress.

"That seems to be the case," Rachel begins to explain but is interrupted by a signal from John's.

"Wait, we have complications outside," John says, listening intently to the device.

"Lota has been destroyed. Suluk will attempt to retrieve the disk from Chang's jacket. Tzabar is severely injured, and he plans to bring him in as well. Victor, you need to help me with Tzabar."

"No, you're too injured. I'll go with Victor," Rachel insists, holding John down to prevent him from getting up.

"Please, be cautious," John pleads, attempting to sit up with Marta's assistance.

Victor and Rachel exchange worried glances, anticipating the dangers that lie outside. Suddenly, the disk materializes before them, crashing to the floor from the wall in front.

They stand in astonishment, gazing at the disk, half-expecting to see Tzabar or Suluk appear as well. However, no one emerges.

"Suluk is not responding. Complete silence," John says sorrowfully.

"Help me. I must place the disk inside that vault," John says, an unexpected reserve of strength helping him struggle to rise.

"Victor, please assist me. Then we can check on Tzabar and Suluk."

Outside, Shaman kneels, desperately searching for the disk. "Damn it. Where is that blasted disk?" He gazes at the wall where he saw Tzabar throw it, but upon approaching, he finds only a solid wall. Confusion clouds his mind as he steps back, bewildered by the perplexing turn of events.

His attention shifts to Suluk, and he notices a chain around his neck with a medallion.

He gazes back and forth between the wall and the medallion, his mind racing with curiosity. Without hesitation, he reaches out and snatches the chain from Suluk's neck, clutching the medallion tightly in his hand.

Victor opens the rectangular blue door and assists John as they step inside. They find themselves in a room with sleek, empty walls adorned only by four towering vertical sarcophagi and a rectangular pillar positioned at the center.

Outside, Rachel and Marta observe with suspicion, maintaining a cautious distance.

"What in the world are these sarcophagi for? And if their size corresponds to the height of their occupants, they must be over three meters tall," Victor remarks as John approaches the pillar.

The top of the pillar splits open into four segments, revealing a circular cavity within.

"I've seen one like it. I believe that's the cradle where we're supposed to place the disk, as Suluk instructed," Victor says, his voice filled with a mixture of anticipation and uncertainty.

John carefully lifts the disk and deposits it into the cradle. Both of them stand there, their hearts pounding, waiting for something to occur.

"Are you certain this was the right place? Nothing seems to be happening..." John utters in disappointment.

"Yes, I believe so. There doesn't appear to be anything else here..." Victor replies, though he sounds far from certain.

Suddenly, a metallic sound interrupts Victor's words. The four segments at the top of the pillar seal shut, and the pillar begins to retract, gradually descending toward the ground.

"It seems like it's done. Let's hope this damn disk remains locked in there for eternity," John says, leaning against the wall, succumbing to the pain that courses through his body.

"Suluk mentioned that afterward, we need to close the door by placing our hand on the green rectangle and waiting for the color to turn orange. This must be it," Victor explains, pointing to a rectangle illuminated in green at the center of the door.

As John extends his hand to touch the rectangle, the color at its base transitions to a gradual shade of orange, spreading throughout. He swiftly withdraws his hand.

"I believe I know how to seal this. Now, you go. Leave," he mutters quietly, ensuring Rachel doesn't overhear.

Victor exits the vault, aware of what is about to transpire. "Thank you, John," he says, his voice choked with emotion, realizing the sacrifice John is about to make.

"John, what are you doing?!" Rachel exclaims in alarm, her heart pounding with suspicion as she witnesses Victor leaving the vault without John.

Suddenly, before John can respond, something thuds heavily onto the floor of the Kernel room, causing Rachel and Marta to scream in fright.

Shaman rises to his feet, a sinister grin stretching across his face as he locks eyes with them. "Well, well, hello, girls. And John, my regards from your dear brother," he taunts, a burst of cruel laughter escaping his lips. He raises his gun, aiming it at John with malicious intent.

"Take cover!" Victor bellows, leaping in front of John in a selfless act of protection.

The gunshot reverberates through the room, and Victor collapses to the ground, his eyes finding John's for one last moment before the light goes out of them. In a frantic panic, the girls seek refuge behind one of the command tables, shaking with fear. John desperately tries to close the door.

"It appears you're trying to escape from me," Shaman sneers, his eyes fixated on John. "You should have seen the look on your brother's face when I struck him."

Unarmed but driven by frantic determination, John desperately searches for anything that can serve as a makeshift weapon while simultaneously struggling to seal the door. Shaman raises his gun, aiming at John. However, before he can pull the trigger, Rachel charges at him, causing him to lose his balance and drop the weapon.

Shaman retaliates swiftly, striking Rachel with a powerful punch, sending her crashing to the ground, unconscious.

Marta seizes the opportunity and snatches the fallen gun from the floor, hurling it towards John, who narrowly evades its trajectory as it lands safely within the vault.

Shaman screams in a violent rage and charges toward John. The two adversaries collide, tumbling into the vault.

Rachel regains consciousness and calls out to John, terror in her eyes as she watches the brutal struggle between the two wounded men.

Summoning his last reserves of strength and driven by sheer desperation, John lands a decisive blow on Shaman, momentarily dazing him. John rises to his feet, his determination burning bright, and places his hand on the green rectangle, initiating the closing mechanism. He casts a reassuring wink at Rachel.

Shaman, seething with rage and desperation, raises the gun, pointing it directly at John as he turns around. The door slams shut with a resounding thud, muffling the sound of the gunshot and Rachel's anguished scream.

Rachel crumples against the door, her body racked with uncontrollable sobs. Marta stands by helplessly, tears streaming down her face, torn between consoling her friend or allowing her space to grieve.

Suddenly, a loud metallic click reverberates through the room, and the vault begins its slow descent, disappearing seamlessly into the floor of the Kernel.

Rachel's cries intensify, her fists pounding relentlessly against the cold metal surface of the door in a desperate attempt to open it. Overwhelmed by fear and anguish, she staggers backward, screaming through her sobs, "John! John!"

Marta watches in sheer horror as the massive vault inexorably vanishes from sight, sinking into the depths of the floor.

"Rachel, Marta, what's happening? Get away from the vault!" Alvin's voice booms, as he rushes toward them, closely followed by Lydia.

"John locked himself inside, he was fighting Shaman," Rachel sobs, collapsing onto her knees and turning to them in utter despair.

"No!" Lydia's cry fills the air, her body collapsing against one of the consoles, her legs giving way beneath her. Her face drains of color, terror mirroring the overwhelming fear that has gripped her.

Alvin, dread etched on his face, implores, "Please, tell me they didn't place the Quantum Spark in the vault.

"Yes, John locked himself inside with Shaman. What's happening? Why are you all so distraught?" Marta asks, struggling to make sense of the escalating panic among them.

The despair and horror etched on their faces seem disproportionately intense to their relationship with John.

Lydia attempts to speak through her agitated state, tears streaming down her face. "When we arrived at the base, we received the final translation of all the characters and symbols on the portal," she manages to say, her voice unsteady.

Alvin, his finger trembling as he points towards the descending vault, continues, "The repeated message was: 'Cradle ready for Quantum Spark.'"

Rachel looks at them, desperately trying to grasp the gravity of the situation. "I don't understand. What does that mean?"

Lydia sits on the floor, staring vacantly into the distance, wiping away her tears. "The vault is the cradle, where the Quantum Spark was meant to be placed to initiate the harvest, the cataclysm," she murmurs, resignation weighing down her words. "The pillar we discovered behind the mirrored wall was where it was supposed to be sealed, inside the mountain.

Suluk and Lota were meant to lock themselves inside, along with two other companions, to initiate the process anew. To begin a new era for the planet after the cataclysm," Alvin adds, joining Lydia and gently squeezing her hand as he smiles affectionately at her.

"But that can't be. It's impossible," Rachel utters, disbelief cracking her voice.

Lydia explains, "The texts mentioned four enablers. They were supposed to be the four survivors Suluk spoke of before."

"There's one more thing," Alvin says quietly, not quite looking at any of them. "Suluk told us, the last time we spoke — the enablers don't just begin the new era. They're bound to it. Whoever seals the Spark walks back to the moment that set them on this path, and lives it again, and again, until the cycle finally takes."

"So, that means John..." Rachel whispers, her gaze fixated on the dwindling visibility of the capsule as it continues its descent.

"That means it's the end of everything," Marta breaks down into sobs, seeking solace in Rachel's embrace. Together, they watch the capsule's slow and somber descent.

A strange tranquility settles over them, their arms wrapped around each other, smiles mingling with tears as the last remnants of the capsule disappear into the ground.

Anxiety creeps into Lydia's voice as she asks, "So, what happens now?"

Alvin glances around, his eyes searching for answers. "I don't know," he replies, his voice thin with fear. "Here, perhaps nothing. But out there..."

He trails off, his words abruptly interrupted by a murmur escaping Rachel's lips. "It's nearly all gone. There's hardly anything left."

Alvin remains frozen, his eyes locked onto the smoldering remains of the capsule. Lydia clings to him tightly, her face buried in his chest as her body convulses with sobs. Rachel weeps inconsolably nearby, while Marta desperately tries to provide some comfort.

As they witness the slow and relentless descent of the capsule, now reduced to a mere gleaming metal cylinder, hopelessness settles over them.

"That's it, just millimeters left," Alvin whispers, resignation heavy in his tone. Rachel and Marta fall into silence, their gazes fixed on the descending capsule.

With a resounding clang, the cylinder collides with the ground, and a metal plate slides over it, sealing it shut.

"And now? What comes next?" Marta asks, uncertainty creeping into her voice.

"I don't know," Alvin replies, his voice barely audible. "I can only assume that the ground plate will close the compartment. As for what lies ahead, I dare not speculate."

"Should we stay here?" Marta asks, her tears subsiding.

"It all depends on what we find outside and what we can do to survive," Alvin responds, striving to instill a glimmer of hope within the desolation that surrounds them.

Suddenly, a dry, metallic clanking sound captures their attention. They watch in stunned silence as the ground plate begins to retract, gradually revealing the rising cylinder.

"He's getting up," Rachel gasps, rising abruptly. Marta follows suit, both transfixed by the sight of the ascending cylinder.

Alvin and Lydia join them, astonishment on their faces as the cylinder continues its ascent.

"What's happening?" Alvin asks, holding Lydia close to him.

The door slowly opens as the cylinder comes to a halt, emanating a soft blue light. They cautiously approach, hope and fear intertwining within them. Rachel is the first to enter, but their hope is swiftly dashed as she emerges, staggering and pale, leaning against a nearby console for support.

"There's no one," she murmurs, her voice barely audible. "There's no one inside."

Alvin and Marta follow suit, confirming the emptiness within. They stand in stunned silence, exchanging incredulous glances.

"No one? It can't be," Alvin says, desperation seeping into his voice.

"And the disk is gone too," Marta says, her voice shaking. "All that's left are bloodstains and a revolver."

"We saw them fighting inside. They were both in there when the door closed," Rachel adds, her voice unsteady. They exchange helpless glances, their despair personified by Rachel sitting on the floor, crying.

#

As I navigate the winding road, the car's headlights pierce through the torrential rain. An eerie foreboding washes over me, and my body shudders involuntarily.

Beside me, a woman sings cheerfully, with a child in the back seat.

I glance at her, and an unexpected emptiness floods through me, bitter anguish twisting beneath it.

Tears stream down my face without explanation and a frigid chill courses through my veins.

The woman stops singing and looks at me with concern. "What's wrong, dear? Why are you crying?"

"It's nothing, don't worry," I reply, attempting to calm her. "It must be the air conditioning," I say, fully aware that it's far from the truth. I grip the steering wheel tightly, struggling to rein in my emotions.

The child in the backseat says excitedly, "Dad, look at me! I solved your puzzle!"

I glance at the rearview mirror and see a strange yet oddly familiar expression staring back at me. A chilling medley of disjointed and hauntingly recognizable images floods my mind.

A pair of gleaming eyes capture my attention, drawing me back to a reality I recognize but find difficult to accept.

The boy, who should be four years old, sits in the backseat, beaming at me. He clutches four interlocking metal pieces in his small hands.

"Well done, Sebastian," I hear myself say, returning his smile. "We'll show it to your uncle Angel and surprise him with your puzzle-solving skills."

A stronger tremor courses down my spine.

"Only 5 kilometers left," I state. "We'll reach there in 15 minutes."

But the sensation doesn't ease. Something pulls at me — not thought, not memory, something older than either. I glance in the rearview mirror.

"Sebastian." His name comes out different this time. Complete, somehow. As if I have been reaching for it for a very long time.

He looks up at me in the mirror. "Yes, Dad?"

"John, watch out!" the woman beside me cries.

By the roadside, drenched by the pouring rain, I glimpse a figure frantically waving on my right — a blonde woman and a child, both hauntingly familiar.

This time, my foot finds the brake.

"John, stop!"